Praise for Eva Salomon's War . . .

"With grace and a good deal of insight, Gabriella Goliger paints a vivid picture of the life of Eva Salomon and her uprooted family during the early 1930s in Breslau, Germany, and then in Tel Aviv and Jerusalem during the years leading up to 1948. This is the story of one woman's difficult and at times painful journey, a journey of rebellion and love, of survival and of 'becoming.' The story takes place inside a broader world of danger and turmoil, and brilliantly reveals the complex relations experienced by the British, Jewish and Arab populations of Palestine. The smells and sounds and sights of the streets and the varied people who populate them during this historic period are brought to life in the strong, assured writing we have come to expect from Goliger." — Frances Itani, fiction writer, poet, essayist, Member of the Order of Canada

"I felt as though I had been on a journey to mid-century Palestine after reading Eva Salomon's War. Every detail is charged and real, the most minor characters speak with compelling voices. This novel is infused not just with Gabriella Goliger's meticulous research, but with her deep sympathy for her subject, a fiercely alive young woman coming into her own in a world where every value is up for grabs." — Joan Thomas, prize-winning author and noted journalist

"A superb account of life in Palestine under the British Mandate between 1938 and 1948 . . . Captures brilliantly the tension between generations, racial prejudice, the atmosphere of the time, the tension between the British and the Arabs or the British and the Jews. With its well-researched natural, political and historical context, the novel discloses in a most truthful, yet unobtrusive, manner a period still unknown to many." — Prof. Dr. Danielle Schaub, Oranim Academic College of Education, Israel

Eva
Salomon's
WAR

Eva Salomon's WAR

Gabriella Goliger

BInk

Bink Books

Bedazzled Ink Publishing Company • Fairfield, California

978-1-945805-81-3 paperback

Cover Design
by

Bink Books
a division of
Bedazzled Ink Publishing, LLC
Fairfield, California
http://www.bedazzledink.com

To the memory of the late Gretel Young (nee Perle)
—more loved and missed than she could have known.

Acknowledgements

Beloved friends and family made my long writer's journey much less lonely than it might have been and also provided invaluable practical help towards the birthing of this novel.

Heartfelt thanks to:

Prof. Ursula Büttner for her enthusiastic encouragement, unwavering faith in me, and so much research assistance. (The books, photocopied memoirs, answers to my questions, corrections of my German and history mistakes, etc. etc.)

Frances Itani, Cheryl Jaffee, Debra Martens, Gila Shmueli, and Barbara Freeman (and Ursula too) for reading and commenting on near-final drafts.

My brother, Dan Goliger, and sister-in-law, Maddy Goliger, for their caring and support and just for being such wonderful people.

My cousins Gila and Michal Shmueli for allowing their mum's photo to be on the cover.

Joan Thomas, Frances Itani and Prof. Danielle Schaub for the lovely endorsements. (And also to Danielle for catching so many typos.)

My Ottawa writers' group for reading early chapters and for not believing me when I said I'd never write another novel.

The many other friends and family who cheered me on over the years. The readers who praised my previous books and gave me heart for this one.

My life-partner, Barbara Freeman, whose steadfast love nourishes me, sustains me and has brought me to this day.

I am also grateful to the City of Ottawa for its financial support and to Bedazzled Ink Publishing for its dedication to books by and about women.

Prologue

Jerusalem, January 10, 1947

IT'S FRIDAY AFTERNOON and the hour of long shadows. Of slanting light that brings out the tarnished gold of Jerusalem stone. As the sun sinks, its amber rays fire the minarets in the heart of the Old City, burnish Suleiman's walls, wash over towers, crosses, and domes, glint on gun turrets, and glance off the upraised bayonets of the sentries on the Hill of Evil Counsel. Throughout the town, both old and new, the day's decline brings a flurry of activity. Jews rush home to prepare for the Sabbath. Arabs flock to the call of the Maghreb prayer. British officials crowd into the bar of the King David Hotel to toast His Majesty with tumblers of gin. Citizens of all three communities hurry their separate ways to reach the safety of their enclaves before the vehement darkness of a Palestine night descends.

In front of a billboard at the corner of Mamilla and Princess Mary Roads, a woman lingers. She wears a fawn-coloured tweed jacket with padded shoulders and a sheepskin collar and a smart, emerald-green wool suit underneath. A gold scarf is tucked around her throat for a splash of contrast and to fend off the stiff January wind. Her trilby hat is angled stylishly, the brim sloping across her brow and tilting towards the sky. She balances on pumps with two-and-a-half inch heels, the highest she could find at the shoe shop on Ben Yehuda Street. She's young, though not in the first blush of youth. A small woman—barely four foot eleven—who dresses to give herself extra inches.

Pausing before this billboard on her way home from work has become a habit. The hoarding, plastered with notices in three languages, is an island of sanity in a city coming apart at the seams. Despite the tensions, sporadic curfews, the possibility of an explosion rending the air any moment, there's much entertainment on offer. Film stars smile or scowl down from gaudy posters. Charles Boyer, Ingrid Bergman, Judy Garland, Danny Kaye. They promise romance and laughter, tears and thrills. Yes, the cinema scene continues to flourish, with British and American films in half a dozen theatres, along with a steamy Arabic love triangle on at the Rex. For the serious minded, there's a talk about Spinoza at the Hebrew University and another on Roman-era pottery at the Museum of Antiquities. Friday night is dead in the Holy City, but by Saturday eve the place will perk up.

What most absorbs the woman's attention are the announcements about music. Jazz at Fink's Bar. The monthly record concert at the YMCA (still accessible, though in a fenced-off security zone). A string quartet in the auditorium of Rehavia High School, which will perform *Eine kleine Nachtmusik* and other Mozart selections. She adores Mozart. Instantly, the lilting melody capers through her mind and she shifts from foot to foot, carried away into dreams of brighter times, another, more vibrant city. Tel Aviv! Tea dances at a seaside café, twirling in the arms of the man she loved. She inhales the tobacco and bleached-cotton smell of him. She feels her cheek against the solid oak of his chest. She hears the bass beat of his heart and conjures his tender gaze and for long moments can forget the aching void in her heart.

Also among the welter of announcements on the billboard are some political notices, which the daydreaming woman has resolved to ignore. There's a stern proclamation from the General Officer Commanding of the British Forces in Palestine and Transjordan. It warns against leafleting by outlaw groups. *"Anyone caught . . . severe prison sentence . . . information rewarded . . ."* Etc. Right below— under the very nose of the G.O.C., so to speak—is a freshly pasted manifesto from the deepest layer of the Jewish Underground. A densely printed page, thick with shrill phrases.

"*The Imperial oppressor . . . The treasonous capitulation of the Jewish Agency lackeys . . . The perfidious proposal to partition the Eternal Homeland. Armed struggle . . . Blood and fire . . .*" And so on.

The trilby-hatted woman doesn't read further, because she knows what the manifesto says and she's fed up to her marrow with overblown rhetoric. Let the street-corner philosophers in Zion Square argue over the militants. Are they heroes or terrorists? Will they hasten redemption or trigger calamity? Pave the way for the new Hebrew state or set the whole world against the Jews, while dragging the entire region into a vortex of violence? Let the heavyweights in Café Atara foam and spar and call each other names. Nothing changes.

But why doesn't the woman get a move on? It's time to leave, for the light is fading fast. Behind the billboard, beyond the street corner, lies an ancient cemetery: a wide expanse of gnarled trees and overgrown bushes, where the Jerusalem darkness always seems dense as bricks. Yet she dallies a bit longer to fish out a pack of cigarettes from the depths of her handbag. To recapture the filaments of her nostalgic dream and to avoid the chill absence that awaits her at home. She floats away on her clouds of what-once-was and what-might-have been, while the streets empty and the last shutters clatter down over the shops.

Soon the townsfolk will have vanished behind their closed doors, their own four walls. Soon clusters of soldiers will be out on foot patrol, exchanging rude jokes to buttress their spirits. An armoured car—a behemoth with a gun-barrel snout—will rumble down the hill from the parking lot beside the King David Hotel. The zealous young men of the Underground will emerge from cellars and alleys. Some of them have barely begun to shave. They are armed with home-made bombs and the fieriest of convictions. Soon the game of the hunters and the hunted will begin.

And that oblivious, day-dreaming woman in the trilby hat?

She is me.

Part I

Chapter 1
The Presence

Breslau, Germany, 1933

WHEN I WAS twelve years old, I was suddenly struck by an awareness of the Divine, a white-hot conviction that fired my soul and changed my entire outlook from one intake of breath to the next. The period of exaltation was absurdly short lived. Nevertheless, the episode knocked me sideways for a long time afterwards.

It was August, towards the end of the school holidays, a tense, in-between period, bloated with idleness and anxiety. It had been a strange summer of deadly quiet spells in the hot streets of our city, spells punctuated by loud marching bands and huge rallies in honour of the Führer. My two best friends had disappeared into the new national youth group—the Bund Deutscher Mädel—where I couldn't have followed them, even if I'd been so inclined. My older sister Liesel was busy with her own preoccupations. I had an inner vacuum to fill.

Prowling about our apartment one day, I discovered that the door to Papa's study had a broken latch and this gave me the idea to spy on him as he recited his morning prayers. I knew that special business duties that week would keep him from the usual service at his synagogue. Shortly after dawn the next day, I crept down the dark corridor and put my face against the gap. There Papa stood, with his back to me, enveloped in his white prayer shawl, nodding towards the wall behind his oak rolltop desk. Right above the desk hung a portrait of Kaiser Wilhelm II in his glory days before the Great War and before he'd had to flee the country. The emperor wore a gold-braided, heavily medalled uniform. His moustache was shaped like two upside-down scimitars spreading across each cheek. The expression on the imperial face spoke of the stern Prussian virtues that Papa prized: discipline, strength, steely resolve and unbending convictions. Papa's moustache was thinner, trimmer, and more modest; still, he too was a man who knew his own mind. But much as the emperor's portrait held pride of place on the wall, it had a rival for Papa's attention in another item just a few inches nearby. This was a framed *yahrzeit* chart with long rows of numbers, the anniversaries of my mother's and grandparents' deaths, projected over fifty years, according to the Hebrew calendar and cross referenced to the secular, ensuring we knew when to light a memorial candle.

I pressed deeper into the doorway gap and my gleeful spying eyes took in quite a different Papa from the one he normally presented to the world. In his white *tallith* and his leather phylacteries he was transformed from an ordinary German citizen and small businessman, into a strange spectre, a shrouded creature that swayed, muttered, and droned. I watched intently, but even more carefully, I listened, absorbing words and intonations. When I'd fixed the scene in my memory, I scampered down the hall to the room I shared with Liesel, jumped onto her bed and bounced my sister awake.

"*Baruch Atah*, blah-blah," I mocked in my deepest, most sepulchral voice. I rocked back and forth, my hands cradling an imaginary prayer book. Liesel blinked sleepily, dropped her jaw, and finally sat up in alarm.

"Eva! Hush! Papa will hear. Or Tilly will at least."

I continued in a frenzy of bobbing, swaying, and ever louder muttering.

"Papa would never *shokel* like an *Ostjude*," Liesel scolded as she wrestled me down and muffled my face with the pillow. We both burst into giggles under the covers at the scandalous notion of making Papa out to be anything like an eastern Jew, those foreign-looking apparitions from the wilds of Poland and Russia.

"God sees everything, naughty monkey."

But I knew my older sister feared our father much more than God. She dutifully recited prayers and blessings for no other reason but to keep the peace.

"Stop spying on Papa. Promise me, Evaleh, please."

Too late. I'd become drunk on the power of mockery, the exquisite pleasure of shocking my sister while treading dangerously close to the volcano of Papa's wrath. My mischief sprang from deep-seated resentment. There were two Papas: the one who ignored me and the one who could explode in fury. Of the two, I preferred the latter, for the distant Papa was hardest to bear. Even when at home, our father was essentially absent—bent over his work desk or poring over his holy books or sheathed in a *tallith* or simply absorbed in his own thoughts at the supper table. Wrapped in a hard, forbidding, inviolable silence. His outbursts were frightening, but his disregard reduced me to ash. And so, every morning for the rest of the week, I returned to my station at the study door. There was a delicious thrill in being an unseen eye, intruding on Papa's private moments, hiding behind the newel post, yet daring myself to make a noise. I imagined him wheeling around, mouth agape, his phylactery box a clownish lump upon his forehead. All a-tremble, I pressed my nose deeper into the gap. The door creaked. He didn't hear.

Papa's prayers never varied, the words, their sequence and rhythm always the same, yet as the mornings went by, I began to notice small things. A sigh at the end of the prayers of gratitude for body and soul. A hum that escaped his lips during an otherwise silent passage. The delicate way his draped figure moved as he chanted. No, he didn't *shokel.* He didn't jerk violently back and forth like those Jews in black caftans and raggedy beards who'd come to our town from their impoverished villages across the Polish border. Papa disdained such displays of naked fervour. Unseemly! Un-German! But he performed his own restrained choreography as he sank into his devotions, head bowing, body swaying ever so slightly like a pine in a breeze.

On the sixth morning of my Peeping Tom game something extraordinary happened. I felt a tingling at the back of my neck and a shudder of my heart in my chest. I became aware that I was no longer just the watcher watching. I too was being observed. Someone—or some Being—saw me as I pressed against the doorpost in my long flannel nightgown. It perceived me down to my tiniest details: that I was absurdly small for my age, that I chewed my thumbnails, that the pink ribbon at the end of my rust-coloured braid was frayed, that my bare toes had turned bluish on the cold wooden floor. This Being read my thoughts too, every whisper that sped through my mind, including the startled realization that I was not alone in the hall. The Presence was behind me, beside me, above and below. I didn't turn my head, but kept my eyes glued on Papa's fringed *tallith* while feeling myself utterly revealed. The Presence was warm. It smiled. Its honeyed light flowed along my spine and illuminated Papa's study. The walls that were normally the colour of jaundiced skin shone like gold.

Papa cleared his throat. I jumped backwards, away from the door, and the Presence vanished. But not quite. As I tiptoed down the corridor, slipped into Liesel's bed, and curled myself against her warm, sleeping body, I carried the dazzling brightness inside myself. It was like a beautiful dream whose details you forget but that is real and vivid nevertheless and makes you glow all over.

That evening, after Liesel lit the Sabbath candles and after Papa intoned the blessings over wine and bread, I announced my desire to go to synagogue next morning. Liesel stared at me in disbelief, while Papa narrowed his eyes. What devilry was I up to now? Meanwhile, our dead Mama, the woman in white on the mantelpiece, gazed out of her photograph with an expression of mild surprise.

Though Papa was strict about many things, he never insisted we accompany him to *shul.* He would have loved to have a son with whom to study Talmud and to stand beside him during prayers, but he only had us: two girls of whom he expected the virtues befitting our sex. Modesty, obedience, unobtrusiveness.

The rare times Liesel and I absolutely had to go to synagogue—High Holidays, a cousin's bar mitzvah—we always died multiple deaths from boredom.

"You want to go to *Shabbat* morning services," Papa repeated slowly, emphasizing every word as his dark gaze drilled into me.

I sat up high in my chair, lifted my chin.

"Yes!"

The word came out louder and shriller than I'd intended, like a challenge rather than simple assent. Papa regarded me for another long moment and though I held his gaze, inside I'd begun to shrivel. I had a flash of panic. Did he know I'd been peeping through his study doorway?

"Hmmf," Papa grunted finally. "Very well. I'll send Tilly to let your Aunt Ida know. She'll come for you in the morning and take you to the Storch."

I opened my mouth to protest. *No, not the big, fancy synagogue with Aunt Ida and Uncle Otto. I want to go with you, to your* shul. But I couldn't get the words out. They seemed too preposterous, even to me.

"Ida will come for both of you," Papa added, with a sharp look at Liesel. It was a look that said he expected her, and not just Aunt Ida, to keep an eye on me. My sister murmured her reluctant assent, for Papa's decisions were final. He nodded towards Tilly, standing in the dining room doorway, to bring on the soup.

Aunt Ida arrived early next day, puffing from the long climb up the stairs, her hand pressed to her heart as she stood in the front hall of our flat. She wore a high-necked purple dress, a bell-shaped hat that sat snugly against her face and long white gloves, *à l'anglaise*. When she'd assured herself she wasn't going to have a dizzy spell, she nodded for Liesel and me to come forward.

"Good morning, dear Aunt," we chanted in unison, as we bent our knees in a brief, respectful curtsy.

Ida leaned forward and turned her face to accept a delicate peck of her powdery cheek from each of us in turn. As I delivered my kiss, I felt Auntie's hand flutter against my spine like a skittish moth. This was Auntie's version of a hug—restrained, cautious, uneasy about flesh-to-flesh contact. Aunt Ida was frightened of the germs that swarmed over human bodies and that might jump upon her during too warm an embrace. She never kissed us back. Still we felt ourselves richly rewarded by those nervous little pats, which we knew expressed genuine affection. We weren't exactly spoiled in that regard.

"What an unexpected pleasure. The company of my nieces at synagogue," Auntie said with an approving nod of her head.

"The *Zwergel* has had an attack of piety," Papa said, with a skeptical noise at the back of his throat.

Zwergel—Dwarfling—was his nickname for me. The moniker always grated for I had reminders enough of my tininess as it was.

Auntie looked at me shrewdly, but with humour and indulgence in her twinkling eyes, as if to say, "I don't care about the depth of your motivation; a morning in synagogue can't do you any harm." Meanwhile, Papa smoothed down his black velvet skullcap, set his Homburg on his head and hurried off alone for the modest, back-alley *shul* he preferred to the more sumptuous synagogue that was the pride of the Jewish community.

The three of us—Auntie, Liesel, and I—walked down our narrow street, across the main thoroughfare, Friedrich Wilhelm-Strasse, and over the lovely stone bridge that spanned the ancient moat that circled the inner town. Past stately statues and the tree-lined promenade and the outskirts of the business district of Breslau. Despite her asthma, her heart condition and her stout legs, Auntie kept up a good pace. I sensed in her, and in the other Jews heading in the same direction, a general unease, an anxiety to arrive at our destination. Everyone walked with straight-backed dignity, outwardly calm, yet twitching underneath: that barely contained urge to send a furtive glance over the shoulder. The mood changed the moment we passed through the arched portal that led to the courtyard in front of the synagogue. A kind of collective sigh of relief arose as voices joined in a happy hubbub. The courtyard was large and airy, but fully sheltered by the backs of buildings, creating a separate, hidden space from the world outside. We were in the heart of town, just steps from one of the large market squares, yet in a private enclave that few non-Jews ever entered. Before us was the grand, pilaster façade of the Weisse Storch Synagogue and beneath us, the smooth cobblestones polished by generations of Jewish feet.

Auntie shepherded us up the stairs to the women's gallery. We sat in the front row, overlooking the great hall below and the backs of hundreds of men and boys in their black skullcaps and white prayer shawls. Uncle Otto had a main-floor seat near the ark of the Torah. Plus his name appeared on bronze plaques and was stamped into the prayer books he'd donated, for he was rich. He was heir to the business my late grandfather had established: Salomon and Sons, Purveyors of Sacks and Twine. Papa could have been an heir too, but he'd quarrelled with his father and older brother over their practice of keeping the factory open on Saturdays. After Grandpa's death, Otto again offered him the partnership but my father adamantly refused. He preferred to earn a modest salary as Otto's employee, in charge of buying torn sacks for refurbishment, rather than share in the sin of desecrating the Sabbath. No one else took such a narrow view of the matter. My uncle's generosity made him a pillar of the community. And, though he was far from ostentatious, Otto didn't mind that his status be known through such small honours as plaques and designated seats. Every so often my father let slip a disparaging remark about "immodest displays" at the Storch. These barbs were never aimed directly at his brother, for to do so would be to commit the sin of "evil speaking." But Papa made it clear that the Storch, with its bronze chandeliers, stained glass windows, and gilded mouldings, was not to his taste. He preferred his dark, shabby, hole-in-the-wall *shul*, where nothing distracted from the word of God. I suppose he thought me incapable of similar devotion.

Slowly, very slowly, the service rolled forward. Though I knew enough prayer-book Hebrew, learned at Auntie's knee, to follow along, the words all ran together, foreign, impenetrable, even the German translation on the other side of the page. *Magnificence . . . Your Throne . . . Rock of Ages . . . Exalted . . ."* None of it meant anything, the dense print blurred and the old boredom settled in, well before we even finished the introductory prayers and arrived at the Torah reading. My eyes watered and my legs twitched, a yawn swelled in my throat. Liesel noticed me jiggling my knees and smirked an I-told-you-so. This made me bend my head back to my prayer book with renewed determination as I tried to summon the Presence beside me again from the distant place to which it had drifted since I'd first made its acquaintance. *I* had the light. *I* was the chosen one. When the congregation broke into song, I joined in, blending my voice with the rest and floating away on the familiar melody. The secret of prayer revealed itself. Not meaning, but repetition; not thinking, but knowing; not coherence, but ecstasy. I sang with my fists clenched and my eyes squeezed shut and my body swaying, as I drew the shining Presence towards me. It hovered just above the grey slate roof tiles of the synagogue.

At table that evening, I chimed in with Papa through the long, long prayer, the *Grace after Meals*. My lips moved as his did during the silent recitations, my voice shrilled through the out-loud parts and my finger followed the printed text on the card, line by line. My eyes shifted from the card to Papa's face to see if he noticed and I thought I detected a glimmer of approval in his dark pupils. Liesel watched me with an expression of exasperation, while the woman on the mantelpiece wore a smile of detached amusement, but whether because of me or Liesel wasn't clear.

After sundown, during the ceremony to mark the separation between holy and profane, between the Sabbath and the ordinary days of the week, Papa allowed me to hold the braided, three-wick candle before he snatched it from my hand to make the fat flame die with a hiss in the spilled drops of wine. Then Papa fetched his violin and I ran for my recorder and the three of us clustered at the end of the dining room table that Tilly had cleared of dishes. Now Papa struck up a German folk tune. I joined in, tootling away, while Liesel sang in her strong, sweet voice, hands behind her back, chest puffed out. Her budding breasts pushed against the buttons of her blouse, but she forgot to be ashamed as her voice, Papa's violin and my recorder wove together like the three wax strands of the *Havdallah* candle. We did a series of melancholy songs: about the lonely rose on the heather, about the silver moonlight in the fields. And when we did a jolly number that too sounded sad because of the slow, sober pace Papa set. As he played, Papa gazed at the photograph on the mantelpiece, his eyes misting over. The concert was for her, entirely for the woman in white with the wistful gaze and doubting smile. The concert lasted exactly fifteen minutes. When it was over, Papa returned his violin to its case, snapped the latches shut, and retired to his study.

Back in our bedroom, I hummed a Sabbath hymn as I peered through the open window, down the street, where people were lined up for the evening performance at the cinema on the corner. The big hit of the summer was "S.A. Mann Brand" about a stalwart truck driver who joins the Brownshirts to defend Germany against communist subversion. The poster showed him holding a huge flag emblazoned with the new national emblem that was like a big, black spider with hooked legs spiralling out in four directions. Mimicking the exalted voice of our synagogue cantor, I chanted some passages from the morning service at the heathen who knew not the name of the Lord. Liesel looked up from her novel, appalled.

"Have you gone mad?"

Yes, I had and I was enjoying my madness. I felt as if I'd grown twelve inches. Leaning farther out the window, I shouted out words that were destined to bring light unto the nations. "*Adonai Elohenu, Adonai Echad . . .*"

Liesel grabbed me by the arm, hauled me back into the room, clutched me close, her heart pounding hard through the thin material of her dress.

"Eva, you mustn't . . . can't you . . . don't you know . . ." She was so upset she could hardly breathe. "Don't you know what's going on out there?"

I knew. I knew everything. I knew just by being certain about knowing. That the Presence would bear me on eagle's wings. That the Messiah would come in his own time. That I would walk with Papa to his *shul*. That at last, after much unfortunate delay, I was chosen.

LIESEL AND I were different in many ways. She was older by three years, taller, almost fully developed and quite lovely, with glowing skin and soft, dark eyes. She was unaware of being lovely, careless with her looks, as if looks didn't matter, or shouldn't. Perhaps she didn't believe what she saw in the mirror—it didn't compute with an inner image. If someone paid her a compliment, she laughed, uneasy, as if she'd accepted a gift she didn't deserve. While I longed for pretty clothes, Liesel was quite content to wear the severe, drab, ill-fitting outfits that Papa—ever frugal—obtained for us second-hand. Liesel wouldn't try to tuck in a waist or improve on a sagging hem. Yet for all that, her beauty shone, which made me both proud to have such an attractive sister but also a bit resentful. I was small, skinny, pale, red haired, and freckled. Liesel had no right to be so unmindful of her blessings. My sister was also better at making friends. She was warm, whereas I was prickly. Practical and down to earth, while I was dreamy. She didn't expect much of Papa, took him as he was, worked around him, avoiding, escaping or manoeuvring diplomatically. She hated conflict. She was water, while I was fire.

Our mother had died during a messy miscarriage when I was a baby. There were two deaths actually. But the other, the foetus, which might have become a third child, was never mentioned in our household. Somehow Liesel and I were aware of the double tragedy. Perhaps Tilly, the maid, had let something slip. We kept this knowledge—too dark for words—locked within our private selves. And there was another secret we were not supposed to know, though we did—its bare bones at least. Our father, the widower, who'd been left with two small children, had become betrothed again not long after our mother died. But who broke it off and when and why . . . over that we could only speculate. Liesel argued the mystery woman had been unworthy, while I insisted it was surely all Papa's fault. As far as we knew, there had been no further attempts.

For me, Mama was only stories and the photo on the mantel, but for Liesel she was real. Liesel had known the late Rachel Salomon, felt her love. Though only four when Mama's body was taken away in the black-draped funeral carriage, Liesel swore she could remember her face and her touch, her sayings and instructions. When we were younger, Liesel had often talked aloud to Mama, and received clear answers whispered into her ear, or so my sister swore. When I was naughty, Liesel scolded me in Mama's voice. When I had a fever, Liesel cooed Mama lullabies and held me tight until I was blazing and gasping for air. Now that we were older, Liesel still often said, *Evaleh, you mustn't! Mama will be twisting in her grave.*

At Mama's *yahrzeit*, when a memorial candle in a tin container burned upon the mantelpiece, Liesel gazed at the photo with yearning and recognition, much as Papa did. To me it was just a flat, grey, enigmatic image of something utterly lost. All through my childhood, the photo annoyed me. The eyes followed me around, the smile unreadable. When I stared closely, the face exploded into a cloud of dots. I had tried very hard to make Mama speak to me. Until recently there'd been nothing but silence. However, now that I'd been touched by the shining Presence, it seemed I could finally detect a spark of life in those paper eyes, a quiver of sympathy about the lips.

FOR A THIRD time I expressed the wish to go to services.

"To your *shul*," I dared to ask Papa.

He gave me a sharp, curious look—still skeptical, but with a glimmer of appreciation, as if I might be more than merely a pale, undersized, impudent, demanding child. Perhaps he'd underestimated me? He considered the proposition for some moments, seemed to weigh the pros and cons, but shook his head.

"No. You'll go to the Storch."

And still I was not discouraged, convinced I could win him over. Next week for sure he would invite me to accompany him to the hidden-away *shul* where the most pious Jews of the city prayed. He would introduce me as his daughter with pride, and sober heads would nod, seeing, not a pint-sized girl, but the legendary "Woman of Valour" of the Friday evening hymn.

"You've gone crazy, completely crazy," Liesel groaned when we were alone. "But it will pass," she added with big-sister forbearance. She meant that I'd had strange notions before and they had all blown through me like an October wind.

As we milled about in the Storch courtyard before services, Liesel got to chatting with a couple of girls who invited her to join them later at a meeting. When we'd returned home she asked and got permission from Papa. It was a gathering of the Ezra movement, she told him, the one for orthodox youth. Everything would be strictly kosher and observant of the Sabbath laws. Before she left, she suggested I come too, but I didn't want to be seen as the little sister who tagged along, and anyway, I disliked the overwhelming chumminess of groups. Liesel warned that I'd be bored and lonely without her, but I haughtily told her I wanted to study, that I intended to immerse myself in the Portion of the Week. Liesel just rolled her eyes.

Alone in our bedroom, I opened a heavy tome: the five books of Moses, annotated by Rashi, our most famous sage of the Middle Ages. The Portion of the Week was *Ki Teitzei*, and it began most fascinatingly about the Israelite soldier taking captives in war.

> . . . and if you see among the captives a beautiful woman and you desire her, you may take her for yourself as a wife. You shall bring her into your home, and she shall shave her head and let her nails grow.

The head shaving and nail growing, Rashi explained, was to ensure that the captive would become ugly and undesirable to the Hebrew soldier so that he would change his mind about marrying a Gentile, however attractive she might have first appeared. I read and re-read and turned the passage round and round and still it made no sense. I tried to continue to other passages, but the commandments and explanations became ever more complicated until my brain came to a shuddering halt. I slammed the holy book shut.

Heavy rain splattered against the window panes. A sad, grey light filtered through the glass. Everything in the room seemed lifeless, while from its corner of the hall, the grandfather clock sent out a mournful bong. Frantically bored, I peered out the window at the street below, where people milled about beneath the shelter of awnings or marched forward with raised umbrellas. They were lining up for tickets at the cinema. They were waiting for the tram on Friedrich Wilhelm-Strasse. My feet chattered against the floor, propelled me to the hall, where I snatched my raincoat from the closet and the nicest umbrella from the stand. The rest of the world was going about its business. Why not I?

Outside, I opened and hoisted the umbrella as if it were a torch of triumph. It was a beautiful thing of deep green material with a band of gold along the scalloped edges and a carved wooden handle from which dangled a silky tassel. The rain had tapered off to a drizzle and the breeze licked my cheeks. A man passing by smiled that amused, patronizing smile adults bestow on entertaining children. Perhaps I looked odd—a slip of a girl beneath a wide umbrella. I refused to care.

Turning a corner, crossing a broad street and a broader plaza, I arrived at the nearby Freiburger Railway Station, a grand old building, ornamented with classical columns, friezes, cornices, winged statues, and a large bronze clock at the very top. Across the balustrade stretched the blood-red banner with the familiar hooked-leg emblem. The black spider was everywhere these days: on the armbands of men in uniform, at the front of newsstands, on billboard notices, on flags big and small. One had to—one did—take it in stride. I sauntered up the entrance steps into the vast, echoing hall, thrilled by the hum of purposeful activity. People rushed about, newsboys shouted, porters pushed hand trucks piled high with suitcases, travellers waved from carriage windows, families embraced on platforms, while overhead, beneath the vaulted glass roof, sparrows swooped and twittered as if drunk with excitement. There was a pretzel stand and a man who sold sausages out of a steaming vat and a one-legged Gypsy playing a plaintive tune on his accordion. Hither and thither, hallos, whistles, tramping feet, the pant of engines. The cacophony was balm to my soul after the loneliness of our empty flat. I'd forgotten my longing for the Presence. Or perhaps my young brain, in which wishing and believing were almost the same, had decided the Presence must be here, amid the bustle, the noise and the heady, unkosher smells.

I watched a tall, svelte woman who was leaning against the post beneath the station clock. She wore a fawn-coloured trench coat with a wide belt and padded shoulders and a saucer-shaped hat with a pretty bow. Hands in her pockets, one leg bent, her pose was exquisite. A man rushed towards her, burbling apologies. She drew herself up, said something which made him wince as if slapped. When he lit a cigarette for her, she blew smoke into his face and laughed and I imagined she must have a low, husky laugh, the kind that made men shiver. After they'd vanished into the crowds, I wandered around dreaming about them: his eager questions, her ambiguous answers. In my dreams, I became tall and haughty, cool and teasing, just like her. Still half in a dream, I drifted out the great arched doorway of the station back into the rain.

But as I began to walk along, a prickly sensation in my spine told me I was being followed. I quickened my steps. The Brownshirts! Were they after me? Had I drawn too much attention to myself while strutting about the station and twirling my open umbrella? Did the authorities know me because of the time I'd yelled Hebrew verses through the open window? Though I itched to break into a run, curiosity won out at last and I turned to see if I really was being pursued. Sure enough, a man was bearing down on me. A man in a black suit, and the face under the Homburg black with fury. Papa! His hat and suit jacket looked damp from rain. His eyes smouldered in a way I knew only too well. Reflexively, I pulled the umbrella close to my head like a turtle retreating into its shell. Papa pushed it backwards and glared down at me.

"Where have you been?" he hissed.

"Nowhere! Just walking."

"With that?"

He grimaced and jerked his chin to indicate something unspeakable, as if a hideous demon were seated on my shoulder, but the only thing on my shoulder was the polished wooden shaft of the lovely umbrella.

"Wretched girl," he snarled through gritted teeth. "You've broken the Sabbath. Again!"

I blinked at him, speechless.

A holy rage flushed his cheeks and sparked his eyes, but all he could do was glare. He couldn't vent his anger to his full satisfaction because we were in the plaza in front of the station, with the well-dressed gentiles flowing by. He turned on his heel and stalked away, as if he couldn't bear the sight of me another moment. I trudged after him with anguished heart. I'd closed the umbrella and let the drizzle fall on my bare head but it was a useless gesture of appeasement. To be carrying any object outside the house on the Sabbath was considered one of the thirty-nine prohibited forms of work and thus a violation of the day of rest. How could I have forgotten such a thing? But I had.

Papa was waiting for me when I entered the flat. The moment I came through the door, he snatched the umbrella out of my hand and called for Tilly to take it away. Give it to the poor, he commanded. To someone deserving. He never wanted to see it again. I felt it was me he wanted to send away, never to be seen again. Tilly looked astonished to have a handsome green and gold umbrella thrust upon her for no discernible reason, but she was used to the strange quirks of her Jewish master.

Liesel came home, exuberant from her time with the youth group and wearing the blue neckerchief of the Ezra movement knotted below her throat. But she sobered up immediately upon absorbing the black mood in the house.

"I told you to come with me. Oh, I should have *made* you come. I could kick myself."

I tried to smile. Liesel's contortions of guilt usually made me laugh, but not now.

"Tell Papa you're sorry. Do," she urged, taking my hand, wanting to lead me to his study door.

"No!"

I couldn't apologize, or rage, or explain. I wanted to be left alone.

Supper was an awkward, painful affair, with Papa, Liesel, and me seated in near silence at the big table facing the empty chairs that denoted Mama's place, the place of the lost child and places of the other children who would never be born. The rituals proceeded as usual: blessings over wine and bread, a cold meal of hard-boiled eggs and pickled beets, and hardly a word passing between us. Papa wasn't much of a conversationalist at the best of times. Tonight, his silence was especially harsh. Meanwhile every small noise I made—chewing, pushing things around on my plate—seemed further proof that I was all wrong. During *Havdallah*, I wanted to disappear into the trail of black smoke that billowed up from the triple wick of the braided candle. After the flame hissed into the spilled wine, our father went straight to his study, skipping the concert for the lady in the white dress. She stared out of her portrait with a vacant look in her eyes and a sickly smile on her bloodless lips.

Papa was right. I'd broken the Sabbath before, more often than he realized. But never so unintentionally as today, never with such a pure heart. There was no justice.

Back in our bedroom, Liesel tried to console me, whispering a secret in my ear. She had not spent the afternoon at Ezra, the movement for Orthodox youth, but with a group of socialist Zionists instead. Papa would call them Godless heathens. There had been music and *hora* dancing and I should have come. Seated on my bed, Liesel sang to me a spirited new song she'd learned about rebuilding the ancient homeland.

> *In the hills, the golden dawn has poured her splendour*
> *In the valley, dew drops glitter still*
> *To you cherished land we tender*
> *Our hearts and hands to serve your will*
> *We shall plant and build, renew the story*
> *What can we offer more to praise your glory?*

Her voice quavered with emotion and her eyes shone, as if that golden dawn had already poured its splendour upon her. As if she could see the desert wasteland transformed into a carpet of green. I let her sing and enthuse, though I was not in the mood. I was trying to understand how the Presence could have withdrawn itself from me so completely.

Chapter 2
Exodus

Port of Trieste, May 1937

"GOOD RIDDANCE EUROPE, you cruel old sow!"

The voice nearby that yelled these words was hoarse and speaking Yiddish, the bastard tongue, which had its appeal even as it scalded my High-German sensibilities. Wheeling round, I spied a pale, gangly, scowling youth who leaned over the ship's rail and puckered his lips as if he intended to aim a gob of spit at the upturned faces gathered on the quay. But no, he merely sucked in air for more salty curses as he invited the jack-booted Italian border control policemen, at that moment marching down the ship's ramp, to lick his royal Jewish ass. I heard him yell something more about freedom and sailing to *Eretz Yisroel* and then his words and his figure became lost in a general roar of goodbyes and the crush of people storming towards the side of the ship. Fiercely I clung to my spot at the rail and jabbed my elbows into the jostling bodies beside me, refusing to succumb to the disadvantage of my smallness. I didn't want to miss a single moment of this grand, forever-after departure that I'd anticipated for so long with a mix of emotions. *Eretz Yisroel* I whispered aloud, rolling the ancient name around on my tongue, trying to get used to the idea of the new homeland. I had only the vaguest notions and forebodings, heightened by Uncle Otto's talk of the wild Orient.

The morning Papa and I had left Germany, Uncle Otto and Aunt Ida had come to see us off at the Freiburger Railway Station. Auntie bent down to stuff an extra woollen shawl and a bag of camomile tea against seasickness into my suitcase. She stroked my cheek with her gloved hand. Suddenly her arms flung open to clasp me to her bosom so tightly that I felt the thud of her heart beneath the stiff cloth of her dress. Embarrassed, or maybe remembering the swarm of germs that could pass between us, she quickly let go again and patted my hair and her own collar as if dusting us off. Her eyes had misted over in a look of sad bewilderment.

If Uncle was sad, he hid his feelings beneath a burst of good cheer, smoothing over the awkwardness of parting with a blanket of words.

"The exotic Orient, what an adventure, ha! You'll be fine Markus, on your feet in no time. I'm a little envious. But it's not for us. Foreign lands. Strange climates. *Ach nein.* Palestine is for the young. Or the young at heart, like you, Markus. Yes, of course, you're young at heart. And used to your Spartan diets. Not like me."

Otto patted the large belly straining against his belt buckle beneath the vest of his three-piece suit.

"What would I do without my Bratwurst and dumplings?"

A sonorous blast of the ship's horn shook me out of my reverie. The deck throbbed beneath my feet as somewhere far below an engine grumbled to life. Slowly our vessel inched away from the quay and a blizzard of waving handkerchiefs filled the air. Trieste's Habsburg-era palaces shrank into doll houses, the people on the quay faded into dots, the coastline under a grey sky became a smudge on the horizon while a pewter-coloured sea stretched all around. I turned and noticed Papa.

He too was leaning against the rail, a few feet away from me, shoulders slumped, Homburg crushed onto his head to keep it from flying off in the wind. He stared down at the wake churned up by the propellers with a stricken look on his face, as if something precious was lost in the foam. As if he were standing by a graveside. I knew what it was. Regret. Homesick already. He missed our home town, Breslau, the city of his birth and that of his ancestors, dating back to a bearded patriarch who'd moved there from the Rhineland in the eighteenth century. He missed the canals, bridges, promenades, linden trees, market squares, street cars, the back alley *shul* with the sloping floor, the leafy cemetery in which our mother was buried along with generations of relatives and acquaintances—all those familiar names carved into marble monuments. I believe at that moment he also missed the Storch synagogue, the one Uncle Otto and Aunt Ida attended and where Papa wouldn't deign set foot because it was too prosperous and showy, and probably he even missed the heathen Christian churches. I wasn't used to seeing my father so subdued. A sprout of pity stirred within me. But his head suddenly whipped around and his expression changed.

"What are you gaping at, girl? Close your mouth before the flies rush in."

His eyes fixed me with his signature harsh, bleak stare that seemed to penetrate my soul and find it nothing but an empty vessel. Then he muttered some curt instructions about our lunch arrangements before turning his back on me again. Though I was sixteen-and-a-half now—almost a grown woman—and though Papa was always thus, his withering glance hurled me back into the helpless rage of childhood. He never saw me as I really was. Always he misunderstood. *Good riddance, good riddance,* I chanted to myself, trying to recapture the euphoria of departure, but feeling mocked by the swooping, squealing gulls instead.

AMONG THE CROWDS of people from many lands who milled about our ship, the SS *Adriatica*, were groups of youths, all of whom already seemed anchored in friendships that had sprung up instantly. Sometimes they took over much of the open deck to form a solid wheel of frantically joyful *hora* dancers. Arms grasping one another's shoulders, feet all stepping and kicking in unison, round and round they whirled to the squawks and squeaks of a harmonica. The same tunes played over and over—an eager, strident, annoyingly hypnotic music in four-four time. Boys whooped, girls flashed open-hearted smiles, hands and shoulders fused more firmly together and no one paid attention to me, hovering on the sidelines, aloof and bitter. I'd barely grown since seventh grade and was still stuck in the same kind of dowdy brown dress I'd been wearing for years, a hand-me-down that bagged around my thin, childlike limbs. I had a stubby braid, the face of a waif. If the happy gang of youths did notice me, it would only be out of pity. The tyranny of the circle. The self-absorption of the group. As I watched the dancers one morning in a confusion of longing and disdain, I became aware of someone else nearby—the boy who'd yelled Yiddish curses towards the harbour as our ship departed. He was a stoop-shouldered angular fellow with a shock of unruly black hair over his brow and, even before I heard him speak, I sensed the blast of scorn emanating from his soul towards the circle dance, a repudiation even greater than my own.

"They think it's a game, a big party. They have no idea about the real struggle. We won't win the homeland by hopping like crickets."

His eyes remained fixed straight ahead, so I wasn't sure if he was addressing me or simply talking to himself. His intensity fascinated me, even as it set off a hundred alarm bells clanging through my already unsettled mind.

"Jabotinsky calls for strength, discipline, fighting fire with fire. What do they know about the great Jabotinsky, those pathetic Labour Zionists?"

I had no idea what he was talking about and though I sensed it was just the sort of story to make me profoundly uncomfortable, curiosity twitched beneath my forebodings. But before I could summon the courage to ask him a question, he'd taken himself away, to another part of the ship. No doubt he too thought I was just a little girl and thus unworthy of his high-blown musings about the great Jabotinsky. During the days that followed, I glimpsed him now and then, his pale, aloof, serious face beneath the tangles of dark hair, but finding him even more unapproachable than the happy crowd, I steered clear. Brittle with shyness and pride, I would drift away to the back of the ship to the safety of solitude and gaze out at the grey expanse of the sea. The journey through monotonous sameness, through the frothy curled tongues of a zillion identical waves became a dreamy in-between time, a state that lent itself to brooding. And since I couldn't imagine the future or the country to which we were heading, I found myself engulfed in the past, just like Papa, but without a hint of honeyed nostalgia.

In those hours, my seventh grade teacher, Fräulein Spitz, returned with a vengeance. I hadn't thought of her for years, but here she was, searingly vivid as a scorpion's sting. She'd come to our school just after that miserable August of my absurd religious conversion, sent to replace the kind, but mumbling, dull-voiced and absent-minded *Frau* Bauernfreund, who had taken early retirement. Fräulein Spitz was young, energetic, and attractive—a model of the new ideal, with straight, athletic shoulders, noble features, blond locks, and keen blue eyes. She had a touch of film star sophistication, but also a sweet cleft in her chin that made her seem just a tiny bit vulnerable and not entirely above us. As she marched back and forth in front of the class, talking about how we were on the threshold of a great era, the air in the room became charged with her passion. Here at last was a teacher who was bold and had something to say. Glancing around, I could see how the others had been instantly smitten. I was almost in love myself except for a creeping sense of dread.

Fräulein Spitz believed in innovation. She wanted to get us out of our seats. She wanted to become acquainted with her pupils. And so, after her opening lecture, she asked that the whole class rise and gather in front of the windows to form a row—tallest to shortest. We were to do this quickly and quietly, with no silly tittering or chatter. She clapped her hands. Everyone rose at once in an explosion of scraping chairs. Without a word, as if we'd done this many times, we sorted ourselves out and glided into place. Not surprisingly, I was at the end of the row.

Fräulein Spitz slowly walked down the line, as if inspecting an honour guard, and asked each girl her name and that of her father. She held an attendance register and ticked off the names as she found them on her list. This procedure took longer than the usual way of reading out the names in alphabetical order. But it allowed Fräulein Spitz to make eye contact with each one of us, to literally size us up. There were two other Jewish girls in class—Beate Friedmann and Lilly Kohn. Fräulein Spitz made check marks on her list, but then suddenly asked them both to step forward and state their nationality. In unison, both girls said, unwavering, "German!" The teacher's eyes widened in astonishment.

"*Ach so?*"

Fräulein Spitz peered carefully at Beate and Lilly as if wondering if they were real or cleverly dressed-up storefront dummies. But after a long moment, she moved on. Everyone who'd been holding in her breath in expectation, exhaled.

At last the teacher stood in front of me. I opened my mouth, ready to state my name. The hint of a mocking smile played upon Fräulein Spitz's lovely lips. She shook her head in disbelief.

"Well, I suppose this one won't be competing in the high jump."

A gust of shocked titters swept up and down the row. The name I'd been about to speak died in my throat. But the teacher already knew who I was. Her ice-blue eyes regarded me from their lofty position near the top of her statuesque body.

"Just how tall are you, Salomon?"

And when I didn't respond: "You don't know?"

In that moment of panicked vertigo, I'm not sure I did. My throat closed, my lungs collapsed, breath failed me and a roaring chaos filled my mind.

"Let me guess. I'd say about one hundred and forty."

The mockery on her lips was now unmistakable.

She called for the girl at the front of the row to fetch the wooden rule that lay on a ledge beneath the blackboard and, with it pressed against my back, she confirmed she'd been close to the mark. I measured no more than one hundred and forty-five centimetres.

Not everyone laughed, but those who did positively shrieked with delight. It was as if the esteemed teacher had released a thought that had been pressing on everyone's minds for ages and was finally being allowed to see the light of day.

A pygmy of the Mosaic persuasion.

I never told Papa. What was the point? He had his own nasty encounters to deal with by then, along with the financial worries that began to plague almost every household in our community. Anyway, he wasn't the kind of father one told things to. Nor did I speak to Liesel. I didn't want her crushing me to her breast in an excess of sympathy or begging me to join the youth group. After another week of tall-to-shortest roll calls, Fräulein Spitz suddenly, without explanation, went back to the usual alphabetical method of taking attendance. Other humiliations were not quite as personal but equally shattering. The lessons in racial studies, for example. Tacked to the wall in front of the class was a chart of sketches of typical heads—Aryan, Slavic, Asian, and so on. Fräulein Spitz lingered over the example of the ideal type, her ruler tapping at the placard. We were to note the Aryan's narrow face, the high-built nose, the strong jaw, and prominent chin, all of which expressed boldness of character. The teacher read aloud from a printed document, labouring through opaque facts such as a "cephalic index of seventy-five," and a "facial index of ninety." Beate Friedmann, Lilly Kohn and I sat on a bench at the back, apart from the others. The Jew bench.

My attention was glued to the ninth and last placard. This face had fat lips, a nose like a claw, a scraggly beard, and squinting eyes that latched onto mine. They stared back at me with a pitiless intensity. I squeezed my own eyes shut but still saw the face—an electric yellow afterimage—the expression jerking through a dozen changes in an instant: from leering, to pleading, to defiance, to tenderness, to deep, pained all-knowingness, and back again to craven meekness. The images pulsed behind my eyelids and finally exploded into a thousand rancid-yellow dots. The face and the explosion of yellow specks pursued me for a long time afterwards.

I came to an iron-clad conclusion in that hard season. There was no justice in this world and certainly no Presence. Nothing, nothing, nothing, whether on high or here on earth. The entire Torah was a sham. The whole, elaborate set of rules served no purpose but to squeeze the few drops of joy out of life. Why such rules were dreamt up and why joy had to be quenched was beyond me, but I could see it was so. And it was not the Jewish religion that was the fundamental problem, I realized. It wasn't Christianity, the Führer, nationalism, Zionism or communism. Belief itself was to blame. Belief gave false hope. All faiths, persuasions, enthusiasms, and models of social order, all were the same, made people blind and cruel. I became more convinced of this truth through the years of dreariness, uncertainty and terror—the mass rallies on the streets, the vicious laws, the ugly songs (*All will be well in German life / When Jewish blood spurts from the knife.*)

In 1935, shortly after the time of my fifteenth birthday, Tilly, our maid of so many years, had to leave our household because of the Law for the Protection of German Blood and German Honour. No German-blooded female below the age of forty-five was allowed to work as a servant in the home of a Jewish male. Somewhat cross-eyed and with a nose like a lump of putty, Tilly was not exactly alluring. Plus, she exuded a stiff, spinsterish reserve—surely one of the features that caused Papa to hire her in the first place. I'd never seen a hint of anything improper between them. Never had it occurred to me there could be anything *like that.* But now the ugly spectre had been raised and visions of Papa and Tilly touching one another in forbidden ways assaulted my fifteen-year-old imagination. I felt defiled by my grotesque thoughts. We were all defiled, as if a foul substance had permeated the flat, penetrating each of us to our inner core. Papa could barely bring himself to look at Tilly, and when she leaned towards him to serve the soup, he jerked away as if stung, while Tilly's face flamed scarlet. Papa sat at the table, fiercely dignified and straight-backed as ever. He recited blessings in his usual gruff drone. And yet I caught an uneasy flicker in his eyes that made me want to sink into the floorboards with shame. And so I became impatient for Tilly to go and knew Papa felt the same. Neither of us could bear her presence any longer—a rare moment when Papa and I thought as one, but it didn't draw us closer together in the least.

Liesel spent more and more time with her Zionist youth group and one day, against Papa's wishes and before I could try to talk her out of it, she'd hitchhiked across the Czechoslovak border and joined a training program on a communal farm that prepared Jewish youth for agricultural settlement in Palestine. I received letters in which she extolled the pioneering life—the rising with the larks, the marching off with her hoe to whatever task was assigned, exulting in what she called the "cleansing force of physical labour."

"The dark stains on my palms are kisses from Mother Earth. How much greater the joy will be when I kneel on the soil of our homeland. Stop laughing, cynical child. One day you too will understand."

Now it was just Papa and me alone together, consuming our supper in silence at the great oak table with the empty chairs and Mama's pale face gazing blankly from the photo on the mantle. A new maid, a Jewish woman, originally from Krakow, rattled around in the kitchen. She was a widow who'd fallen on hard times and who spoke German with an accent that made Papa grit his teeth. Cowed by his grim demeanour, she spent any free time she had sequestered in her room. Sometimes I heard weeping from behind her closed door, a sound that sent me into a strange, excruciating rage. I'd fling open the window of my room and lean far out over the sill, gulping oxygen. Or I'd crawl into the closet and play my recorder in the dark, amid the company of a few sad bits of clothing Liesel had left behind.

Eventually, Papa transferred me from the German public system to the Talmud Torah, a Jewish school, which, in normal times, accommodated about three hundred students. But in this new era it held twice that number—refugees from the public system from all over town and surrounding villages. Pell-mell, we were thrown together: orthodox and secular, rich and poor, boys and girls, old-stock German Jews and *Ostjuden*, whose parents had come to the country in recent decades and who still clung to their foreign ways. Classes were crammed, books and equipment lacking, the teachers harried. As the atmosphere outside the walls of the Talmud Torah went from bad to worse, the classrooms buzzed with talk of emigration. To Palestine. To the four corners of the earth. Our school set up extracurricular vocational programs and encouraged us to learn a trade that would help our prospects for future employment. The accent in all the classes was on stuffing our heads with practical, utilitarian knowledge, but the teachers themselves were uncertain what that might be. The geography of Argentina? The American constitution? Who knew where any of us would wash ashore?

One by one, teachers and students left the country, the classes thinned out and the sad, restless atmosphere of a way station permeated our school. At Liesel's training program, the girls chose boys' names out of a hat and they all got married in an assembly line of weddings amid much hysterical laughter. It was a ruse to make the most of scarce immigration certificates. A married immigrant was allowed to bring his bride into Palestine. Aboard the deck of a ship bound for Haifa, Liesel and her "paper husband" and all the rest of her group had danced a joyous *hora*, no doubt to the same harmonica-wheezed tunes that I now heard on the SS *Adriatica*.

For the longest time, Papa had refused to consider joining the tide of emigrants. He clung to his consolations. At least we had order, he said. No more street brawls between the Brownshirts and the Communists. Across the border, in darkest Poland, a mob could boil over at any moment, but not here. Not in Germany. And though certain park benches, swimming pools, theatres, restaurants and so on, were now forbidden to Jews, the parks were spotless at least, one could still swim in the river, the shows were dreadful anyway and restaurant meals were a pure waste of money. Moreover, trains ran on time and the station master at Freiburger Bahnhof still touched his cap in a smart salute at the start of every journey. But there could be no denying the steady decline of business at Salomon and Sons, Purveyors of Sacks and Twine. Day by day, customers switched their loyalties to the Aryan competition. Papa could no longer comfortably travel around the countryside, buying up used sacks. His familiar face in the villages—his very Jewish face—had become a liability. This truth bit hard into Papa's heart, as did the prospect of having to give up our flat and move in with Uncle and Auntie to make ends meet. Uncle had other business interests to keep him afloat, but Papa saw his savings ebb away. With great reluctance, he finally appealed to foreign embassies, including the office for British Palestine. By that time, because of unrest amid the Arab population, the British authorities had imposed strict quotas on Jewish immigration. To qualify for a "Capitalist" certificate, Papa needed 1,000 pounds sterling to bring into the country. The only way he could afford that amount was to borrow from Uncle Otto. Papa loathed debt. The fact that his own brother would do the lending didn't lesson the shame in the least. He filed his application with a heavy heart, half hoping it would come to nothing. As for my wishes (which didn't count, but I had them anyway), I was torn. Though I longed to see Liesel again, I was more drawn to the civilized West—America, England, France— than the exotic East.

Months went by, bringing letters of refusal from a string of countries and no word on Palestine. Then, one day, the amazing news arrived from His Majesty's Government in Jerusalem. Papa's application had been accepted. I heard him muttering to himself as he paced around like a trapped fox. What was the lesser evil? To borrow Otto's money or accept his hospitality? Visions of the four of us under one roof, trying to step around one another, must have sprung to his mind. Thoughts of Otto's kosher laxities settled the question.

Just before we left Breslau, I received a letter from Liesel, postmarked Palestine and written from a settlement by the shores of the Sea of Galilee.

Ein Rachel - May 11, 1937
Dear Evaleh,

Forgive me for my long silence, but the days wring me out and leave me like a schmatte flung into a corner. Two months ago, three from our group, Trudi, Hans and I arrived in Ein Rachel, a settlement in the lower Galilee. We travelled by train, donkey cart and finally on foot guided by a couple of boys with rifles. For miles we saw nothing but stony earth and thistle fields until a ribbon of green— the vegetation along the Sea of Galilee shimmered on the horizon like a mirage. Our first glimpse of the settlement was of the top of the tall wooden watchtower looming above the compound walls. As we tramped through the fields to the main gate, a couple of "old-timers" leaned upon their hoes to look us over. The woman had skin like an old shoe and straw-like hair poking out from under her kerchief.

"Shalom comrade," I said and stretched out my hand. Her grip was so hard I almost shrieked.

"Ha," she chuckled. "You'll soon lose your rosy cheeks and baby fat."

She meant no harm—it was just kibbutz humour: frank, a bit brutal. At the time, the remark felt like a slap in the face, especially after our exhausting journey, but I'm getting used to these little shocks. With Trudi and another girl, Doreet, I share a tent furnished with cots, sea-grass mattresses, orange crates (for stools and storage) and a hurricane lamp. It's by the flickering light of this lantern that I'm writing you now. There's so much to tell—about our living conditions, the work, the climate. Briefly, it's all very hard but I am trying to toughen up and conquer hardship—that's the

Zionist way: to prevail through sheer force of will. I have come, as
we say in the movement, to "build and be rebuilt." I so much want
to be like the others.

How wonderful that you and Papa are finally coming to Palestine.
You can't imagine how relieved I am. And dying to see you again. But
I can't possibly meet the ship in Haifa. It's too far and too expensive.
Only the old-timers are allowed trips out and even so there has to
be a vote on the request at the weekly communal meeting. But we
will get together as soon as I can manage, perhaps after the grape
harvest. In the meantime, a fat kiss on your dear cheek. The lantern
is smoking, my eyes are watering. I simply can't write another word.

Your loving sister,

Liesel

ON THE SIXTH day of our journey, a cry echoed from the upper deck to
the lower, from bow to stern.

"Land!"

People streamed out of the cabins and lounges to witness the miracle—the
land of Palestine taking shape, like the birth of a star.

I climbed onto a bench to see over the crowd of heads. Some chalky streaks
appeared—beaches perhaps. A curved shape emerged out of the sea, grew into a
hill haloed by the golden rays of the sun, rose higher and sharpened in outline.
The misty gold turned to dusty green, white humps became buildings and thin
ribbons became roads.

"Mount Carmel," someone shouted.

"*Eretz Yisroel!*" someone else called and the triumphant cry echoed around
me—*Ha'aretz, Ha'aretz!* The Land.

Finally the captain cut the ship's engines as a tug arrived to pull us towards
the harbour. A hush ensued, a few moments of awed silence magnified by the
swish of waves against the ship's prow. Someone on our deck broke out into
the Zionist anthem and more and more voices joined in, gathering strength. It
was a slow, majestic melody with echoes of Smetana's *The Moldau*—very Slavic
to my ears and haunting, with an irresistible pull like the flow of a great river.
Soon the stirring words, which I knew from the Talmud Torah school, insinuated
themselves to my lips.

*The hope of two thousand years / To be a free people / In our land / The
land of Zion and Jerusalem!*

I saw the disdainful youth with the unruly mop of hair standing ruler-straight at attention and singing for all he was worth. I saw the target of his mockery, the Labour Zionist group, clustered nearby and doing the same. And mothers of young children and grown men, with tears streaming down their cheeks. This grab-bag of rumpled, care-worn Jews had coalesced into a sea of brotherhood, and, I, Eva Salomon, in my dowdy brown dress and lumpy, dirty-carrot-coloured braid, for the briefest moment was carried along with the tide. Then it was over. People mopped their eyes. They started milling and murmuring, became ordinary again as the euphoria of arrival dissolved into the scramble to disembark. Papa was beside me, nervously patting his pockets for papers, his Homburg askew, the top of his starched, buttoned-up collar gone soft with sweat. Now that we'd left the breezes of the open sea behind, the air had become heavy and the morning sun beat down with remarkable force. With the rest of the immigrant contingent—the largest group on board—we shuffled through the gangways, down the stairs.

When it was Papa's turn to present papers, I got my first good glimpse of the British authorities. The two men with the peaked caps and insignia on their square shoulders did not speak roughly. They showed more politeness than we were used to, nevertheless they subjected both Papa and me to a hard, official scrutiny—passing our documents between them, peering at us through narrowed eyes. Papa stammered his answers in awkward, heavily accented English, and suddenly obsequious, mentioned that his daughter could speak the language well. It was true that the one subject at the Talmud Torah school I'd enjoyed was English because of a teacher who'd had a dramatic flair and read Hamlet aloud to us in his rich baritone voice. Though I'd barely understood, still I was able to envision the tormented young prince before me and became enthralled with the cadences of the language. I'd even enjoyed the more tedious exercises, such as the Imperial system of weights and measures, soothed by words with an archaic ring that seemed to stem from a language of gnomes: *furlong, fathom, stone, ell.* Those were the preposterous words that now sprang to my mind as I tried to think of how to impress the officer with the red-veined face and squinting eyes. Before I could arrange my thoughts, he'd turned to his mate.

"'Ow old's this one supposed to be? Sixteen? Hmff. Bit queer that. Usually they pretend to be younger than they are. But the papers are in order. Right then. Off you go."

He gave us a last glance of blank indifference as he smacked the rubber stamp to our documents. I looked away quickly, my face flaming.

We emerged onto a noisy, dusty, crowded quay, presided over by armed British soldiers with sun-broiled faces, who barked at people to move along.

I saw donkey carts, swarms of flies around the beasts' quivering flanks, dark-skinned Arab porters in odd, ballooning trousers. A wiry little man staggered by, doubled over by a huge load of boxes strapped to his back. Foul smells simmered: of donkey dung, latrines and some other kind of rot. Papa and I shuffled into a cavernous grey customs shed and joined a long, buckling line in front of a table where more officials sat checking papers yet again and examining the contents of people's luggage. We stood and stood, the process taking forty years, it seemed to me. Moisture beaded in the furrows of Papa's cheeks and brow. My heavy brown dress stuck to my skin. Liesel would not be among the throngs outside waiting for their loved ones. We would have to face the wild Orient on our own.

Chapter 3
White City

IN A CITY of dazzling light, my father managed to surround us in gloom. He found us a basement flat in the older, shabbier part of Tel Aviv near the bus station, the railway tracks, the Yemenite district and an Arab neighbourhood that I was warned to avoid. Two tiny, dim rooms and a galley kitchen in a narrow building sandwiched between a hodgepodge of others in a warren of pot-holed lanes. After the porters dumped the last of our boxes onto the floor, I looked about in shock. How could we live here? When we'd packed up our apartment in Breslau, I'd thought Papa far too ruthless. So many precious things we were leaving behind! The china cabinet. The grandfather clock, whose deep-voiced chimes had parcelled out the hours for as long as I could remember. Now I wondered what we'd do with the abundance crowding around. Heaped up-crates and the jumble of furniture took up almost all the space in the main room and seemed to suck up the available oxygen too.

A high window, level with the lane outside, let in a modicum of light. A large crack snaked down the wall beneath the window. Something moved in the crack: a procession of ants. Papa rummaged through packing straw until he found the framed chart of the *yahrzeit* dates of my mother and grandparents. With a grunt of triumph, he held it up against the teeming crack.

"Yes. Right here," he muttered to himself.

Pleased to have found a spot for his beloved memento and a way to cover up an unsightly flaw, he gently leaned the chart, with its heavy frame and glass, against the wall. But this effort seemed to take up the last of his energy. He groped for the dining room chair that had been shoved into a corner, collapsed onto it with a groan. The other seven chairs sat up-ended like dead beetles on the great, oval-shaped dining room table. Of all things, Papa had decided we could not be without this massive piece of furniture, which had been in the family for generations and on which he'd taken his meals since childhood. Made of dark, heavy oak, it had ornately carved legs that culminated in stylized claws. The porters had struggled mightily to manoeuvre it down the stairs and squeeze it through the doorway of the basement flat. The table, which I hadn't seen since Breslau, got me thinking about the routine of meals and other domestic realities.

"Who will cook and clean for us?" I asked Papa.

Papa's chin, which had sunk towards his chest, jerked upwards at my question.

"Why you, of course," he snapped. "Did you think I could afford servants? Did you think the streets would be paved with gold? I have to start from nothing. And you will have to do your part too. No more mooning and dreaming and frittering away your time. It will do you good."

So much for Papa, the capitalist, with his apparent fortune of a thousand pounds sterling. Much of the money never left Germany, I learned. Like many others, he'd been forced to invest in German exports, the result of a complicated arrangement between the Nazi government and the Zionist leadership, which allowed Jews to access their otherwise frozen bank accounts and the Nazis to circumvent an international boycott. Papa had purchased an inventory of electrical goods—light bulbs, batteries, fuses, copper wire—which he intended to peddle around town, though he knew nothing about electricity. The crates of inventory now jostled for floor space with the heaps of furniture and other belongings in our shoebox of a home.

WHAT DID I know about keeping house? What did I understand about the ways of the Levant? And who was there to teach me? My teacher would be trial and error.

The torment of every greenhorn in those days was the three-legged monster called the Primus. It was a small kerosene stove, the kind one might take on a camping expedition. I was dismayed to learn that this little one-burner device was to be my sole cooking appliance. Very few households in Palestine had anything else. The fuel for the stove was delivered to our neighbourhood by a man with a mule-drawn cart, on which lay a cylindrical tank with a spigot.

"*Neft! Neft!*" he called out, while clanging a bell.

People ran into the street with their jerry cans, then lugged the sloshing cans back home through lanes and up stairways.

To get the Primus going, you had to pour a small amount of alcohol into a circular spirit cup just below the burner and light that with a match to pre-heat the burner assembly. When the burner was hot, you pushed a little hand pump to force kerosene from the tank at the bottom, up through tubes to the burner head. At that point, if you were lucky, a ring of blue flames blossomed. By turning a screw, you could adjust the size of the flames. All this was theory. In reality you could fiddle and pump, fiddle some more and hold your breath, and still the thing would sputter out or else belch great gusts of soot into the air. My early attempts produced smoky explosions.

"*Gevalt!*" screamed Hannah, the Russian lady who lived one floor above. "You'll set the whole building on fire."

"How long did it take you to learn?" I asked her tearfully.

She shrugged. "I don't remember. But it doesn't matter about learning. The beast will always have a mind of its own."

There were so many other skills to master: where to shop and what to buy and how to haggle. How to build a wood fire under the boiler for hot water, how to spot the bad eggs from the good, what to do with an eggplant, how to stretch our meagre housekeeping money. And the use of a scrub board, the saving of precious water, the tackling of assorted insect invasions. Cockroaches the size of mice paraded over the cracked floor tiles. The walls of our flat spewed ants and smelled of mildew. The lane- way showered dust through our window. The market clamoured with languages I could not understand. I struggled through my tasks in a daze of shock.

To Papa's credit, he ate everything I put in front of him without complaint. Rubbery omelettes, scorched soups, milk that had been boiled into little clumps. One time he bit down hard on a stone that I'd neglected to sort out of the lentils. He spat it into his hand, tucked it under the lip of his plate and continued to eat, methodically, silently, with a calm air of martyrdom. His manner didn't change much with my more successful creations. But though Papa made little fuss about the quality of our meals, he did, of course, insist on a kosher kitchen. We had two sets of dishes for meat foods and for dairy. Two sets of utensils, dish towels, wash rags. Separate areas in the minuscule cupboards. Papa hovered as I washed the dishes, making sure nothing got mixed up.

Hannah and other women in the building offered advice, but they were busy with their own households or jobs, or both. They patted me on the shoulder.

"All will be fine," they said. "*Yiyeh tov.*"

This expression was the first bit of Hebrew a newcomer learned, after the greeting, *Shalom*. No matter what my trouble, no matter how desperate my straits, people were always ready to respond with a smiling, bland and useless "*yiyeh tov.*" From early morning to late in the evening I was busy: schlepping, scrubbing, chopping, grating, dusting. Every day brought new frustrations. I heard the iceman's bell and ran out onto the street with the other housewives, but I had brought no tongs. The women laughed when I struggled to carry my block of ice wrapped in the bottom of my skirt.

"Next time you'll know," they assured me. "*Yiyeh tov.*"

If I lamented, I reaped superior smiles. Didn't Papa and I enjoy luxury accommodations compared to what other newcomers had? Two whole rooms for just the two of us! Many families with flocks of children had to crowd together in smaller spaces. Many had to use an outdoor privy. A kitchen? We had a kitchen with a sink? Others had to fetch water from a hose in the yard. And this too was luxury compared to conditions faced by the original wave of immigrants. All around us now, a fine, modern city was rising up—shops and cinemas and even that wonder of wonders, a traffic light. Thirty years ago, what could you find here? Nothing but shifting sand. When neighbours heard my German accent, a particular note of scorn entered their voices. According to the local wisdom, German Jews were notoriously spoiled and demanding. I soon stopped expecting sympathy from our hardscrabble neighbourhood.

Astounding to think that our two-storey building was less than thirty years old. Everything moved fast in Tel Aviv—new construction, but also decay. The sea air and the harsh sun took their toll on façades so that yesterday's bright surfaces became pockmarked and weathered into a yellowish grey. Rickety sheds made of shipping crates clogged backyards. Litter abounded in lanes. Flies blackened rotting scraps. Feral cats prowled. Still, there was much that was fresh and fine in the city. Despite all my housework, I managed to slip away now and then to explore.

Walking along Nachlat Binyamin Street to Allenby Road in the centre of town, I discovered the Tel Aviv of its nicknames: the White City, the First Hebrew City. I saw sparkling, clean-lined, efficient buildings made for the sunny climate with small windows, curved balconies, and shady arcades. I saw sidewalk cafés with striped awnings and cane chairs and tables, to which waiters delivered milk-coffee and Viennese torte. There were delicatessens, pharmacies, and smart clothing shops, with imitations of the latest Parisian fashions artfully arranged in the windows. Cheek-by-jowl with these better establishments could be a hole-in-the-wall workshop or a grocery—plank shelves cluttered with inventory, pickle barrels and tomato trays spilling out onto the pavement. But this added to the vibrancy. Tel Aviv was raw, hectic, alive. People rushed about, faces full of purpose. On every corner, construction and scaffolding. Everywhere, crews of sweating, sun-bronzed youths in undershirts. *Jews! They were Jews!* The roads were a patchwork of newly laid asphalt, rubble, and sand. Smells of industry mingled in the air: freshly poured cement, whitewash, exhaust fumes. Horns tooted, hammers rang out, traffic rumbled. *Jewish traffic!* Buses and motor cars of every description, bicycles, wagons drawn by horses and donkeys, handcarts and wheelbarrows and the occasional flock of goats. Escaped our dingy flat, my feet stepped faster and my heart beat in happy concordance with the brash Tel Aviv rhythm. Others had found their place in the new Hebrew city. Perhaps, my heart whispered, so could I.

Meanwhile Papa saw only negatives. That buses came late, that passengers pushed and children yelled without being restrained. That many businesses ignored the Sabbath, that people bought on credit and that women smoked out in the open in the broad light of day. And that both women and men paraded their half-naked bodies along the beach. Also he vehemently disapproved that Hebrew, the holy tongue, was merely an everyday language here, used for notices about garbage collection and polluted with slang by louts on the street. Near dawn each morning, he set out to trudge the pavements, lugging two suitcases packed with his wares. At first, despite the climate, he dressed exactly as he had back in Breslau: dark suit with waistcoat, knotted tie and Homburg. The heat grew from week to week through the summer, until it melted patches of asphalt and made sparrows gasp. Other businessmen wore open-necked, short-sleeved shirts, and even short pants. Eventually, Papa gave up on the waistcoat and tie, but he retained his jacket. One had to maintain some standards! Despite his knowledge of Biblical Hebrew, he had trouble with the everyday language. He insisted on addressing people in German. Those Ruskies and Pollaks knew perfectly well what he was saying, Papa fumed. They laughed and called him *Yecke*, the consummate, unbending German Jew. Even fellow *Yeckes* shook their heads over his stubborn ways. From dawn to dusk, Papa made his rounds of radio shops, lighting shops, appliance factories, and bit-of-everything establishments. He came home parched, sweat-drenched, sagging, and bitter. He lacked what it took to succeed in this new land. He wasn't a schmoozer, a hustler, a dealmaker. Still he trudged, redoubling his efforts. And the household money dwindled.

One evening, as we sat at table over chicken feet soup, I broke our customary mealtime silence.

"I could go to work," I said, as casually as my thumping heart would allow. "I could earn some money to help us out."

Papa lowered his soup spoon and stared at me in astonishment.

"I won't neglect the household. I'll do both."

"You? At a job? And what do you think you could do?"

A picture from some magazine sprang to my mind. I remembered a smartly dressed woman perched on a swivel chair with a phone wedged against her shoulder. Her head was tipped at a coquettish angle. Her exquisitely manicured fingers danced over a typewriter.

"I could . . . I would like to become a secretary. I could answer phones and type."

"Is that so?" Papa laid his spoon down beside his bowl. A sarcastic gleam came into his eyes and the left side of his mouth twitched in a smirk.

"You have skills I'm unaware of? You have learned how to type and how to speak to strangers over the telephone?"

I squeezed my hands together under the table but met his gaze head on.

"I'll go to the Jewish Workers Federation and ask them to send me for training."

Papa erupted in a series of mirthless snorts.

"The Jewish Workers Federation! Why, your stupid Papa has been slaving like a mule when all he had to do was go to the Federation."

"But all immigrants go there for help. Why shouldn't we?"

"Because they are scoundrels! Party hacks. Socialist *machers*."

His fist smacked down on the table, making the cutlery rattle.

"Loud-mouthed boasters who act as if they can bring forth water out of stone. You think you know more than I do? You know nothing. First thing, they'll ask you where your father is from and how does he lean: left, right, centre, *nu*? Is he one of our men, or beyond the pale? Training! Ha! That's for girls whose fathers have *Protekzia*. Same as in the alleys of Lodz. That's how this country of heathens and scoundrels works. A wink here. A back slap there. You know what jobs that they find for girls like you, fresh off the boat? House cleaning! They'll send you to scrub floors in the home of some Labour Zionist *macher*. Some big shot who doesn't keep kosher. You'll earn a few piastres and many pinches of your bottom besides."

He turned back to his soup, shovelling the broth into his mouth with brisk determination.

"But I want to try," I squeaked.

He jerked his chin towards my neglected meal. "Finish up. It's perfectly good food. Don't waste. You're worried about money? Then eat what's in front of you. I worked hard enough to put it on the table."

The smell of boiled chicken hung heavy in the air along with the stifling heat. I pushed my bowl away.

"I want to try," I said again, more firmly. For response Papa took each of the long yellow chicken toes into his mouth to suck the nourishment out of them. Afterwards he finished my soup as well, and then, glaring at my downcast face, muttered to himself the Grace after Meals.

"So, you have time on your hands? You want to make yourself useful? Fine. You can help me with my business. There's plenty more you can do right here in this house."

That evening Papa had me sort and organize inventory—separating tiny screws from larger ones, winding copper wire into neat coils, tucking light bulbs into cardboard sleeves, labelling packages. Cinderella work. We sat together at the dining room table, which we'd covered with a protective layer of newspaper, working by the light of a single twenty-five-watt bulb to save electricity. Papa pored over his order books and accounts while I performed the fidgety tasks. In another flat somewhere, a radio blared peppy marching band music. Feet shuffled by in the lane. But in our flat, there was only the rustle of turned pages and the click of metallic objects as I sorted, for Papa was a locked vault. The crushing silence bore down on me. An old restlessness, an electric crackling, pervaded my limbs. Of its own accord, my arm made a violent sweeping movement that sent three precious sixty-watt light bulbs sailing off the table and onto the terrazzo floor. Papa reared up and raged, calling me a clumsy cow, the bane of his existence and a dozen names besides, but I barely heard. My mind reverberated with the delicious sound of the light bulbs exploding into showers of glittering shards. Something in me snapped awake.

IN THE MORNING, I left the dishes on the counter, the laundry in the tub, the shopping bags in the drawer, the floor unswept. I marched away from our quarter to the heart of town, to a big, bright, modern building with broad steps, a maze of halls and swarms of people. The Jewish Workers Federation. For two-and-a-half hours I waited my turn in a crowded corridor where people shifted from foot to foot and surged towards the employment office door whenever it opened and a shrill-voiced secretary called out, "Who's next?"

The man in front of me wore a wrinkled linen suit and clutched a briefcase full of credentials. He was a philology graduate from the University of Heidelberg. There was a woman who'd been a district school inspector back home. Another woman had training as a legal secretary. All around me people showed off their certificates and letters of reference while lamenting the lack of work in their fields. Skilled tradesmen were the new gods of Palestine. A truck driver could get the officials of the Federation to bow down to him, but a white-collar professional faced rejection and scorn. These stories nibbled away at my resolve, as did the remark, kindly meant, from the legal secretary. "A sweet young thing like you should be in school."

At last I was ushered into a small office with tall filing cabinets, a desk piled high with assorted papers, notebooks, and newspaper clippings, and a sweating official whose glasses had slid to the end of his nose. On the wall behind the man's head hung a stylized poster of a heroic figure with a sheaf of grain in his upraised hand. "Arise Worker," said the caption. "Rejoice in the sweat of your brow."

Hesitant and stammering, in a mixture of Hebrew and German, I told the official all about myself. I made it clear I wasn't interested in agricultural work. I stressed my secretarial ambitions. He didn't seem to be listening, kept his head ducked down, reading some letter, as the blunt fingers of his left hand—all the nails chewed down to the quick—did a restless dance on the desk. Every so often he nodded and sighed. Over the contents of the letter, I presumed. From the corridor conversations, I'd gleaned that it was important to sound firm and determined before these officials. I leaned forward and clutched the edge of the desk.

"Sir! Please! Listen to me. I need your help."

He looked up in surprise.

"Of course you need help. Why else would you be here?"

The question hung in the air as he peered severely over his smudged glasses. When I failed to answer, he broke into a pleased chuckle.

"Your Hebrew is horrible. Simply horrible! You say you're seventeen? You don't look it. Not a bit. Never mind. You'll grow older. Guaranteed! But listen, you could be a pretty girl if you put some meat on your bones. Ha, it's a joke. Don't be so offended. You won't survive in this country with such a thin skin."

I began to tell my story again, starting with my hopes for a secretarial training program. He waved his hand impatiently.

"There's no such thing. Not that we fund, anyway. Do you have money? No? Then you need to work. Or go back to your father. A simple choice. Believe me, that's a blessing: a simple choice."

As he spoke his hand scrabbled around in the sea of papers, searching for something, which he finally found—a folded note tucked into the frame of the desk blotter.

"Aha, here we have it. The perfect fit. *Mr. Mandelmann on Rothschild Boulevard seeks domestic help three times a week.* A golden opportunity."

I stared at his triumphantly smiling face in disbelief.

"But that's not what I want to do! I'd prefer something else."

"You want? You prefer?"

The official threw up his hands.

"You're not in a position to prefer. The professor who was here just before you was grateful to get work in the brick factory. You've taken care of your father's house for a few months so you know how to shake a carpet and wash a floor. Tell Mandelmann you have experience in domestic labour. Don't tell him it's your first job in this country."

The man peered at me again over his glasses. "Or in any country."

Before I could say another word, he'd come around from behind the desk, thrust the note in my hand and was ushering me towards the door. He propelled me out of his office with a parting pat on the shoulder.

"Don't worry. *Yiyeh tov.*"

DOMESTIC HELP. THAT was all I was good for. Exactly as Papa had predicted. I'd be rubbing my knuckles raw on washboards, but instead of being the mistress of the house, I'd be a servant, sullied with all the shameful connotations of that word. Back home in Germany we'd always had a maid, more than one in our better years, and they were part of the household and of course they were individuals with rights and needs. Papa treated them correctly, always. Yet it was understood they were on a different level. They had their place and we had ours. As I stood on the outer steps of the Workers Federation, I squeezed my eyes shut against the sunlight, but there was no hiding from the blinding glare for it pulsed behind my lids. Simple choices are blessings, the man had said. I could hurry home and cook an omelette for Papa's midday meal and he'd never know I'd left the flat and it would be easy to slide back into the embrace of the familiar.

No, not easy. The familiar was a noose. I could barely breathe when I returned to the warm, mildewed basement that smelled of yesterday's soup and the sour residue of this morning's yogurt on the unwashed bowls. The dining room table that I'd just polished to gleaming the day before had dimmed under a fresh coat of dust. The metal washtub sat, where I'd left it, in the middle of the kitchen floor, and it was full of soapy water in which Papa's shirts lay soaking, the sleeves floating upwards to nudge ribbons of grey scum on the water's surface. It seemed particularly evil to leave his shirts like that, but there was nothing else I could do. I packed my little bag in haste, stuffing things in, willy-nilly, as if the flat were the hull of a sinking ship and I only had seconds to save myself. I scribbled a note so that Papa wouldn't think I'd been abducted by a gang of hoodlums. Up the stairs to the main-floor landing I ran, not knowing where I was going, just that I had to listen to the inner voice screaming, *get out, get out, get out.*

Chapter 4
Malka

I WALKED WEST and north along Allenby Road, the main artery of town, ducking into side streets, searching for signs for a room to rent. I inquired in shops, checked notice boards, and knocked on doors at random. Those who answered were not unfriendly or even surprised to see a girl with a suitcase on their doorstep. Refugees were common as sand flies in the city. People gave me tips.

"I've heard of a room on Melchett Street."

"Go to that grocery on the corner and ask Pnina. She knows everything going on in this neighbourhood."

"Try the workers' district on Ben Yehuda. There's always coming and going in those flats."

I did find vacancies, but even the cheapest was far beyond my means. All I had was a small heap of coins—housekeeping money stolen from Papa. The proprietors wanted a deposit, or at least more proof that I could pay the rent than a scrap of paper with a Mr. Mandelmann's address scribbled upon it. Towards evening, I found myself come almost full circle, back near the train tracks, drifting up Lilienblum, a street of money-changers, tailors, and fabric shops, where bolts of cloth in every conceivable pattern and colour stood braced in doorways and leaning against walls. Footsore and parched, I flopped down onto the curb and pressed my face against my weary arms.

When I looked up again, I noticed a woman with a glass in her hand, standing by the wrought-iron balustrade of a second-floor balcony across the street. The woman blew into the glass, took a sip, bent sideways for a moment and returned into view with something in her other hand—a bread roll, perhaps, out of which she took a lusty bite. I watched her eat and drink. Though I was too far to see what was in the glass, I decided it must be coffee with steamed milk. During my tramp through the city, I'd passed many a café and inhaled the smell of freshly ground beans and salivated at the sight of mocha topped with milky foam. But I couldn't dream of splurging on such luxuries. Despite my parched tongue, I hadn't allowed myself even a glass of *gazoz*. The woman on the balcony seemed queen of all she surveyed as she finished her small meal and lit a cigarette. She had a regal set to her shoulders. She wore a nice dress: lemon-yellow, with puffy sleeves. Watching her made me thirstier, hungrier, and sick with envy. I rose to get away from a sight that demonstrated all that I lacked. Instead I found myself right below the balcony, calling up.

"Excuse me, Madame. Could I . . . Would you be so kind as to give me a glass of water?"

I'd thought my Hebrew perfectly clear, but she stared down as if I'd spoken a Martian tongue.

I STOOD IN her narrow kitchen, trying not to gulp the tap water too quickly. This time I was the one under observation. Hand on her hip, head slightly cocked, it seemed the woman was taking in every detail of my pathetic appearance. My straggly hair. My dented suitcase. My dusty, down-at-heel shoes. My faded blue smock, marred with white blotches, the result of an accident with bleach. A mocking twinkle lit her dark eyes as her finely shaped eyebrows arched.

"So? What else do you want?"

The corners of her mouth twitched with amusement as if relishing my humiliation.

"Nothing!"

I banged the glass down on the counter and turned to leave.

"If you ask for nothing, you get nothing, and you sink like a stone in this country, little *Yecke*."

She spoke to me in German, with a rolling, singsong accent that drew out the word "*Yecke*," making it sound like a cackle of glee. I didn't know what to say. She had no trouble filling the silence.

"You're a mess. Miserable. Down on your luck. Right? Desperate for help. I'm probably the first person who's offered you anything all day, right? So let's hear your story."

She crossed her arms against her ample chest and leaned against the kitchen doorpost in an expectant, listening position.

I dropped my chin. I dropped my suitcase onto the floor and gave it a violent kick. The ill-fitting clasps sprang loose and the lid popped open, revealing my sad pile of bunched-up clothes with the pairs of greying underwear on top. The woman threw back her head in a peal of laughter.

Thus began my friendship with Malka, the seamstress.

SHE WAS A Hungarian Jew from Budapest, twenty-six years old, with shrewd eyes, a smirking mouth and a plump, curvaceous, languid body that was aware of its own charms. She had married a man from Vienna, had come with him to Tel Aviv three years earlier, but they'd separated, and he was living in Haifa now. They were not entirely disentangled, for he returned once a month to tend to some business he'd established in the city and in which Malka was still partially involved. The flat had two rooms—the bedroom, with Malka's double bed, and a slightly larger room, which served as her work and living space. Here were all the accoutrements of her profession: a table made of boards on trestles for cutting cloth, a dress-maker's dummy, a treadle sewing machine, an ironing board and iron, well-thumbed fashion magazines, shelves with spools of thread, bobbins, scraps of material, scissors, baskets of sequins, and buttons. There was a wicker screen, behind which customers could change, and a full-length mirror on the wall. Another corner of the room held a writing desk and stacked wooden crates. Squeezed into the middle of everything was a sofa where customers could sit while Malka made adjustments. And on this sofa, Malka offered me a place to sleep. Not just for one night, but for as long as I wished. The rent she proposed for the use of sofa, kitchen, and bathroom seemed very reasonable—1.5 Palestine pounds per month—but still completely beyond my means.

"No money and no work," I said, and shook my head.

Malka made a dismissive noise with her tongue against her teeth.

"You'll get work. You'll pay me when you can."

Now it was true that all of Tel Aviv lived on credit. Every grocer had a notebook with pages devoted to different customers and what they owed, the payments crossed off and the new debts marked—masses of scribbles that surely only the proprietor could decipher. Or else, the shopkeeper collected slips of paper—*petakim,* as they were known. Drawers full of I.O.U.s. throughout the town. But, despite our differences, I was still my father's daughter. Papa staunchly refused to take advantage of the credit system, which he called "theft, pure and simple." We only ever bought what we could pay for on the spot in cash, even though this meant forsaking all but the barest necessities. Precisely because Malka was so kind, it seemed a sin to accept her offer. What if I failed to find work? There wasn't just the rent to consider. Water. Electricity. Food.

"And besides, I'll be in your way," I protested, gesturing towards the sewing machine and the cutting table, on which lay a half-finished garment.

"What? The arrangement isn't good enough? You think you can do better elsewhere? Go ahead. Find that bed of roses at half the price."

Malka stiffened with pretended offence. Darkness pressed against the windows. Hunger gnawed in my belly. In addition to *"yiyeh tov"* there was another Hebrew expression that newcomers quickly learned and that helped them bulldoze through obstacles. *"Ein breirah"*—no choice.

Shortly afterwards, Malka and I sat together at the corner table in the kitchen over a light supper of bread, cheese, yogurt, and salad—the first food I'd had since breakfast, the first meal that someone else had prepared for me since I'd arrived in the country. I almost felt compelled to say a blessing before I dove in.

"I've been thinking of getting a roommate," Malka said in a manner that brooked no further argument.

"If I get work at all, it will be as an *ozeret*." I sighed.

I used the Hebrew word to avoid the German word for "maid," with all its negative connotations. Malka picked up my tone at once. She jabbed her fork in my direction.

"There's no dirty work in this country except for prostitution, and you're hardly the type for that. Don't look so shocked. Yes, we have whores in the Holy Land. Same as everywhere else. The country is crawling with British army and police. Marching around in circles mostly. They have to ease their urges somehow. They don't have much success with normal Jewish girls and they don't dare even look at the Arab ones, or else . . ."

Malka made a throat-cutting gesture with her forefinger. Her eyes darkened for a moment as if contemplating one of those gory Arab daggers, but she gave herself a shake.

"Where were we? We were talking about your prospects. You won't get paid much as an *ozeret*. So what? You'll get by. Almost everyone in town is just a few coins away from disaster—including me, by the way—but we manage."

Again I brought up the issue of being in her way.

"A little *puppik* like you? You won't take up much space."

Oblivious to my wince of pain at being called a *puppik*, a bellybutton, she went on. " You'll be out of the house during my business hours with your own work. And if you happen to come home early, so? You can sit on the balcony or in the kitchen. You can make my customers a glass of tea. You can keep me company. You can . . . do you know how to darn socks? Nothing to it. I can show you in minutes. I won't teach you more though. Don't get ideas."

She looked at me sharply, as if she read plots in my head.

"I don't have time to teach. And besides, a little sister seamstress competing with me, I don't need. There's already too much competition, workshops like mine on every second street. But if you learn to darn socks, I can give you something to occupy your hands with when you aren't washing floors. I take in darning orders from the laundry. Doesn't pay much, but you'll make a few piastres. All adds up."

My eyes filled with tears of gratitude. Darning socks. A few piastres. My expectations had fallen mightily since the morning's visit to the Jewish Workers' Federation.

After Malka had gone to bed, I lay awake on the sofa, knocked about by competing emotions—in awe over my new friend's generosity, but anxious over all the unknowns. At the very least, I needed to earn two Palestine pounds a month to get by. The sum seemed astronomical. And would we really get along? Could I stay out of her way as she so confidently assumed? And what about Papa? Would he seek me out and drag me back? Stupidly, in my haste to get away, I'd left some things behind, including my identity card. It was in one of the pigeon holes of Papa's roll-top desk. The document showed I was underage—legally still his ward. At some point I'd need to collect the card. Would he refuse to relinquish it out of pure spite?

I SLEPT LATER than usual next morning. At six-thirty a.m., I found Malka in a flowered housecoat in the kitchen, already finished her own breakfast and enjoying a cigarette. She waved towards the pot of coffee on the Primus and the chair across from her between the table and the wall—my seat for ever after, her gesture seemed to say. There was a basket of sliced bread on the table and real butter and a jar of aromatic apricot jam.

"So, today you go job hunting," she said. "You can go to that address they gave you at the Federation. But unless they put you to work right away, you can knock on other doors too. Try offices, shops, residences. Start with the better neighbourhoods."

Her heavy lidded eyes became animated. Her chest swelled with advice. She had three years in the country, which made her a seasoned veteran, a brilliant expert, compared to me. On the back of a used envelope, she drew a rough map of Tel Aviv, marked with asterisks and X's—where to go, where to avoid—as if I'd just come off the boat.

"Stay out of the Arab districts. There've been riots, stabbings. The British call the Arab terror *disturbances*. Ha! A *disturbance* is a ripple in a pond. But that's how our British lords want to view things. Nothing serious. All under control, so let's drink another gin, chin-chin. Anyway, here, by the mosque, is Manshia. And here, behind the railway station, starts the road into Jaffa."

I bristled.

"I've been here three months. I know my way around."

Blowing a plume of smoke between her ripe lips, Malka gave me an amused, pitying look.

"All right. Let's talk *tachlis*. What's your price when they offer you the honour of cleaning their toilets? You don't know? But you have to know. You have to say. Otherwise, they do the saying, and it will be less than what you want. Twenty mils an hour. That's where you start and maybe come down to fifteen to show your good will. And you talk about all your wonderful experience with mops and washtubs."

Act determined, but not desperate. Lie through my teeth about prior experience, which wasn't lying, Malka insisted. It was necessary embellishment, and necessity was the law of the land. *Ein breirah.* Her lazy drawl, the expansive wave of her hand, made all this sound like an excursion to the beach, but I was not reassured. A quaking fear of the test to come hollowed my stomach and jellied my knees.

Malka cocked her head to one side, appraising.

"Let's get that braid pinned up. It will make you look older. I'm glad you're wearing a different dress today. Not what I'd call stylish, but it fits the role. A sober, working girl. A new Hebrew."

She fussed with my hair, straightened my collar and pushed me firmly out the door, for she had to get started on her own workday.

MRS. MANDELMANN'S MOUTH pursed into an expression of profoundest doubt when she found me on the landing of her Rothschild Boulevard flat. She had the look of someone who's been offered a wooden piastre. My tongue had gone to clay, but I forced myself to speak.

"I *can* work hard. I can cook and clean, whatever you need. I've had lots of experience. Mr. Vitsky at the Workers Federation recommends me highly."

With my every squeak of protest her lips screwed up more. She had a pale, doughy, tired face.

"You don't look any older than my son. He's having his bar mitzvah in October."

"I'm eighteen," I insisted, feeling my jaw tighten and my face flush. "I have papers to prove it, if you don't believe me."

The treacherous words popped out of their own accord. Panic had made me say something so stupid, and in panic I tried to think of how to take it back. Even if I could produce the identity card, it would show I was a good year shy of my eighteenth birthday.

But Mrs. Mandelmann merely sighed. "It's not just the housework. There's my mother-in-law. She's old. She needs help with the bath and moving around. Do you understand? She needs someone to support her."

"I'm very strong. I take care of my father and he's very old too."

The audacious lies blossomed in my mouth. I'd gone so far down the road of falsehood, what did another one matter?

Mrs. Mandelmann sighed again at the sight of me nailed to her doorstep, gazing up at her, my hands clasped in supplication.

"At least you speak German," she acknowledged. "That's something."

She allowed me to step into the hall, questioned me about where I was from, how long I'd been in the country and was about to launch into the stickier questions about my so-called experience when a creaky voice called out from one of the rooms.

"Greta! Who's there? Who are you talking to?"

"I'm busy *Mutti*. Wait. I'll come in a moment. *Mutti*! For God's sake! You're not supposed to walk on your own."

A bird-like, bent-over creature shuffled towards us. One hand pressed against the wall, the other groped and flailed at the empty air straight ahead. Mrs. Mandelmann rushed forward and grabbed that outstretched arm, hooked it firmly under her own, letting out a grunt of irritation.

"My mother-in-law. She's blind."

"I am not blind," the elder *Frau* Mandelmann rasped. "My eyes are dim, but I see shapes, I see movement. Who's there?"

Her face lifted and her glaucous eyes fixed upon a point past my shoulder. I introduced myself in my brightest voice, adding a small curtsy. At the old lady's beckoning I approached to let her touch my hand, my face. Hunched, shrunken with age, the woman was no taller than me, with withered flesh hanging off limbs like sticks. I'd have no trouble supporting her.

"You say you're from Breslau? We're from Frankfurt, my son and I. We came here together four years ago. My son is a lawyer. A very good one. After only two years in the country, he was able to pass the British bar exams and plead cases in the Palestine courts. Greta is from Meissen. A small, nothing place. You probably haven't even heard of it. I don't know anyone in Breslau."

"My Aunt Ida is related to someone from Frankfurt," I said, scrambling around in my mind to remember the connection. "A Mr. Something-sohn."

"Rabbi Jacobssohn?"

"Yes . . . maybe . . . I think that's the one."

"Imagine that, Greta!" The elder *Frau* M. turned towards the younger. "A relative of Rabbi Jacobssohn."

"She only thinks . . ." the younger woman began but her mother-in-law interrupted.

"She's from a good family. Yes, I like her."

The younger Mrs. M. pursed her lips, but shrugged.

"All right, let's see what you can do."

I detected a hint of respect in her tired grey eyes, that I'd won over the old lady so quickly. We agreed I would come three times a week for four hours while Mrs. Mandelmann was at her teaching job at the high school. During that time, I was to clean the flat, cook a hot meal for the old lady, tend to her needs generally, and on Fridays, help her with the bath. If time remained after all the chores—but only then—I could entertain her with conversation if I wished. Erich Mandelmann was a busy man and the two boys were away at school or youth club most of the day. *Mutti* could get lonely. I'd be paid on Fridays, the money left for me in a cup on the dining room table. I could let myself in when I came. The door would be unlocked. But I was to call out so that the old woman wouldn't get a fright. Most likely, she'd be waiting for my arrival anyway, hopefully safe and sound in her chair and not hovering in the hallway. Greta Mandelmann gave her mother-in-law's arm a warning squeeze as she said this. I could start tomorrow. Oh yes, the amount of payment. Ten mils an hour. That's what the last girl got. I opened my mouth and closed it again. I'd missed my chance to bargain, but, in truth, I was much too relieved to care.

Ein Rachel, August 14, 1937
Dear Evaleh,

It's all harder than I ever could have imagined. Stumble to my feet before dawn. Gulp down tea and bread rusks. Trudge to the fields to chop at the iron soil with the turiya, a hoe with a short handle and lead-heavy head. After half an hour, my back aches, my temples throb, my eyes burn from trickles of sweat and the glare of the risen sun. Before noon I'll have fainted at least twice. Since coming here, I've lost three kilos and I haven't had a period in months. But I'll grow stronger. I will. I must. I so admire Shuli, the woman who greeted me with the fierce handshake when I first arrived. She lifts the turiya as if it were a matchstick, moves her arms rhythmically and hums as she sails along the furrow. She's much older than me, 30 at least, but her strength and resilience put my youth to shame.

Back at the training farm in Czechoslovakia, I could keep pace with the boys. Here I'm the weakest among the girls. Even Trudi from my old group does better than me. It's because of the savage heat. At 6:00 am, the sun crouches on the horizon, bares its teeth, regards us with pitiless fury and pounces. By 6:30 I'm mauled. Each moment a more intense heat pours down, the air steams, the eastern hills wobble as if about to melt. And yet I know all this is nothing. Twelve years ago, Shuli and the other founders came from Russia without tents, with hardly any tools and transformed a

*wasteland into planted fields. They all got malaria, but they worked
on anyway. You must have heard the teasing question by now:
"Have you come here out of conviction or out of Germany?" I must
prove that devotion to the cause, not just the need to flee Hitler
brought me to The Land.*

*I've run out of paper and my head sinks. A big hug for my darling
Mouse. I know I'm not supposed to call you that, but I was just
remembering about how you'd used to make me shriek by sneaking
up on me and going "kribbly-krabbly" with your little fingers across
the back of my neck. Just like a naughty mouse. I miss you dear
Sister-ling.*

Your Liesel

Tel Aviv, August 21, 1937
Dearest Donkey,

*Just like you, I now earn my bread by the toil of my hands and
the sweat of my brow. Maybe you wouldn't consider it productive
labour, scrubbing the stains out of a heavy linen suit belonging to
a bourgeois lawyer on Rothschild Boulevard. Or beating the sand
out of their plush carpets. All the same, I'm "conquering work" as
it says in the Zionist posters. Or rather, work is conquering me. My
fingers are swollen, my nails cracked, my back sore. I run around
all morning—the washing, the beds, the carpets, the floors, the
dust on the books and the ornaments! Fetch this and that for the
old girl. She interrupts me a dozen times an hour for trivial things.
But she's all right really. The other day she insisted I read aloud to
her from the English newspaper, The Palestine Post. I said I hadn't
finished the sheets, but she nagged until I sat beside her armchair
and laboured through the front page. She corrected me and
explained words I didn't know. How she enjoys playing teacher! I
enjoy the break and the chance to learn. But the sheets! The rest of
the cleaning! "You'll just have to stay longer," she said with a crafty
smile. I left a note for Mrs. Mandelmann explaining the problem and
asking whether I could have extra hours. Her reply was negative. I'm
caught in the middle between the two. Luckily, I have a second client
now as well, but still not nearly enough work to pay off my debts to
Malka.*

In the Post, I read about attacks by Arab gangs on Jewish settlements, which raised the hairs on the back of my neck. Your little colony must be terribly vulnerable. And the work in the fields sounds like pure slavery. Can't they give you an indoor job? So what if you're more delicate than the others? It's nothing to be ashamed of, Dearest Donkey. Come visit me soon. Leave that pioneering paradise in the swamps and come to Tel Aviv-Babylon. I'll take you to the seashore. I'll feed you ice cream. Come!

Love,

Your Eva

Ein Rachel, September 6, 1937

Dear Evaleh,

My head swam when you gave me the figures. I can hardly imagine problems like rent, bills, the price of tea, etc. Here, though the work is brutally hard, all our needs are provided for. I sleep in a tent and the food is plain, but I never have to think where my next meal is coming from. Everything is communal and allotted to me, down to my shoes and socks. I'd be lost in the city now. Are you sure you did the right thing by leaving Papa? I could write to him and beg him to let you learn a trade. Don't stay away from him out of sheer stubbornness. He might listen if I reason with him. Should I try? I hate to think of you in debt to a stranger. Malka sounds nice, but she's not family. Even if you find more paid hours, I can't see how you'll manage.

You say there's no disgrace in being delicate, but there's no glory either. And having I fainted once too often, I've now been transferred to inglorious kitchen duty, which is a step downwards, though no one would say so, since all labour is supposed to be equal. We're sheltered from the sun here, but it's still stifling hot with the wood fire in the stove and the pots on the boil. Constant explosions of temper too. Three girls, plus 15 different ideas on how to cook the soup. Actually, I have no opinion, so the fights are between Ruthie and Pnina, with me trying my best to stay neutral. Even in the kitchen, I disgrace myself, for the other day I went green trying to clean a fish.

As for the danger from our "cousins," please don't worry. Yes, we do get nighttime "visits" now and then. But all the male

comrades and, some of the girls too, take turns standing guard and
will blast away into the darkness if anyone tries to set our fields
alight. You'll be relieved to hear that I'm not among those on the
watchtowers. Much too clumsy to be trusted with a rifle.

    Ice cream! I can't imagine that anymore either. I'd love to visit,
but as I told you before, it's not so easy to get away.

    Love, Your Liesel

MRS. MANDELMANN SENT me to the Kuchinsky family. Kuchinsky put a word in for me with Mrs. Kleiner who ran a pension near the sea. This lady liked to keep her establishment according to old-world standards—starched tablecloths, silver service, thick carpets, furniture with intricate carvings and glass surfaces, on which the dust from all the surrounding sand dunes and construction sites loved to cling. Having stepped across the threshold of Pension Kleiner, the guests must feel that they'd left the primitive Levant and returned to the bosom of civilized Europe. The hired help had to work silently, unobtrusively, so that clean sheets appeared on beds, and gleaming plates on the table, as if by magic. Here I truly felt like a servant, a *"Dienstmädchen,"* but I did what I had to, because *"ein breirah."*

Now I was on the go all day, whether working, or rushing through the steaming streets to my next job. At day's end I trudged home to Lilienblum Street, tired to my marrow and sticky with the day's waves of sweat. Occasionally, out of the corner of my eye, I'd catch a glimpse of a dark figure, a man in a black suit and Homburg. Was it Papa? Was he following me? I'd continue along, trying to dispel the notion that he'd pop out of a doorway any moment to block my way. Malka couldn't understand why I'd hesitate to just go to his flat for my identity card, my recorder, and the other important things I'd left behind.

"You look him in the eye and tell him what you want. What can he do? Refuse? Lock you up? He can only hurt you if you give in to your fears."

"I'm not afraid. I just don't want to see him."

But I did see him lurking like a feral cat in the dark corners of my imagination, eyes ablaze with accusations.

DURING A STEAMY night in September, Malka told me about her adventures with men. We sat on either end of the sofa, Malka with her bare feet up on a crate, a glass of beer in her hand, me hunched over the darning egg. I hated the finicky business of weaving threads across a hole in a sock. I was too slow to make it a lucrative sideline. But I laboured away, while the sweat trickled behind my ear lobes and down my neck.

According to Malka, there were two types of men: the wolves and the dogs. The wolves took you on exciting adventures, but devoured you afterwards. The dogs, though reliable companions, shadowed your every footstep to an excruciating degree. With both, you had to hold something of yourself in reserve. Even dogs would turn on you if they thought you helpless.

"I was this close to disaster," she said, holding her thumb and forefinger up, almost touching. She told about the affair that shook her out of youthful naivety.

"He got me pregnant, the filthy devil. Said it was safe, that he would spill his seed in the last minute. What did I know? I was a girl from a nice bourgeois Jewish home, sheltered. He was an officer in the gendarmes whose barracks were close to where we lived in Budapest. Terribly handsome and charming, but of course he vanished as soon as I told him of my condition. I'll never forget the look in his eye: pity mixed with a gleam of triumph for having brought me low. There are men like that. They want a woman on her back and in the dirt, but then of course, they lose interest. Maybe they're all like that a bit. Luckily, I had a miscarriage."

Malka exhaled a long, thoughtful plume of smoke and studied her glittering fingernails. They were recently manicured with red polish, only slightly chipped from the work at the sewing machine.

The miscarriage had been a painful and a bloody business, but it saved her from the predicament of a bastard child. Her family arranged for her to meet a man in Vienna. Eleven years older than her and a decent, solid type from a good Jewish home, but broad-minded enough and smitten enough to overlook her youthful misadventure. She fell into the marriage without knowing him well, pressured by her family. Career prospects were turning sour in Vienna for Jews. Kurt was keen to try Palestine. He wanted them both to leave the past behind, have a fresh start. In Palestine, after a few ventures fell through, he set himself up in—of all things—the condom business, as agent for an English manufacturer.

"He's a smart man, hard working. Not a prude or narrow minded. He stumbled upon the condom idea and realized the potential with so many young singles in the country, plus the British army detachments. Our best times were building up the business together. In between my sewing, I helped him with the packaging. We would receive the goods from overseas in bulk, not individually wrapped. I had to put them into little packets. Kurt went around making sales pitches to pharmacies and private doctors and some of the army doctors. But Kurt is also a difficult man. Reserved, inflexible, brooding, jealous. Work is his god, but as for me, I like a bit of fun in between slaving for my keep. To drink, to dance, or just to dress up and mill around on the streets. Kurt would go crazy if another man just looked my way. He'd come home from his sales rounds and want me to account for every minute of my day. Who did I see? Who did I talk to? What about that handyman at the Sapir? Did I smile at him again? I mustn't go to that café anymore, or any café without him. He forbade it. Forbade! As if I was a child! Well, one day Amnon, who had been doing some repairs in the Sapir's kitchen, bought me a mocha torte and sat down at my table to chat. And I thought, why shouldn't I have a friend? I'm lonely for some real company. I can't talk to Kurt anymore. So . . . that's how we started to unravel."

"But you still see him?" I asked.

"Who? Kurt? Oh yes. The flat is his. He's moved to Haifa but he still does business in Tel Aviv. He stays here. On this sofa. Oh don't look so worried. I won't send you out into the night when he comes. You'll sleep in my bed with me."

She smiled at the thought of this arrangement. For the first time I realized, this was the most important asset I had to offer: being a buffer between her and her ex-husband. A way of keeping him at bay.

"But isn't it terrible for you to have him here? And why does he let you stay?"

Malka flopped her head backwards, closed her eyes. The cigarette burned towards her knuckles and I wondered if she'd fallen asleep. Suddenly she jerked forward to crush the stub, smeared with her lipstick, into the ashtray.

"He wants me back. He's trying to be nice. Who knows? Maybe he can change. He's been very humble lately."

"But who are you in love with? Kurt or Amnon?"

"In love!" Malka snorted. "What does that mean? It's not so simple—in or out, this or that. By the way, Amnon takes me places and we have fun, but we never come back here, not even for a coffee." She laughed and touched her nose. "Dogs like Kurt have a good sense of smell. Here! Give me that. I can't watch anymore how you're torturing that sock."

AT THE END of September, just before my seventeenth birthday, I triumphantly poured a handful of crumpled notes and coins onto Malka's kitchen counter—all that I owed from the past two months and enough to cover the next two weeks besides. We were fair and square and I was finally debt free.

"Ha, little *Yecke*! So worried about debt. What did I tell you? Didn't I say you'd get work and pay me soon enough?"

She put my money into her purse with the snap clasp and shook it to hear the pleasant jingle of coins. "I'm rich. We should go out and celebrate. To a bar at the beach for drinks, or maybe. . . ." A sly smile blossomed on her lips. "Or maybe we should finally get you something decent to wear. I can't stand that sack you've got on. Don't take it so personally. It's not you I can't stand, it's your dress. Come with me."

"Where?"

"Never mind. Just come."

She grabbed her handbag, stuffed the fattened purse into it and pushed me out the door. On the street she hooked her arm into mine and steered me into a nearby shop, crammed floor to ceiling with bolts of cloth, where she bought her supplies.

"My friend here needs material for a new dress."

The owner, a bald-headed man with a pencil moustache, nodded and raised his eyebrows approvingly.

"Malka, I can't let you buy that for me."

"Who said I'm buying? You are. I'll put down a deposit, and the rest you'll pay. On credit. Enough with your *Yecke* complexes. My friend has a steady job," she said to the owner. "She's a work horse. You'll get your money, *chick-chack*. Before you get around to making a note in your accounts book, she'll be running in here with a fistful of cash."

"*Giveret* Malka, your word is as good as gold." The man flashed a smile, waved his hands expansively, inviting us to look over his wares.

I started to protest, but there was so much good will in Malka's sparkling eyes and she looked so well turned out herself in a new blue dress she'd recently made and I was much sicker of my dowdy rags than she was, so I let myself be led around the shop. We examined all kinds of fabrics—cotton, linen, silk, wool and blends, in all kinds of patterns—until I spotted a print of red polka dots on a cream coloured background.

"Hmm," Malka murmured, contemplating first the material, then me, with her head on one side.

"Too loud?" I asked.

That settled it.

"Too loud!" she exploded. "There's no such thing. Not here, not now. No more whispering, hiding, trying to appease the *goyim* by blending into the shadows. No more wearing *schmattes* to please your fanatic father. You must shout your womanhood to the rooftops."

My heart danced a tarantella as she spoke.

Back upstairs, she measured me—shoulders, bosom, waist, and hips—with her yellow tape measure, while her twinkling eyes assessed my strengths and weaknesses, what to accentuate, what to conceal. Her deft, soft hands with the needle-pricked fingertips flew about, pinning, patting.

"Aha, Miss Salomon," she declared. "You'll be the princess of Moghrabi Square."

"I just want to be less of a mouse."

"Aim high," Malka chided. "Do clothes make the man? Maybe yes, maybe no. But for sure they make the woman."

Over the next week, after she'd finished with her regular orders, Malka worked on my dress late into the evenings, but I was not allowed to watch. Banished to the kitchen or the balcony, I listened to the whir of the sewing machine and the snip-snip of her scissors, eager as a child waiting for Hanukkah to arrive. Seven days after we'd gone shopping for the material, Malka called me into the room to see her masterpiece: a chic, close-fitting, calf-length frock with a wide red sash, big red buttons, and a matching bolero jacket. The neckline was just deep enough to create allure without vulgarity. The jacket had padded shoulders for elegance and heft. I tried the outfit on, and though the size was right, a tide of disappointment flooded my heart. The image in the mirror showed an imposter with a too-small head and out-sized feet, the ugly stepsister instead of a transformed Cinderella. The dress needed someone finer looking, someone with the natural elegance to highlight its lines and textures.

"Nonsense. That's not the problem," Malka declared.

She took me to Allenby Road where we hunted through the shoe shops for the highest heeled pumps we could find. Again she put down the deposit and talked the merchant into opening an account for me. Again I wrung my hands, but I'd weakened enough that my reservations were more pro forma than real.

"Now we'll go to Schatzi's and get your hair done. Yes, of course. A grown-up woman needs grown-up hair. What's the problem?"

Wordlessly, I shook my head. I couldn't let Malka spend another mil on me. It wasn't just debt I feared. A spot in my soul that had rotted through habitual dread over the years sent out vapours of warning: beware of too much happiness.

"You look like a schoolgirl, but you act like an old woman," Malka scolded. "All right. Forget Schatzi. I'll do your hair myself. I can't possibly make it worse than it is now."

That evening, with her own hands, Malka undid my severe braid for the last time, washed my hair over the kitchen sink and set to work with scissors, a curling iron and potions to shape and sculpt a dreamy set of waves. The result, Malka swore, was as good as anything that Schatzi's Hairdressing Salon could provide and gratis to boot. As a finishing touch, she made up my face with her own cosmetics—powder, rouge, eyeliner, mascara, cherry-red lipstick. She clutched her hands to her bosom and beamed. Once again I put on my new outfit, slipped on the heels, and turned to examine myself in the full-length mirror.

"Nu? What did I tell you? The new princess of Moghrabi Square."

A stranger stared back at me from the glass. She had shapely calves and hips and a real bosom instead of girlish bumps, all swathed in red polka dots that seemed to pulse with light. Her hair was short and glossy and artfully waved to create a charming frame for her pretty face with its arched brows and crimson, cupid mouth. Though that face had freckles, they were nicely muted by foundation powder. Best of all, this lovely, grown-up lady was three inches taller than dowdy little Eva of not so long ago. The mirror lady stared at me uncertainly, broke into a grin and welcomed me into her storybook life. I wobbled shakily in my new spiky heels along the tiled floor as I danced towards Malka to give her a hug. She laughed until her eyes disappeared into the folds of her plump cheeks.

"I must owe you . . . You must tell me exactly how many hours you spent . . . Oh Malka, how can I ever pay you back?"

"You can't. You owe me from here until the world to come. Ha, ha, silly *Yecke*, you still can't tell when I'm joking. Go out and dazzle the boys of Tel Aviv. Wait! No, not yet. Practise walking in those heels first or you'll never make it down the stairs without breaking your neck."

Ein Rachel, Oct. 5, 1937
Dear Evaleh,

You ask what keeps me here in this Godforsaken place buried between malarial swamps and scorched hills? In a word: the group. Everything we do is for the group, this small band of comrades, held together by noble ideals and a vision of a better world. Each gives what he can and takes what he needs and no one must have more than another and all have a say in the collective operations. Every week we meet in assembly. I must admit, my attention wanders during these meetings when the smallest detail gets examined under a microscope. For example, whether to wash the dining room floor twice a day, as Pnina proposes, or only once, as Ruthie insists. The comrades take sides, argue, quote the spiritual founders of the movement, probe practicalities (hygiene vs water conservation) and principles (Is floor washing productive labour? Is the obsession with cleanliness a bourgeois habit?) until late at night. All in flowery Hebrew, of course, which I struggle to grasp. The debates become heated, which I find painful. I plead for a more civilized tone and the room erupts in laughter. "Poor Yecke. We forgot our 'pleases' and 'thank yous.'" I sit down feeling stupid.

Other aspects of the collective life come more easily to me. The sharing, for example. We share everything, including work clothes, which lie in baskets in the laundry room, each basket labelled according to type, gender and size—male shorts, medium sized, and so on. Eva, do you remember how each year at the beginning of the school term we received a package of hand-me-down clothes? Papa had no idea how to make a girl look nice and absolutely no interest either. He wouldn't dream of spending extra for something new and pretty. You would howl your disappointment. I pretended I didn't care so as to keep the peace, but, truth is, I didn't enjoy the pitying looks of our classmates any more than you did. And now I'm in a place where everyone wears hand-me-downs, where simplicity of dress is normal, natural, celebrated. In fact, if some fancy city lady arrived here decked out in fripperies, we'd treat her with scorn.

The group encourages us to take Hebrew names to show we are no longer in Exile. Hans and Trudi now call themselves Hanan and Tamar. I try to remember, but before I can stop myself, the old names jump to my lips. And what name shall I take? I keep putting off the decision, because I can't decide.

Have I mentioned that Trudi and Hans have become a couple? It makes me a bit sad because I'm not keen for Trudi to move out of our tent. That won't happen right away, since accommodations for couples are scarce. But sooner or later Trudi won't be here in the cot next to mine and I will miss her terribly. I dread the day.

I've run out of paper. Goodbye for now.

Your loving sister,

Liesel

(Or perhaps, one day, Yonati, Daphna, Aviga'il, D'vorah. Who knows?)

Ein Rachel, Oct. 14, 1937

Dear Evaleh,

I didn't expect you, of all people, to be so scathing about my possible name change. You, who have transformed yourself into the "Moghrabi Square princess" with one outrageously expensive new dress! Even if I do adopt a Hebrew name, you have my full permission to call me Liesel, or Donkey, or whatever you want. Nor was I thinking of you with my comments about the "fancy city lady."

I didn't know anything about your metamorphosis. Our letters crossed, as you'll realize if you check the dates. Of course, I can't help but be concerned about the debts you've racked up with your landlady and all those shopkeepers. Still, I'm glad you are so happy with your new clothes. Though when I try to imagine what you look like now, all I see is little sister with the impish, freckly face and the schoolgirl braid. A comforting picture. Allow me to hold onto it for a while longer. Anyway, let's not quarrel. It frays my nerves and they're already in a delicate state for Trudi and Hans are talking about moving to a new settlement on the east side of Lake Kinneret that is in desperate need of extra hands. The conditions there are even more primitive than here, so I couldn't go too. I couldn't endure the hardship. The thought of them leaving fills me with gloom.

Write soon. Tell me everything. Don't hold back.

Hugs and kisses,

Your Liesel

Ein Rachel, Oct. 20, 1937

Dear Evaleh,

Trudi and Hans are gone. The cot beside mine lies bare. The pegs where Trudi's clothes hung are empty. Another girl will soon move in, but no one can replace Trudi, my best friend for so many months, nor Hans, who was like an older brother. I feel as if I've lost a piece of my body. Now, no one here speaks my language. No one shares my memories of that place we once called home.

As for a love interest of my own, I haven't found it. People here mate without much formality. Sometimes the overtures can be a bit coarse. The other day as I was standing on the kitchen porch, taking a breath of air, this fellow—Dov Kalisch—ambled over, plunked himself against the post opposite and proceeded to look me up and down with a gleam in his eyes—a mix of appreciation, calculation and raw appetite. He cleared his throat as if to say "Well, what about it?" but didn't actually speak. He'd been doing some heavy work in one of the sheds, and his shirt was open to his navel, exhibiting a sweaty chest covered with thickets of black hair. I should mention that Dov is Ruthie's man—at least as far as she's concerned—and, despite all the mocking of bourgeois conventions, *she would dig my eyes out if I let him come within spitting distance. Which I have no intention of doing.*

"I have to get back to work," I said, turning to go inside.

"No you don't," he grunted, grabbing my arm to yank me back. "You're on break, so finish your break. Don't be such a scared rabbit. I'm not going to force myself on you like a Cossack. That's not how we do things here. If you're not interested, just say so. You don't have to beat around the bush."

This little outburst, delivered in an aggrieved voice, as if I'd insulted him, left me speechless. Falling into silence, he stroked his stubbly chin and seemed to be ruminating about something.

"Tell you what," he finally said in a tone of someone who's been asked for a favour which he's trying to accommodate. "We have a new man coming soon. Maybe he'll be more to your taste. He's from your home country, from Berlin, I think. In any case, a Yecke. And I suppose Yecke needs Yecke."

Having offered me this man neither of us knew, Dov Kalisch beamed mightily and took himself off, to my great relief.

I hear from Papa every two weeks, like clockwork. His letters are brief and always the same: general comments about the bleak news in Europe, a quote or two from his holy books, etc. But at least he does maintain contact. Evaleh, I know he would like to see you again, though he's much too proud to say so. Can you not bring yourself to drop in for a visit? You are practically neighbours. I can't understand how your paths never cross. By the way, Auntie's letters are terribly brief and vague. As if she doesn't want us to know what's really going on back home. What have you heard?

Your loving sister,

Liesel

Tel Aviv, Oct. 25, 1937

Dear Liesel,

Your life in that swamp sounds so harsh and joyless. Yes, I know. You have hora dancing and cultural nights and the spiritual rewards that come from self-sacrifice to that marvellous, mystical entity called "The Group." All right, I'll bite my sour tongue. But if you ever want to leave, you'll have my full support.

As for me, during the week, I'm mousy little Eva in my ugly sack and scuffed-up shoes, a cotton square tied over my head against the dust. Grubbing and scouring, schlepping and mopping. (I'm slowly whittling down my debts, so don't worry.) But Saturday nights, after a day of rest, I get dressed in my polka dot frock. And with my hair washed and waved (Malka taught me how), prancing on my high-heeled shoes, I'm ready for adventure. Sometimes I go out with Malka and Amnon and their crowd—most of whom are in their thirties, but still very lively. Sometimes I go out on my own. I join the parade of Tel Avivans just milling around the avenues. In my womanly clothes, I draw notice for the first time in my life! Such fun, though somewhat overwhelming too, to feel men's eyes upon me. "Let them look, let them want, let them spoil you rotten," Malka says about men. My inner self hasn't caught up to my glamorous appearance, so I hold myself aloof. For the moment, I'm happy just seeing and being seen.

Liesel dear, I know you'd like me to visit Papa, but it's out of the question. Why should I expose myself to his meanness and rage? I had enough throughout my childhood. If he wants to see me (which I don't believe), let him make the first move.

Love,

Your Eva

Chapter 5
Kowalski's

MY REFUGE, MY paradise, in those days was a cluttered little shop on Nachlat Binyamin Street with the name "Kowalski's" astride a treble clef, painted in gold on the dusty plate glass window. I'd discovered the place one stifling September afternoon during the siesta hour, when I was in between clients and drifting up the empty street, seeking shelter in the islands of shade offered by canvas awnings that stretched over the fiery pavements. Palestine kept Levantine hours, with most businesses closed and tightly shuttered between one and four p.m. But here was an establishment with the shutters rolled up. And from the dark cave inside came the loveliest music, a melody that wrapped its arms around my neck and drew me over the threshold. I found myself surrounded by shelves of sheet music, tuning forks, metronomes, musical instruments, packets of violin strings, and stacks of records in paper sleeves standing upright in wooden crates. On top of a broad counter sat the most marvellous item of all: a gramophone in a handsome console of gold-brown oak, its lid open, a record spinning. And no one was in sight so that I was all alone with this divine device that seemed set up and running specially for me. I stood still in the enchanted gloom. I listened to the deep-throated voice of a cello, answered by the plaintive cries of a violin. Time and the whole wide world vanished. Yet it turned out I was not alone, for when I inched closer, I saw, behind the counter, a fat, jowly man on a swivel chair with his feet up on a box, eyes shut, hands folded over his ample belly. I began to back away, not wanting to wake him, but the mouth beneath the drooping moustache opened.

"Brahms' *Double Concerto*," the man declared in a tone of deepest reverence, followed by a long, contented sigh.

Was he fully awake? Was he aware of my presence? Yes, he was, for after some moments his left eyebrow arched comically upwards, while his right eye squeezed shut in a wink. Chaim Alexander Kowalski, late of Odessa, was no ordinary shop owner, but rather, in his own modest way, a patron of the arts. Though I couldn't possibly afford his wares, he made no move to shoo me away. I never saw him exert himself to sell anything to anyone. The business was his excuse to indulge in and share his musical passions. Let all who are hungry for music come and feast, his signature siesta-hour, feet-up posture seemed to say. And so I did. And

I learned. During my brief respites in Kowalski's shop, I became acquainted with works of the great European composers and with some of the brilliant recording artists of our time.

Some weeks later, towards the end of October, I arrived as usual during the midday closures, when scarcely another soul was about on Nachlat Binyamin Street. The weather had turned pleasant—bright sunshine and neither hot nor cold—yet the city lay in a dreamy lassitude as if still in the grip of summer's inferno. Kowalski was at his post in his armchair with his chin on his chest. I took up mine, leaning against the counter, my head thrown back, my eyes shut, and directed towards the ceiling where a strip of flypaper twirled lazily under its weight of dead flies. On the console spun a recording of selections from Mozart's *Don Giovanni*, featuring the magnificent bass voice of Ezio Pinza and the pure soprano of Rosa Ponselle. The sumptuous duet, "Là ci darem la mano," burst into the room.

> *Give me thy hand, oh fairest*
> *Whisper a gentle "yes"*
> *Come, if for me thou carest*
> *With joy my life to bless*

Behind my eyelids I saw them, clearly as if they were standing before me: Don Giovanni, the handsome seducer, and Zerlinda, the lovely maiden, as they approached one another, drawn by irresistible attraction. Closer, closer together they came, their voices urgent, entwined in a perfect blend of high and low, male and female, robust and tender. Two beings transformed into a single soul by love. For it must be love, not mere lust, they felt at that moment to sing with such passionate joy.

> *With thee, with thee, my treasure*
> *This life is nought but pleasure*
> *My heart is fondly thine*

Under the spell of the exquisite harmonies and the vision of the rapturous lovers, I was lost, lost, soaring to the heavens. And then I had the eeriest sensation. That I was not alone. That something outside me beheld the swaying, humming, dreaming Eva and viewed her with a benevolent and cherishing gaze. As this thought took hold, my palms began to tingle and a sweet warmth infused my chest. I knew this sweetness from somewhere. I wanted more. I shut my eyes tighter, tilted my chin higher, willed the feeling closer.

A harsh sound—a grunt, or a snort, animal-like—pierced my reverie. My eyes flew open to behold a tall man in uniform filling the doorway. Because of his peaked cap, pulled low on his forehead, and the strong sunshine outside that made his figure a dark silhouette, I couldn't see his face clearly. But I could sense his scrutiny, his taking me in from head to toe. His fist rose to his mouth and again he made that sound. "Hack, harrumph." Clearing his throat. He stepped forward and I found myself looking up at an officer of the Palestine Police Force.

He wore the pressed summer khaki of the Force: crisp shirt and shorts, knee-high socks, and thick-soled shoes, wide canvas belt with a large brass buckle. A truncheon dangled from the belt. An entwined double "P" of white metal emblazoned the peaked cap that shaded his eyes. Those half-hidden eyes looked down on me now, took me in, read me for information in the manner of a person of authority, forming judgments. I shivered. While I'd been swaying to "Là ci darem la mano," in my free hand I'd been holding another of the records in the Don Giovanni set. I flung the thing, still in its paper sleeve, onto the counter, as if caught with stolen goods. The policeman's lips twitched in a smile or perhaps a sneer. He came closer without breaking his gaze. My work clothes—shabby cardigan and skirt, sweat-stained blouse and dusty flat-heeled sandals—stamped me for what I was, someone barely eking out a living. At least I wasn't wearing the yellow *schmatte,* which normally covered my head as I pounded carpets and bent over washtubs.

"Hullo Miss. Haven't seen you here before. New in town?"

The voice was exactly a policeman's: stern and crisp. I thought of the illegals, the many Jews who had slipped into the country in defiance of the quota. Officials like this one were sent to hunt them down. Though I'd come into the country legitimately, with my father, I had no papers, for these were still with Papa and I'd run away from him.

"Constable Duncan Rees," the policeman said as he stretched out his hand. I could see his eyes now. They were an uncompromising blue.

Unsure of how to answer, I said nothing, pressed my back against the counter, which caused the constable to drop his hand from the air between us to the truncheon at his side. He fiddled with the heavy stick while the tip of his tongue explored his upper lip, as if relishing my discomfort. On the record, they had skipped to much later in the opera. Don Giovanni was in the throes of his final scene in which he refuses to repent, hurling defiance heavenward, while demons approach to carry him to hell. It dawned on me I was being a fool, acting as if I were back in Germany, where men in uniform swaggered down streets and smashed skulls. I was behaving like the nervous Diaspora Jew instead of the new Hebrew, free and bold, in her own homeland. I said my name, but not loudly enough. The constable shook his head as he cupped a hand behind his ear. Shouts, pleas, and orchestral crescendos were issuing from the gramophone.

"I say! What a racket!"

The constable leaned forward to lift the needle from the spinning disc, chuckled at the sight of Kowalski, sprawled on his chair. The room was suddenly quiet, except for Kowalski's gargled snores.

"Trusting bloke that. Anyone off the street could rob him blind."

My back stiffened, my heartbeat quickened. Did he consider me such an "anyone" with thieving designs? But I refused to be cowed.

"It's not a racket. It's an opera."

He had a look of blunt, goyish ignorance, this uncouth policeman with the stick out ears beneath his cap. This man who'd intruded on my privacy and made me afraid.

"By Mozart!"

My voice rang out through the stillness of the store. The man's blue eyes widened.

"A world-famous composer," I added sternly.

"You don't say!"

"I *do* say!"

His eyebrows rose, but otherwise his face remained impassive and inscrutable. After a long moment of thought, he rapped his knuckles on the counter to rouse the store-owner's attention.

"Hoy there, my friend."

Kowalski acknowledged the policeman with a grunt, but didn't stir.

"Can't we have something more up to date? How about some jazz?"

The constable snapped his fingers to an imagined rhythm. Kowalski lifted one hand from its resting place on his stomach and waved it lethargically as if to say, "Whatever you wish."

Snatching the Mozart record from the turntable, the constable placed it back in its sleeve and walked his fingers through a stack of albums. He had long, sun-reddened hands, with blond hairs sprouting from the knuckles. All his exposed skin had been similarly roasted: his nose, cheeks, ears, and knees. The music he chose was fast and brassy, with bleating horns, crashing cymbals, and rattling drums. I'd never cared for jazz, finding it too foreign and manic: the music of jungle Hottentots. The man could read the distaste on my face.

"Not to your liking, Miss?"

A teasing smile curled his lips. "It's Duke Ellington. Never heard of him? My, my. Thought you Jewish girls knew everything."

"I know a bit about real music," I declared. "I don't bother with noise."

I pushed past him and marched out of the shop in a rage. My small scrap of pleasure—a bit of recorded opera to soothe the workday—had been snuffed out by a churlish stranger with a badge on his cap. His cold eyes had observed me at my most unguarded, while I'd hovered at the edge of rapture. While I was about to tumble into mystical delusions I thought I'd long ago outgrown! Self-disgust stabbed along with resentment. Hearing his footsteps behind me, I quickened my own. If he had official business, let him say so or leave me be. I was sick to my marrow of men in uniforms.

In a moment he was by my side, my short legs no match for his long-limbed stride. He began to whistle a familiar tune—the opening of Beethoven's *Fifth*. More mockery. I kept my head high and continued to steam down Nachlat Binyamin, which was just coming to life again as the siesta hour ended. A few automobiles chugged by. A donkey pulling a cart loaded with sacks of onions shuffled along. Meanwhile, the policeman kept up his whistling rendition of the *Fifth*, progressing through the more intricate bars of the movement, a cascade of melodious notes. I looked up. He slowed his pace and my feet followed suit of their own accord. He came to a standstill and so did I. Hands behind his back, rocking on his heels, he continued to produce theme and variations, managing to suggest the tremolos of a violin and the tinkle of piano keys. In mid-note he burst into laughter.

"You look as if I'd banged you on the head, Miss."

"How do you do that?"

I'd never seen nor heard anything like it.

"Rubber lips. It's all in the lips."

He shaped them again into a moist cherubic *O*.

It was my turn to laugh.

"Right then, let's try this again. I'm Constable Duncan Rees."

The constable removed his cap, revealing a mop of pressed-down hair the colour of beach sand and sun-bleached eyebrows. He stretched out his hand and it enfolded mine.

"Eva Salomon," he said slowly, as if tasting my name.

He looked fairly human without the cap and not exactly ugly despite that pair of stick-out ears. High cheekbones and a full, rosy lower lip gave him a jovial, boyish air. He was older than me, but not by much, I guessed. His eyes, I saw now, were a brilliant, piercing blue, almost the same shade as the radiant sky overhead. He replaced his cap, but at a less menacing angle.

"So, Eva Salomon. From Germany, right?"

"You can tell from my accent, I suppose?"

"But your English is excellent," he said quickly.

I was flattered, despite myself. We'd started to walk again, but at a more conversational pace now.

"So, Miss Salomon-from-Germany. You're a dedicated fan of serious music. Not surprising. Great music's in your blood."

I wasn't used anymore to hearing the words "Germany" and "blood" twinned in a way that included me and that made me feel good. His compliment pleased me more than I'd want to let on. I switched the focus away from myself. He must love the classics too, I said, if he could whistle whole sections of symphonies by heart.

"Guilty as charged."

His hand snapped to his temple in a mock salute.

So we talked as we ambled across Magen David Square and onto Allenby Road, northward, towards my next cleaning appointment at Frau Kleiner's pension by the sea. The constable had a commanding way of walking: easy and relaxed, but alert, with sharp glances this way and that. He looked as if nothing escaped his notice. He looked as if he owned the street, which I suppose he did in a certain way, being a member of His Majesty's Palestine Police. As he slipped deeper into his story, his accent became more pronounced, vowels running together, consonants dropped, but I had a good ear and could follow his words.

In his childhood, he told me, he'd been a choir boy and he'd studied the piano for a number of years, though he gave that up when he'd made an ass of himself at his first major recital.

"I wasn't ready. My dad pushed me. Not that he had any interest in music—it was my mum's doing, the lessons—but dad wanted to see results for his money. Moment I got out on stage my hands shook like a drunk with the d.t.'s."

He stretched out his hands in front of him as if to demonstrate. They were long, strong, finely shaped hands, and they remained perfectly still in the air.

"I whistle for me supper now," he said.

He came from an industrial town near London called Slough, a word that meant "a low muddy place."

Someone who didn't care for all that sprawling industry had recently written a funny poem about his town, the constable told me. He stopped abruptly again at an intersection, put his hands behind his back, and recited in a schoolboy singsong:

> *Come friendly bombs and fall on Slough*
> *It inn't fit for humans now*
> *There inn't grass to feed a cow . . .*

I told him I was from a slough too. "Bre–slau.

The constable threw back his head and laughed. "Very good, Miss Salomon. Capital!"

There was a factory in Slough that made Horlicks, a powdered drink supposedly delicious and good for anything that ailed you. According to Constable Rees the brownish brew tasted like dirty feet. His father was a foreman at Horlicks and his older brother worked there too. It was the expected thing. Get a job at Horlicks, put in your time on the shop floor, find a girl, move into your own little patch of the housing estate—row upon row of soot-washed brick boxes with tiny squares of garden, all fenced in with brick walls. The younger son balked.

"I tried for a scholarship to a technical college. Blew it. Went on a tear to Brighton. Dad told me I was good for nothing and tossed me out of his house. I was dead broke and he thought I'd come crawling back to him on my knees. Would have rather thrown myself under a train."

A recruitment poster for the Palestine Police had saved him from Horlicks and humiliation and more drastic choices. The poster, which showed a drawing of an officer in a pith helmet mounted on a camel aiming his lance at a wild boar, promised a life of adventure, plus room and board and 11 Palestine Pounds a month.

"Made it look like we were joining a happy hunting party. Foxes and hounds sort of thing, but more exotic. Ha!"

He described the training depot in Jerusalem: the dusty parade ground on a bare, exposed hilltop, daily drills with full kit bags under the blazing sun. The bawling sergeant. (*Come on yew lily-livered ladies, lift yer bloody feet!*) And then, initiation by fire. The Arab revolt had begun. In his first month after being posted to Jaffa, Duncan had to help quell a riot. Stones rained down from all directions, the air rang with blood-curdling yells and there was nothing between him and the seething mob save a thin wooden shield and a rifle he wasn't allowed to shoot until the order came.

"Nice chap on his own, Johnny Arab," he told me. "But a mob is a wild beast."

When he first arrived in Jaffa town, Duncan said, the place was near ungovernable because of the maze of winding alleys and the dense housing, piled up like matchboxes one atop another, that gave escape routes for mischief-makers, enabled barricades and put a copper in danger every time he turned a corner.

"Then the Royal Engineers gave the town bit of a face-lift. Blasted two new roads, east to west and north to south and got rid of lots of those rat's nest houses. We had a long spell of quiet after that. But the troubles have heated up again all over the country, including Jaffa. There's many days when work is humdrum. And then suddenly, out of the blue, comes an ugly wave. We're up night after night. No time to catch a kip, or if we can, we're fully dressed, ready for the next emergency call. Worst mischief happens in the dark, but daytime too, we've got to be on our toes."

I tried to imagine what it was like, patrolling those crowded souks of Jaffa town, never knowing when a dagger might flash from under a robe. I'd asked if he was sorry he'd joined up. The constable stared at me as if I'd missed the point. As if I'd questioned something sacred. His shoulders straightened as he tried to explain. He loved the job. Even on quiet days, it was never a bore. One did one's bit to serve and protect. And where would the country be without the Palestine Police—a small force of excellent men, a thin blue line between civilization and chaos? I could see he felt anchored among these "excellent men" and full of pride at the order they managed to achieve despite the plotting of the desperadoes. His words implied that the normality we observed around us—Tel Aviv clattering awake after the midday break, shutters rolling open and shopkeepers setting out their crates of wares—was very much thanks to men like him. I thought I understood. Still, it would be a long time before I could grasp what it meant to him to be a member of the Palestine Police.

We arrived at Moghrabi Square where the afternoon bustle was now in full swing. On one corner, half-naked men poured concrete for a building site; at another, a mob of people swarmed the door of the bus that had just rolled to a stop, while three barefoot Yemenite women, adorned with strings of coins around their temples and carrying baskets on their heads, strolled across the street amid honking horns. Other people were clustered under the marquee of the Moghrabi Theatre, waiting for the matinee. The cinema was an imposing structure and the focal point of the square. It had tall, stylized, rectangular columns and a pyramid of steep steps, as if designed to suggest a latter-day temple. And it was a temple of sorts to the newest of the arts, to modern life. The three Yemenite women had positioned themselves on the steps and offered oranges from their baskets to film-goers and passersby. They formed a tableau of the old world amid the new. Constable Rees told me that he and his mates came often into Tel Aviv from Jaffa or stations farther afield for rest and recreation. All this, he told me, with a sweep of his hand to indicate the various scenes of human activity in the square, couldn't be more different from stodgy old Slough. How it pleased me that he loved this new Hebrew city—and at that moment it became *my* city—an outpost of European culture built by *my* people upon the Levantine sands.

He wanted to know more about me, so I told him my story, the basic outlines—coming with Papa, leaving his house, Malka, my work as a char. I didn't try to use a nicer word to describe what I did and braced for his reaction, expecting a flicker of distaste to appear in his eyes, but there was none. On the contrary.

"You're a plucky girl," he said, with a nod of approval. He knew about the hardships of the country, especially for newcomers. He had respect for anyone who made a go of it. I spoke of my ambitions to take secretarial courses as soon as I was able.

"You'd be a natural for a government job with your English, Miss Salomon. May I call you Eva?"

Oh yes. He could.

He listened to all I said with keen attention, absorbing every detail, locking each away in his memory, it seemed. And it seemed too that he read between the lines, guessed at the deeper stories I didn't tell: about my troubles with Papa, about the big things I wanted out of life. So that when he said he had to return to his beat, I couldn't help a small sigh of disappointment. He coughed into his fist. Would I like to accompany him to a concert next week, he asked. He had tickets for the Palestine Symphony Orchestra. He looked down at my face intently, eagerness in his eyes, a masculine longing I recognized.

I was stunned. Though we'd been chatting in such a friendly way, it hadn't occurred to me he'd find me attractive as a woman. Here I stood in my grubby *ozeret* attire. My hair was a squirrel's nest, though I'd tried to pat it smooth on catching sight of myself in a window glass as we walked. Seeing my hesitation, his expression changed. He asked whether my religion prevented me from stepping out with someone of a different faith. My face burned, for the fact of his goyishness now flashed through my mind. He seemed suddenly very tall, stiff, foreign and policeman-like again.

"I'm not religious," I said quickly. "It is the individual that matters to me. And besides, I didn't flee a country with racial laws to become a person of prejudice myself."

I don't know how I found the words for such a high-minded speech. I'd never formulated such a principle to myself before. The proud, stern glint that had come into his eyes melted into a warm bath of blue. He bent forward and thanked me as if I'd given him a lovely gift, and it felt delightful, intoxicating, to be in the position of a giver. Plus, he'd invited me to a concert, this big, commanding, whistling, music-loving, goyish policeman. He'd invited me to the best concert in the land—a performance of the Palestine Symphony Orchestra.

Ein Rachel, Nov. 18, 1937
Dear Evaleh,

The rains have finally come. The dusty tracks and yards have turned into rivers of mud. I've moved from a tent to a wooden hut, an improvement, but nevertheless the wind howls through the cracks, making the flame of the hurricane lamp shiver (and me too). Rain drums down on the corrugated tin roof. I wake and fall asleep to the sound of vibrating metal and also to the tap, tap, tap of a drip from a leak in the corner. Everything is damp: my work clothes, the newsprint we use as toilet paper, which turns to pulp between my fingers. I never thought I'd say this, but I miss the sun. Still, I'm lucky not to be in the fields. The comrades out there get drenched to the bone.

I've left the kitchen for a new job and made a new friend in the process—the mild-mannered, easy-going and very lovely Becka. She listens sympathetically to my laments. She regards me with her big, sweet brown eyes. She makes contented noises when I entertain her with an old German wandering song, never insisting, as the other comrades do, that I address her only in Hebrew. She never criticizes at all, though she does let me know when these clumsy paws of mine make a mistake. What she lacks in conversational skills, she more than makes up in good will and an instinctive understanding of my moods. She's a sturdy, stalwart, productive member of the settlement and a beauty too, in her own cow-like way. Yes, Becka is a cow. She's the most placid of the dozen in our modest herd and therefore the one who was chosen to teach me the fine art of milking.

My other teacher is Shlomo, a boy built like an ox, patient and good-humoured, who fits in well here with these big, slow beasts. He explained to me the basics of cow biology and psychology and then let me go at things at my own pace, Once I got over my fear of the stamping hooves and developed the right muscles, I found I had the knack for milking. In the pre-dawn darkness, my eyes barely open, I slosh through the mud and manure to grope for Becka, always going to her first. She shuffles in her stall and lets out a plaintive moo as if to say: "I've missed you so. It's been an eternity since we last saw one another. How could you abandon me to the loneliness of the night?" But as soon as I rest my forehead against her warm, quivering flank and we settle into our rhythm, she snuffles with content. She offers me not just her milk but her soothing animal presence too. Afterwards, I help milk the others, prepare the feed, and clean out the stalls. At first the stench bothered me, but now I barely notice it.

The new comrade, the fellow Yecke that Dov Kalisch wants to match me up with, is due to arrive in another week. Everyone reminds everyone else about this piece of good news several times a day. Though no one knows much about him, the whole settlement yearns for his arrival as for the coming of the Messiah. Of course, no one would admit to such feelings, yet everyone talks, speculates and pesters Dov Kalisch for information. Nu? Any word? And I'm as anxious as all the rest. It's because we have few visitors, little contact with the outside world, and a prospective new member only once in a very long while. The odd thing is, even as Dov Kalisch's casual suggestion annoyed me, I began to weave fantasies about this new man from Berlin. That's loneliness speaking, I suppose. The hard work, harsh climate and dangers strip me bare, make me hungry for a deep and intimate friend.

Hugs and kisses,

Your Liesel

Chapter 6
Palestine Symphony

"A POLICEMAN? A *British* policeman."

Malka screwed up her lips. She'd been about to light the Primus, but now leaned up against the kitchen counter to study me, head to one side.

"He's not like that," I said.

I placed my slice of bread and butter back on the plate and turned in my chair to meet her eyes.

"Like what?"

But I refused to descend to her level and use her coarse terms. Or even think them.

"He's a nice man. A good man."

"My little chick, all men are 'like that' to some extent when it comes to women, even the good ones. Unless he's a castrato or a homo, and it doesn't sound like he is . . ."

"Stop it! He's perfectly decent. A lot more decent than those two married men you set me up with."

Heat rose to my cheeks.

"Me set you up? What are you talking about? I introduced you to some people at a café. Did I say you should step out with anyone? You made your own decisions. And when you did, I gave you good advice. And anyway . . ."

Malka paused in mid-speech to fill the kettle. The stream of tap water sang inside the kettle's metal belly. She clapped on the lid and turned back to me.

"Anyway, how do you know this policeman isn't already hitched up himself with a wife back in England?"

"They don't recruit married men for the police force," I shot back. "Yes, he told me so. Just in passing. When he told me the criteria for recruits. He's honest and kind. What have you got against a man you haven't even met?"

Malka didn't answer right away. Instead she devoted some moments to coaxing the Primus to life, working the fuel pump, muttering curses or incantations under her breath. When the flames were right, she balanced the kettle on top. She lit herself a cigarette and offered me one. I shook my head.

"I'm not against *him*, my dear, I'm *for* you. Trying to be a friend. Just keep your eyes open. Don't decide he's an angel based on one brief chat. I know a bit about these British. How they think."

She held up her hand, seeing I was about to protest. "Let me finish."

She sucked her cigarette, allowed herself a long, thoughtful exhalation.

"He may be very nice, but to him you're a local girl. A native. A foreigner. Not equal to one of his own. The British consider themselves the chosen people as much as we do and they've got a lot more to show for it—a whole empire. He may not even be aware that's how he thinks, but he does. You're not the type he'd take home to mother. And since mother is thousands of miles away, the matter will never be put to the test. Very convenient. You're someone to have fun with. Fine. Nothing wrong with that, as long as you understand where you stand. Have fun too. Just make sure you handle him like a smart hunter with big game—aware of your strengths and weaknesses."

"I'm not like you," I spat.

We eyed one another.

"And what exactly do you mean by that?"

Malka's lips curled in a half smile. Her voice now had an edge. She drew hard on her cigarette.

She meant well in her own limited way, I knew. But how I loathed her crude calculations. As if every human interaction—even the finest—had to be like haggling over vegetables at the souk. What mean assumptions about Duncan Rees. A petty, provincial streak ran through Malka, bred by generations of *shtetel* folk—for that's where her family came from originally. They came from some little Jewish backwater town, sunk in the mud of its prejudices and fears. I was convinced too that she wanted to mould me to her image and resented my refusal to swallow her every nugget of advice. All this swam through my head, along with calculations of my own. She was my only friend. I owed her a lot. She could throw me out on my ears. So she reduced me to her level after all, for I bit my tongue and murmured a vague apology.

THE WEEK CREPT by, oh so slowly. As I scrubbed and wrung out the Mandelmanns' bed sheets, as I dusted *Frau* Kleiner's porcelain knick-knacks, I sifted in my mind every word Constable Rees (he was not yet Duncan to me) and I had exchanged, every gesture he'd made. How he'd taken off his cap. How he bent forward to listen. Malka's warnings, designed to make me wary, had the opposite effect. I defended him against her in my thoughts, producing Constable Rees' sincere remarks, his open, upright manner, as evidence. Such warm blue eyes he had. *True blue.* I'd heard that English expression somewhere and it seemed just right.

At the appointed hour on the Saturday night, those eyes drank me in as I stood at the door. They saw me exactly as I wanted to be seen. Though it was a bit light for the season, I wore my best outfit—the cream-coloured dress with red polka dots and red belt and the matching red jacket. I'd done my hair and face. I stood tall and confident in my high-heeled shoes. His stare of surprise turned into a gleam of appreciation and a flush of pleasure, as if he'd stumbled upon a gold coin on the ground. He raised his eyebrows and darted his tongue against his upper lip. But all he said was, "Fetching outfit."

"What does it fetch?" I asked.

I'd become a woman of the world, ready with coquettish remarks.

"A lucky dog," he answered without hesitation.

He too had dressed for the occasion. Gone the khaki uniform and visored cap. He wore a smart navy blue blazer, white shirt, and grey flannel trousers. His hair was neatly parted and wetly combed against his head and it seemed to me he'd had a haircut since we'd last met. He had no hat, just an umbrella in one hand.

"Is it raining?"

"Not yet, but it might. There's a nasty wind though."

His brow pleated in concern over the summertime lightness of my outfit.

"I'll wear a coat," I assured him.

Such commonplace words we spoke, yet they seemed code for a conversation taking place beneath the surface.

"This is my landlady . . . my friend," I corrected myself. "Malka."

She'd emerged from her bedroom to inspect my cavalier for herself. She gave him her thinnest smile, but I could tell from the appraising light in her eyes, that, despite whatever else she thought, she found him handsome. I swelled with pride.

He helped me on with my brown wool coat, held it open for me with such gallantry, I forgot to be ashamed at its drabness.

"Thank you Constable Rees."

"Duncan!" he chided.

On Allenby Road, we boarded a jam-packed bus, Duncan creating space for us amid the press of bodies with a firm "Excuse me!" and subtle shoves of his hips and shoulders. The crowd parted to let us through. Even minus his uniform, Duncan commanded respect through his height and bearing, his assumption of status. People seemed to know who he was and allowed him to pick his choice spot for us in the aisle near the back door. As we bumped and lurched along,

Duncan held my arm in a protective grasp to help me keep my balance, his own feet planted squarely, immovable, against the floor. And every time I almost stumbled, he murmured an apologetic "Oh dear!" as if he were solely responsible for my staying anchored. I wasn't used to being treated like a precious vase. It made me giggle and blush.

All the length of Ben Yehuda Street we travelled, to the outskirts of town, to the estuary where the Yarkon River meets the sea. We disembarked into darkness and uneven ground, for the road had ended, and, again, Duncan held my arm in a firm, solicitous grip. After wading through sand for some minutes we arrived at the strangest place: a ghost town of low, wide, silent buildings. Here and there, lights glimmered and torch beams bounced, allowing us to see the outlines of hard blank walls that loomed out of the darkness. A few voices echoed and died away. Figures popped up in front of us and vanished. The hush-hush of waves lapped a nearby shore and the smell of salt was in the air, but the sea was utterly hidden from view.

"I've never been here before," I confessed. "It's a bit eerie."

"Not been to the Levant Fair grounds?"

Duncan tucked my arm more tightly under his, guiding me along the asphalt paths between the shuttered buildings. He explained that this had been a bustling trade fair a few years back. The pavilions had been built to showcase the products of Palestine and launch Tel Aviv as *the* commercial centre for the whole Middle East.

"The Arab troubles put the kibosh on dreams like that. Bleeding shame. So now the pavilions are warehouses or stand empty."

"But there are concerts?"

"From time to time, in one of the buildings, yes."

We turned a corner. An oasis of light leaped out of the darkness, a brilliantly lit doorway towards which people streamed. Suddenly there was life, hubbub, a kernel of downtown Tel Aviv in this abandoned complex. We joined the crowd filing through the entrance of the illuminated building. We found ourselves in a large, stark, rectangular room which reminded me of the customs shed in Haifa port, except for the bright white walls and ultra-modern chandeliers hanging from steel rafters spanning the ceiling. Bleachers of wooden chairs filled the sold-out hall from end to end. Our places were near the back, but central, giving me a good view of the audience—a happy, animated crowd, some people dressed in their best suits and gowns, others in simple attire: workers' caps, plain shirts, and trousers or skirts and blouses. People shouted to one another across the rows, laughed, waved, jostled, fanned themselves with their programs. Duncan helped me out of my coat and carefully hung it over the back of my chair, his gentle, attentive movements adding to the bubbles of excitement dancing beneath my ribs.

"Isn't this wonderful? Have you ever seen anything like it? I've never been to a symphony before."

I said it all in one breath, like a gushing schoolgirl.

"How is that possible?" Duncan asked, amazed.

It pained me to explain how things had been back in Germany and how little money I had for luxuries here. But Duncan's response was to become even gentler and more gallant.

"What an honour then to be the first to bring you to a symphony," he murmured.

He spread the program open between us, his long forefinger running down the list. The *Fidelio* overture by Beethoven, selections from Mendelssohn's *Midsummer Night's Dream*, Tchaikovsky's *Violin Concert in D major* and Mussorgsky's *Pictures at an Exhibition* to end the evening.

"A first-class selection," he declared. "I see they've dropped the lighter works introduced last year. There were complaints. No Strauss waltzes for this sophisticated audience."

Despite the commotion around us, he pitched his voice low—his British reserve, I assumed—so that I had to lean close to hear. He had a clean, manly smell, of shaving soap and fresh laundry with a hint of sweat underneath.

"The conductor is superb. Michael Taube. You've heard of him? He was with the Municipal Opera of Berlin before he came to Palestine. A great catch. But of course, there are so many brilliant musicians here now. Thank you, Herr Hitler."

I winced, but Duncan seemed not to notice.

"The violin soloist is Moshe . . . what? How do you pronounce this?"

Duncan pointed at the printed name. "*Sztyglic.*"

"I have no idea," I said and began to giggle.

"Is it Chiglik, Stiglich? Come, you must know. You Jewish girls know everything."

Which made me giggle harder, rolling in my seat, knocking against him. Duncan snorted too and for some moments we were two naughty schoolchildren at the back of a classroom. Abruptly, Duncan stopped. He went from hilarity to composure in what seemed a split second, startling me into silence. I put my hand over my mouth and looked around but nothing had changed. The rest of the audience was still babbling away. Duncan smiled. There was no censure in his eyes, just a grave look, as if to say "enough is enough." This made me aware of how much more confident he was than me, how sure of his place in the world and precisely what behaviour was required from one moment to the next.

The lights dimmed, the hubbub abated and, as the musicians began to file onto the stage, the audience exploded into thunderous applause. All through the tuning of instruments—the squeaks of strings, the blats of horns—the clapping continued sporadically. When the conductor—dressed impeccably in a black suit and black bow tie—arrived, the applause became a roar, with shouts of "Bravo! Bravo!" as if the perfect performance had already been delivered. I understood. Before us was nothing short of a miracle. These ordinary-looking men and a few women fingering their instruments, mopping their brows, constituted an achievement that went far beyond their musical talents. They were an orchestra composed, as Duncan had noted, of top-ranking musicians from across Europe who'd fled Hitler to be gathered together in this raw young land. A Jewish orchestra performing for Jews in the first Hebrew city of modern times! The orchestra was almost two years old, yet still took people's breath away. As for me, new to the land, new to orchestras of any kind, I couldn't help the tears that sprang to my eyes nor the frenzy of my own clapping hands. I paused to peek at Duncan. He sat with his hands resting on his thighs, a faint smile on his lips, as if waiting patiently for the crowd to come to its senses. Could he appreciate what the euphoria was about? He smiled at me through the half-light. Yes, yes, he too understood. He was part of all this. Revolt might be brewing throughout the country. Europe might be going up in flames. Never mind. Here in this hall we would rise above chaos to savour the golden fruits of Western civilization. We would answer madness with brilliance, destruction with creation, banishment from Europe with establishing the best of Europe on the Levantine sands.

Mr. Taube leaned forward. The audience held its breath. The bold first notes of *Fidelio* thundered through the room, followed by the gentle strains from the wind section. I forgot the audience, forgot Duncan, was swept up in the majesty, the poignancy, the great, all-encompassing Beethovian sea. The music was everywhere: behind and in front, above and below. Different instrument sections popped up suddenly to surprise me and then all blended together into magnificent crescendos. My whole being became the music—the surge and crash, the golden call of the horns. My heart ached with feeling, part pain, part delight, an emotion so big I thought I might explode. As the final notes died away and the roar of applause began, I opened my eyes to see Duncan peering down at me with a surprised, tender expression on his face. He took a pressed white handkerchief out of his trousers pocket and touched it to my cheek where a tear had fallen.

"What a sensitive thing you are, Eva Salomon," he whispered. Though startled, I warmed to the touch and the look.

When the music resumed, he enclosed my hand in his own in a gentle, though possessive grip, while staring straight ahead, deeply attentive to the orchestra. He held my hand as if doing so were the most natural thing in the world. As if our hands were autonomous beings that could behave as they wished. He kept his gaze on the stage but the skin of his palm and fingers spoke, their heat travelling up my arm and into my chest, making my breath catch in my throat. The experience was part pleasure, part panic. All my being was now my hand, it seemed—small and helpless, enfolded in his masterful grip. A mastery he could conjure without thinking, without trying. Meanwhile, the Mendelssohn I'd so been looking forward to had become muted and discordant like the chatter of remote starlings. It was all too much, too soon, and, with an effort of will, I jerked away.

"I'm terribly sorry," he whispered.

"It's all right, I . . . I just want to listen," I whispered in return.

"Of course."

Our hands returned to our laps. We became two separate entities again. After some moments the jittery, fearful, distracted feeling dissolved, the musical notes fell back into their places and I melted away into the Mendelssohnian extravaganza of sound.

AFTER THE CONCERT, we agreed to take the bus only as far as Keren Kayemet Avenue and to walk the rest of the way. The rain had held off, the wind had died down, the open space and bracing air were divine. Scraps of clouds raced across the face of the moon. It was a gibbous moon, Duncan told me, this ripe, bright shape, lounging on its side like a pregnant lady. He could name stars and planets, could point them out above, the night sky not a vast emptiness for him, but a kind of map. At the police training depot, they'd learned to find their way in the dark by the position of stars in case they ever got lost in the wilderness. "There's Venus," he said, indicating a jewel of light near the western horizon. Just then I stumbled at a break in the pavement, of which there were many in this city-in-a-hurry, this city whose roads still included yawning gaps of sand. Duncan caught me with a lightning swift movement of his arm, pressed me close for a moment. His manly warmth reached me through the cloth of his blazer.

"Steady," he said, with a small chuckle, releasing me only reluctantly it seemed. I liked the warmth. I liked the reluctance. I liked that he knew when to let go.

Never before had the night sky seemed so close and vibrant. Never had it possessed such a glittering depth. We ambled past sandy lanes, past small houses half hidden by the shrubbery of front gardens, past new buildings, whose white-washed walls gave off a muted glow in the dark. We went by the lane that led to

Frau Kleiner's pension, but I didn't mention this to Duncan. I wanted to cling to the now, not be reminded of my work-a-day life.

"The concert was so wonderful," I said for the umpteenth time.

"What was wonderful was seeing you so carried away. You were quite in a trance. Thought I'd lost you altogether at one point."

He sounded amused, but also intrigued.

"Music is my religion, I suppose. My only religion."

The words seemed affected no sooner were they out of my mouth. I struggled to think what I really meant and decided to change tracks.

"What about you? I suppose you're a Christian. Do you go to a church?"

"Oh, I'm Church of England, of course. I make it to a pew on Christmas and Easter and the odd Sunday now and then, like any other bloke. Otherwise . . ." He shrugged. "Wouldn't call myself pious. Can't stand those solemn, prudish, fall-on-your-knees folk. They give me the willies. But . . ."

"But what?"

"It's quite something to be smack dab in the land of the Bible. You wouldn't think you were while muckin' about in Tel Aviv, but other places . . . well, it grabs you: this is where Jesus walked, this is where it all happened. Can't help but feel moved to your bones. So much of the country looks frozen in time, exactly like it must have back then. It's ancient and it's so . . ." Duncan waved his hand, at a loss for words and then laughed. "So Biblical!"

He'd seen a lot more of the land than I had and listed places that had impressed him—the Old City of Jerusalem, the Judean desert, Bethlehem, Jericho, the Sea of Galilee, the Crusader fortress of Acre. I was touched by his enthusiasm and stirred by the thought that this land of historic riches was part of both our heritages—his and mine. As we continued to walk southward, we could see the lights of Jaffa quite clearly in the distance. They formed a bright, separate constellation on a hill above the sea.

"I've never even been to Jaffa," I said, vexed. "I shouldn't be such a coward perhaps."

"Yes, you should." Duncan's voice was stern. "I hope you'd never dream of going alone. You need a male escort. Even in peaceful times you'd need one."

I asked him what the town was like and to tell me more about his work. Generally, there was respect for the uniform, he assured me, and even gratitude because Arabs were more likely to be killed by fellow Arabs in the disturbances than anyone else. He described the gracious villas of the effendis and the densely packed poorer houses. The ancient, narrow lanes, chock-a-block with little shops, the bazaars, noisy with the shouts of hawkers, swarming with townsfolk, camels, and donkeys, and, of course, the flies. The cafés, with men playing *sheshbesh* and smoking their hubble-bubble pipes. All very colourful and Oriental. Trouble? Yes, a copper had to have eyes at the back of his head. Mostly he was on the lookout for concealed weapons—not so easy to spot beneath those long robes some Arabs wear—and for hotheads trying to stir up a mob. Many incidents were pure mischief, like when boys scattered nails and broken glass on the Tel Aviv-Jaffa road. At night a patrolman had to watch out for curfew breakers of all stripes, vandals, arsonists, and those turds—pardon the expression—who liked to cut government telephone wires. There was all the ordinary crime to deal with too. Knife fights. Domestic brouhahas. Thievery. Cheating scales. Smuggling. Counterfeit money. Never a dull moment. His speech became more rapid. He sounded as if he savoured every one of those not-so-dull moments. The only time he'd ever been truly upset, it seemed to me, was when he'd witnessed a donkey being flogged within an inch of its life. Put the man in the clapper overnight for that, he said. Slapped him with the maximum fine.

"How long do you expect to stay in Palestine?" I asked.

He was surprised at the question. He had no plans beyond his present career with the Force. And then he told me a saying that was often repeated around the billets and canteens, sometimes jokingly, sometimes in dead earnest: *There is no promotion beyond Palestine.* The place was so remarkable, and protecting the Holy Land—the land where Jesus had lived and died—such a privilege, that no other posting would do.

We walked and we talked. He towered above me, yet it didn't seem so, for he would bend towards my face as he listened, diminishing the distance between us. Every so often we paused to gaze out at the vast, dark sea. The waves heaved in and out, a steady rhythm like a heartbeat, filling the silences between our words. At Allenby Road we turned inland towards Moghrabi Square, to find ourselves amidst the clamour of a city that had roared to life. Hundreds of Saturday night revellers milled about the square, eating ice cream and sunflower seeds and boiled corn on the cob. Parents pushed prams. Bands of youth with arms around each others' shoulders stretched across the sidewalk. A large group of *hora* dancers had taken over a section of the road in front of the theatre. There was clapping and singing and bouncing strains of accordion music. Car horns tooted in solidarity or frustration—it was hard to tell which—as traffic inched around this obstacle. We moved closer to watch the leaping bodies and animated faces, bobbing in and out of the wash of neon lights. The same chords played over and over in a monotonous but compelling rhythm. My toe couldn't help but tap against the pavement.

"Lively tune, that," Duncan said. "Did you want to dance?"

I looked up at him in surprise.

"Do you?"

"Me? Lord no!"

He laughed as if the idea was absurd.

"I only meant you should go ahead if you want to. I'll be happy to watch."

"But you don't dance?"

"Not this!"

There was something odd in his vehemence. And then he explained. It would be unseemly—it would simply not do—for a member of His Majesty's Palestine Police, even if off-duty and in civvies, to link arms with the Jews in their Saturday evening nationalistic fervour. For that's what this *hora* dancing was about. A statement of allegiance. Not merely a bit of fun. If I wanted to jump into the circle, I'd have to do so alone. But I had no wish to do so.

As we were leaving the square, an adolescent boy horsing around with a group of his friends, jostled against me.

"Hey there, mind the lady," Duncan said sharply, in English.

He drew himself up to his full height, towered over the boy. The youth stared, first at Duncan, then at me. He pulled off his cap, held it against his heart.

"Oh please, my lady, please excuse me."

He spoke in English with a heavy Russian accent, drawling the words. There was no mistaking his mockery and that of his friends, who cackled to one another, *My lady. My lay-ay-dee.*

"That's enough," Duncan said, taking a step forward. In a flash, the youth and his gang vanished into the crowd. Duncan made a disgusted noise and muttered about bloody rascals under his breath. I had the impression such encounters with mischievous youth were everyday fare for Duncan, flies he regularly had to swat away. Now, hooking my arm firmly into his own, he guided me across the square, people moving aside to let us through. I felt a mix of emotions: pleased to be so protected and cherished by this man who cared about a boy treading on my toes. Vaguely ashamed, as if I'd betrayed one of my own. Duncan was telling me about his barracks and the mess, but I hardly heard, for uncomfortable questions buzzed around in my mind.

"What do you think of Zionism?" I suddenly blurted out.

He came to a sudden halt. Peered down at me. "What's that got to do with anything?"

"I'm just curious to hear your views."

He made some vague, polite comments about admiring the drive and energy of the Jewish cities and settlements. He called it "bulldozer drive."

"But?" I challenged.

"But what?"

"I sense a reservation."

"Then you're being touchy. My admiration is entirely sincere."

He pressed my arm, a gesture that was supposed to convey affection, but felt more like reproach. I pulled away and we continued to walk some moments in awkward silence. I tried a more tactful approach.

"You must sometimes find it hard to be in the middle between the Arabs and the Jews."

"Are you questioning my allegiances, Miss Salomon?"

"I'm trying to understand what it's like for you."

Duncan looked down at his shoes. Then at me.

"I uphold the law. Detect and prevent crime. I'm here for all citizens."

"But some laws aren't so nice. Like the ones against refugees. And against Jews defending themselves when they're attacked."

"Whoa. Hold on there." He stopped again to face me.

"It's not so simple . . ."

But I jumped in before he could continue, sparks let loose on my tongue.

"It *is* very simple. It's simple if you're a refugee risking your life to get here in a tin can boat and you're caught and put in a detention camp. It's very simple if you're a settler and have to guard your colony from Arab raids."

Why I was talking this way I don't know. It wasn't as if I was such a big Zionist myself. But reading the newspaper almost daily with Mrs. Mandelmann had made me more aware of the uncertainties we all faced and the contradictions in British policy. And perhaps something of Malka's poison had entered my veins.

"We coppers don't make the laws," he said in an even tone. "Just uphold them. Can be sticky sometimes when those chaps in Whitehall make a mess. We have to pick up the pieces."

"So you're against the cruel immigration laws?"

"I didn't say that," he said stiffly. "Look here, there has to be fairness. There have to be limits. We can't just let in the whole kit and caboodle. And we can't let 'em in any old way. There's a queue. We can't let people jump the queue."

"You think like the Arabs do. That we don't belong here. So where do we belong, tell me? What scrap of this great earth should be safe for the Jew?"

"Good bloody grief!"

He jerked his head impatiently. Despite the dim light, I could see his jaw tighten. But he took a breath, cleared his throat, collected himself.

"I didn't say Jews don't belong here. Just maybe not all Jews. Think of it! There are millions in Europe. They can't all come to this little strip of land. And what about the Arab citizens? I can understand their point of view. The Arabs see the Jews pushing them aside in their own country . . . wait, let me finish. They're a completely different people. The Arab is attached to his dreamy ways, his ancient, sleepy rhythm of life that's been the same for centuries and here the clever Jew comes along, buying up his land from under him, bringing the modern world roaring down upon him. One has to go slow with the Arabs. Prod them gently into the twentieth century. It's all the rushing that leads to the troubles. Your people don't know how to slow down and relax."

He was attempting a more light-hearted tone. A reasoning tone. It only upset me more.

"But we have to rush. We're being driven. It's unbearable in Germany. You can't imagine. Do you think people like me would have left otherwise? And you said yourself that it's hotheads stirring up the Arab masses, causing the trouble. Not anything we do. And . . . and what about the question of arms? At my sister's settlement, British soldiers came and took arms away from the men guarding their homes. Would you do that too?"

"We have to appear even-handed," he said softly. "So we disarm Jews as well as Arabs. But some orders are . . . well, the brass makes mistakes, I'll give you that. Still the men in the trenches have to follow through. An order is an order, otherwise the whole system breaks down."

We'd come to a halt at the intersection with Rothschild Boulevard. There were benches and young trees along the walkway that divided the road. Duncan drew me towards one of the benches beside a shuttered kiosk.

"Let's sit."

A deep darkness had settled over this part of the city, broken only by scattered street lamps and a few lights in the upper stories of the building blocks.

"Look, if I were a Jew," Duncan continued, "I'd do exactly what your people are doing. I would tell his Majesty's Government, as Mr. Weizmann does, that we were here first. We've belonged to this land since biblical times."

But you're not a Jew, I thought. Aloud I said, because I couldn't help myself, "I just want to know whose side you are on. In your heart."

"Why, yours of course," he said, cupping my face in his hands and tipping it upwards. "I'm on your side, Eva Salomon."

"Me as just me, or me as one of the Jews?"

"What tormented thoughts you have, Eva! How am I supposed to answer? It would take me a whole day to figure it out. I'm not a diplomat. Just an ordinary bloke."

I felt his breath on my face. I trembled in anticipation and in fear of something that felt inevitable, irreversible.

"You have to admit," I said with a silly laugh, "we're not an easy people to get along with."

At which he pulled me closer.

"Eva Salomon! I have to admit, I don't want to be chums with the whole of the Jewish people. Just with you."

Ein Rachel, Dec. 7, 1937

Evaleh, forgive me. I didn't mean to offend you and I never dreamt you would take my words like that. It's a misunderstanding born of my clumsy way of expressing myself.

Of course I have faith in your judgment and realize you're not the young thing I left behind when we parted two years ago. Well, to be honest, it is hard to picture my baby sister in her chic lady clothes, stepping out on the town with her handsome cavalier. Of course, I don't regard you as "desperate for male company." And yes, you're right, he has a name: Duncan. I'll stop calling him "your policeman." I do apologize for that. But you are quite unfair to compare me with Papa. I'd never judge you, as he would. Nor was I suggesting you go crawling back to him. It just would be nice if you could maintain some contact. He's the only family we have here, after all. And if you do see Papa again, you don't need to mention Duncan. Why get into a terrible argument? It would serve no purpose. You and I should certainly not quarrel. I'll try not to be an awkward, bumbling mother hen. So please don't be angry.

Love,
Liesel

Ein Rachel, Dec. 17, 1937
Dear Eva,

At last he's here—the new volunteer, whose name is Manfred Glatt and who, at first sight, was pure disaster. He arrived curled up in a foetal position on top of sacks of supplies in a donkey cart. Stricken by a migraine, of all things. When the cart bumped to a halt, he clutched his head as if he wanted to bury it under the potatoes. Only after he heard people shouting "What's wrong? Has he been shot?" did he stagger to his feet and face the welcoming committee. I wasn't there, but I heard the story and can imagine how dismayed the others must have been when they caught sight of this doubtful scrap of pioneering material. In the evening during

supper, I got a chance to form my own first impression. *There he sat,
pressed between Dov and Shlomo on the bench, like skimpy filling
in a thick-bread sandwich, his face a blur of misery, accentuated
by round, steel-rimmed spectacles on a long, sad nose. Every time
someone came over to clap him on the shoulder, which is the usual
style of greeting here, he winced with pain as if they'd stabbed him
with knives. Finally, he extracted himself from the Dov-Shlomo vice
and hurried out of the hall. A buzz of commentary filled the air.*

"He's fragile as a moth."

"He won't last a week."

"A week! I'd be surprised if he hasn't vaporized by morning."

*Yet next morning he trudged off to the fields with some other
men to dig a drainage ditch. People say he attacked the muddy
ground with his shovel as if it were a personal enemy. The others
had to warn him to pace himself. That evening, Dov Kalisch
welcomed him officially with a little speech about the history of
the settlement. A comrade stood to correct Dov on the date when
the cowshed went up. Ruthie rose to put in a few words because
it wasn't right that only the men should speak. Then we pushed
chairs and benches against the walls, Shlomo hooked his arms into
the straps of his accordion, the instrument burped, wheezed and
exploded into melody and the hall vibrated with the stamp of feet.
Manfred Glatt, in whose honour we were dancing, gamely joined
the circle and allowed himself to be swept along. His legs jerked like
those of a badly handled puppet.*

*And now I'm coming to the crux of my story. Next day, in the
murky light of early morning, I was in the cow shed, shovelling dung
pies while entertaining the dear beasts with a good old German
hiking song. As I paused for a rest, I heard a noise by the open door.
A rustle or a footstep that signalled a foreign presence in the shed.
I had the distinct feeling of being watched, but saw no one. My first
thought was Arab infiltrators, who are never far from our minds.
With shaking hands, I hoisted my shovel over my shoulder like an
axe and moved cautiously towards the entrance. "Who's there?"
I yelled, fiercely as I could. A pair of glasses glinted. The new man
stepped forward with his palms upraised in surrender.*

*"Good morning, Comrade. I know I look like vermin, but I hope
you'll spare me."*

He was dressed in the mid-week pickings from the communal clothes basket—a flannel shirt several sizes too big for him. Sleeves flopping past his wrists. Work pants cinched at the waist with a makeshift belt of rope. His thick, wiry black hair stood up from his narrow head like a cluster of exclamation marks. He looked like a bedraggled tramp, a Charlie Chaplin with spectacles. All that was missing was the toothbrush moustache. I let out a hoot of laughter, partly out of relief that he wasn't the knife-wielding raider of my imagination.

"I didn't mean to startle you. Just wanted to listen. I like that song you were singing. I know it well."

He offered a thin, shy smile.

"We haven't been properly introduced," he continued. "I know you are Liesel Salomon from Breslau. I'm from a town not so far down the road Görlitz. Though I've been living in Berlin until recently."

His shoulders stiffening, he bent forward in mockery of an old-fashioned bow. Except that it wasn't pure mockery, for there was something reflexive in the movement, as if he'd been schooled in proper, bourgeois, last-century manners by some ancient aunt. Again, when I laughed, he only allowed himself a tight smile without parting his lips. But now, at least, he stretched out his right hand like a regular human being. Despite the dim light in the shed, I was able to get a good look at that hand. Small, pale, blistered from digging. A city man's hand. My own was a rough paw in comparison, plus, I realized as I dropped my shovel, it was filthy with cow dung. I was about to apologize, but a mischievous impulse took hold of me. Let's see what this greenhorn is made of, I told myself. I expected him to hop backwards in disgust the moment his fingers touched mine. But he didn't. Instead, he took my hand in his and held onto it in a firm, lingering grip. Was it really so long we stood like that, or did it just seem so—a moment suspended in time? Our clasped hands grew warm and sticky, glued together with cow muck. He was either strangely oblivious or wanted to let me know he'd taken up my challenge and intended to prove himself worthy. And he gazed at me in a way that seemed both gentle and sad, his eyes older than the rest of him. There was something dignified, solid and reassuring here, despite the nebbish appearance. I felt ashamed of my dirty trick. But I didn't want to be the first to pull away either. When he *finally released my hand, I wiped it belatedly against my skirt. He just dropped his arms to his side and finally gave a full smile. His front teeth are bent inwards slightly, as if in apology at being teeth that can bite and tear. I couldn't help but like him. I led him to the sink outside the shed and we took turns having a good scrub under the trickle of cold water.*

"Well, what do you think of Ein Rachel?" I asked, as we splashed along the muddy path towards the dining hall for breakfast.

He looked about at the rows of small, wooden huts and canvas tents, sunk into rivers of churned-up ooze.

"It's certainly not Potsdamer Platz," he sighed.

"But if it were, you wouldn't feel like a pioneer," I said heartily.

I proceeded to chatter about the ideals of the collective as if I were delivering one of those Saturday night spirit-rallying speeches in the dining hall. He nodded respectfully, but when I paused for breath he confessed, "I'm not really a socialist."

I stared dumbfounded.

"You're not? Then what are you doing here?"

We'd arrived at the porch of the dining hall, and stood aside as others streamed in from their various workplaces. In a few sentences, Manfred told me his story. Visas to Palestine—to anywhere—are rare as pearls now. The illegal route is the only way for many to find refuge. The Haganah organizes passage, but mostly for its own people—long-time members of Zionist groups—and Manfred had never joined. But he had a good friend who was high up in the movement and this friend arranged for Manfred to be taken along on a tramp steamer set to cross the sea and run the British coastal blockade. Manfred's part of the bargain was to pledge to volunteer in a settlement for at least a year. He described to me the conditions on the boat. Horrible. Not enough food and water. Hundreds packed together in the stinking, airless hold for days on end. The steamer was detected by a British police patrol vessel and stopped before it reached the Palestine shores, but a few lifeboats put out to sea and Manfred in one of them made it to land. He has nothing good to say about the British authorities. Says they are like officials anywhere: hearts of stone. Anyway, Manfred is neither a socialist, nor much of a Zionist, though how one can be anything else in these times of persecution is beyond me. He plans to do whatever is asked of him here for a year, and then start over in one of the cities. It's noble that he does this much, because he could have just melted into the streets of Tel Aviv; no one could force him to fulfill his pledge.

"Maybe you'll be seduced by the communal spirit," I said to him as we entered the dining hall.

He gave me a warm, wistful look as if to say: "Maybe I'll be seduced by something quite else entirely."

There. I've told you everything, and I'm written out. Did you receive the letter with my apology? Are you still seeing Duncan, or have you made new conquests?

Love, Your Liesel

Chapter 7
Love in Tel Aviv

AND SO I had a man-friend, a *gever*, as they say in Hebrew, though I thought the term crude. I preferred a gracious, old-fashioned term to refer to Duncan. He was my *beau*. Together that winter, we discovered the sweetness of intimacy and the pleasures of the raw, bold, half-baked city—the new Hebrew city—of Tel Aviv. He took me to concerts at school auditoriums and workers' halls and again at the Levant Fair. We heard Sacha Parnes play Schumann's Concerto for Violin and Joseph Tal perform Chopin and the Palestine Symphony in a wonderful Mendelssohn program and recitals by students from the Tel Aviv Conservatoire. We sat or stood in drafty rooms with terrible acoustics, drinking in the music and each other's presence, our heartstrings plucked by sweet awareness and brilliant sound. He took me to the pictures. The city boasted five cinemas, with films from America, Britain, France, Austria, and even Germany (re-runs of classics from before the Nazi takeover). We saw *The Last Days of Pompeii*, *The Prince and the Pauper*, *I Met Him in Paris* and *Seventh Heaven*. With Duncan's arm draped over my shoulder and our heads close together, we floated into the cinema glow, into the stories on the screen and the murmurings of our bodies in the dark.

On Saturday nights, if it wasn't absolutely pelting with rain, I'd wait for him on the balcony that adjoined Malka's kitchen. I'd gaze up and down the dimly lit street, dashing from one side of the narrow structure to the other while pedestrians sauntered by below. Neighbours on nearby balconies shook out the crumbs from their supper bread baskets and called across teasingly, "*Nu*? What's keeping your *gever*?" No matter how carefully I kept watch, I never saw his approach, for that was his game—to catch me by surprise. Out of the darkness of a side alley I'd hear him whistle the opening bar of Beethoven's Fifth, which had become his trademark signal. I'd grab my bag and dash to the front door, and maybe bump into Malka, who'd roll her eyes and tell me it was the man who should be kept on tenterhooks and be made to run like a dog at the sound of his master's whistle. When I came tripping down the stairs, Duncan caught me in his arms, his warm blue eyes aglow.

He bought me chocolate torte at Café Sapir and ice cream and lemonade and peanuts and flowers and anything else I might have wanted from the kiosks on the seaside promenade. When I worried at the extravagance, he'd laugh and say money was meant to be spent, not hoarded. He loved to squander his hard-earned policeman's salary on me. He liked to feed me rich desserts and said I could eat myself silly because I was such a wee, slender thing. He loved that his hands nearly fit, fingertip to fingertip, all around my waist and that he could lift me into the air without the slightest effort. I told him Papa used to call me *Zwergel*—Dwarfling—which I hated, as I hated being so small.

"But Missy, don't you know, the best things come in small packages? Once, when I was a young squirt and had the measles, my mum read me stories. There was one about a tiny princess, no bigger than a thumb, who lived on a lily pad. I can still see that picture from the book—her sweet pixie body. Her name was Thumbelina. That's you. You're my darling Thumbelina!"

Thumbelina. If anyone else had called me that, I would have smacked him in the face. Out of Duncan's mouth, it sounded lovely.

He kissed me on the beach below the seaside promenade and beneath the young trees on Rothschild Boulevard and in the stairwell of the building on Lilienblum Street. His hot, urgent lips pressed against mine, forgetting to be tender, our teeth knocking together awkwardly, and then his "sorry, oh so sorry, my dear!" as his arms held me tighter and then his hands slipped under my blouse. Outside, beyond the entrance, furious rain smacked the pavement and gusts of wet wind howled into the stairwell. There was nowhere to go because Malka was home. But even if she'd been out, I'd have resisted—shy about Malka's sudden return and afraid of all that fierce male need, despite the new, disturbing hunger between my own legs. And so another time when she was gone, I refused to bring him up to the flat. He coaxed, but he let it go. He thought I was being strong. He thought I was doing what girls had to do. I suppose I was.

Then one night he took me to the San Remo Hotel, a swanky, three-storey establishment at the end of Allenby Road, near the beach. It was like something out of the Riviera: white and wedding-cake grand with umbrella-shaded patios and attentive doormen. The lounge had cane chairs, glass-topped tables, potted palms, lacquered wood ceiling fans that swept in lazy circles, a wide dance floor and a raised dais for the band. A jazz quartet—piano, bass, clarinet, and crooning vocalist—served up sentimental favourites, along with lively tunes that had reached our shores from America. *It don't mean a thing, if it ain't got that swing. Do wap, do wap.* The crazy Negro rhythm set my toes a-tapping, fit my mood exactly. How could I have ever thought jazz beneath me? Duncan was right. The music was all snap and joy and effervescence. In front of the dais, a few couples flung themselves about with an ease and abandon that seemed utterly beyond anything I could ever achieve. At least I looked smart in a new dress of soft green wool, while Duncan, in his navy blue blazer, his hair wet-combed off his forehead, looked a dream. All around us were other well-turned-out couples, older than us, mostly, and with a prosperous sheen for Tel Aviv standards: the bourgeoisie of Jewish Palestine. They appeared to be businessmen or lawyers out with their wives—the kind of people who hired me to scrub their toilets and floors. I half expected the pudgy figure of Mr. Mandelmann, my Rothschild Avenue employer, to breeze in from the lobby. There were some British too, off in their own corner, easy to spot by their pink, gentile faces and by the women's white gloves. No one in Palestine wore white gloves except the Brits.

The San Remo's drinks cost more than at regular bars, plus there was a cover charge, making it an expensive place for a simple constable to bring his girl. The waiter, wearing a black jacket, bow tie and a long white apron around his waist, as at the best European restaurants, finally drifted over to our table. He was a swarthy young Jew with a mop of dark curls and bored, insolent eyes.

"Yes sir, what can I get you?" he asked in English before Duncan had a chance to open his mouth. The lad knew his clientele.

Duncan looked at me with eyebrows raised. "What will it be?"

"Lemonade?"

"Lemonade!" Duncan snorted. "That's for schoolgirls. How about a gin fizz? You'll like that, Eva."

The waiter turned to me with a hint of a smile curling his lips "So what do you really want?" he said in Hebrew. He stood back, hands folded against his belly—a pose of apparent deference. But the way he tilted his head and narrowed his eyes and the fact he'd addressed me in Hebrew suggested something else altogether. As if he were thinking, "I know who you are; you're one of us; you can't fool me." My cheeks grew hot. I'd started to notice such looks on the street when I walked with Duncan, my arm linked with his. People's eyes sliding from me to Duncan and back to me again. The shrug that was supposed to mean, "Feh! It's your business!" while clearly doing the opposite. Making it theirs.

"Gin fizz sounds excellent," I said, enunciating every word in my best English. "I shall have a gin fizz."

The waiter nodded in a way that also seemed mocking. "And you, sir?"

"Scotch on the rocks."

"Right away."

After he'd turned and gone several paces I called out in my most commanding tone, again in English, "Please also bring some water with ice."

Duncan seemed quite unaware of anything untoward, but several heads from neighbouring tables turned. The British *goy* and his wayward Jewish girl, that's what the glances seemed to say. My neck stiffened with irritation, anxiety. I felt relieved that at least I didn't know any of these people and then annoyed with myself for being relieved. I turned my attention to Duncan. His eyes meeting mine made me conscious of every inch of my body, from my flaming ear tips to my jittery toes. My heart squeezed, grateful, happy, determined not to care about anything else. The drinks arrived, mine served in a tall glass topped with thick white foam and garnished with a twist of lime. I took a sip and then another, pleasantly surprised at the taste: tart, sweet, perfumed, and not too much alcohol flavour at all. Like lemonade, only better.

"Chin-chin," Duncan said, raising his glass, which struck me as terribly funny so I began to giggle behind my hand. The gin rocketed to my head, but what did I care, I was having fun. Duncan didn't crack a smile, instead contemplated me with a serious air that I knew was meant to make me laugh harder and so it did. I cackled. Heads turned our way again. I took a big gulp out of defiance of these small-minded Tel Aviv burghers.

"My, my, Miss Salomon, aren't you full of surprises? But perhaps you should slow down just a bit?"

A pang of guilt stabbed me.

"Oh dear. I'm sorry. The cost . . . I'm not making the drink last."

"Nonsense. Why should you?" Duncan asked, reddening. "Plenty more where that came from."

He downed his entire Scotch in a couple of smooth swallows and his arm shot up for the waiter again. The man came, once more wearing that barely suppressed smirk, which Duncan noticed this time. He subjected the man to a hard, contemptuous stare that did the job, for the fellow swallowed his insolence and his manner changed to stiff, distant, self-effacing. No more trouble from that quarter. With an air of cool authority, Duncan ordered another round, along with cocktail nuts. When the second order arrived—more promptly than the first—Duncan flung his coins on the tray as if they were nothing more than sand. He bade me to enjoy my drink, but to eat something too, to anchor the liquor. An awkwardness had descended upon us. Clearly I'd offended him by my concern for his purse. He chatted and smiled, but I could see by the strain about his brow that something rankled. I apologized for my gaffe, which only made things worse as he waved my words away. Self-consciously, and then more recklessly, I sipped my lovely gin, much of the first gone now, the second waiting. I drank to show him I wasn't holding back. The nuts were more trouble though, for I was too wound up to eat. I pretended to nibble and when he wasn't looking, I slipped a few under the table.

"Let's dance!" I said, leaping to my feet with a sudden impulse.

"But of course!"

Duncan steered me by the elbow between the tables. A dreamy foxtrot was playing. The vocalist was a dapper little man in a white jacket and black tie who sang a velvet tenor. He purred into the microphone about waiting, longing, praying, being blue…and then finding, oh finally finding, someone "Exactly Like You."Duncan placed one hand at the small of my back, held my left palm against his right.

"Our first dance," he murmured, smiling down at my face. "Let's show 'em how it's done, Thumbelina."

As his feet began to move, our knees collided. My hands turned to ice and my limbs to wood.

"But I can't. I never learned," I wailed. "What an idiot I am. Oh Duncan, I'm so sorry."

Around us couples twirled, fused together as single entities of grace and skill, those stodgy burghers I'd inwardly sneered at a few moments ago. They swerved past Duncan and me, an obstacle in their midst, and glanced sideways, superior, and amused, at the oddly matched pair we made: he so tall, me so short, he so British, me so Jewish. How could I be so reckless as to propose a dance? My head reeled, my stomach soured, and I gazed with longing at our empty table near the potted palm, but Duncan resisted my attempt to draw us back to that safe harbour. He held me firm, his eyes laughing.

"So now you'll learn, Thumbelina. There's no time like the present. Follow me. Watch my feet. Step, step, slide, together. Make yourself loose like a streamer in the wind. Feel the rhythm. Never mind how it looks. We don't care a fig what people think, do we?"

No, now I didn't. Duncan's gaze lifted me up and trumpeted our indifference. His blue eyes obliterated everyone else in the room. Soon I could foxtrot, or thought I could, which was nearly the same thing. We bumped into one another and laughed and it didn't matter. Our silliness on the dance floor dispelled the little embarrassment about the drinks. Duncan bent low to shape his body to mine, while I stood tall in the circle of his arms. Sweat trickled down my sides and I was as dizzy and fizzy as my gin. We drank and danced, danced and drank. Duncan's movements became more fluid, his squeezes somewhat tighter, but aside from that, I would have never guessed he'd consumed anything stronger than tea. I, on the other hand, was fairly stewed. Tottering back from the powder room, I almost knocked the glasses off the table as I collapsed into my chair. I raked my teeth over my lower lip, which I'd just caked with lipstick and must have given Duncan a grotesque, red-toothed smile, for he threw back his head in a hearty laugh. When I reached for my unfinished drink, he stopped my hand.

"Come on, let's get you some air."

Outside, on the promenade by the sea, the wind blew brisk, fresh, wet, and sobering. Ragged clouds sped across a crescent moon.

"Your girlfriend is a drunkard," I moaned.

"Right. A rip-roaring drunk. Shocking!" He pressed my hand to his cheek. "Sweetheart, you don't even know what that means."

His arm around my waist, pinning me to his side, we marched and swayed and swerved around the puddles on Allenby Street. In the dark stairwell of Malka's building Duncan's voice became husky.

"Let's go up."

"But Malka's there."

"You're fibbing!"

"How do you know?"

"I'm a policeman and you're a lousy liar. Come on, Eva. I'll be gone before she gets back and if not, what's the harm? What's it her business?"

So we groped through the darkness of the flat, for I didn't let him put on a light and we tumbled down upon the sofa and he fumbled with buttons, belts, our wet shoes, and I remembered the crate of condoms in the corner of the room. But I didn't say a thing because that would have been too awkward and awful and, besides, I wanted him to go fast. But once he started, I wanted him to go slow. He drew my hand down to his groin. I curled my fingers around that strange, solid, powerful yet vulnerable thing: his sex. His nakedness, his manhood. It twitched at my touch and he groaned. Then he was on me, inside me, hurting me very much, but not so much really, since I was still numb from the gin. The hurt seemed part of the wonder. It amazed me that I could hold his bigness inside me, which must mean I was bigger than I thought. I was just as big as he was, only in reverse. He shuddered. He called out my name. He collapsed with his full weight crushing me into the sofa, but that was all right too for I was strong enough to bear him. When his organ shrank and he withdrew and the aching place he'd awakened inside me felt bereft and hollow, I couldn't help but think: Is this all? Is this the great event? A clinging, whining disappointment dribbled through my veins. Yet mostly I was proud. I'd had him. He'd been in me. He'd long to return, again and again. My head sideways, my eyes open, I discerned familiar obtrusive shapes in the crowded room: the grotesque torso of the dressmaker's dummy, the sewing machine, the cutting table. They were their old lumpish ordinary selves, while I was reborn into glorious womanhood.

A verse from the *Song of Solomon* that I didn't even know I knew floated into my mind.

My love is mine and I am his
He grazes among the anemones

MALKA SOON GOT wind of what was what. Did she see the loss of innocence in my face, or did she get a whiff of Duncan's seed in the air?

"You don't have to sneak around me, *Bubbeleh*. I don't judge. Sorry if you got that impression. Is he a murderer, a criminal? Of course not. He's a policeman. A British policeman. What could be more respectable? Ha! Oh well. Bring him here when you need a place for whatever. Look how you blush! As if I'm speaking of something unnatural. But you better be prepared. I won't have you growing a belly."

She briskly strode to the far side of the room, to the packing case under the window. She rummaged a moment and returned to me with a small paper envelope in her extended hand. I opened it to find a yellowish rubber disc that looked like some dead creature washed up onto the beach from the ocean depths. I almost flung it away from me in a frisson of disgust. Malka had a good laugh.

"That little rubber is your best friend, my dear. Keep one about at all times—in your pocket, your purse, your brassiere, if you must. I've got lots more. I'll sell you a dozen at a discount. Give it here. See, this is how it works."

Malka held up her index finger and unrolled the little disc down over it and waggled what now looked like a shiny fat worm in my direction. I nodded, promised to stock up, though the sight of the rubber sheath quite unnerved me. I was hardly as modern and sophisticated as I wanted to appear.

The first time I produced the packet, after recovering from his surprise, Duncan chuckled low in his chest and kissed my hand.

"What a dear and clever Thumbelina you are!"

He knew exactly how to use the rubber, for I was not his first girl. But I was the most precious to ever come his way, he warmly vowed, and I knew it to be true.

Ein Rachel, Jan. 22, 1938
Dear Eva,
The whole settlement assumes that Manfred and I are a couple, or that we will become one very soon. Dov Kalisch's phrase "Yecke needs Yecke" has made the rounds. When I tell people not to be ridiculous, they smirk knowingly. I'm enveloped by collective relief, a sigh in the air that says: "We don't have to worry about that one anymore; she's found a mate."

They knew I was depressed after Trudi left, which is partly why, I think, I was transferred from kitchen to cows. Their watchfulness comes through in oblique looks and wordless gestures. In the dining hall, comrades slide over on the bench to make a space beside me that Manfred can fill. All quite touching really. Shows they consider me one of their own—or almost. It takes a long time to truly be a member of the group, but with each passing day the threads between me and them become stronger, my ties to this place—this clutch of primitive buildings and patch of wilderness—become deeper.

Yes, but how have things progressed between Manfred and me, you want to know. Are we indeed a couple? I'd say we are friends. I'm not in a rush to get on with it (Dov's words again), and besides, are we really so well suited? I'm not sure. I'm drawn to him, and yet . . .

The other day, on Friday evening, Manfred did something unheard of. He piled the cabbage stew onto two plates—one for me and one for himself—and led me out to the back steps of the dining hall where we perched for a private picnic under the fading sky. I didn't want to follow him at first, but he looked at me with such eagerness and appeal that I couldn't say no. He has nice eyes. Small and hidden by his glasses, but when the light is right and I'm standing close, I see them clearly: hazel, with flecks of green and gold, giving an impression of layers and depth. Besides, I didn't want to embarrass him in front of the others. Heads turned, the comrades stared, but no one said anything outright. Once outside, as we sat with our plates on our knees, I explained to Manfred that what we were doing went against sacred settlement custom and perhaps even against a sub-paragraph of a written policy. We always eat as a group, every single meal, except for Saturday morning breakfast, when the comrades drift in and out of the dining hall as they please for a cold buffet. Friday evening it's especially heretical to desert the dining hall.

"But Ein Rachel is unreligious!" Manfred protested.

"Yes, of course. This is about the collective spirit, group solidarity, not about the laws of Moses."

I knew Manfred had already broken with tradition a number of times by stuffing bread and cheese into his pockets and wandering off on his own. There were unkind jokes that he was afraid of having his dinner stolen, that he had the hoarding instincts of a burrowing animal. But then a comrade would wink at me, as if to say: "You'll break him of such unsocial habits." They expect me to have a positive influence.

Hearing my lesson on settlement etiquette, Manfred now made a doubting noise in his throat, laid down his fork and offered a rebuttal. I could tell he didn't want to offend me, but that he had his convictions. He pointed out that some people barely glance at their neighbours during mealtimes, while others shout across the table in heated debate and that all this forced togetherness is as likely to cause friction as to inspire brotherly love. He said something more about explosions, the law of nature. But then he looked at me and his brow knitted.

"Do you want to go back in? I don't want to put you in an awkward position."

He was anxious for me, only me, not the collective welfare. His fine, deep eyes conveyed a gentle regard.

"They can manage without us for one meal." I laughed. "Group solidarity doesn't crumble that quickly."

"You don't look comfortable," he said, still apologetic. He was watching me try to balance the plate on my knees, his hand shooting out just in time to catch it as it slipped and threatened to spill my dinner onto the ground. "I would have preferred to take you out to the restaurant at Hotel Kaiserhof, but this is the best I can do."

"You've been to the Kaiserhof!"

I was amazed that he could have ever afforded to go to one of Berlin's finest locales, or that they would have let a Jewish face like his across the threshold.

"No, of course not," he said, and we both laughed and then we were quiet for a while, busy with our greasy cabbage and black bread. The light was fading fast, painting the clouds a dreamy shade of purple, while the distant hilltops stood etched against the dim horizon. Lake Kinneret had already vanished from view and there was no moon to offer a glimmer on the waves. After a few more minutes, all I could see was the small area illuminated by the dim light bulb on the post above our heads: the outlines of the path, the steps, Manfred's hunched figure and the crazy moths smashing themselves against the caged bulb. Normally I dislike this time of day, when black night gobbles up our little world. Fear creeps into

*my heart. How small and feeble we are, despite our watchtowers,
guards and dogs. I'm seized by childish dread, not just of Arab
raiders but of the vast, impenetrable darkness itself. But now
was different because of this man beside me, shooting quick, shy
glances my way as he daintily mopped gravy with pieces of bread
at the end of his fork. His Adam's apple leaped up and down as
he ate, a huge thing—that Adam's apple—in his scrawny throat.
As if he's swallowed a frog. The sight touched me, comforted me,
and I thought: yes, maybe, perhaps he's the one. Who can explain
such things? We'd been having a warm spell in the region. The air
that night was soft and still. Apart from some insects inspecting
my plate, I thought that Hotel Kaiserhof couldn't offer a nicer
atmosphere. I said so to Manfred, which produced another skeptical
snort. But I think he was pleased. From behind the closed back door
of the dining hall, came the muffled clatter of dishes and buzz of
voices.*

"One needs a bit of privacy now and then," he said.

*He's an only child. Grew up quite solitary, without brothers or
sisters, a father who was distant and a mother who was sickly.
The group togetherness at Ein Rachel is harder on him than on the
rest of us. All the more he deserves our respect for giving it a try. I
assured him the collective life becomes more natural with time as
old habits of a decadent, inhibited culture fall away. I spoke of the
deep fulfillment that comes of self-sacrifice. I noticed him suppress
a smile. He regarded me with his chin in his hand and I thought at
first he was mocking me. But no, I felt the intensity of his gaze,
though his eyes were hidden by the darkness and his glasses. At
that moment, I knew he would never become one of us, that our
friendship was destined to be temporary, and the thought hurt.
Maybe he was thinking the same, for he said, very wistfully, as if
asking for a parting gift:*

"I'd like to photograph you. Would you let me?"

"I don't like being photographed," I confessed.

*And then, to change the subject, I expressed surprise that he
would possess such a luxury item as a camera. It seemed a strange,
frivolous thing to bring over the miles to a rural settlement where
so many more practical items are needed. He told me it's his most
prized possession. He'd managed to save it by holding his knapsack
above his head when he'd had to wade ashore with the other*

refugees upon arrival on the Palestine coast. His dream is to start a photography business in one of the cities after he's done his year of service in the settlement. The camera has become a bone of contention because we are supposed to relinquish all private property. While he lives here, Manfred's camera should belong to the group. But he refuses to let anyone else touch it.

Eva, I'm very glad that your "beau" (not a word we'd use here) treats you well! So he should. You sound quite giddy about him. Must confess, I was a bit shocked to hear how far things have gone between the two of you. That you're careful about pregnancy is a relief, for sure. But dear sister, there's more to be careful about. If you tie yourself to this man, you can't help but cut yourself off from your own kind. And does he offer you anything other than the pleasure of the now? Can you really see a future with someone like him? I'm sorry, but I have to ask such questions for they weigh on my heart with every letter you write. I try to view your affair with an open mind. It's hard. But that's only because I care so much about you. Do write soon. And tell me all. Always.

With love,
Your Liesel

Chapter 8
A Visitor

AFTER A FEW days break, the rain returned, slashing against the window panes in nasty gusts. It was the kind of weather that usually made *Frau* Mandelmann's joints ache and her mood sour. But that Tuesday, she was mild as a lamb, content to smile at me from her nest of shawls and wave me off into the kitchen. With my hands in the dishwater, scouring congealed egg from the frying pan, I sailed off into dreams of the next rendezvous with Duncan. As I scrubbed, I hummed the stirring Hebrew Slaves' Chorus from Verdi's *Nabucco* that I'd recently heard on a recording at Kowalski's. A knock at the front door made me freeze in mid note. I ripped the *schmatte* off my head and gave my hair a quick pat as I ran to answer.

I wished I hadn't. I wished I'd pretended that no one was in, for on the landing stood my father. Water dripped from the hem of his black overcoat and the brim of his Homburg. The briefcase he gripped in his hand was wet too. Clearly he'd been walking through the downpour, perhaps tramping the streets with his little packages of electrical wares. His dark eyes raked me with cold fire, the familiar, scathing stare. I hadn't seen him for months, but at this moment those months vanished and I was little Eva again, quaking before Papa. I had the impulse to slam the door.

"You better let me in," he rumbled. "*Frau* Mandelmann invited me."

He cleared his throat in a satisfied manner. I was too stunned to do anything but step aside. After wiping his shoes with fastidious care, he entered and, with a jerk of his head, indicated I should lead the way to the living room.

"*Herr* Salomon, how kind of you to drop by."

The old woman's wrinkled face was all craft and feigned innocence. She tilted her head upwards so that the dull coins of her half-blind eyes caught a gleam of the wintry light.

"My nephew, Eliezer, works in the Philips shop where your father sells his bits and pieces," she croaked. "Isn't that a happy coincidence? Do sit down, *Herr* Salomon. Eva, will you make some tea?"

Wordlessly, my father handed me his wet coat and hat to hang up in the hall. As if we were still living under the same roof and I was still his handmaid. He seated himself on the straight-backed chair, the one I usually used when I was reading aloud from the newspaper to *Frau* Mandelmann. As I lit the Primus and put on the kettle, I heard them exchanging small talk, my father making polite inquiries about the old woman's health, sounding quite civilized. And then it was all about the mutual acquaintance from Frankfurt, Rabbi Jacobssohn. What had become of him and where had his children gone?

When I brought in the tray with a plate of almond biscuits and two glasses of tea—one with lemon and sugar for *Frau* M., one black, as Papa liked it—she said, "But you should have made some for yourself too, dear. You don't want? Why not? Well, all right. But you must sit and have some biscuits or your father will think we work you to the bone. In fact, I will take my tea in my room. Yes, I must. I must lie down. Come, child. Help me to my feet. And then you two can have a nice chat all on your own. You must have so much to catch up on."

As my father made no comment and as her bony hand was reaching out for me, I had no choice but to do as I was told. Levering her upwards, making sure her slippers were on right, I supported her as she shuffled with tiny steps to her bed. With her arm firmly tucked under mine, I must have seemed the soul of patience and care, but for the first time I wanted to give that trembling, fragile, conniving old woman a violent push. On returning to the living room, I lowered myself onto the edge of the sofa and waited for Papa to explain his business. He was in no hurry. He sat quite still, staring at an engraving of the Loreley cliffs over the Rhine on the wall above my head. His jaw worked slightly, as it did when he was lost in thought. I noticed his suit hung more loosely on his limbs than when I'd seen him last and that creases cut deeper into his cheeks and brow. Perhaps, as Liesel had suggested in a recent letter, he'd been ill. But if so, he was quite recovered, his bearing stiff and severe as ever, the knot of his cravat tight against his throat. The silence grated on me, the sense of waiting for a judgment.

"Aren't you going to drink your tea?" I said at last. "It's getting cold."

A flicker of a smile passed over his face.

"I don't like it too hot. Have you forgotten?"

As if only to oblige me, he lifted the glass from the tray and took a few gulps of the dark liquid, but didn't touch the biscuits. Nor did I. Replacing his glass, he now looked me over from top to toe. My limp hair—flattened from the *schmatte*—my grey work dress, my worn shoes. I must have appeared like the drudge he'd predicted I would become. How I would have preferred to confront him in my polka dot frock and heels. Harlot attire to him. He would spit with contempt, but I would flounce and strut in glorious defiance. In my shabby work clothes, I couldn't muster such confidence. He, on the other hand, looked quite tidy despite the residue of mud from the rain-flooded streets on his trouser cuffs.

Otherwise not a thread or button was out of place. Somehow he'd managed for himself without me.

"What do you want?" I finally blurted.

He bent down and snapped open the briefcase that he'd placed beside his chair, taking out a package, loosely wrapped in brown paper.

"I brought you some things you left behind."

My identity card, a couple of books, and my recorder. The books I didn't care about—they were silly romances—but the sight of the recorder warmed my heart like an old friend. My fingers strayed over the tone holes and mouthpiece, over scratches and dents in the wood, where, many years ago I'd bitten down in fits of frustration.

"I haven't played for so long . . ." I stopped myself. I didn't want to give him the satisfaction of hearing me admit that I'd left his house in hurried distraction or that anything was the least amiss in my current life.

"I haven't either," he said. "My violin sits in the closet and absorbs the humid air of this accursed climate. I should sell it while it still has value."

"Don't," I said, appalled.

He smiled bitterly. "Perhaps if I had someone to play with, I would be tempted. I miss our little concerts."

He looked at me directly, a question in his eyes, an appeal—something I wasn't used to. It was unsettling, disarming. I looked away. The concerts belonged to another time, to my childhood, when I'd had to be content with tiny crumbs of happiness. What did it matter to me what he did with his old fiddle? Yet the thought of that beautiful instrument, a long-ago gift from Uncle Otto, leaving the family circle made my heart ache. And the thought that he'd want us to play music together again pleased me despite my dismay at his presence. It was my turn to fall silent as I turned the recorder around in my hands and stared at the floor. Why had he come now, after all this time? Was it just because of the good excuse of *Frau* Mandelmann's intervention? The first weeks after I'd left Papa, I'd often felt I was being followed, though I'd never caught him in the act, and perhaps the feeling was only the product of my overwrought imagination. With time the sensation subsided. I stopped turning cold whenever I caught a glimpse of a black-suited man of his height and build. I'd assumed he'd given up on me as I on him. But maybe I'd been wrong. Maybe, as Liesel often suggested, he'd just been waiting for an opportunity to make a connection.

"So! I see you're getting on!" Papa said.

His tone was hearty, not ironic. He glanced around the room, taking in the mahogany table I'd recently polished to a rich gleam and the Mandelmanns' new

HMV wireless set, housed in a case of lovely wood veneers and shaped like a miniature cathedral window, in pride of place on the buffet.

"The Mandelmanns are good clients."

I emphasized the word clients. It had a fine sound, as if I were a professional of some kind. I began to speak of them, inflating my employer's stature in the land and his mother's kindness (never mind her treachery for the moment). I was prepared to lie about my wages—to double them—if Papa asked. But he gave an impatient jerk of his chin and tapped his knees. Something else was on his mind.

"I heard from your Aunt Ida last week."

"Is she all right? Is uncle?"

Papa shrugged and pressed his lips together to express his uncertainty and forebodings.

"She does not complain. She does not say much about the atmosphere, but it can't be very comfortable back home, never knowing what that madman will do next. There are only old faces at the synagogue now. The young folk are all gone abroad. She asked after you, by the way. Wondered why you haven't written for so long. I suppose you have your reasons."

He gave me a sharp, reproachful look. How could I be so cruel as to neglect auntie? Indeed, how could I? A flush of shame rose to my cheeks.

"I was writing every week and then . . . I got so busy this past month . . . I'll write tonight. I will. The minute I finish work."

"And what will you tell her? Nothing to upset her I hope?"

His odd question took me aback.

"Of course not. I write nice letters. Pages and pages. About the Land. About my life here, my work, but also what I do for fun."

It struck me that Aunt Ida was much more *au courant* about my life than Papa was. I'd written in great detail about my quarters at Malka's, my employers, the concerts I'd attended and of course my new frock.

"Hmm." Papa snorted. A triumphant gleam lit his eyes. "Fun! I suppose that includes consorting with a *goy*?"

If his skullcap had sprouted horns, I couldn't have been more surprised. I felt the blood drain from my face.

"What are you talking about?"

"Do you think it's a secret? That nobody sees or talks? Tel Aviv is a village. Even the blind can notice such things."

I remembered the heads that had turned to stare at Duncan and me at the San Remo. Fists clenched, I tried to meet his gaze without trembling. But I felt sullied. As if he were shining a merciless, powerful lamp into the hidden-most corners of my soul.

"I can spend time with whomever I want. I am an adult."

"You are still my daughter," he snapped. He opened his mouth to blast me some more, checked himself, chewed the inside of his cheek. "So you don't deny this . . . this liaison?"

"I don't."

I pressed my arms against my chest. He was silent, his mouth working to an obsessive rhythm. The real reason for his visit was now clear. It had nothing to do with reaching out to me, making amends. Even the news about Aunt Ida and Uncle Otto had been calculated to exact guilt and compliance.

"You left of your own volition," he said at last. "I wasn't going to chase after you. I knew it would be useless anyway. Adult. Ha! This is a land that worships youth. Every bed-wetter is superior to his elders. Parents dare not open their mouths. Of course you fell under the sway of such thinking. You were always a stubborn, rebellious girl. You wanted neither my advice, nor my protection. Fine! I let you go. I didn't try to interfere. Let her make her own bed in this workers' paradise, I said."

Here he gave me that once-over look again, taking in my shabby dress.

"I knew you'd make mistakes. I feared you'd join some outrageous movement, like your sister has. Let yourself be exploited. And I knew you'd turn your back on our religion. You'd eat *treif*, break the Sabbath. Plenty of opportunity to do that here in this Socialist homeland. Plenty of company for Torah scorners."

His voice was rising, gathering force.

"But never did I imagine you would give yourself to a *goy*. Even the girls of loose morals here don't do that. Even they still have a shred of pride and decency."

"Don't shout," I pleaded. "*Frau* Mandelmann . . . she's trying to sleep."

I imagined her taking in every word, nodding in agreement with Papa.

"Break it off," he abruptly commanded.

"No!"

I jumped to my feet, my nails digging into the palms of my balled fists. Papa rose too. He was nowhere near as tall as Duncan, but still he looked down on me. Then he said what I'd heard in various ways from others—from Malka, even from Liesel.

"This liaison will lead to nothing but trouble. You think you are having a bit of harmless fun, but he wants just one thing from you and he will exact his price and leave you ruined. Break it off before it's too late."

Before I lost my virtue, he meant. An uncomfortable heat crept up my neck and into my face.

"I can't. I won't. I don't expect you to understand."

I tried to sound strong. My voice came out like a mewling kitten. His insinuation made me feel naked, though I had nothing to be ashamed of. I was a modern woman in a free society, free from old-fashioned taboos.

"I'm giving you one more chance," Papa rasped. "I'm not asking you to come back to my house but promise me, swear to me, you will end this affair immediately."

A trembling coursed through my body but I forced myself to keep my eyes level with his.

He glared fiercely, and I saw a suspicion dawn on him; that it was indeed too late, that I was already "ruined." His face darkened into a mask of cold contempt.

"I never imagined you'd make the worst mistake of all. Betray the most sacred duty of a daughter of Israel. In these times when the name of Israel is being trampled into the dust you would add to the agony."

Abruptly he turned away and began to mutter. I recognized snatches of a passage he liked to quote from Isaiah, "*Because the daughters of Zion are haughty / and walk with outstretched necks / glancing wantonly with their eyes . . . The Lord will smite with a scab / the heads of the daughters of Zion.*" It was a comment on my iniquity. A prophecy of my doom. A dirge for a daughter who was dead to him. It was also an absurd piece of theatre and yet, as he droned on in his venomous way—*Instead of perfume will be rottenness . . . sackcloth . . . shame*—I felt a chill, as if from the cold breath of a tomb.

When he was gone the demon rage that had been pressing against my rib cage broke its bounds and flooded me entirely. I ran to the bathroom, stuffed my mouth with a towel to keep from screaming like a wild animal. A part of me—a tiny, cold-blooded homunculus—stood apart and asked why I was behaving like a crazed hyena and what else did I expect from Papa? When at last my energy flagged and my heartbeat began to thud back to a normal rhythm I tried to reason with myself. Hadn't I triumphed? *He* was the one forced to leave, defeated, powerless. Then why did I feel as if I'd drowned in the sea and been spat up like a piece of flotsam on the shore?

Chapter 9
Copper's girl

"IF YOU'RE GOING to eat pork," Malka liked to say in her crude way, "the pig fat should drip down your chin."

What she meant was: If I had to step out with a gentile, he should at least provide unremitting pleasure.

But it wasn't all songs and roses, being a copper's girl. There were times when I waited and he was unbearably late. Times when I paced the little balcony, straining to hear his Fifth Symphony whistle, but all I heard was the flap of canvas awnings down below and the rattle of shutters in the winter wind. There were times he didn't show at all.

One Saturday evening, not long after the outing to the San Remo, we'd agreed to meet at Café Sapir at eight p.m. By design, I arrived ten minutes late, but he hadn't yet come, so I allowed myself to be seated at a table for two. There I waited while the waiters rushed about taking other patrons' orders. While laughter, chatter, and the merry clink of crockery echoed around me like a mocking chorus and while the minutes ticked by so slowly, each one heavier than the last. I ordered Turkish coffee and apple strudel. I drank the coffee all in one gulp, but picked at the pastry, the sugary flakes sticking to the dry roof of my mouth. *You don't know him*, Malka's cold warnings had hissed. *But I do, I do*, my heart now insisted. I knew the smell of his shaving lather and his warm blue gaze, his sun-burnt ears and his impish lower lip, the attentive tilt of his head and the sweat in the creases of his neck and most of all the way he kissed me in the dark stairwell of the building on Lilienblum Street. Kissed me with such a fierce and pleading hunger.

At a neighbouring table, a man lifted a spoonful of sour cream, stained and dripping with blood-red borscht, to his lips. The sight snuffed out my last trace of appetite. Duncan was never coming. I was alone with an apple strudel on a Saturday night, humiliation coursing through my veins. Finally, I signalled the waiter for the bill. Of course he had to comment, for people do in the New Hebrew City. No one minds his own business.

"So where is he, your *gever*? Only a louse would leave a cute thing like you stranded. Stay, why don't you, sweetheart? Have another coffee on me. Hey, don't leave in such a hurry."

For I'd slapped my money on the table and jumped to my feet.

"Sweetheart, he's not worth your tears," the waiter called out after me, loudly enough for the whole room to hear.

Through the driving rain, I walked and walked, down Bialik Street, Pinsker Street, around Dizengoff Circle, a wide plaza with a few pathetic saplings pretending to be trees. On and on, splashing through puddles, unconcerned about wearing down my heels or soaking the leather of my precious going-out shoes. *He'd forgotten. He didn't care. A louse, like the waiter said.* But simultaneously another possibility tore at my heart. *He'd been hurt.* There were daily reports of clashes between Arab malcontents and His Majesty's forces. Most of the incidents occurred in the countryside, on isolated roads where marauders struck in ambush. But Jaffa town held perils too, trouble simmering just below the surface in the bustling bazaars, in the cafés, blue with the smoke of hookahs and hot with the voices of shouting men. Paired with an Arab constable, Duncan would patrol the maze of streets, on the lookout for rabble rousers, and at night they walked the border areas between Tel Aviv and Jaffa, where sheds and factories were often set alight and a straggler might get a knife in his back.

I reached Ha'yarkon Street, with its string of bars on one side, music and laughter spilling out of doorways, and the other side edging the black, hard-pounding sea. Rain penetrated through the cloth of my shawl, trickled down the back of my neck, though I pulled my coat collar tighter. No one was mad enough to wander the beach on such a night, only me, drawn to the thick darkness by my gloomy thoughts. For the first time I grasped what the "thin blue line" meant—the small force of uniformed men who protected their colonial masters and the law-abiding citizenry from the fury of the mob. The blue serge, the badge on his cap, and the number on his jacket collar made him a target, his long, lanky body an invitation to bullets and knives. I turned my head to the south where the lighthouse above Jaffa port swept its beam, warning sailors of treacherous rocks. If something had happened to Duncan, I'd be the last to know. The news would fly from ear to ear among his mates. His mother in England would receive a telegram. But I was no one official, just some Jewish girl he stepped out with. If he was hurt, I'd have to read about it in *The Palestine Post*.

NEXT DAY MY head ached and a lump of soreness clogged my throat, but I had to rise nevertheless. Six a.m. the clock said. Sunday morning, start of the Jewish work week. Malka needed her sewing room and I needed to earn my daily bread, so I dragged myself to the Mandelmanns. A basket of wrinkled laundry awaited in the hall, along with a list of other chores. But before I did anything else, I pounced upon the folded newspaper on the dining room table beside Mr. Mandelmann's jam-smeared breakfast plate. A small paragraph on an inside page told of one constable in Jerusalem killed and another injured. Nothing about Jaffa. Somewhat relieved—though not entirely, for sometimes news of casualties appeared a day or two late—I was ready to tackle the chores. As I coaxed stubborn wrinkles into smoothness, I was grateful for the heat of the iron, but shivered with the chill that crept up my legs from the frigid tile floor. Outside, the blustery wind rattled the panes and blew through the gaps. In the living room, bundled in shawls, *Frau* Mandelmann dozed in her armchair. And then came the urgent tinkle of the little bell she kept by her side. Slowly, we shuffled down the hall together, her trembling arm hooked in mine. I stood outside the WC door from behind which I heard the rustle of her garments, the groan as she lowered herself, the trickle of urine and the creak and splash as she flushed.

"Ready now," she croaked.

I opened the unlocked door, helped her to her feet, and pulled up the underpants that had fallen around her ankles, averting my face from the smell, for of course there was an old-person smell even though she'd wiped and though she bathed once a week. It penetrated through the congestion in my nose. She always let me help her up from the toilet, but insisted on going in alone and closing the door while she did her business. That was one of the few scraps of dignity left to her and I understood.

"You're a good girl," she said, brushing my cheek with her knuckles. Her withered-apple face with the dull, sightless eyes was tilted towards me trustingly, gratefully.

"Are you crying *Schatzie*? Is something the matter?"

"No. I just have a sniffle."

I wiped my nose on the back of my hand. I tried hard not to breathe my germs towards the bobbing head beside me as we shuffled back to her armchair.

"Shall we read the paper, *Schatzie*?"

"All right. Just a little bit. And then I'll have to work."

I blew my nose into a rag and stuffed the soggy thing into my apron pocket. I read aloud from *The Palestine Post*, "Two convicted men were hanged in Jerusalem Prison yesterday morning for the murder of British archaeologist Mr. J.L. Starkey. Hussein Ahmed el . . . el . . ."

I struggled with the difficult Arabic name.

"Never mind," *Frau* Mandelmann broke in. "It's English you must learn to pronounce. You can call them all Ahmed if you like. I won't remember one from the other anyway."

I continued through the entire newspaper—page one to page eight—reading the highlights in my congested voice, pausing often to take a breath and wipe my dribbling nose. *Frau* Mandelmann settled back into her chair, her eyes shut tight as if asleep, but harking to every syllable. News of the troubles across the country and news of calamities around the world.

Another Arab had been sentenced to death for firing on police. A Jewish-owned brick factory was gutted by fire—arson suspected. Armed brigands had held up an omnibus on the Hebron-Jerusalem Road. Police cars mounted with Lewis guns were now escorting buses on Mt Carmel in Haifa. An Arab government clerk was detained in connection with a bomb thrown at a lorry of Jewish workers. Two Jewish youths were sentenced to five years imprisonment for carrying pistols—the first such case in the land. And then there were those Jerusalem constables.

When I stopped again to snuffle and snort, *Frau* M. suddenly reared up in her chair.

"But what's the matter with you child? You are not yourself today."

Her blank, rheumy eyes stared past my shoulder, but her face was all vibrant attention, as if absorbing impressions through her skin.

"I have a cold . . ."

"Yes, yes, but it's more than that. I'm an old dog, I smell feelings and you, my dear, stink—pardon the expression. You are upset. But of course . . . that man. He is still . . . Tell me *Schatzie*. You can open your heart to me."

"There's nothing to tell. I should get back to work."

"No, no. Stay. Read some more. Greta won't be home for hours."

A sly, conspiratorial grin stretched across her wrinkled face.

"Read!"

So I continued. Polish Jews were protesting the immigration restrictions to Palestine, as were various American Jewish organizations. Roumania now had race laws similar to Germany's. Beyond the Jewish sphere, there was fierce fighting between rebels and General Franco's forces in Spain, continued war between Japan and China, and fractious negotiations between England and Ireland. On a happier note, the orange export market was booming, the teachers' strike was called off, huge crowds, including His Excellency the High Commissioner and other dignitaries, had attended a spirited program of horse racing at the grounds between Jaffa and Tel Aviv.

As I read, my thoughts flew to forebodings, like a fly to bad meat. The stories about the Jerusalem constables weighed on my mind. I had visions of Duncan face down in a pool of blood. Eventually, my dull, laboured voice put *Frau* M. to sleep. With a sigh of relief, I returned to the ironing board. As I ironed, I dribbled into my nose rag and fretted. When I was almost done the pile, a knock came at the door. Who at this hour? A peddler perhaps. Tel Aviv had legions— immigrants who, for lack of other options, set themselves up in business to bring all manner of goods door-to-door: bread, fruit, home-made preserves, soap. There was even a one-man mobile lending library, created by a fellow who rented out books from his personal store. With another hasty wipe of my nose, I rushed to the door to prevent more knocking that would wake the old lady. I opened up and got a shock. On the landing, cap in hand, stood Duncan, a sheepish smile on his lips. The hair on his forehead was wet and his blue serge uniform soaked through in places, but otherwise he looked hale and hearty as ever.

"Hullo, Eva. So sorry about last night. May I come in? For a moment?"

I was too stunned to say yes or no.

"How did you find me?"

I'd never given him the address of my employer.

"I'm a policeman," he chuckled. "It's my business to find things out. You look a bit peaked. You all right?"

"A cold."

Relief swept through me, followed by acute embarrassment that he should see me like this—my maid's apron, my thick shoes, my straggly hair, my red nose. Heat rose in my cheeks as I sniffed and stepped aside to let him in.

"You shouldn't be here."

I pitched my voice low and motioned towards the living room where *Frau* Mandelmann slept.

"What happened?" I hissed. "I thought you'd been hurt. I was planning to go to the Tel Aviv station right after work to ask if they knew where you were."

"Glad I got here first, then. Never hear the end of it from the mates if you'd done that. Promise me you won't. Eh, love? There's no need."

"But where were you? How could you . . . ?"

"T'were the races yesterday. Lots of bigwigs came from out of town. Had to do extra duty with the armed convoy that accompanied the mucky mucks back to Jerusalem. Slept at the billet on Mount Scopus and only returned this morning. I knew you'd be browned off when I didn't show. But I couldn't help it."

He said he was sorry, but he didn't look it. He looked quite at ease, cheerful and pleased with himself, this man who'd turned me inside out over the past twenty-four hours. A steaming fury rose in my chest.

"You could at least have sent word," I hissed.

"Sorry. But no, I couldn't." His smile shrank, ever so slightly and his body stiffened. "The order to put extra men in the convoy came at the last minute.

There'd been a spot of trouble on the Jerusalem road earlier in the day. The brass didn't want to take any chances. We had to move fast, before dark."

Duncan's brow furrowed. Displeased at my displeasure.

"The High Commissioner was with us. His Excellency, himself. "

As if that explained everything.

"Did you even ask them to send someone else? Did it even occur to you?"

His laugh was sharp and derisive.

"You think that's how it works? That we pick and choose our orders? The Force is stretched thin. A few thousand of us expected to keep the peace in every rat's nest and gully. There's the army and there's Special Constables—volunteers—but it's not enough by half. The thing you must understand, Eva, is that duty comes first. Now and then I just won't be able to come when I say. When that happens, don't wait around. Find something else to do. I'll catch up with you later."

"You're joking," I spat. "You think I'm willing to have things so casual? Maybe you'll come, maybe you won't. Have you any idea what an idiot I felt like last night? Sitting alone, people watching me?"

A creaky voice from the living room called out, "Who's there?"

"Damn. She's awake. You better leave." I gave him a shove to push him towards the door. He grabbed both my cold hands in his big warm ones and bent towards me.

"May I see you later?"

I wrenched my hands free and pushed him again.

"Get out!"

When I went to explain the disturbance to Mrs. M., a crafty, knowing look came over the old woman's face. She arched her thin, pale eyebrows.

"Why are you so angry with this poor peddler? He sounded quite sweet to me. Or does he offer shoddy goods?"

Later, as I trudged home through the rain-washed streets, I heard footsteps behind me. A whistled theme from Schubert's *Trout Quintet* ambushed my ears.

"I'll make it up to you, darling," he said. "Name your fancy. Dancing. Dining. Or, next sunny day, I'll take you rowing on the Yarkon River."

And he did just that. On a mild Sunday afternoon, Duncan rented a rowboat from an Arab fisherman, who also supplied cushions, a blanket, a picnic of pita bread, *leben,* and cheese. The man dragged the boat through the mud and rushes to the open stream and, as he sent us on our way, his dark, seamed face broke out into a smile so warm and brilliant, it was like a blessing. The cutthroat bandits, the hate-mongers and violent ruffians I'd read about in the newspaper seemed like a bad dream, or a slanderous tale, set beside this simple, peaceable fellow. We slipped through a watery, whispery paradise, a world removed from the clatter and stinks of the city. Propped on cushions, wrapped in a blanket, I lay back and drank in the sun while Duncan rowed. The oarlocks creaked, the reeds rustled, ducks splashed out of our way, and Duncan whistled for my entertainment the exquisite Andantino from Mozart's flute and harp concerto. How cheekily handsome my oarsman looked, his coat thrown aside, his sleeves rolled up, his lips wet and rosy from whistling. The afternoon lay suspended between river and sky, between Mozart and the swish of the breeze in the rushes. Could Cleopatra floating down the Nile amid her opulent entourage have been any more pampered or cherished?

Chapter 10
Call of duty

A SMALL WHITE envelope, addressed to me, lay on Malka's kitchen table. I recognized the handwriting in a flash, the neat, strong, forward slanting letters. There was no stamp or postmark, meaning it had been hand-delivered. My first thought: So when you want to, you *can* send word! I tore open the envelope and read.

March 16, 1938, Jaffa Central

Dearest Eva,

I hope this letter gets to you before Saturday so that you don't have to wait around wondering where I am again. I'm sorry—oh so sorry—to say that I won't be able to take you out for quite a while. When you read this, I'll be on my way to Lydda, Ramleh, and points beyond to help beef up the patrols that protect the convoys travelling the roads. There's been such a spate of trouble from armed marauders lately and, despite the arrival of fresh army battalions in the country, the Force needs every able man it can spare at the pressure points. After months of taking it on the chin, our men are finally getting the chance to bring the battle to the Arab gangs. My new posting as a roving reinforcement will last two or three months until we've re-established law and order in the district, or until the bloke I'm replacing is out of hospital. Oops, that came out wrong—as if I'm likely to end up there too. Not at all. The chap got banged up in a freak motorcycle accident that had nothing to do with the rebels.

Wish I'd had time to see you again and tell you all this in person. I'll miss my lovely, sweet Thumbelina. In fact, I miss you to bits already. But I wouldn't be honest if I didn't say I'm rather chuffed about the posting. Things were getting ho-hum in Jaffa town. The real action is in the countryside, on the roads and in the rough hills and villages. I'm keen to prove my mettle, put my training to the test. Besides, service with the convoys and hunting squads will be good for my career. All-round experience, that sort of thing. Plus, since the peasant folk in the rural areas speak nothing but Arabic, some of it might penetrate my thick skull.

I do hope you won't forget me, Eva, and that we can take up where we left off when I'm back. Please write whenever you can. I'll be starved for your letters. Oops, there's the horn. The lorry taking us to Lydda just pulled up in the courtyard. Got to rush. Will write again soon as I can manage.

Lots of kisses on your dear lips,
Your Duncan

The air in Malka's kitchen lost its substance as I stood in the doorway and read this letter—once, twice, three times, and with each reading, the breath more ragged in my chest. "Two or three months" it said. "Lydda, Ramleh, and points beyond." It had been bad enough that until now Duncan was stationed in Jaffa, and so, just out of reach. He would not allow me to seek him out anywhere near his place of work. Not safe for me to come alone, he'd said, and, besides, not done, to mix duty and private life. So always when we met it was he who came to me, in Tel Aviv. But at least in the intervals between one Saturday night and the next, I could, if I wished, walk to the end of Allenby Road, stand on the beach and look south towards Jaffa. I could gaze across the long, curving stretch of sand and make out a cluster of dun-coloured buildings, the hint of vessels in the port and the ancient bell tower that seemed to float above the promontory. I could imagine Duncan on patrol, walking in his masterful policeman's way—not too fast, not too slow. And I could imagine myself one day throwing caution to the wind, disobeying his "orders." I'd simply march down that strip of coast and take him by surprise, as he so often did me. Three or four kilometres along the shore. An hour's walk. But where Duncan was headed now might as well have been Mars, a world unknowable and completely out of reach. Risky too, despite his pooh-poohing the dangers to himself. I refolded the pages and tucked them into my dress pocket, where my fingers could seek them out again during the long hours of my workday. So that I could re-read the lines, splash my tears upon them, mull over every phrase. These pages, these words, were all that I had now of my Duncan, and so began a new phase between us. A time of waiting, not for his whistle beneath the balcony or his knock on the door, but for the blessing of a letter in the mailbox.

Lydda Station, March 24, 1938
Dear Eva,

Getting settled after a week of slogging in the trenches. I'm only half-joking when I use that term. Same day I arrived here, I was assigned to a squad protecting construction at the airport just outside of town. The Jewish labourers work on the new runway at night when planes don't fly. The arc lights that allow them to see what they're doing make them brilliant targets for Arab snipers. We hoped to surprise the bandits with an ambush of our own. We lay on dew-damp sand, in the pitch dark, rifles poised and waited. And waited some more. Cramp in our muscles, cold in our bones. Howl of jackals in the distance. I drifted off and jerked awake as the hours crept by. Nothing, nothing. We returned to our transport bleary-eyed, stiff-limbed and in sour spirits. The bandits must have got wind of our presence. Next three nights, more stake-outs, but again, no action. So we've left the guarding of the airfield to a couple of Jewish ghaffirs (that's the term for locals recruited for special duty with the Force).

The rest of the week I've been at Lydda Station, my days filled with briefings, refresher training and orientation to the town. The reception area of the police station has a "rogues' gallery"—a wall of "Wanted" posters of the most notorious gang leaders in Palestine. Kauwakji, Abu Dorreh, Abdul Razzek, Al Battat. They're wily, determined, ruthless scoundrels, posing proudly in the photos with rifles in their hands and bandoleers of bullets across their chests. They instill fear and awe among villagers and townsfolk. To bag one of those big fish would be a prize indeed.

How's my dear little Tel Aviv Miss? Still enjoying the lights of the big city? Through all those long nights of lying in ambush the thought of you kept the blood running in my veins. And in between briefings and duties, the vision of you comes. You, in your smashing red-polka-dot dress and how you look up at me sometimes with that sweet but doubting smile, making me wonder what I said to put my foot in it. Oops, I'm revealing how smitten I am. Thank you for your long letter and for being so brave about our separation. Hope you're not too, too lonely without me or you might find another fellow to snatch you up. I can't compete with the cheeky blokes in Moghrabi Square while I'm out here in the sticks.

Oh so fondly and jealously,
Your Duncan

April 10, 1938

Dear Eva,

I'm hale and hearty, my darling, so don't you fret. Had my first whiff of action on convoy duty, which, believe it or not, is easier on the nerves than those dreary stake-outs. Our armoured patrol vehicles accompany a string of lorries that take milk and produce from Jewish farm colonies in the north down to Jerusalem for breakfast deliveries. It's a long, winding journey in pre-dawn darkness through the gorges between craggy hills. The rebels hide in the hill clefts above a narrow curve in the road and, when our convoy snakes into sight, let loose with their rifles. We answer with our Lewis gun, an automatic rifle that can deliver about 50 rounds. Bam, bam, bam, bam, blasting away towards the sound of their fire. The hills echo with the noise that must seem to our attackers to come from all directions. The steel box of our patrol car allows us to duck and take cover from their shots. I mention all this to point out we are well equipped, so the danger's not as great as it may seem. Soon enough the attackers quit and the convoy continues. Before you know it, the first rosy rays are peeping over the hills. Breakfast at the Mount Scopus billet. Showers and a kip, and then back north with a daytime patrol.

Dear Thumbelina. I say your name often to myself. It's like a little song in my head that I hear as I stand in the rattling, swaying patrol car with the dark landscape whipping by.

A long, long kiss my darling. And another, and another.

Your Duncan

April 15, 1938

. . . A few nights on special assignment: lying in ambush by a newly repaired railway bridge, waiting for the rebels to try their tricks. They have a whole bag full, the crafty devils. Sometimes it's gelignite on the tracks or under a bridge. Sometimes they wrench the bolts off a couple of fishplates, and presto: a treacherous gap that causes a train to fly off the rails. We waited patiently for them to come. No luck. The hills must have eyes and ears . . .

April 24, 1938

. . . It's touching that you worry so about me, but you mustn't. We're a well-trained, well-equipped force and we have military troops to back us up. Our adversaries are a varied lot. Some chaps are fanatically committed to the cause, some are in it for booty and adventure, and some are just poor peasants, pressed into service by threats, or loyal to their leaders. If every bullet they fired was aimed well, we'd be in trouble, but they produce far more smoke and noise than harm.

A favourite technique of the gangs is to pile rocks across a strategic bend of road in a narrow ravine and then, when the convoy comes to a halt before this blockage, to open fire on the "sitting ducks." If the rebels time it right, the convoy arrives at sunrise, when the light enables them to see their target, but blinds the defenders looking up to the eastern hilltop sniper nests. The other morning we ran into just such a trap. Trained in counter measures, we were ready. As soon as the driver slammed on the breaks, yours truly and two other chaps jumped down and began clearing the rocks off the road at a feverish pace, while the Lewis gunner provided covering fire. It was pretty lively for a while. One of the drivers took a bullet in the shoulder and a fellow constable broke a toe when a rock fell on his foot. That was the extent of the damage, for we managed to get moving again in fairly short order. Well-earned rounds of Johnnie Walker when we got to Jerusalem. I'm chuffed that I was able to keep my cool on the battlefield. . . .

May 29, 1938

. . . Please understand, Eva. I'm not bloodthirsty. Just that I want to do my bit for the honour of the Force. When our lads have a chance to fight the rebels out in the open, man for man, we leave the field triumphant. They do their worst in road ambushes, when the advantage is all theirs. All we can do is fire back defensively. One just itches to have at them. We should be the chaser, not the chased.

Excellent news about your plan to study typing and shorthand. I have full confidence that you'll learn in no time. Then you'll get a desk job—maybe even in government—and your sweet little hands will be spared the laundry tub. When I'm back to civilization we'll go to the rooftop terrace at the Savoy. Nothing but the finest for my princess Thumbelina . . .

Kfar Yusef, June 12, 1938
Dearest Eva,

I'm afraid I won't be back for a while yet. I've been sent to a
small police post near a rural railway station on the Lydda-Jerusalem
line in the Judean Hills. Filling in for a man on home leave. Bum
luck. Wish I could fly across the miles and drop in for a surprise visit
beneath your balcony. It's not to be. Not for a while yet.

Around here are several Arab villages, plus a Jewish colony. The
closest Arab village, Kafr Yusef, consists of stone and mud-brick
houses bunched together on a rise. From a distance, just looks like
a tumble of rocks, as all these places do. Not much to our station
either. A two-storey building with a front counter, office and a lock-
up on the ground floor, living quarters above and sentry posts on
the roof. There's a dirt courtyard for drill, a garage and a stable for
the horses. A senior constable is in charge of three British constables
(including me), two Arab constables, plus two ghaffirs. The station
has recently come under attack from marauders, so must be
carefully guarded at all times.

Yesterday, Senior Constable Charlie Ryan took me "sightseeing"
in the village. I saw men, children, donkeys, goats and dogs, but not
a single human female over ten years old. Ryan says they scatter
at our approach. I suppose they spy on us from their hideouts for I
did hear a few giggles from inside the houses as we strolled about.
The little children stared at us and the bolder ones clutched our
pant legs, shouting: "Hallo, hallo, hallo, sir! How 'wa you?" They're
barefoot and filthy, but have the most beautiful big dark peepers.
The mukhtar—the village chief—had us over for coffee and sweet
cakes in his simple mud-brick home, where we sat on cushions on
the floor and were served by a veiled old woman, one of his two
wives, who padded in barefoot with the copper tray and padded
quietly out again. A gracious, dignified chap, the mukhtar. Leathery
face, twinkling eyes, white moustache. He chatted about crops and
horses and the heavy responsibilities he bears keeping the peace
between a couple of feuding families in the village. Ryan translated.
He's what we call an Old Sweat, been in the Force for years and
knows the native lingo well. I can manage the basics but soon as the
locals yammer fast, I'm lost. This mukhtar seemed to be on our side.

But Ryan says to be careful with assumptions. The village chief has to tread a fine line between us and the gangs, for they can cause him much trouble. He can end up kidnapped for ransom or tossed into a pit with snakes and scorpions. Generally, Ryan says, the people in the area only care about village life. The world beyond doesn't exist for them. Yet, they do fear the encroachment of the Jews and so get pulled into the national cause. Our motto: smile and watch your step.

Time and distance and the distractions of duty haven't made you fade from my thoughts one tiny bit. The moment I can get back to Tel Aviv, I will. Please wait a little longer . . .

I ACHED FOR Duncan. I chafed for his return. The months went by bringing only letters and loneliness and vague predictions about when he'd be back in Jaffa. Yet there was also something intimate and precious in separation and in getting to know one another through the written word. Each one mattered, each had weight. Every endearment written down in black and white became a seed that planted dreams in my mind, certainty in my heart. Though I trembled for Duncan's safety, I thrilled to the stories of his exploits on the convoys and the outpost in the Judean hills. I sent him small gifts: biscuits, socks, a book I bought from a peddler—*Innocents Abroad*, Mark Twain's witty account of his travels to the Holy Land in 1869.

Dressed in my polka-dot frock, I went to a photographer's on Dizengoff Street, and posed on a stool in front of a painted backdrop of palm trees as the flash bulb popped. I wasn't satisfied with the photo, which cost a full week's salary. Thought my nose too long, my freckles obvious, and my smile strained. At an extra charge, the photographer made another copy that whitened my teeth and improved my complexion. Duncan thought it perfect. *Your lovely photo is under the cover of my policeman's manual which I keep beside my bed. I'd pin you up on the wall except that I don't want the other fellows gawking. You're mine alone.* At my begging, he finally sent me a snap in return. It was done by a visiting sergeant with a camera and it showed Duncan, along with the other British constables, standing in the station yard in Kafr Yusef, their baggy shorts and khaki shirts blending with the dusty grey of the ground, their four faces squinting into the sun. Duncan had a pipe in his mouth that made him look as if he was grimacing. He'd grown a moustache that hid his upper lip, and his hair was badly in need of a cut. The rest of his face was a blur in the poor-quality shot. And yet it was clear to me he was the handsomest man of the outpost.

Malka emphatically declared—and Liesel hinted—that I should sniff out the "other fish in the sea" so as not to deprive myself of male company. After all, "my policeman" had vanished into the wilderness, who knew when to reappear, if ever. But I couldn't imagine flirting with another man. Duncan was mine and I was his, and never had I felt such a fierce sense of belonging, and Duncan would return—surely it would be soon—so that we could take up where we'd left off—the handsome policeman and his dear, plucky Thumbelina.

Ein Rachel, July 20, 1938
Dear Eva,

Manu—that's what I've taken to calling Manfred Glatt—is allowed to hang onto his camera in exchange for taking photos of Ein Rachel for the movement newspaper in Tel Aviv. After work, he plods around the settlement pointing his lens at the tractor, the fishing boat, the comrades trimming dead banana leaves off the trees with machetes. I still refuse to let him point the lens at me, despite his silly, embarrassed, begging half-smile. Despite what happened between us the other day. Yes, I won't beat around the bush any longer. We were intimate. Now I've caught up with you, little sister. I too have been with a man.

Last Shabbat afternoon, when he asked if I'd like to go out on the lake in the rowboat, I said yes in a kind of dream. I wasn't suspecting or wishing anything, even though much of the courtship in the settlement occurs in that rowboat. It's become a code word for a certain kind of invitation. And still, I swear to you, I had no intention . . . Because I considered him a friend, nothing more, and all I thought was how nice to have an outing. The water was calm, like molten glass under the burning rays of the late-afternoon sun. Manu worked the oars with earnest vigour, pulling us towards the centre of the lake where the choking heat engulfed us with all its force. Not a breath of breeze stirred. I splashed my face and neck, yet I could barely breathe, while Manu was sweating so hard his glasses slid to the end of his nose and his eyes blinked furiously with the salt. Still, I was enchanted by the beauty all around and told him not to move, to let us drift. I can see the Kinneret a million times and always it seems like a vision—the wide blue water embraced by a semi-circle of low-slung yellow hills. And the air so still we could hear the thin piping of a shepherd's flute from one of the far-off Arab villages. Finally, I took pity on Manu and

let him row us closer to shore so that we could swim and cool off. We
plunged in with our clothes on, laughed, splashed like children. And
then he led me under some eucalyptus trees by the shore and drew me
down onto the bed of sweet-smelling leaves. Without his glasses he
looks vulnerable, boyish, full of awe, or at least he did then as he asked
with his eyes, the question that was in his heart. We were shy and
awkward together and not quite successful, for which he apologized
profusely, as if it mattered. It didn't. Not at all. What mattered was
how he held me tenderly afterwards and sighed into the nape of my
neck and stroked my body as if memorizing every inch of my skin.
Between one murmured endearment and another, the black Palestine
night descended. I looked up from the crook of his arm and was blind.
A cold dread ran through me.

"How will we get back?"

"Don't worry. The moon is on its way."

His voice is very deep. Did I mention that? A quiet bass.

And then, indeed, a silver light poured down between the leaves.
He shook out my still-wet clothes, helped me dress and led me by the
hand back to the boat which he'd tied to a tree root. He rowed us
through the moonlight while a multitude of cicada voices rose up in
their chirping chorus. Luckily we hadn't yet been missed and luckily,
the guard on duty was Shlomo, who just gave us a scolding for putting
ourselves in danger. Manu apologized to me the next day. It was a
stupid, reckless act, to be out beyond the settlement perimeter after
dark in these days of terror. He took full responsibility. I told him that
was nonsense. We'd both lost track of time.

More news soon.

Love,

Your Liesel

Chapter 11
Miss Blatt's Academy

DETERMINED TO IMPROVE myself, I enrolled in an evening course for typing and shorthand offered in German and English by a Miss Blatt from Berlin. Three nights a week, at the end of a long day of drudgery, I joined five other girls in a hot, crowded room for lessons we all hoped would catapult us to that ultimate paradise—an office job with a regular salary of at least five pounds a month. Miss Blatt's "academy" was on the third floor of a building on Balfour Street, in the back office of a recently established importing firm, where our teacher worked during the day and with which she had an arrangement for after-hours use. As soon as we arrived for the lesson, we'd help Miss Blatt bring desks and chairs from other rooms until we had our makeshift classroom, which we dismantled again before we left.

Crammed into this airless space, we thumped away on real and dummy keyboards. Because the firm owned only three typewriters and there were six of us, we had to take turns. While waiting our turn for a machine, we would practise on "Qwerty" keyboard models drawn upon planks of wood. The painted keys sat mute and still and deceptively obedient as we tapped away with the fingers of the left hand—"asdf," "fdsa"—and with those of the right—"jkl;" ";lkj". I copied the diagram from the plank onto a separate sheet of paper so that I could practise at home. Two cups anchoring the page on the kitchen table, my eyes closed so that I wouldn't be tempted to peek, I tapped and I memorized until I could do the exercises in my sleep. My sweat-damp fingers soon wore away the letters in the circles on the page. That hardly mattered because the practice keyboards—both my own clumsy version and the one at the school—only gave the illusion I was mastering a skill. When I tried the exercises on a real machine, I found myself producing blotches, wrong letters, and jammed keys. I needed the feel of the metal keys and the spaces between to achieve the fine tuning of muscle movements. Still, by the end of the six-week session, I could type passably well. The next six weeks were devoted to short-hand, which required only notebooks and pencils and therefore was taught much more efficiently.

Our teacher was a pale, reedy, flat-chested woman, soft-spoken to the point that, even when she bent near, I often had to strain my ears to hear her instructions over the creak of chairs and the peck-peck-peck of the typewriters. Her watery brown eyes and tentative smile gave her a lost soul look, an air of homesickness and anxiety. When someone asked a question, Miss Blatt hesitated, sucked in her breath, as if about to take a plunge into the unknown. Of course, she knew the answer. She knew the secretarial profession up and down. She possessed highly impressive credentials, including nine years as personal secretary to a sales manager at the famous Wertheim Department Store on the Kurfürstendamm in Berlin. That Miss Blatt was now reduced to giving evening lessons in this awkward setting for a paltry thirty mils each from a total of five students (one dropped out after the first week) signalled something was seriously amiss. The import firm that employed her and whose offices we used clearly didn't pay enough. So why didn't she find a better job? Why didn't she seek employment with His Majesty's government in Palestine, or with the Jewish community administration or at least with a more prosperous company? We discussed Miss Blatt's plight and shortcomings among ourselves as we stood on the street corner after class.

"She's too delicate and timid to make a go of it here. She lacks chutzpah."

"Yes. Psychological problems. I think something bad happened to her back in Germany."

The girl who said this lowered her voice as if we were still in Germany, where those who did bad things could overhear.

None of us were willing to admit the truth. Miss Blatt had to struggle because everyone did. There were too many brilliant candidates for too few office positions in a city stuffed with uprooted immigrants from Europe. You just had to glance at the "Work Wanted" ads in *The Palestine Post* to get discouraged.

> Woman, 31, experienced secretary, 10 years with Hamburg shipping line, including 3 as assistant to vice president.Man with experience in insurance and sales. Speaks four languages: English, Hebrew, Yiddish, Roumanian. Every offer welcome.

And so on.

At the end of my three months at the makeshift secretarial course, I received a "certificate" of proficiency, typed on a crisp sheet of white paper by Miss Blatt herself and signed by her too. I took it with me as I went knocking on doors after checking the ads in the *Post* and the flimsy little notices tacked up on billboards. I haunted the doorsteps of firms large and small, introduced myself in government offices, hunted out shaky (and perhaps shady) concerns at the end of dusty corridors in half-finished buildings. No one was interested. No one had a job to offer. And I had to do all this job hunting during moments snatched in between my hours as an *ozeret*, and without my employers' knowledge. Because if I wasn't eager and grateful for the cleaning work, they could easily replace me with some new, desperate refugee with more realistic ambitions.

Despite the strict quotas and border controls, the refugees kept coming. They came in sardine-can boats that managed to elude the coast guard and limp to shore in the darkness on lonely stretches of sand to the north. Aided by an underground network of volunteers, they melted into the community, the *Yishuv*. Those caught by the British patrols faced jail or deportation. They were our brethren and they had nothing. I felt guilty that even a tincture of resentment should enter my heart about the newcomers offering themselves up for any kind of employment at any price. Yet so it was.

While I searched for work that summer, I tried to study Hebrew too, at evening lessons given by a man who'd once taught at the prestigious gymnasium in my own hometown of Breslau and who was now a mere elementary school teacher by day. Mr. Falk's evening students sat at children's desks in one of the school's classrooms. Though this stifling room had windows, they seemed to let in dust and flies only, rather than air. Beads of perspiration glistened in the seams of our teacher's ruddy face. The chalk grew damp in his hand so that the verb conjugations he drew on the blackboard came out faint as wisps of evaporating clouds. His voice droned. Ten minutes into the lesson, my eyelids grew heavy and my head dropped. I was so tired after a day of fighting with carpets, sheets, and toilet stains, and Hebrew was so foreign. Not like English. On the bus home one evening, as I chatted in German with a classmate—a woman from Königsberg—a man in front of us barked, "Speak Hebrew, not Hitler's language." I shot back that it was also the language of Schiller and Goethe. I almost wanted to stop the lessons with Mr. Falk out of spite.

"*Don't lose heart, Thumbelina,*" Duncan wrote. "*You're such a plucky girl and have a head for languages. Not like me. I'm still struggling with basic Arabic. As for their squiggly writing, forget it! Don't know that I'll ever learn enough to earn my sergeant's stripes. But your English is so excellent, Eva. You should be able to find a government post. Lots of those don't require much Hebrew.*"

A job with His Majesty's administration in Palestine! In an office with a ceiling fan, among men and women who said "beg your pardon" and "oh terribly sorry" in crisp, educated accents. How all Miss Blatt's students and Miss Blatt herself, and no doubt Mr. Falk too, longed for such a position. Along with civil servants sent out from the mother country, the government did hire plenty of "locals," both Jewish and Arab, striving to maintain a balance between the two. But many, many applied for such jobs and very few were chosen.

Hebron, Aug. 14, 1938
Dear Eva,

Finally seen some action again. Was sent with a search party to hunt the rotters who've been cutting telephone wires along the Hebron-Jerusalem road. Six of us went out with a tracking dog, a fine black Doberman named Matey. Hot work under the blazing sun, clutching our Lee Enfields in one hand, swatting flies with the other, ammo pouches and water bottles smacking our butts. We followed the scent through the rough hills to a village, Matey panting harder by the minute as we wound our way through the narrow, cluttered lanes. Not a soul among the villagers stuck his nose out, but we could feel eyes watching from the windows. Suddenly bullets whistled past my head and I heard a heart-breaking yelp as Matey took a hit. We dove for cover and returned the fire, which was coming from just one of the houses. There was quite a lively exchange for a while. Presently, the house went still, the door opened a crack and a white sheet was thrust out through the gap. A man and a boy of about 10 emerged with their hands up. Inside we found a wounded man bleeding profusely on the floor, and a woman and three girls cowering behind a table. In a cupboard we found a big cache of arms. The story told was that four rebels had commandeered the house—the father swore he and his family had been forced to shelter them. Three had managed to escape through a back door while the fourth, the wounded man, had covered their flight. Gone to the hills. We'd never find them without our dog. But at least we'd bagged one of their lot, plus a nice pile of arms. The house has been blown up, following the policy of punishing those who harbour rebels for whatever reason. I feel badly for the family, but we have to set an example. Unless we act firmly, we'll never get the country back under control.

A big kiss on your dear lips,
Duncan

I never mentioned Duncan to any of my classmates, even when I went out with a couple of the girls for a *gazoz* by the beach and they burbled about their own little passions and misadventures. Soryl had something going with a handsome though bitterly depressed actor from Prague. Miri had set her sights on Mr. Falk, of all people, convincing herself our Hebrew teacher wasn't as dull as he appeared. Sensing I too had a love interest, they prodded me to 'fess up but I laughed them off. I didn't trust their reactions, anticipated the slant-eye skeptical glance and the half-hidden sneer of judgment. Or a flurry of warnings as I'd had my fill of from Malka and Liesel. No, my Duncan was not for sharing, not even his name. The more he was my secret, the tighter, I felt, was our bond.

Chapter 12
The Thirsty Hart

IN MID-SEPTEMBER, DUNCAN returned to Jaffa for a week of leave and arranged to meet me on the Saturday morning by the lifeguard tower at the beach. The usual crowd milled about the strip of sand below the end of Allenby Road—people in bathing costumes and beach robes, toddlers stark naked except for floppy white hats on their heads. The deck chair loll-abouts, the paddle-ball players, the exercise fanatics performing jumping jacks. I tried not to race across the road, but to walk with a casual air, all the while my heart pounding, my eyes searching. And there he was. In the tower's shade, both arms waving wildly. At the edge of the sand, I bent down to take off my shoes, my galloping heart aware of him streaking towards me, closing the distance between us. He lifted me right off my feet, swung me around, and crushed me to his chest.

"Eva! Sweetheart. Is it you? Are you real?"

We touched foreheads. We laughed and laughed.

"You look different," I said, running my fingertip over the bristles of the thick moustache he'd grown while away.

"You look wonderfully the same."

The fierce-looking moustache wasn't the only change. His face was the colour of dark brick and leaner than I remembered. The cheekbones more prominent and the jawline more defined, while his eyes held a guarded, watchful light. Months of missions in the hills had whittled him down to a tough inner core and swept away the last traces of boyish softness. For a moment I drew back from this rough-hewn stranger. But he was so happy to see me that my uneasiness vanished.

"What shall we do, darling? Would you like an ice cream? A drink? Shall we walk? Shall we go dancing? So what if it's nine in the morning? I'll bang on the doors of the San Remo Hotel and tell them to wake up the band."

We decided to stay just where we were—on the beach, in the midst of the merry Sabbath morning crowd. Hand in hand, our two pairs of shoes in the crook of Duncan's other arm, we strolled barefoot along the glistening sand at the water's edge. Gulls mewed, children shrieked, waves splashed, peddlers called out their wares, and the smack-smack of paddle balls rode the salty air, and all these sounds mixed together in a natural ode to joy. There was no high or low on the Tel Aviv beach on a Saturday morning. Money didn't matter. Race, religion, age didn't matter. Everyone was equal, free to strut, to yell, to be. Here all milled about in states of innocent half-nakedness, and a Brit copper and his Jewish girl could hold hands in blissful anonymity. Here, by the sea, time stood still. Hitler's evil machinations in Czechoslovakia vanished. The Arab revolt melted away. Jaffa town was a postcard view, with the bell tower of St. Peter's Church in the hazy distance. And besides, the only Arabs on the beach were harmless hawkers and curious urchins.

As the sun climbed higher, its searing heat beat down on our heads and snaked up from the baking sand. By that time, the hem of my skirt had been soaked by rogue waves, and so had Duncan's rolled-up trouser legs.

"We should go for a swim," he said. "Did you bring your bathing suit?"

I had. In my straw handbag lay the emerald green costume I'd bought some weeks before, anticipating Duncan's return. After changing in the wooden shed beside the lifeguard tower, I stepped gingerly across the hot sand towards Duncan as he watched me, his eyes intense, squinting against the glare. Beneath his gaze, I felt exposed and lovely in the green costume that hugged my body and contrasted with my pale, delicate skin. He stood with his hands on his hips, his ruddy muscled shoulders and naked chest open to the sun, and I noticed how the sprinkling of brown hair that began below the hollow of his throat trailed down to the waistband of his bathing trunks. When he rubbed oil over all my bare back and shoulders, I leaned into his hands. I could barely breathe, a sensation both painful and exquisite.

We dunked into the cold, leaping sea. I paddled in the shallows, while Duncan swam with strong, vigorous strokes far out enough to make me anxious and then returned, snorting like a playful porpoise. At one point he had me hang onto his shoulders, my front against his long supple back, as he ferried me over the waves. After the swim, we lay side by side in adjoining deck chairs, topped with canopies that made a nook of shade in which to nestle together. Duncan bought us each a lunch of corn on the cob from the vendor, who forked the golden cobs out of his steaming kettle, wrapped each in a leaf and lavished it with butter and salt. I'd brought almonds and a milk chocolate bar that had softened in the heat and that we licked off the silver foil wrapping in turns. We washed down our feast with lemonade fetched for us by an Arab peddler boy Duncan befriended. The boy returned at a run with two large cardboard cups sloshing their contents onto his hands and bare feet. His eyes were dark as coffee, his hair matted with dirt. Duncan chatted with the boy in his own language and gave him a coin and finally another so that he would go away. In the distance, near the Yarkon estuary, a train of camels carrying *zif-zif*—construction sand—plodded along the shore.

Slowly, as the hours drifted by, the sea turned from deep blue to a molten bronze and the sky to polished zinc. Duncan fell asleep while I fanned his hot cheeks with pages of *The Palestine Post* I'd brought along in my handbag. His long limbs spilled over the deck chair to rest in the sand. The beach had become quieter, for many people had gone home for a long Sabbath afternoon siesta. The day stretched out before us like the hazy mauve horizon above the gentle heave of the sea.

Two gulls fought over a chewed-up cob of corn that some careless picnicker had flung into the sand. I was about to shoo them away and dispose of the cob in a litter box when one of the birds uttered a piercing shriek. Duncan reared up from his dead-to-the-world slumbers, his whole body instantly rigid. His eyes narrowed in a look I'd never seen on him before: something between fear, fury, and disgust. He grabbed his shoe and hurled it at the gulls.

"Bloody vermin."

"It's the litter. People are so thoughtless. I'll get rid of that thing," I said and started to scramble to my feet.

"Leave it."

He pushed me back down into the canvas chair.

"It's not your job. You're off duty now, Miss Scullery Maid."

The expression stung me. His eyes shifted as I stared at him, stunned. He rose, stretched, went to retrieve his shoe, and to pitch the filthy cob far into the sea. When he returned he was all smiles and tenderness again, as if the person I'd glimpsed a moment before had been an illusion. What dark thought had flashed through his mind as he'd heard the gull's scream? To what place of danger had he been transported? Beneath the warmth in his eyes lay something tense, a warning, and so I didn't ask. I sighed when he settled back in his chair and enfolded me against his bare chest. We lay together in a hot, sticky, sandy embrace, our hearts beating the same hard rhythm, a single two-sided pulse.

I FEIGNED ILLNESS, skipping work that week to be with Duncan, indifferent to the loss of pay. Each moment of togetherness shone deliriously bright, like sun on water. Yes, though a couple of times, as we lay entangled on Malka's sofa, he seemed to slip away from me, taut, alert, distant, already back in those fascinatingly dangerous eastern hills, where the bandits roamed and the Force gave chase. Those absences didn't count, I told myself. All that mattered were the many moments of his sweet, living presence. And yet the week waned and anxiety about the approaching end nibbled at my heart. One afternoon, two days before his departure, as we sat together at a quiet spot on the north end of the beach, I tried to steer the conversation into comforting waters.

"Wouldn't it be lovely if you'd be posted to Tel Aviv?"

He took a swig from his hip flask of Haig's Scotch, something he wasn't supposed to do out in the open, even when off duty. But who was going to challenge him here on this peaceful stretch of sand, far from the eyes of some rule-obsessed sergeant?

"S' not likely, Eva. Not unless I get in with C.I.D. The ordinary beat cops in this town are mostly Jewish chaps."

"C.I.D.?"

"Criminal Investigation Department. The detective section. I wouldn't mind, but I'd have to get my sergeant's stripes at the least. I'd need quite a bit more to show for myself. To have cracked a big case. To be really strong in Arabic or Hebrew, which I'm not."

"I heard you speaking to that boy on the beach the other day. Your Arabic is very good."

He chuckled.

"Easy to impress you, my dear. How much Arabic do you know? '*Yalla! Yalla!*' That's the extent of it, right? No, I'm still far from fluent. As for my Hebrew, it's even worse."

"So you'll go back to your beat work in Jaffa?"

"Hope not. No fun going backwards."

He took another mouthful, rolled it around on his tongue before swallowing. He shook the flask and sighed at the small amount left. Turning to smile at me, he saw my questioning eyes.

"If I'm posted back to Jaffa, they might put me with the Inlying Pickets. That's a special squad for riot control. The training and the base are at the Ajami barracks south of Jaffa. I'd get intensive training for a few weeks in busting up mobs. They've got this new stuff now—canisters of a gas that's not real poison, but makes people choke and their eyes smart. The squad is deployed to different hot spots around the country—short assignments—and then returns to base."

"*If I'm posted back to Jaffa!*" I'd barely heard a word he'd said after that, as I hugged my knees and ground my bare heels into the sand. Straightening up, I assumed a false, bright, joking tone.

"I'll learn Hebrew properly and then I'll teach you. And then you'll get posted to the C.I.D. in Tel Aviv and then we'll live happily ever after."

He laughed and draped his arm around me.

"Don't know if you'd really like that, Eva. I'd be hunting Jews. I'd be searching out the fanatics who are trying to stir up revenge against the Arabs. Like that fellow Stern. Total nutter that one, so I've heard. Talks about driving out the British and setting up a Jewish kingdom. They're small fry, those lunatics, but still, they must be nipped in the bud. And when we lock them up, there'll probably be an outcry in the Jewish streets."

He shook his head.

"Like when the chap who threw the grenade at the Arab bus got hanged and all of Jewish Palestine went into mourning. It's ok to hang Arab criminals, but not Jews."

He was talking about Shlomo Ben Yossef, a militant youth, who, together with a couple of others, had plotted a desperate act of retaliation for an Arab terrorist attack on Jewish passengers in a taxi some months ago. The boys had targeted innocent Arabs, but they'd botched the deed, for their grenade failed to explode. No Arabs had been killed. Nevertheless, Ben Yossef, the oldest of the three, was condemned to death. Black flags draped over balconies in our city when the news of his hanging broke. People railed at the British authorities and old Mrs. Mandelmann had sobbed as if her own flesh and blood had died on the gallows. He was the first Jew to have been hanged in the Holy Land since Roman times. Somehow this was a source of shame for the whole *Yishuv*. Plenty of Arabs had swung for much less. And still. At the time I too had felt a flare of anger at the heartless authorities. But I said nothing of this to Duncan.

"I don't mind if you lock up the Jewish fanatics," I said. "They deserve locking up."

Duncan held me close. I smelled his skin and his whisky breath. For some time, we gazed seawards in silence as the fiery sun approached the horizon.

"What I wouldn't be so thrilled about," I finally said, choosing my words carefully, "is if you were tracking down refugees. I mean, I'd understand if you did it. You have to do what you're told. But I'd be sad because they've suffered so much, those people escaping Hitler."

"But they can't all come here," he said softly.

He held my hand. His warm skin thrummed against mine.

"To be honest, Eva, I wouldn't want that job either. Chasing after those poor blighters. Anyway . . ." He gave my hand a good squeeze. "Hitler might have done his worst by now. He'll back down when he's confronted at the Munich meeting."

"You think so?"

"Mr. Chamberlain will tell him he can't have Czechoslovakia. That better be the message. Otherwise we'll have another wave of illegals heading for these shores."

Golden snakes of light writhed over the waves. The red ball of sun bled towards the horizon, slowly first, then faster, so that we could almost see the motion as it sank into the sea. A fresh breeze sprang up. In a few minutes, the water turned inky and then darkness gobbled up everything, turned the other sungazers around us into indistinct humps on the sand. Duncan's arm around my waist guided me northwards into the greater blackness, away from the glimmers of the city lights. We stumbled along dunes whose contours became visible for a brief instant in the faint sweep of a searchlight from a government patrol boat, one of those on the look-out for illegals. Duncan drew me down into the soft sand that still held the warmth of the sun.

ON THE MORNING of Duncan's departure, we were to meet at Kowalski's for a brief goodbye before he'd join his mates in the police car travelling east. I'd not slept well and was in a prickly mood as I smudged my mascara, had to wipe it off and start again. Precious minutes slipped away. My dawdling before the mirror was eating into our last morsel of time together. My nervous fingers dropped the open lipstick tube, which fell into the sink with a clatter and a smear of red on the porcelain. I stamped my foot. *Let him wait.* Let *him* be the one to wonder what had become of me for a change. I imagined him gazing at his watch in dismay as he fidgeted in Kowalski's shop. There was a danger that he'd leave in despair of my coming, but, though waves of anxiety rolled through my gut, I refused to rush. Even when I saw him outside the shop door, peering down the street, I kept my pace steady. I braced for a scolding. It didn't come. His tense face simply melted with relief as he took my hand to pull me inside.

The shop was unusually quiet for the hour—no record on the gramophone, the only sounds being grunts and sighs from the back office as Kowalski hunched over his desk and struggled through his accounts.

"Pick something to play," Duncan said.

His arm made a grand sweep to indicate the crates of records that lined the shelf behind the counter.

"Don't you have to leave?"

"Soon enough. But there's always time for music."

His smile was calm and sweet and held a trace of tease, as if he'd seen through me, refused to be ruffled by my little games of delay.

The crates were marked alphabetically under the names of key composers: Albinoni to Bruch, Chopin to Dvorak, and so on. The records were in paper sleeves with a hole in the middle to show the label. It still seemed magical to me that these thin, fragile discs could hold entire orchestras in their tiny grooves. The breadth of choice overwhelmed me, and then I had the sense my choice might become an omen, which made me hesitate all the more.

"You decide," I said, with a shrug of feigned indifference.

He plucked out a collection of choral music by Mendelssohn. I made a face.

"Oh, church music. How very Christian," I scoffed.

Hurt clouded Duncan's eyes. But he quickly recovered. He would not be provoked.

"Mendelssohn was Jewish."

"Not very. He was baptized."

"Bully for him. He composed like an angel. You'll love this. Psalm 42."

Duncan stepped over to the gramophone, wound the crank, slipped the record from its sleeve and gently lowered the disc onto the turntable. Static crackled, followed by the first searching notes of an orchestra introducing its theme. The choir began to sing. Both the words and the melody were sublime.

Wie der Hirsch schreit
Nach frischem Wasser

Duncan bent towards me to murmur the translation.

As the hart pants
For fresh water

"Screams," I corrected him. "As the hart screams. It's much stronger in German."

The blended voices rose, resonated with anguish and longing and etched in me a vision of a gaunt beast alone in the wilderness. Parched grey wasteland. Merciless sun. The antlered head rises, the neck stretches, the black tongue hangs out, the beast bellows for the water that can't be found, while the heavens gaze down in insufferable silence. I'd never seen a desert in my life, yet I knew this harsh, dry eternity of stone and sand. Perhaps my Jewish genes held the memory. Perhaps some of the Bible's fearsome language lay lodged in the recesses of my brain. The psalm went on to lines of hope and solace and the music was exquisite, but I couldn't get past the vision of the desperate hart, its helpless, agonized scream. When the piece ended, I realized I'd been standing there with my fists pressed against my cheeks. Duncan was gazing down tenderly.

"Told you it was lovely. Even if it *is* church music. Dear Thumbelina, my sensitive girl."

When the time finally came for us to part, I couldn't help but cling. I knew he really did have to hurry now to catch his transport, but as we stood outside on the street, I asked trivial, last-minute questions to draw out the moment. Did he have water for the journey? Would he write soon?

"Can't I come with you?" I finally wailed.

He laughed and kissed the tip of my nose.

"Don't know that I'd want to share you with the mates. They'd eat you up with their eyes."

He kissed me long and sweetly, one last time, as the stream of pedestrians detoured around us and bicycle bells rang, and as, on another street nearby, a donkey brayed in distress. Then I watched him stride away, his arms swinging freely as he whistled the melody of the thirsty hart.

Part II

Chapter 13
Ill Winds

May 1939

THE MONTH OF May brought *khamsin*—sultry winds from the Sahara that transformed the sky into a dusty yellow haze. I'd wake at dawn to a heavy presence in the air, a stealthy, oppressive occupation that pressed me down into the sofa before I even tried to raise my head. *Khamsin* had a bad effect on everyone; it made tempers blow, spirits wilt, bowels rebel, migraines flare and limbs grow lethargic. During *khamsin*, *Frau* Mandelmann became listless and distant, her love of chat stilled, her face a grim, grey mask that barely registered a flicker as I washed the floors around her and carried away her untouched apricot compote. Malka complained about her aching head, but she had no time to nurse her temples with wet washcloths. She had an exciting new customer, an Englishwoman, Mrs. Millicent Hollingsworth, who needed a gown for the king's birthday ball. From early to late, the sewing machine chattered, Malka sweated and cursed, and the component pieces of the Hollingsworth project—swathes of taffeta, billows of chiffon, packets of sequins—took over every surface of the main room. This alone would have driven me outdoors in the evenings, but the *khamsin* did as well. The weather enervated me one moment and filled me with a rank, twitchy energy the next. I would have liked to sink my nails into Duncan's back as he lay on top of me and crushed the agitation out of my chest, but Duncan was elsewhere that week. On duty with the Inlying Pickets. Perhaps he was in the Ajami exercise yard, at drill with shields and batons, canisters of gas and the close-range riot gun. Or sent with the squad to test out their techniques in some town where the Mufti's men, the followers of Haj Amin Al Husseini, continued to stir up trouble. I didn't know for sure. Only that I wouldn't see him until Saturday next. Still, he had come back, hadn't he? After all those months of remote postings, after all Malka's cynical comments and Liesel's anxious entreaties, aimed at persuading me to give up hope, he'd proven them wrong by returning to Jaffa and to me. And I could prove that I had what it took to be a copper's girl. So I taught myself to have faith in the next Saturday, or whatever day it was he could get away, and to keep myself occupied in the meantime.

When *khamsin* lay dense upon the city, I itched for the seaside, where the view opened up and a breath of fresh air blew off the water. As I headed in that direction one evening, I noticed something amiss. My neighbours weren't out strolling or sprawled on their balconies. The street was almost empty, except for a subdued crowd gathered around the newspaper kiosk on the corner. Approaching the huddle of people, I heard the thin metallic tones of a radio broadcast and I remembered that tonight the British government was announcing its new policy on Palestine. For weeks there had been rumours and forebodings. For months, Weizmann and the other Jewish leaders had poured their arguments into British ears. Now we would learn if they'd been successful. I pressed closer to the kiosk with the radio and listened to the clipped, oh-so-civilized voice reaching us from the Palestine Broadcasting Service studio in Jerusalem amid spits of static. The news was worse than anyone had anticipated. People around me gasped as the announcer made his way through section after section of His Majesty's Government's White Paper. Jewish immigration to be severely restricted. Illegals to be deducted from the annual quotas. Land sales to Jews to be banned altogether. In ten years hence, if peace and good order prevailed, Palestine would become independent, with a guaranteed Arab majority of at least two thirds over a one third Jewish minority. The broadcast ended with a restatement of British intent to do justice to both peoples and urging both peoples to live together in harmony for their own sakes and for the sake of the millions of Muslims, Jews and Christians the world over who revered the land and prayed for its peace.

Mirsky, the kiosk owner, snapped off the radio on the shelf behind him. For a moment all was silent. Then the lamentations and arm waving began.

"A stake in the heart of the Jewish national home!"

"Surrender to Arab terrorism!"

"So that's what the British promise is worth! A heap of dung!"

"But from the British point of view it makes sense," said a round-faced man I recognized as Mr. Pinsker, the optometrist on Nachlat Binyamin Street. "If the British go to war with Germany, they will need Iraqi oil and quiet in her Middle East dominions. So they court the Arabs with a sacrifice of the Jews."

"Wrong thinking," shouted Mirsky, thrusting his head and shoulders through the window of his little hut. Above him, the newspaper and magazine display, pegged to a string with clothespins, quivered as he shook with indignation.

"The Arab countries won't lift a finger to help Britain and in the meantime the British spit in the face of their real friends."

"The Arabs don't have to help," Pinsker continued, in the reasonable, almost cheerful tone of someone in possession of an airtight argument. "They just have to stay out of the way. The British know we can't do anything more than scream and when we're finished screaming we'll feed their army and even give them our sons for the war. Would we fight the British? Of course not. Not with Hitler's boots on our brethren's necks."

Mirsky thumped the heel of his hand against the window ledge. The newspapers on the string twitched.

"We must resist, resist, resist!"

"I agree with you absolutely, my friend. Of course, we must resist."

Pinsker looked left and right at the straggle of people who'd remained for the discussion before spreading his arms wide and delivering his stinger.

"But how?"

Such talk made me jumpier than I'd already been. I didn't wait to hear more. I turned the corner, strode along Nachlat Binyamin Street, across Magen David Square, and up Allenby Road until I came at last to the edge of the sea. The vast dark expanse of gently rolling water calmed me, and so did the soft, cool sand beneath my feet. I wandered up and down, south to the outskirts of the Arab quarter of Manshia, and north again to the safer stretches. And, as always when I was at the edge of the sea, I lost all sense of time until, when I turned once again, I noticed a strange yellow flicker in the sky to the southeast, the direction of our neighbourhood. Dark smudges sank and rose and revealed themselves as billows of smoke, while tongues of orange flame danced along the rooftops. I watched in stunned awe as the smoke ballooned and the flames stretched higher. Finally, propelled by foreboding, I hurried back whence I'd come, towards the source of that lurid yellow light. Magen David Circus was deserted. One lone figure appeared out of a side street and, catching sight of me, hesitated before proceeding briskly across the empty intersection. It was a matronly woman in a light-coloured dress and sturdy shoes.

"What's going on?" I asked, pointing towards the southern sky.

"You didn't see them? You didn't hear them? There were thousands gathered outside the Great Synagogue and then they marched with raised fists, looking for trouble. They're not our people."

She saw me staring, trying to understand.

"Revisionist scum!"

Her shrill voice echoed about the empty square.

"They were chanting 'Down with Weizmann! Up with Jabotinsky!' After all that Weizmann has done for the Jewish people! And who is Jabotinsky? A madman, a fascist. Him they adore, those ignorant youths! The last thing we need is a Jewish riot. Divisions."

She sucked in a deep breath, smiled, and her tone changed.

"I've just come from a meeting at the Labour Hall with the real leaders and we have a plan, a day of defiance and unity, a great day, but you'll find out . . . tomorrow . . . there will be notices. I have to go . . . work to do."

She charged past me up Allenby Road, while I continued in the opposite direction. Arriving at Lilienblum, I half expected to see our building engulfed in flames, but no, the street was dark and quiet and everything normal, except for the acrid smell of smoke. When I strained to listen, I heard muffled shouts from the direction of the bus station. Papa still lived down there in the ramshackle neighbourhood behind the station. I imagined him standing in his doorway, muttering curses against this unholy land of no-goods and ruffians until clouds of smoke blocked up his throat. In this season of sultry heat, a fire could spread fast, jump from lane to lane to devour the shipping-container shacks, the cheek-by-jowl houses. I shuddered at the vision I'd conjured and rushed forward with the hope I might spot him on the street from afar and know he was safe after all.

Down Herzl Street, down Yehuda Halevy. More shouting now and the sound of gunfire and the sting of smoke in my eyes. Well before the bus station, I arrived at the scene of the trouble and knew it wasn't Papa I should be worried about. The intersection in front of the District Government Office was blocked by police lorries. The top floor of the building was on fire, flames leaping out of the upper windows and thick black smoke pouring heavenwards. Beyond the barrier of trucks, I saw violent movement—people running, shoving, surging towards the uniformed constables. Duncan! Duncan! Where was he? Was he in the melee of swinging fists and batons? Or in the midst of the fire? Someone grabbed my arm while I stood and gaped. A soldier. He bent down to peer into my face.

"What's your business here, Miss?"

When I couldn't answer he gave me a shake, none too gentle.

"Go home. Or you'll be under arrest."

I spent much of the night on the balcony, listening as the muffled commotion a few streets away gradually died down and the last of the police lorries rumbled off. I listened for Duncan's whistle on the street below. In the delusional fog of half sleep, I thought I heard his soft call of "Hullo, Thumbelina." But it was only the yowl of feral cats fighting over the garbage.

THE NEXT DAY'S *Post* reported on the assault against the District Office by a disorderly crowd of five thousand strong, mainly youths, who'd smashed furniture, burned records, and set the building alight. The nearby Land Registry and Migration Offices had also been hit. A similar ruckus had occurred in

Jerusalem. But all this was a side story. The main news was the protest against the White Paper—now dubbed the Black Paper—from the mainstream organizations of the *Yishuv*. The *Post* carried verbatim statements from the Jewish Agency and the National Council—paragraph after paragraph of resolute, righteous prose. The chief rabbi called the policy "a sin against God." The leadership vowed resistance, starting with a country-wide general strike, a day of "solidarity and resolve." It must be peaceful, of course. Anything less would undermine the moral superiority of the Jewish cause and play into the hands of our enemies.

By the time I'd scanned the newspaper I'd bought at Minsky's kiosk, the general strike had already begun. An ominous quiet lay over the city, with shops shuttered, schools closed, traffic stilled and construction sites abandoned, the naked skeletons of half-finished buildings looking strangely reproachful under the sun's harsh glare. Even Malka, after some hesitation and knuckle-gnawing, decided to stop work on the Hollingsworth gown for twenty-four hours— deadline be damned. No, on this day she would not sew a stitch. The national cause was greater. We had to show those callous British, those two-faced back-stabbers. Besides, Mrs. Millicent Hollingsworth was getting on Malka's nerves with her fussy demands and hoity-toity English lady ways.

"She's wife of a Deputy District Superintendent in the Palestine Police, so only one step removed from the Lord Almighty. When she came for a fitting she held herself all squeezed together as if she was afraid she'd get infected if she rubbed up against anything in the flat."

Arms stiff at her sides, Malka sidled between the kitchen counter and the table to illustrate Mrs. Hollingsworth's fastidious manner. Then Malka noticed the time.

"It's late! Never mind your coffee. We have to go. The meeting!"

All over the country, in synagogues and halls, Jews were gathering together to hear speeches and declare their readiness for the struggle against the White Paper. I didn't want to get personally involved, but Malka hooked her arm in mine as if my coming with her was beyond question, so I allowed myself to be hurried out the door. Though she normally walked at a languid pace, especially in hot weather, Malka was now so fired with zeal that she steamed along the streets towards the Moghrabi Theatre, while I trotted beside her, trying to sort out my thoughts. In theory, of course, I agreed with the protest. What else could we do? But the anti-British sentiment in the air weighed heavily on my heart.

The Moghrabi was packed. Standing room only, five rows deep at the back, with many people squashed into the aisles and bunched up outside the main doors. Malka elbowed us forward until there was no use to even think of escape, pressed as we were between the mass of bodies. My dress clung to my damp skin. My head rang with the cacophony of voices in the hall. All around us heads bobbed, arms waved, and paper flapped as people fanned their hot faces with the handbills that had been distributed at the door. On the stage was a podium, a microphone, and a huddle of men, nose to nose in agitated discussion as if nobody else existed. Finally one of them tapped the microphone, which crackled and let out an ear-splitting screech. Instantly, the hubbub in the room subsided. Another man, introduced as a representative of the Jewish Agency, stepped forward. He was short, heavyset, with a gleaming bald head and owlish glasses, and he was dressed in a suit and tie for the occasion, attire that surely burdened him in the steam-bath heat of the hall. The man mopped his face with his handkerchief, adjusted his glasses on his slippery nose, rustled through his papers. And then he began.

"Comrades. Citizens of the *Yishuv*. My fellow Jews."

The speaker's voice was raspy, as if he'd recently smoked his throat raw. It began slow and weary, but quickly gathered strength and energy.

"Yesterday the colonial secretary in London issued a policy of betrayal. He has torn up Britain's sacred pledge. Today, the Jewish people here and the world over answer him. We will not bow. We will not submit. We will continue to build, to plant, to settle, and to welcome our persecuted brethren to this land. The scattered, the exiled, the homeless will come. For two thousand years the Jewish people have aspired to the rebirth of its homeland and the era of redemption is at hand. I ask you comrades, can it be stopped by a decree from the colonial secretary?"

"Never!" the audience howled.

"Will we tolerate this treacherous policy?"

"No!" came the thunder of five hundred voices.

The Jewish Agency man peered left and right over the rim of his glasses before looking down again at his papers.

"No power in the world can destroy the natural right of our brethren to enter the ancestral land . . ."

As I stood at the back of the hall amid the crush, several streams of thought ran through my mind at once. I took in every word of the speech. I envisioned a crowd of "brethren," including Uncle Otto and Aunt Ida, pressed up against a closed gate labelled "Palestine." I saw Duncan cock his head mockingly at the speaker's florid statements. I imagined him with that funny helmet of the Inlying Pickets on his head. It was shaped like a tin soup bowl and held in place with a strap under the chin and somehow made him look like he was dressed up for Purim. I imagined the approach of a swarm of protesters. *A mob is a vicious beast.* And also, at the same time, Pinsker's pained words came back to me. *Of course we must resist. But how?* Who were we, a motley collection of Jews, against the might of Britannia and its colonies and dominions, the biggest empire in the world?

" . . . and we will not surrender to a policy aimed at shattering the last hope of the Jewish people," the thickset man declared.

"No surrender," the audience chorused without needing to be prompted.

"No power on earth can stop us."

"No power," the shout rose up.

The small *were* standing up to the mighty. The mad daring, the just cause, the righteous fervour in the room became a powerful wind. My lips parted of their own accord and a concurring murmur escaped my throat. *No surrender.*

"And now Comrades, I will ask you to take an oath. It is the same solemn oath your fellow Jews are taking this very hour in towns and settlements around the land. This vow is comparable to the great pledge our ancestors took when they faced exile to Babylon, and it has never been forgotten to this day."

The speaker's gravelly voice was the voice of the people—flawed, scarred, raw, but unquenchable.

He bade us raise our right hands, and so we did, five hundred of us in the same posture, palms upraised, five hundred voices enmeshed—mine among them—as we swore, *For Zion's sake, I will not hold my peace and for Jerusalem's sake, I will not rest.*

What did the words mean exactly? It wasn't clear. It didn't matter. Here we were, all together, swearing a pledge, as in Babylon, as at Sinai, and the enormous resonance of this antiquity shivered my bones. For the first time in my life I felt an unflinching solidarity, an exalted sense of belonging. This stubborn, beleaguered people. My people! I had come to the Moghrabi Theatre as a spectator. I left as part of a mass procession.

We poured out of the wide double doorway, down the steps, and into the intersection, which was free of vehicles and completely taken over by the crowd. Malka grabbed my arm. We linked elbows, and then linked with our neighbours on either side. The slow, dignified march of thousands began. Men and women, young and old, workers groups, youth groups, professionals, black-garbed rabbis and women with prams. Up Allenby, up Ben Yehuda, towards the exhibition grounds in the north of the city. We were a force. We were a sea. We were the new Hebrew nation. The way was long, the sun hot, and the going painfully slow because of the huge numbers.

"You'll continue to the end? You're not tired?" I asked Malka when our section of the column paused to let those behind us catch up. Malka never walked anywhere if she could help it, preferring to ride the bus or on the handlebars of Amnon's bicycle.

"I'll go all the way to Jerusalem if I have to. Yes, to the High Commissioner's door! I'll stand before his mansion and scream the walls down."

I laughed, but her fevered eyes said she was serious. What had happened to my scoffing, cynical, practical-minded, physically lazy friend? She puffed out her bosom, squeezed my arm tighter, and we moved forward again with this great tide of Jews.

Now and then came a spontaneous outburst of *Hatikvah*, amid much waving of the blue and white flag. But mostly the procession wound its way through the dusty streets under the blazing sun with grim and quiet dignity. At one point, I glimpsed a cluster of police at the mouth of a side street, the bored red faces beneath their stiff, peaked caps. My heart leaped. My eyes searched for Duncan. In vain. All in all, few police were about and those who were kept their presence low key. In my mind, I spoke to Duncan. *This is what Jewish protest looks like*, I told him. *Not an ugly beast.*

THE NEXT DAY, a Friday, was back to normal in our city, with markets bustling, labourers trundling their wheelbarrows, barefoot peddler boys yelling themselves hoarse. Everyone was out to recoup the losses of the general strike. The day of protest had proceeded peacefully all over the country, in every town, village, and settlement except for one place: Jerusalem. There, as dusk fell, an ugly mood had possessed the crowd gathered in Zion Square. *The Palestine Post* reported that a hundred and twenty people had been injured, including a number of coppers, one of whom, a British constable named Harold Lawrence, had succumbed to his gunshot wounds. My hands shook as I stood in the Mandelmann's kitchen and read the front-page report from top to bottom and then searched for more news in the inside pages. Other than Constable Lawrence, none of the police casualties was mentioned by name. Once again, I experienced that helpless dread. How could I find out if Duncan was all right? It was a Friday morning. He was due to fetch me at Malka's on Saturday evening, which was more than 24 hours away. Many a time, I'd scanned the casualties lists like this, and it was always hard, but this time harder still. A Jewish riot was not supposed to happen. When I read the story aloud to Mrs. Mandelmann, she insisted the constable got hit by one of his own.

"None of our people would take guns to a protest rally."

TO MY HUGE relief, Duncan did arrive at Lilienblum Street at the appointed time on Saturday evening. I stood on tiptoe and flung my arms around his neck. He grinned at my shriek of delight. Though lines of weariness crinkled the corners of his eyes, he looked quite well. Clean shaven. Hair wet-combed. Ready for the bright lights of Moghrabi Square. Yes, he'd been with the Pickets in Jerusalem on Thursday night and yes, it was messy, but he'd managed fine and he didn't want to talk about it further. He seemed a touch quiet, but that didn't alarm me for sometimes he needed time to switch from the tensions of active duty to the simple pleasures of ordinary life. So trotting at his side, I filled the vacuum with my own little adventures. I chattered about the speech at the theatre, the street procession to the exhibition grounds, the suffocating ride back on the overcrowded bus. Malka moaning about her blisters for the next two days. And, since he still remained quiet, I nattered some more. About Malka's fury of activity on the Hollingsworth gown. She had to make up for lost time, for the king's birthday ball was fast approaching. Dizzy with joy to be with Duncan again, it took me a while to notice something was wrong. His silence cut deeper than usual. His mind was elsewhere.

"What's the matter?"

"Nothing's the matter."

"You haven't been listening to a word I said."

"I've heard every word. What would you like to drink? Just lemonade? Nothing stronger? All right then."

We stood with a cluster of people before the *gazoz* kiosk, watching the man wheel from one task to the next. He rinsed glasses, wiped them with a rag, poured syrup from his bottles, added spritzer, handed glasses to customers, and snatched up the payment coins, all done in what seemed like one fluid motion. Our turn came. We took our drinks to the wide pyramid steps of the Moghrabi Theatre on which perched a flock of Saturday night revellers eating, drinking, smoking, chatting. With a deft movement of his own, Duncan poured out some of his lemonade and replaced it with contents of his hip flask. He took a gulp.

And then, verbatim, he recited the oath of resistance I'd sworn on Thursday morning, with all those others in the Moghrabi Theatre. *For Zion's sake, I will not hold my peace* . . . He knew it by heart, though in my chatter I'd not mentioned the oath except in the most general way. His voice was flat, neutral, but I could feel the accusations underneath. What had made me think that I could swear to struggle against the British masters and that everything would be the same with Duncan? It wasn't logical, but I couldn't accept any other possibility.

"The protest isn't against Britain. It's against the new policy."

He looked down at me, his jaw tight.

"We're just exercising our democratic rights," I pleaded.

"What about the abuse of those rights?"

"What happened in Jerusalem was awful. No one condones it. Not our real leaders, nor the vast majority of the community."

I spoke quickly, repeating phrases from the editorial from *The Palestine Post* about the unruly elements amid the protesters, their inexcusable rowdiness, the deplorable incidents.

Duncan didn't answer right away. He finished his drink without a word. When I finished mine, he took our glasses back to the kiosk. He seemed in no mood for all those young people around us, chirping away like intoxicated starlings. I suggested a walk to the sea. As we walked he finally broke his silence.

"A mob is an abomination. No difference between an Arab or a Jewish mob. Bunch of wild hyenas."

I reached for his hand but both were thrust deep into his pockets.

"What was it like? For you. Tell me."

He lengthened his stride just a bit as he began to talk, forcing me to trot faster.

"It was just what you'd expect for the first few hours. Mass of people in Zion Square. Blokes with bullhorns stirring up the crowd. The usual slogans. 'No capitulation. Free immigration.' You know the drill. You've done it yourself."

He turned his head sideways to look at me, but it was too dark on this stretch of the road for me to see his expression.

"We had orders to stand firm across Jaffa Road. Not to let anyone get past to the District Commissioner's office and other government buildings. Whenever a few hotshots tried, we pushed them back. The bullhorn blokes should have told their people to disperse once they'd made their point, but no, they let the crowd hang about. They encouraged the lingering and the milling. People get restless and rowdy when they've got nothing better to do. I was in the front row of the cordon, so I had a good view."

"The front row. Oh Duncan!"

"Well, where do you think I'd be? The Pickets are always up front. Anyway, when they'd tired of singing their patriotic songs, the taunts started. And, by the way, it wasn't just nasty boys yelling in our faces. You should see the women go at it. Screaming their bloody heads off. Calling us Nazis. But we're trained to let insults roll off our backs. Yeah, but then the shoving started. That we don't tolerate. Captain issued an ultimatum, and when the crowd kept testing us, we conducted a baton charge. Knocked a few heads that needed knocking. That should have been the end of it, but wasn't. The more reasonable folk took their placards and went home but the worst elements stayed. Stones flew. Shop windows shattered. Placard poles used as weapons. We charged again and again. By that time night had fallen. Some of the rowdies smashed the streetlamps so that the whole downtown area was dark as hell. We could have scattered the herd if we'd used live fire, but we don't do that. Not unless it's the last resort. *We* were the target, but *we* held back."

Duncan and I had arrived at the end of Allenby Road. A low concrete wall stretched along the promenade between the roadside and the beach and we sat on that. Our legs dangling down towards the sand, we stared out at the dark, murmuring waves.

"Maybe I shouldn't have begged you to come back to Jaffa. I wouldn't have if I'd known what it would be like for you with the Inlying Pickets."

Duncan gave a short bark of laughter. He patted my knee.

"You're not entirely to blame for my postings, my dear. Anyway, I like the Pickets. Very fine crew. Brave lads. Two of them are in hospital because of the riot. Luckily they're not too bad. At least they didn't take any bullets."

His hip flask was out again. He tipped his head back to drink.

"Oh Duncan! How awful . . . that there was shooting."

"Yes," he spat. "A fine young constable killed. We held fire, but not them. Not the hooligans. Sticks and stones is one thing. But live fire! No concern for human life, those yobs. None whatsoever."

I hesitated, knowing I was treading into delicate territory, but his account was so different from what I'd read in the *Post* that I had to voice my doubts.

"More than a hundred-and-twenty Jews were injured, some quite badly . . . so . . ."

"So what?"

"So maybe the police weren't all that restrained. And then the police did shoot, didn't they? At some point they fired bullets."

"Yeah? Were you there, Miss? Were you an eyewitness?"

This said through gritted teeth.

"Duncan, I'm not blaming the police if . . . if things got so out of hand. There was confusion, it was dark, it's understandable you'd have to try . . . and I suppose it would be justifiable for the sake of regaining control, and yet it's so awful . . ."

My voice trailed off.

"A good copper shot down in cold blood," he hissed. "Five others badly hurt. While doing their duty protecting life and property. Shot by vermin who bring pistols to their protest. The cowardly brutes. And then the Jewish community cries police brutality. That's too rich."

"Was it certain that the shots came from the crowd?" I whispered. I knew the question would incense Duncan more, but I had to ask, had to plead for the benefit of the doubt.

"The bullets that hit our lads came from a Mauser pistol. A German Mauser. Understand? We don't use 'em. We use British weapons. And even after being provoked the way we were, we didn't fire back. We tried to minimize loss of life. Precious little of that story got written up in the Jewish press."

"I'm sorry about those men . . . your comrades." I touched Duncan's arm but he remained aloof, his hands balled into fists. We looked away from one another to gaze at the neutral sea. The moon had risen. It drew a milky path across the waves and bathed us in its soft illumination. At some distance north on the beach, someone had lit a bonfire and the sob of a harmonica drifted towards us on the balmy air.

"Did you know the constable who was killed?" I finally asked.

"Nope. Not personally. Doesn't matter. We're all brothers. Those leaders you think are so noble. They're the ones whipping up the populace, turning people against their government."

"But they called for peaceful protest. And it was almost all peaceful. There were masses and masses of people on the streets all over the country and no provocations except for . . ."

"Except for the attack on the District Office here in Tel Aviv on Wednesday night, the smashing up of the Land Registry bureau in Jerusalem, and yesterday's mayhem in Zion Circus."

Duncan counted off the three incidents on his fingers and his lip curled in a bitter smile. I saw the gleam of his teeth beneath his moustache. "Not bad for three days work, I'd say."

A cold dread filled my heart. I felt I knew exactly what we were going to say to one another next—word for word—as if there was a script we had to follow and there was no going backward or forward. We were stuck with these hurtful, inadequate lines.

"Duncan, there's been so much violence from the Arab side. Three years of knifings, shootings, bombings, vandalism, against us, against the British. The Jews have acted with restraint." My voice rose as I saw he was about to interrupt. "Yesterday shouldn't have happened. But why can't you see it as set against the background of Arab terror and this new policy on immigration that is . . . that is . . . a knife in the heart of the Jewish homeland?"

"Ha! That's exactly the kind of language I'm talking about when I talk about whipping up the crowds. *A knife in the heart of the homeland.* That's taking the most extreme view of the new policy."

"But there's no other way to take the policy. It's disaster for us."

"And, of course, that justifies riots. That justifies a bullet in the brains of a constable."

"No. You're twisting my words."

We stared at one another for a moment. I think we were both appalled at what we were doing. But Duncan wasn't ready to let go. All this time that we'd been talking, Duncan hadn't touched me once. I reached for his hand again, but he'd started to dig savagely with his thumb at a pebble lodged in the wall. Pick, pick, pick, until he pried it loose and clenched it in his fist. He was more upset than I'd ever seen him. I wanted to make it good between us. All I could think of was to ask again about the fallen comrade. Constable Lawrence. Harold Lawrence. The name came back to me.

"Poor blighter. Twenty-one years old. New recruit. Just finished his training at the depot. He was a good batsman, Harry was. They had high hopes for him on the district cricket team."

"I thought you didn't know him?"

"Didn't. But stories go around in the canteen after these things happen."

Duncan flung the stone he was clutching into darkness below the wall.

"They say that directly after training, he went out on a tear in the Old City of Jerusalem. Spent a few nights in lock-up for drunk and disorderly. On duty though he was rock solid. He faced that crowd unflinching. The best sort of chap. Now gone. Like that."

Duncan snapped his fingers.

"Oh Duncan, I'm so sorry, so terribly sorry. I wasn't there in Zion Square. I wish I had been. I wish I'd been next to the man with the Mauser pistol for I would have thrown myself against him. I would have tried to wrestle the gun away."

Duncan turned quickly, grabbed me by the wrists, stared at me fiercely. The dark sheen of his eyes came through in the moonlight. The thrust of his jaw.

"You'd do no such thing. You'd get the hell out of there if you're in a crowd where someone has a pistol. Better still, don't ever get into such a crowd. A little thing like you could get trampled in no time. Do you hear? Do you understand me, Miss Salomon? You better, or I'll turn you over my knee and whack your bottom good."

His face remained tense and angry, for several moments, and then we both erupted into crazy laughter. I pressed my face against his chest. He held me tight and nuzzled his face in my hair. We rocked together for a while as the sea sang its soothing song against the shore. He hadn't wanted to talk about the protests and he was right. Why had I started us along that path? I should have realized that what he'd lived through Thursday night was still too raw. I should have changed the subject. *I'll know better next time,* I pledged to him silently, in my heart. And then we were walking hand in hand over the moonlit sand, moving with a brisk urgency, searching for a secluded spot amid the dunes.

Chapter 14
Strange Letter

THE *KHAMSIN* ENDED. The skies shook off their film of dust and the naked Middle Eastern summer took hold. By seven in the morning the sun was already hard at work, beating down on heads, sucking sweat from pores, stupefying donkeys, and exciting flies. I continued to clean houses, but in between, I rushed through the baking streets, ran up long staircases, knocked on doors in search of that elusive piece of paradise—an office job. In the evening, at Malka's kitchen table, I practised on my paper Qwerty keyboard, trying to hang onto the little bit of skill I'd gained in Miss Blatt's secretarial course.

"Don't give up, Thumbelina," Duncan said. "Someone's bound to recognize your talents. All you need is one person to say yes."

But the government wasn't hiring and businesses hung in limbo. Three years of unrest had taken a toll on the economy and now this other dark cloud loomed on the horizon: threat of war. All that summer Britain and Germany did the dance of building alliances. Britain wooed Russia, but halfheartedly, dragging out the process, like a man forced to consider an ugly wife because of her money. Meanwhile Hitler bellowed warnings against being encircled by enemies and signed his pact with Mussolini.

"Britain must deal a quick, decisive blow," Mirsky pronounced from the window of his newspaper kiosk to anyone who would listen. "Stamp the Nazi snake into the dust." He ground the heel of his right hand into the palm of his left to demonstrate.

Pinsker waggled his head, expressing doubt. If only it were that easy. Once the dogs of war were unleashed, who knew what they would tear asunder and how they could be kennelled again? Which was why Chamberlain had to exercise caution. Back and forth the street-corner philosophers debated the possibility of war, their talk edged with excitement and dread.

All that summer too, resistance continued against the White Paper. More declarations, demonstrations, oaths, and pleas. Behind the scenes, the underground militia—the Haganah—stepped up its smuggling of refugees, leasing any boat that would float. Rickety freighters, crammed to bursting with their desperate human cargo, crept up to the Palestine shoreline in the dead of night. Some managed to disembark their passengers without detection. Some were caught by the Marine Patrol and refused entry, or towed to Haifa port for legal proceedings against the captain and the processing of passengers. Every refugee admitted meant one deducted from the quota.

Early one morning, a distressed vessel on the verge of breaking apart limped towards Tel Aviv and received permission from the British authorities to weigh anchor forty yards from the central beach. Everyone had heard about the travails of the SS *Marianna*—sixty-eight days at sea, shunted from one port to another, six hundred passengers stuffed into a hold barely big enough for half that number. The news of the unusual landing flew through stairwells and streets. It was a rare chance to witness the arrival of one of those "Death Ships" with our own eyes. To welcome those poor souls. To search for a familiar face—a relative, an acquaintance from "back there," the town we'd left behind.

Since I wasn't due at the Mandelmanns for another hour, I flung some oranges and half a loaf of bread into my cloth bag and hurried towards the beach. A large crowd had already gathered on Ha'yarkon Street, held back from descending onto the sand by a line of police and soldiers. Hundreds of others stood on balconies and rooftops, craning their necks for a glimpse of the drama unfolding below. I looked around for Duncan, but he wasn't among the men in the cordon, so I peeked as best I could between jostling bodies. Government lighters were ferrying the passengers from the stranded steamer to the shore. Troops and police stood by to help the arrivals clamber out of the small craft and make their way through the last feet of water. The refugees were bedraggled and dirty. Some shivered violently, despite the strong morning sun. A woman with a small child clutched to her breast staggered through the shallow waves and fell to her knees. A policeman sprang forward to lift her to her feet. He tried to take the child from her arms, but she pushed him away with all her feeble might. So he turned to a woman too weak to offer resistance and supported her to a waiting ambulance. One man was covered with boils: red, pussy eruptions all over his face and neck. I saw a gaunt elderly man pull down his rolled-up trouser legs and adjust his shirt collar before stepping forward onto the shore, with the air of someone mounting a stage and determined to make a good impression. The spectators behind the police cordon cheered. They applauded everyone—all the wretches with small bundles and dripping clothes who plodded towards the line of buses that would take them to the Sarafand army base. The crowd shouted, waved, and flung gifts over the shoulders of the police. The refugees bent down and collected the offerings and some managed a smile and a wave. Some stood still, transfixed, staring back at us. *Where are you sisterbrothermotherfatherchild? Where is my family?* The man with the boils snatched the orange I'd tossed at his feet and, without first peeling it or brushing off the sand, bit savagely into the fruit. Until that moment, I'd cherished the fantasy that auntie and uncle might somehow manage to join one of the clandestine groups sneaking into Palestine. Now I knew for certain it couldn't happen. They would never undertake such a journey and I was glad they wouldn't. For they would never survive. Satisfied, that I'd done something at least, I left my food with the woman next to me to distribute and headed off to work. As I walked down Allenby Road, I heard the crowd singing *Hatikvah*. Later I learned that the refugees had had nothing to eat for days except mouldy biscuits full of maggots.

THE ULTRA-NATIONALIST PARTY, the Revisionists, pursued its own brand of protest that summer. Bombs against Arab and British targets in markets, cafés, and government buildings. The official Jewish leadership protested the "outrages," but the condemnations failed to impress Duncan, and I stopped bringing them to his attention.

"Just as we're making headway with the Arab gangs, the Jewish scum rears its head," he said. "Sure, sure, your rabbis and mucky mucks make all the right noises. Such fine speeches in the Jewish press. No one knows anyone who sympathizes with the terrorists. Course not."

I let him rail. I didn't try to plead mitigating circumstances: misguided youth and the effect of fevered desperation. For, really, what was there to say about an explosion that ripped open the bodies of men, women, and children in a marketplace? About a banner across Allenby Road proclaiming, "Death to traitors"? About a bomb that killed the woman who hosted the Children's Hour on the radio? There were no words, no coherent thoughts, that could contain such actions—just a kind of ritual tongue wagging. And afterwards one went on.

Across the land, the king's birthday was honoured with marching bands, parades, church services, hoisting of flags, and the closure of banks and government offices. To my delight, Malka bought a wireless set with her earnings from the Millicent Hollingsworth ball gown commission. Now she could listen to music and amusing talks as she snipped and stitched, and I could enjoy the offerings of the Palestine Broadcasting System in the evenings. During that season, Duncan and I went to hear a special performance of Beethoven's *Ninth*, with the PBS Orchestra and a local choral society. We sat rapt through the stormy cascades and lyrical passages, the movements building in intensity to the grand finale, the "Ode to Joy," with Schiller's sublime words and Beethoven's immortal music. The blended voice of the choir became the voice of all humanity, flying us to the heavens with the promise of universal brotherhood and the triumph of good over evil. Two days later a series of explosions ripped through the main hall of the General Post Office in Jerusalem, killing a constable and wounding a number of other people, including a high-ranking officer of the police. The Revisionist underground took the credit. The political storms flowed and ebbed and everyone went on, including Duncan and me. Hand in hand along the beach, while the waves hissed onto the sand and the Marine Patrol searchlights raked the dunes beyond the city's northern edge in the relentless hunt for illegals.

ONE EVENING IN late August, coming home from work, I saw a blank, pale blue envelope on the doormat and my heart stuttered. I feared Duncan had written another apologetic letter like the one many months ago that told me of his posting to Lydda. I pushed open the front door, went into the kitchen, sank down on my chair in the corner. I extracted a thick packet of folded pages and exhaled a sigh of relief. The letter was not from Duncan, nor could it be for me. The writing was all in Hebrew in a neat, dense, pencilled print on lined paper that seemed torn out of a copy book.

"This must be for you," I said, holding the envelope with its re-stuffed pages in front of Malka's face. "I opened it by mistake. Very sorry."

Her dark eyebrows arched in surprise. She put down her pinking shears, took a couple of pins out of her mouth, and stabbed them into the pin cushion on the cutting table. I was on my way out of the room when I heard her make a loud noise of disgust.

"*Pfui*! What *drek*! Have you read this? No? Of course not. You still don't read Hebrew, little *Yecke*. Well, in this case you're not missing much. Throw it away. Straight into the trash, where it belongs."

She held the letter with the tips of her fingers and waggled it in the air as if it indeed was a piece of stinking refuse. When she finally agreed to read it aloud, she did so in a scornful, melodramatic voice, with jabbing forefinger, a parody of the demagogue. The first few lines gave me the gist.

Victory or death . . . British oppressors . . . craven Jewish leaders . . . noble Jewish youth . . .

A zealot manifesto.

Throughout the summer such missives had appeared—pasted on walls or exploding as "leaflet bombs" through the air in a darkened theatre. You could be watching a film, immersed in the drama on the screen, when a shower of handbills would rain down from the balcony to the main floor. After the lights came on, the flyers underfoot would be kicked aside or picked up and glanced at before being crumpled up in a fist. At best, the ravings on the page would elicit an indulgent shake of the head as if to say, "Poor deluded soul, but I know the torments that drive him."

"Why did this come to our door?" I interrupted, as Malka drew breath. She shrugged, slapped the letter back down on the cutting table.

"Heard enough?"

"But who is it from and who is it for?"

I went over to the table to take another look at the salutation, sounding out the syllables until I had it. The political diatribe was addressed to "The Faithless Harlot." As I said the words aloud a strangled laugh escaped my lips. My face must have been a picture of hurt and confusion, because Malka came around from the other side of the cutting table to give my shoulder a squeeze.

"I told you. Filth. I'm going to tear it into little pieces and flush them down the toilet."

"No. Read it to me again. Slowly this time. The whole thing."

Read in a normal voice, without mockery, the words had a passionate, almost persuasive logic. It began with an explanation of first principles. The land of Israel belonged to the People of Israel—solely and absolutely—by virtue of our historic ties to the soil, our two thousand years of longing for the Return, and our indisputable right of nationhood. Here and here alone could the People defy persecution and once again become a great nation. Britain was an alien presence. She had driven out the Turks, not for our sake but for her own imperial interests and now was playing a double-dealing game, pretending to be our protectors but secretly encouraging the Arab atrocities. Worse still was the dastardly immigration quota, designed to keep us a weak minority in our own land. But the strategy would fail. Israel had conquered by the sword in the past and would do so again. The Arabs, like the Canaanites of old, would be subdued. The British, a corrupt, foreign, imperial presence, like the Romans, must be resisted and expelled. How could a small people prevail against a world power, the writer rhetorically asked. Through unity of will and purity of purpose. Through heroic deeds and selfless acts. The great power was solid only on the surface. Underneath was frailty, lack of cohesion, and the moral collapse of a tired, overreaching empire. Against this rotten corpse the People of Israel had only to be fearless and steadfast. Every man, woman, and child had a role to play. The People of Israel could afford no traitors, doubters, turncoats, collaborators or shameless fornicators with the enemy.

And now, in the last few lines, the author came to the point. The style became more lurid.

> Oh woe the Daughter of Israel who spreads her legs for the foreign ruler. Cursed be the harlot who succours the enemy. She is, as the prophet warns, a wild ass that snuffeth up the wind in her desire. And

though she might sneak about in the dark with Albion's henchman, she cannot hide her faithless deeds. The avengers of Israel are watching.

The letter bore no signature.

In the silence, after Malka's reading, I sat on the edge of the sofa staring at my feet in stupefaction.

"All right, you've heard it. Now forget it. Burn this trash. It's the ravings of some madman. There are cranks and crackpots in this town, like everywhere else. Maybe more than anywhere else. There are lost and broken souls. You see them wandering around the bus depot muttering to themselves, plucking at their own sleeves, begging for coins. And some of these lunatics can write Hebrew and quote scripture and put their ravings down on paper. So what?"

Malka sat down beside me and gave me a shake.

"But how would someone like that know about me and Duncan?"

Phrases from the letter hissed about in my head. *Wild ass. Albion's henchman.*

Malka flung up her hands.

"You don't keep it a secret, do you? So people know! Tel Aviv is a city but also a village. People talk. I don't mean you're the subject of eager gossip. Don't flatter yourself. Still, a neighbour might make a casual remark. Maybe some screwball has put two and two together. Don't make yourself sick over this stupidity."

Malka didn't dispute that the letter was meant for me. All these months, I'd assumed my neighbours had been neutral about Duncan, minding their own business, not giving us a second glance. We were just part of the landscape, I'd thought. *Casual remarks!* Maybe Malka indulged in them herself. And somewhere nearby was the raging soul who'd penned this poisoned letter. Perhaps he'd been following me around. Peering at me from alleys. *The avengers of Israel are watching.* The letter was a lucid diatribe, despite the overblown language. The author didn't sound like a lunatic beggar, but rather like one of those fervent youths from the Revisionist movement—the ones in brown shirts, who marched around with a flag that showed a closed fist clutching a rifle. I imagined him as intelligent and earnest, with round spectacles over burning eyes. And he'd have allies—a whole gang of eager avengers.

"Should I show it to Duncan?" I said, more to myself than to Malka, but she made a face, as if she'd swallowed something sour, and rose briskly to return to her work at the cutting table.

"Your choice," she muttered, and I understood it wouldn't be hers. Much as she despised the letter, exhibiting this bit of dirty linen to an outsider went against her deeper principles.

Over the next few days I looked over my shoulder as I trotted off to work or my errands. I studied the faces of the young people wending their way in the morning down Herzl Street to Herzliya Gymnasium. They were fresh, eager, open faces, ordinary adolescents in khaki shorts and white shirts, chattering among themselves, jostling one another, and kicking tin cans with their sandaled feet. Even the quiet loners, absorbed in their own thoughts, seemed far too wholesome to have anything to do with those pages dripping with fanaticism and threats. Discreetly, I studied the Kurdish porters, lounging in a row beside their handcarts, at the bus depot. And the loiterers who poked for cigarette butts in gutters. And the blind, pock-marked beggar, cross-legged on the edge of the road rattling his tin cup. He shouted verses from the prophets at passersby in melodious, Yemenite-accented Hebrew. He might have been acquainted with the line about the wild ass that snuffeth up the wind. But was such a wretch capable of putting pen to paper? As for the porters, the loiterers, and the odd prostitute, blinking and dazed in the morning sunlight—surely they were all illiterate.

I didn't destroy the letter, as Malka suggested, but I didn't mention it again, not to her, nor to anyone else. The blue envelope lay in the inside pocket of my suitcase, while its message burrowed down into the recesses of my thoughts. I would find my heart beating unaccountably fast as I bent over the sink full of breakfast dishes at *Frau* Kleiner's Pension. A movement behind me would cause me to start and the plate to slide from my fingers back into the basin of soapy water. What was troubling me, I would ask myself. And then I would remember. Oh! That. Every evening, when I climbed to the top of the stairs to our flat, my eyes anticipated a second letter on the doormat. But none arrived.

Because of his heavy schedule, it was another two weeks before Duncan was able to come by. Happily, Malka was out with her own boyfriend. I threw myself into Duncan's arms with something more than my usual joy, aching for his touch. Yet as he slipped my blouse off my shoulders and pressed his lips to my neck, a numbness overcame me and my craving for intimacy vanished. I felt strangely empty and absent. Not wanting to disappoint him, I feigned pleasure while giving him his. Afterwards, we tugged on our clothes again in case of Malka's early return, and snuggled up on the sofa in the dark, smoking, listening to big band music on the wireless. Duncan launched into a story about a drunken soldier found buff naked one night, roaring out dirty songs on a rooftop in Jaffa. When I didn't laugh at the right places, he unwrapped his arm from around my shoulder to touch his forehead against mine.

"What's wrong?"

"Nothing."

"Come on. Something's up. Am I boring you, Thumbelina?"

"You never bore me."

That was true. Even when he talked about the latest match between the army and the police cricket teams, he made me happy just by the sound of his voice—animated, engaged, but always with a touch of that English self-mockery.

"Come on. Out with it," he said, his lips close to my face. "You weren't yourself before. Shall we . . . ? Is there something I can do?"

"No. That doesn't matter. That's not it."

With some reluctance I told him of the letter, summarizing the contents in general terms, and leaving out the nastier bits. Even just telling this much brought an intrusive presence into the room and made me feel sullied. I was glad of the darkness. Like the clever policeman he was, Duncan probed, gently, relentlessly, until he had it all—the threats, the reference to the "faithless harlot." I felt him stiffen beside me and go quiet.

"Damn vermin," he growled.

"I shouldn't have let it bother me. It's just a silly prank."

"Of course you're upset, darling. What a low, cowardly, underhanded business! If someone has a bone to pick with the police, all right, let him step forward and do his worst. But to bully you under the guise of championing the Jewish people—it's the action of a rat. "

"Just some schoolboy mischief," I whispered and groped for his hand.

"A schoolboy who needs a flogging. I'd like to whip his arse myself 'til it bleeds. You've still got the letter? Let's have a look. Never mind that it's in Hebrew. Let me see with my own eyes."

He leaned across to the cutting table and switched on the goose-necked lamp. I held my hand over my eyes against the glare. Instantly the room became that cluttered, utilitarian place with the headless dressmaker's dummy, the sewing machine, and the piles of cloth. With some reluctance I fished out the blue envelope from the suitcase that served as my catch-all drawer beneath the sofa. Duncan studied the pages intently, turning them over, rubbing the paper between his fingers, noting the sharpness of the pencil, even bringing the envelope to his nose for a sniff, his anger transformed into keen professional interest. Duncan had even less Hebrew than I did so he asked me to read whatever parts I could. I tried to adopt the mocking tone that Malka had used. Duncan sat attentive, his arms crossed over his chest.

"Standard fare from Jabotinsky's followers," he said when I was done. "But usually it's not so personal and usually they've got bigger fish to fry than a harmless girl like you. My guess is that the cockroach who wrote this is an outlier, someone who wants to be part of the gang but hasn't quite made the grade. I'll tell my mates in Tel Aviv station to keep a watch on the neighbourhood. I'll be on the lookout too. And I'll take the letter for our men in forensics. They probably can't trace the origins, but it might be useful to keep on file. If you get another one of these you must tell me right away. Keep your eyes open when you're out and about. Close the shutters in the evening. Just a precaution my love. Don't you worry. Mr. Lowlife is a coward through and through. He won't come out of the shadows. Gets his jollies by sneaking up and scurrying away."

Duncan deposited the letter in his trousers' pocket, pulled me to my feet and proposed we go out to a café, enjoy the city lights. He was right. I needed distraction—laughter, music, the chatter of a happy Saturday night crowd. I went to the bathroom to freshen up, already relieved that the letter was no longer in my possession. On my return to the room, I found Duncan standing before the sofa, strangely still, his lower lip thrust out, as happened when he was particularly peeved. I started to tell him to take his own advice and put the unpleasant letter out of his mind, when he lifted up a forefinger to silence me. He was listening to the radio. The late evening news had come on. I heard something about Russia and a pact and profound disappointment at 10 Downing Street.

"What's it about?" I asked.

"Stalin's double-crossed us. Signed a non-aggression pact with Germany behind our backs. All these months he's been leading us on, pretending he wants to become our ally. Now, without a word of warning, he's switched sides. Who would have thought . . . Stalin and Hitler in bed together?"

I pressed my knuckles to my face. I could not take this in. *What now?*

"Never mind. If that's the stuff those Bolshies are made of, we're better off without them. They can go to the devil. Ha! They *have* gone to the devil."

Duncan came close and took my hands in his.

"Now don't let that nonsense spoil our Saturday fun. Chin up, darling. England will manage. We'll put Mr. Bully-man Hitler in his place and we'll do it on our own if we have to."

He smiled down into my face, drew me into the steady blue lighthouse beam of his eyes. This was real—his muscled arms and solid chest and the sunburned stick-out ears, that stuck out more than usual because he'd just had a haircut. This was what mattered—so much more than some lunatic ravings in a letter or dark news on the wireless.

Chapter 15
War Comes

I STOOD THE iron on its heel. I went into the sitting room, where *Frau* Mandelmann waited, her hands gripping the armrests of her upholstered chair, her head cocked towards the side of the room where the wireless sat on the oak buffet.

"Turn it up louder," she croaked, leaning forward. Her cataract-clouded eyes were open wide as could be. I fiddled with the dial to ensure the best possible reception for the special broadcast. A voice entered the room, deep and measured, pained and weary—the Prime Minister of Great Britain, Mr. Neville Chamberlain.

You can imagine what a bitter blow it is to me that all my long struggle to win peace has failed.

He went on, in a painstaking manner, like a defendant reading out his testimony, to explain how the latest diplomatic steps had fallen through. Britain's efforts to make Hitler see reason had met with nothing but wilful belligerence. There was no point any more in expecting this man to give up on the use of force to impose his will. As if any of this needed saying. Only at the end did the Prime Minister's weariness lift a little and firmness enter his voice.

And now that we have resolved to finish it, I know that you will all play your part with calmness and courage . . . It is the evil things that we shall be fighting against —brute force, bad faith, injustice, oppression and persecution—and against them I am certain that the right will prevail.

Everyone in the Hebrew city had been expecting such an announcement. Yet the declaration of war felt terrible. So terribly final. As I took in the news, the announcer on Jerusalem Calling promised a special broadcast by the King later in the evening. Then, the Strauss concert, interrupted by Mr. Chamberlain's speech, resumed. Tears streamed down the gullies of *Frau* Mandelmann's face. I brought a fresh handkerchief from the heap on the ironing board and wiped her chin. Her cold, dry hands wrapped themselves around mine as if seeking warmth, despite the thick heat in the room.

"There is no other way. But I'm too old for another war," she sobbed.

In the evening, together with Malka, I listened to the wireless again as the King in Buckingham Palace addressed his subjects throughout the empire. I thought he did better than Mr. Chamberlain, whose laboured explanations could barely veil a deep reluctance and horror. The King's speech had more spirit, and, despite his speaking deficiency, he managed to pull it all off without a single stammer. And yet. Such long pauses between each phrase. Such unvarying modulation. Such mild, gentlemanly words. Screwing up her face with impatience half-way through, Malka stomped off to the balcony for a breath of air. But I remained indoors to hear the entire message. His Majesty warned of dark days ahead. He suggested that war might no longer be confined to the battlefield. He appealed for calm, unity, and readiness for sacrifice. He asserted that "with God's help we shall prevail." And finally he called on God to bless and keep us all, echoing the ancient words of the Aronite benediction.

Switching off the set, I couldn't help thinking of the fierce harangues thundering through loudspeakers into German ears. The electrifying exhortations. The promises of glory, triumph, rebirth, and conquest, delivered at fever pitch with unwavering conviction and greeted by the roars of the masses. Those much-amplified, fire-breathing orations would carry no appeal to a divinity other than the one the people could see and hear and reach out to touch. On that side there were torch-light processions, armoured vehicles, marching phalanxes. No need for prayers to the great Non-presence on high.

DUNCAN HEARD THE same speech that I did, but its effect on him was very different. On September 3, he and his mates at Ajami billet had gathered around the wireless in the mess hall. They were joined by the officers of the station, who descended from their dining quarters on the second floor, where they normally took their meals apart from the rank and file. For this special occasion, in a show of unity, they came to stand with their men. Everyone was on his feet, not exactly at attention, but attentive, silent, taking in the words of His Majesty. At the end, the entire station broke out into a spontaneous rendition of "God Save the King." Duncan told me the story as we sat together on a bench on Rothschild Boulevard. While he spoke, his shoulders straightened and his chin lifted as if he were still singing the anthem. The leaves of the young ficus trees rustled in the evening breeze. A scent of jasmine floated in the air, mixed with the salt of the sea and the aroma of roasted coffee from a nearby kiosk. Everything seemed poignant and fragile, though to outward appearances nothing much had changed. I'd been brooding about the state of war, but Duncan exuded confidence and pride. Finally, we were going to give Hitler a drubbing, he said. At last the arch-bully would be laid low. He raised his arm in the Nazi salute and uttered a series of gurgles from the back of his throat and mock German phrases.

"Uber Alles Kaka-Meister Sieg Heil der Fatter-land."

He succeeded in making me laugh.

"A bully soon wilts when you stand up to him. Hitler's ninety-nine per cent hot air."

Duncan expounded on Britain's strengths: her superior navy, army, air force, leadership and imperial resources and riches, and, most important, the quiet courage of the British race. Plus, the war would be good for Palestine, Duncan argued. Yes, there might be some economic consequences in the short term, but these would be soon overshadowed by a new spirit of cooperation. The petty quarrels between Arab and Jew would vanish in the face of the greater cause. Signs of this new unity were already manifest with the Jewish Agency's promise to support Britain and a similar declaration by the Emir of Jordan.

"What about the Mufti?" I said.

Haj Amin Al-Husseini, the Grand Mufti of Jerusalem, had gone into exile and aligned himself with the enemies of Britain and the *Yishuv*.

"What about him?" Duncan scoffed. "A spent force. All bombast and Oriental deviousness. He's in Berlin. Lovey-dovey with Hitler. So what? He'll never return to this country. He'll have no more influence here. The Arab revolt is finished."

Duncan gave my cheek a playful poke with his knuckle, a "chin up" gesture, to brush away my cloud of doubt. Though I thought him overly optimistic, he swayed me into a muted echo of his enthusiasm for the war. He looked so fine when fired up. Yes, perhaps a nation of Duncans could hold their own against Hitler.

NOT MUCH HAPPENED those first weeks of September. The newspapers told of a few naval skirmishes in the Atlantic, daring raids by the Royal Air Force on German war vessels in the North Sea and the brave stand of the Polish army against the German aggressor. Then the Russians threw in their oar and Poland was crushed, divided up like a tasty pie between the victors. People with relatives stuck in that defeated country spoke of their fate in bleak whispers. Still, the war was more than two thousand miles away. I tried to picture the ships doing battle on the grey Atlantic, but the heat and brilliance of the Levantine sun made it hard to imagine anything else.

On a balmy Saturday evening, Duncan and I sat on the sidewalk patio of Café Sapir ready to dig into a magnificent dish of ice cream. He'd ordered a special treat, three giant scoops—vanilla, chocolate, and almond flavour—for us to share. I loved ice cream and the Sapir's was the best in town. The place was busier than ever with the usual crowd of hedonistic Tel Avivans, along with a party of newly enlisted British soldiers in uniform, being feted by their friends. The khaki cloth of their military tunics still looked stiff and untested. Duncan kept cranking his head around to smile at the group and add a jovial word. He vaguely knew a couple of the enlisted men. They'd left their mundane civil service jobs to answer the higher call, he told me.

"I'll be joining them soon," he said.

"You'll what?"

"I'm enlisting. Don't look so thunderstruck. I couldn't possibly stand by when my country needs me. We've all got to do our bit."

"But you *are* doing your bit. You're serving in the Palestine Police."

"That's yesterday's work. Today the need is for fighting men in Europe."

There'd been talk of nothing else at Ajami billet. A number of the lads were ex-regulars from the British Army and officially still in the reserves. Naturally, they wanted to get back to their regiments where they could contribute directly to the war effort and see action against a real enemy. Duncan's eyes lit up and he crossed his arms over his chest as if trying to contain the emotion that fizzed beneath his breastbone.

I laid my spoon down against the side of the dish we were sharing. I tried to keep the distress out of my voice.

"You always tell me the Force is stretched so thin."

"Pah! The Arab troubles are in hand. The Palestinian side of the Force can take over directing traffic and catching thieves. Every Briton should be free to follow his conscience."

It wasn't just his mates who were signing up for the war effort. His older brother Paul had been accepted into the R.A.F. His dad would be in the Home Guard. Even his mother would make a contribution by taking a job on the Slough Trading Estate, much of which would soon be converted to war industries.

"Fancy that! Mum making machine guns!" Duncan chuckled. "And Dad letting her. Maybe for once he had nothing to say in the matter."

He talked about the enlistment line at the newly opened army bureau, the forms, and medical tests. Because of his police training, he'd have an advantage over the men coming in from civilian life. A ship in Haifa port was already being hastily converted into a troop carrier to take the recruits from Palestine to bases in England, and, after they'd been whipped into soldierly shape, off to the front, wherever that might be. A tightness gripped my heart as I realized how much he'd already thought all this through. But Duncan was oblivious, talking, talking. Perhaps he misread my numb bewilderment for rapt attention. In between sentences, he urged me to eat my side of the hill of ice cream, though he neglected his own, so intent he was on telling me everything. I tried to fathom what made him not merely willing to enlist, but eager. He'd been disappointed with himself for not doing better in the Arabic exam and vexed he'd been passed up for promotion. Also, his stint with the Inlying Pickets was over, for that unit had been reduced in size, and he was back on regular beats in Jaffa, a sign that his career was stalled. None of which mattered now. Only country mattered. Standing up to the bully with all of Britain and its empire. Here was a cause that would give him heart, just as it would hack a piece out of mine.

"And what about us?"

I tried to give the question a coquettish lilt. I tried to be that grand, sophisticated lady who'd made such an impression on me many years ago in the Breslau railway station. I was anything but.

"Oh Eva, don't be sad."

He leaned across the table and took my hand. His eyes softened with tenderness.

"We'll be all right, Thumbelina. The war won't last forever. Maybe a year. Two at the most."

"That *is* forever!"

He gripped my hand harder and smiled. I hated him then. I could have flung the dish with the puddle of ice cream in his face.

"You don't care about us at all. You're just looking for an excuse to be rid of me."

He let go of my hand. Leaned back in his chair.

"Now darling. That's not fair. You know I do care about you, very, very much. I would have thought you of all people would understand that Britain must win this war. And we *will* win. I have absolutely no doubt. It means though that personal considerations have to be put aside. Our own futures are on hold."

"There must be thousands of men all over the world dumping their girlfriends with just those words."

He gazed beyond my shoulder, ran the tip of his tongue along the edge of his moustache, quiet and thoughtful. Perhaps a bit distressed? Good! He *should* feel distress.

"There are enlisted chaps rushing to the altar before they're sent off to battle," he mused. "Settles things, I guess. And if something happens, at least the wife gets a pension."

He brought his gaze back to me, his eyes holding the reluctant question. I could have got him to pose it. He would have. It would have been part of "duty" and "sacrifice" and "putting personal considerations aside."

"How romantic," I sneered. "You think I'd marry under such circumstances? I'd be thinking the whole time I'd jinxed my husband and he'd be sure to die. A widow's pension!" I was almost shouting now. "The idea makes me sick."

He sighed like a man who'd escaped the axe. The moment of the question passed. It was understood we'd carry on as before in the hazy realm where it wasn't necessary to "settle things" and where dilemmas such as whose rites to marry under didn't exist. He dipped his spoon in the melted ice cream and brought it to my lips.

"Won't you have a little more, darling? I left the almond for you. Your favourite."

I turned my face away.

"Doesn't taste the same when it's left standing so long. Gone to soup."

"Then I'll buy you another."

"Don't waste your money."

We looked beyond one another in awkward silence for a moment. The soldiers at the next table broke out in hearty, masculine laughter. A pack of boys eating sunflower seeds and shouting at the tops of their voices sauntered by. A young peddler selling flowers waved his wares under the noses of patrons at the café across the street. My thoughts were a-boil. Duncan wanted me to be plucky. I would oblige.

"I might volunteer too," I said. "The Jewish Agency is calling on people to sign up for national service."

"There's the spirit! But you know . . ."

He put his hands behind his head, touched his tongue to the bristles of his moustache again, working out some equation in his mind.

"Now's the time for you to go back to those government offices that shut their doors in your face. With so many men enlisting, there'll be vacancies all over the place. You'll have your pick of jobs, Eva. This is your chance to put the drudgery of manual work behind you forever."

Duncan could only see the war in a positive light. He spoke again of his mother, who'd been itching to get a job for years and now finally had her chance. And Paul in the R.A.F., the lucky dog. What a lovely bunch of opportunities this war with Germany presented. I flung my spoon down on the table.

"You talk as if it's all a big lark. Like a football match. Soldiers get killed. They get maimed. Oh Duncan! It could happen to you."

For an instant, I thought I saw a ghost of doubt in his eyes—the look of a boy who's about to plunge off a diving board and taken a nervous glance downwards. I'd seen glimpses of this child in Duncan before, torn between excitement and fear. Nothing tugged at my heartstrings more than these lapses he'd be horrified to admit. After a fraction of a second he became his grown up self again, confident, calm, resolved.

"Dear, silly goose. Don't worry. I've told you before, they teach us how to take care of ourselves in the Palestine Police. I expect it will be the same in the army."

A FEW WEEKS later, the tables turned, with me relieved and Duncan disconsolate, me trying to soothe and Duncan choking back bitterness. The Palestine Police would not release him from the three-year contract he'd signed. Not him, nor hardly any of his mates. In fact, contracts were to be automatically renewed. It turned out that half the British Section of the Force consisted of former soldiers and if they were to rejoin their old regiments *en masse*, as they seemed bent on doing, the Inspector General would lose half of his best men. The IG would be left with a police force in which the locals—the Palestinian Arabs and Jews—outnumbered the British, and that wouldn't do at all. So Headquarters issued an order that blocked the men from leaving—all but a few lucky sods who'd managed to move faster than the IG and were already on trains or ships travelling away from the country. Duncan and his mates felt hugely wronged. Stuck in Palestine—once a place of high adventure to them, but now a backwater—thousands of miles from the main action. They would miss out on the biggest drama of their lifetime.

Duncan spoke of his disappointment as we once again sat across from one another at a glass-topped table at the Sapir. He'd brought along a flask of Scotch, from which he poured a generous stream into his coffee cup, while fixing the waiter with a hard stare. The man didn't object. He knew very well that Duncan was a copper.

"Doesn't make sense to keep us from our duty. We're fighting men."

"But you're needed here, Duncan," I argued. "There's important work here in Palestine."

"There's nothing left to do in this back of beyond but hunt for smuggled hashish stuck up donkeys' arses. We've broken the Arab gangs."

"But isn't that a good thing?"

He shrugged. Clearly, quelling the Arab unrest was yesterday's accomplishment.

"Aren't you just a little glad that we won't be separated, Duncan?"

He seemed taken aback at the question, looked over at me strangely as if he hadn't been fully aware of my presence until this moment. Embarrassment flooded his face. But he quickly recovered to give me a smile, half-tender, half-apologetic and sad.

"That's the only thing I am glad about, my lovely Thumbelina. You're the silver lining in this black cloud. But I'm browned off just the same at the dirty trick the brass pulled. I wouldn't be straight with you if I said otherwise. Paul in the R.A.F. and me breaking up petty argy-bargies and handing out fines in the souks of Jaffa."

He had picked up a cigarette butt from the ashtray as he spoke. He was squashing it to bits between his fingers, scattering shreds of blackened tobacco over his side of the table and onto his lap, oblivious of the mess.

"Let's get out of here, Duncan," I murmured. "Let's go somewhere we can be alone."

He nodded and paid the bill. In near silence we walked down to the seashore, along the hard-packed sand at the water's edge, away from the city lights to our spot in the dunes. He fell upon me with his usual, worshipful passion. Everything will be all right, I told myself. His discontent will pass. The main thing: he won't go to war. As I lay on my back in the cool sand, staring up at the distant stars and feeling Duncan's heartbeat thud to a slower pace against my chest, my relief soured. Doubt returned. I was his silver lining, he'd said. A consolation prize of sorts. Was that enough for him? Was it for me?

Chapter 16
War Years

Tel Aviv, March 9, 1940
Dear Liesel,

This last while has been a time of both triumph and misery for me. I'll start with the good news.

My months of knocking on doors finally yielded fruit in the form of employment in the parcel inspection division of the main post office on Herzl Street. There didn't use to be such thorough searches, which goes to show Duncan was right when he predicted the war would create job opportunities. Poor Mrs. Mandelmann dissolved into tears when I told her, which choked me up as well, but, still, I wasn't sorry to be leaving. Goodbye ozeret aprons. Goodbye schmatte on my head. Good riddance to washboards, carpet beaters, dishpan hands. Hello to regular work hours with long midday breaks and time off both Saturday afternoon and all of Sunday. I had to go through quite the stringent interview to determine that I'm loyal to His Majesty's government in Palestine and have no subversive skeletons in my closet. The character reference from Duncan, plus my good English, along with my ability to make a proper pot of British tea, gave me a leg up over other applicants. My new duties include opening parcels for the inspectors who search for suspicious materials, filling out forms, typing up answers to queries, and explaining the complicated regulations over the telephone to harried businessmen, who just want to get the widgets they've imported into the shops. Oh yes, and making that nice pot of tea for the chief in time for "Elevenses." (The tea served in Tel Aviv cafés—in a glass, with a slice of lemon, instead of in a cup, with milk and sugar—causes the Brits of Palestine no end of anguish.) I'm busy from the moment I walk in the door, until I leave, which is good, for it takes my mind off sorrows of the heart—during the daytime at least.

Duncan and I have had a falling out. Things were already a bit shaky between us because of a restlessness that's come over him since the start of the war. And then, feeling I needed to see him without delay, I decided to pay him a surprise visit at his station in Jaffa. I knew he'd be there because he'd been assigned to indoor duties that week. Since I'd be walking through Arab areas, I took pains to look modest and inconspicuous, wearing my raincoat, shawl and flat shoes. To be honest, I felt nervous at first, but all was fine as I made my way with my head down past the smoky cafés and bustling market stalls. No one paid me much attention. Being a "wee thing" (Duncan's words) has its advantages and I blended with the droves of schoolchildren, long-robed women and men, the occasional nun and other holy folks and the donkeys, camels and goats squeezing through the alleys. At last I arrived at the central square of Jaffa with the clock tower and the thick-walled stone building I knew to be the police station and prison. The Union Jack floated above the high, arched doorway. Two police constables stood guard and searched any men who wanted to enter, but let the women pass with just a brief glance and a nod. Ducking behind a pillar, I pulled off my shawl, patted my hair, dashed on a bit of lipstick and then approached the information desk to ask for Constable Duncan Rees. The officer behind the desk wanted to know my business. Personal, I said with a smile. The man looked back at me with a cool, guarded expression and, for the first time in my limited dealings with the British, I felt like an untrustworthy "native." His tone, when he told me to wait to one side with the cluster of Arab women and their children, rang icily correct and aloof.

And then I saw Duncan. He was striding towards me, his footsteps echoing through the long, vaulted corridor. I wanted to throw myself into his arms, but something about his approach made me cautious. And, oh my, I was right to hold back. His manner with me wasn't much different from the fellow behind the desk: stiff and remote, a mask of unfeeling propriety. Actually, he was feeling a lot. Fury! How dare I do this terrible deed: arrive uninvited at his station! He scolded me for taking an unconscionable risk by walking alone through an Arab town, but that was just a smokescreen for what really bothered him. Somehow I'd trespassed on holy ground by coming to where he worked and lived. I belong over there. In Tel

Aviv. With all the other Jews. We argued and I wept and he shushed me and I told him I couldn't bear this state of affairs any longer. Still in high dudgeon, he whistled for a cab and paid the driver to take me back to Tel Aviv right away. Through the window of the taxi I told him not to bother coming round to my door ever again.

We have not seen one another since. This news may give you some satisfaction, because you were always against the affair. But I am wracked in heart and soul. If not for the new job, I don't know how I'd go on. During the day I'm able to keep despair at bay; at night it gnaws deep.

Do write soon, dear Donkey. How are things progressing with that nice Yecke boy from Görlitz? Will you and he marry? Don't hold back. Tell me everything. How I wish you were here.

Your rather tear-sodden sister,

Eva

Ein Rachel, March 16, 1940

Oh Evaleh,

I'm so terribly sorry for your heartache. There's no satisfaction whatsoever in knowing you're unhappy. Even though I had my concerns about your affair with Duncan, I always delighted in your joys. And now I'm cast down by your sorrow and wish I could take you in my arms. But at last I feel I can be completely frank, for, all this time, I bit my tongue. I'll speak freely now, not to say "I told you so" but to bolster your decision to break it off. Suppose the relationship had continued. Where would it lead? It's nice to have a boyfriend to take you out and lavish you with attention. But eventually it has to go one way or another. Could you really become serious with Duncan? Aside from whether his regard for you was ever deep enough (which it clearly wasn't), could _you_ have brought yourself to walk down a church aisle with him? Marry under Christian rites, renounce your Jewishness? I'm not talking about religion. I'm talking about heritage, nationhood, that deep, ancient bond one feels in one's bones as well as the need to keep faith with the Jewish people, especially now, when we face so much hatred, but also the prospect of rebirth.

I've posed these questions to you in my thoughts many times and heard you answer "love conquers all." Well, yes, love conquers *dry reason. Love ignores obstacles. But what happens when the obstacles refuse to go away? In story books they melt into nothingness. In real life they wear you down. In real life, as a Mrs. Duncan Rees you would no longer be one of us. Many of our people would shun you outright. But even those with kinder feelings would feel that you've crossed over to a foreign place, that you no longer share the same fate and aspirations as the rest of us. On the other side of the equation: How fully would you be accepted by the British? Could you become one of them with your German accent, your very Jewish face, your so different lineage and experiences and way of thinking? Can you see yourself mingling on equal footing with the wives of British civil servants? There's a lot more to it than knowing how to make a pot of tea. The British are no keener to see the boundaries between nations erased than anyone else. And what about children? What would they become? Neither fish nor fowl.*

So you see, it really is for the best that you and Duncan part ways. The pain is very deep and will be for quite a while, I fear. But it will subside, Eva. Time will heal the wound. And you will find someone else who truly makes you happy. You are still so young: a mere 19 years old! Just get through your days now and your future will embrace you. Courage, dear sister. Courage!

Your Liesel

P.S. As for me and my "Yecke from Görlitz," we too have our complications. Manfred doesn't want to stay in Ein Rachel. He doesn't have the deep convictions that help one overcome the hardships of pioneering life. He is a man of the city and wants to try his luck in Tel Aviv, Jerusalem or Haifa. Meanwhile, I feel I've found my place among the comrades. It would be awful to abandon them now. Also, I can't imagine starting from scratch among strangers in one of the towns. I have you and Papa in Tel Aviv, but no one else, and Manfred doesn't even have that much. Here we have a community. So, though Manfred and I are very fond of one another, we too face what appears to be an insurmountable dilemma.

Ajami Barracks, April 12, 1940
Dearest Eva,

I'm leaving Jaffa within a week, having received a posting to Jerusalem, and would like to see you once more to say a proper goodbye. And to apologize for any pain I've caused you over the time we've known each other. I'd like us to part as friends rather than with the bad taste of that absurd scene of your visit to Jaffa station in our mouths. I think so highly of you, Eva dear, and value your friendship too much to be content to leave things in such a muddle. By the way, after you departed, I wanted to run after the taxi and explain why I was so upset, while at the same time being touched to the core by your sweetness. I understood your desire to come and see me and why, from your point of view, there was no harm in doing so. Stupid pride kept me from acting on the impulse. Also, I took to heart your request that we never see one another again. But if you'd be willing to hear me beg your pardon in person, I'd like to do so. May I come by at 7:00 p.m. this Saturday evening? And afterwards I promise, you really will be rid of me forever.

 With deepest respect and affection,
 Duncan

Tel Aviv, April 15, 1940
Dear Liesel,

 Last night, Duncan came to say goodbye before leaving for his new post in Jerusalem. He was warm and gentle and I felt terribly torn. But we agreed it would be best to set one another free, his posting to Jerusalem being an opportunity to make the break. Duncan asked permission to write me from time to time. A modest request. You needn't worry that this will lead to our getting back together again, for I doubt very much he'll send many letters. He'll be absorbed by his new surroundings and duties. As you no doubt can tell, I'm still heartsick. Yet his goodbye visit did lift my spirits. Like him, I hated the ugly way we'd left things after my fiasco at Jaffa Station. It was good to be reminded of all the happy times we'd shared. We couldn't continue together—that was becoming increasingly clear. He can't give me enough of himself, which is not his fault. He's just not ready to be tied down. Neither am I, for that matter. But neither am I content to be relegated to the edges of his life. We talked all this through for the first time and came to an understanding and that felt good.

 All that you wrote about the difficulties of marriage to a gentile is quite true. And that's why I never pushed Duncan in this direction.

I just wanted to savour the sweetness of my first love, and I did. If I contemplated the future with him at all, it was to dream of somewhere else entirely. Some other country like America, where you can start fresh, be anything, anyone, you want. But of course Duncan is deeply tied to everything British. I'm fully aware that, as Mrs. Duncan Rees, I'd have to live in a unit of the Palestine Police married quarters, thrown together for company with a small clutch of other wives. Their lives revolve around their little church activities and charities and having one another over for tea, with strict attention to gradations of social status always at play. I'd be expected to hand out finger sandwiches at functions dominated by types like that snooty Millicent Hollingsworth. No, no, no. Impossible. I miss Duncan terribly. But I'm a free woman. Better that way.

And now, let's talk about you, stubborn donkey. So your paramour wants to try his luck in one of our centres of bourgeois decadence? What a wonderful idea. Go with him. Come to Tel Aviv. I'll soften you up with hot baths, fatten you up with ice cream from the Sapir, and dress you in clothes that show off your natural beauty. You've been a severe socialist long enough. If you've got the courage for the swamps of the lower Galilee, you'll find Tel Aviv is a piece of cake—quite literally. The Sapir serves excellent Viennese torte. Do come! And soon.

With much love,
Your Eva

Jerusalem, May 19, 1940
Dear Eva,

I'm settled in the billet in what they call the Kishleh, the former Turkish police station just inside the Old City walls. Four lads to a room, hard beds and a damp chill that seeps out of the ancient stones. The Old City of Jerusalem is like nowhere on earth: half heaven, half hell. You walk down the central alley, find yourself in a covered market like a vault, with the only light coming from smoky torches and small slits in the thick stone overhead. Take another step or two and you're lost in a mess of narrow passageways and dead ends. Would require a lifetime of shoe leather to know all the corners and crannies, though the whole of the old town is crammed into an area of less than half a square mile. Practically every inch is chock-a-block with churches, mosques and synagogues built out of each other's age-old, battle-blasted rubble. Quite the mish-mash of humanity too. Arabs, Jews, Greeks, Armenians and Ethiopians who live in their separate nooks, plus soldiers from all over the Empire on leave, poking their noses into the shops. Keffiahs, monk's robes, stove-pipe hats, knickerbockers, jalabiyas, veils, corkscrew side curls and those big saucer-shaped fur hats the religious Jews wear on their Sabbath—every kind of costume you can imagine. Plus scrawny, scampering, bare-footed, fly-infested children in between the striding feet. Plus the donkeys, the goats, the women with baskets on their heads. And the smells! One moment you're salivating, next you want to retch. A mad, fascinating piece of the universe. The town's a warren, but climb a set of stairs and suddenly you've got a glorious view of rooftops. Of the hills beyond the city— the near ones terraced with olive groves, the far ones, a stark desert brown. One day you must come and see with your own eyes.

I'm teamed up with an Old Sweat called Bertie, from Belfast. Tough bruiser, a veteran of the Black and Tans and schooled in the art of "gentle persuasion." He's not the type to meet in a dark alley at night, but precisely the bloke to have on your side in this scorpion's nest of a town. Our duties are to watch out for the usual murder and mayhem, but also for profiteers and black marketeers. So we poke about, make sure shops use the ration system, see whether chappie's got a load of hidden goods under that blanket or if he's charging twice the going rate for his eggs. At a drop of a hat, an ugly hullabaloo can break out in this so-called City of Peace. Never mind Arabs and Jews. All the different Christian sects can't abide one another either. Worst blow-ups happen at Easter in the Church of the Holy Sepulchre when the place teems with worshippers jockeying for space. Every inch of the church has been apportioned between the sects according to rules that go back to the Crusades. If some chap from a rival religious order steps over a line or touches a curtain he's not supposed to, it'll launch a brawl worthy of the Liverpool dockyards. We can't knock their heads together either. Got to use a light touch, else we could start another world war in addition to the one we're already in.

Our beat includes the Wailing Wall, a narrow, squalid place where ragged, bearded Yids howl and bump their heads against the stones, while Arab clerics in look-out posts above hover like greedy crows waiting for someone to transgress their time-sanctioned rules. See, by law it's Arab property, all of it. By tradition, the Yids are allowed to visit, but they mustn't act like they're moving in. Just let one of the old geezers try to bring a chair to sit on or put up a screen to separate himself from the women! That could start a country-wide riot. Matter of fact it did a while back.

When on night patrol, we enforce the blackout orders. It's eerie here after sunset, for the whole city, both old and new, becomes still and dark as a tomb. Bertie says there wasn't much difference before the war. Jerusalem always rolled up its sidewalks after dark. According to Bertie, Jerusalem is half the size of a Dublin cemetery and twice as dead. Of course there's stuff going on: concerts, cinema, some bars, but it can't compare with lively Tel Aviv. There's a good side to the quiet. With the nightlife so subdued, I can buckle down to my Arabic studies once more. Being a beat copper in this extraordinary town is a lark for now, but I hope to make it into the C.I.D. Since Jerusalem is the site of HQ, I feel my chances to get noticed by the right officers are better here than in Jaffa.

Now for news from the home front: morale is high, despite some setbacks in France. Our gallant R.A.F. bombers have delivered brilliant blows against enemy targets in Hamburg and Bremen. My brother Paul's still in training—for a mechanic's job, not as a pilot. Turns out his eyesight isn't quite sharp enough. Though Mum would have been very proud if he'd got his wings, she's relieved. She doesn't have to worry about either of her sons in battle. As for me, I still envy the fighting men, but the change of scene has soothed the sting.

Hope you're still enjoying the post office work as well as the cafés of T.A. Do let me know how you're getting on. If you ever need another character reference, just tell me. Don't be Miss Independence, all proud and stubborn. I'd be glad to help you in any way I can.

Your friend, always,

Duncan

Tel Aviv, June 3, 1940
Dear Liesel,

I've heard of some interesting job openings at the General Post Office in Jerusalem, and I'm tempted to apply. Yes, I know what you'll say: that I'm asking for trouble. But, really, I'm quite sure Duncan and I can just be friends. He's not the reason I would go. Though I can't say I'm entirely over him, I'm not pining either. I'm too busy to pine. The parcel inspection division has enlarged its activities to examining all imported newspapers, magazines and journals for seditious material, which has inundated us with extra duties. Quite fascinating work, really. The job in Jerusalem would be related, but with even wider and more interesting vistas. I can't say more at this time, because there are security implications. But if I do seek the transfer, and succeed, of course I'll let you know. It would be a pity for me to miss out on such a fine opportunity just because of some old baggage with Duncan. I think we would both make the effort to respect the boundaries of our friendship. Besides, he never stays long in one place. I wouldn't be surprised to hear that he's been sent to Gaza or the Galilee.

As for the "other fish in the sea," I haven't found any, but I haven't been looking either. I'm not ready for more romance. And anyway, there's no point starting something new in Tel Aviv if I'm leaving for Jerusalem. In fact, I'm quite restless to get away from this city. Everything here seems a bit flashy and false to me lately. The too-familiar streets get on my nerves.

Much love,
Your Eva

Ein Rachel, June 18, 1940
Dear Eva,

I'm pregnant. There! It's down in black and white: two words that mean my world has changed forever. Yesterday I saw a doctor in Tiberias who confirmed what I already suspected. Both Manfred and I feel a whirl of emotions: delight, pride, wonder, anxiety, confusion, doubt. Since we'd been taking precautions, this came as a complete surprise and it puts the dilemma of our future together in a whole new light. Now there's no longer a question about our separating. We'll get married without delay, making our little Sabra-

to-be a legal citizen of Palestine and a celebrated member of the Jewish people. Though Manfred still wants to leave the kibbutz, he's agreed we will stay until at least three months after the child is born. I hope by then, when he sees the benefits of communal support in child rearing, he'll change his mind. We are both happy, nevertheless Manfred worries. Is this a good time to be bringing a Jewish baby into the world? In the middle of a war that's going so badly? He's very distressed over the news of Germany's stunning advances through the Low Countries and France. Not that he discusses such things with me—doesn't want to upset me—but I've heard him making pessimistic remarks to others.

For me, Europe and the war are too big to think about, so I don't. I keep my eye on the here and now. I don't want to leave. Is this the time—with an infant in the womb—to try to make our way in the rough and tumble of the city? Here we have all our needs taken care of and our child will receive the best the community can offer. No expense is spared for the children. They are housed in a fine, spacious, white-washed building—the first permanent living quarters that were erected in our settlement and that have been improved many times. They are never alone—always together with other children and supervised by caregivers—and educated according to the most modern, progressive ideas. Parents have to make sacrifices, it's true. At age three months the infants go to live in the nursery, while the mothers return to work. Visits between parent and child become limited, regimented. I've seen mothers creeping around the Children's House at night, trying to hear if their own little one is crying. Yet everyone agrees communal child-rearing is for the best, nurturing confidence, self-reliance and group spirit. Even with your help, dear Evaleh, I wouldn't want to have to learn how to care for a baby all by myself in a strange city, while Manfred casts about to start a business. As for the wedding, though I'd be content with a quick, simple ceremony in Tiberias, we'll marry in Tel Aviv for Papa's sake. I know that might be awkward for you, Eva, but perhaps my wedding would be just what's needed to make you forget your quarrel and bring you two together again.

Because of my news, I've been talking only about myself in this letter. But I have been thinking of you. A lot. I'm concerned about your idea of running off to Jerusalem. You've not been separated from Duncan long enough. You'll be tempted to invite him back into your life for the wrong reasons—loneliness, old habits—and you'll be back in that hole. Now you are free and can have your pick of the handsome cavaliers of Moghrabi Square, if only you would give them a chance. Please, don't do anything rash. Wait at least until after my visit. How I look forward to squeezing my little sister in a real, live hug.

   Much love,
   Your Liesel

Tel Aviv, June 26, 1940
Dear Liesel,

   What delicious news! My sister to be a mama and I an aunt! Come live in Tel Aviv immediately. Forget everything negative I said about this city last time. I was in a funny mood. Don't give that horrid Children's House another moment's consideration. How could you even think of letting caregivers raise your own flesh and blood? A child needs its mother. Was our own miserable growing up not lesson enough on that point? Of course you will know how to care for your baby by yourself because the mother-instincts will flow along with the milk. And I will help. How I'm looking forward to spoiling you both. If you come here to live, I'll abandon all thoughts about those job possibilities in Jerusalem. I forgive you for thinking me so weak that I would let myself get back together with Duncan. Believe me, it's over. You don't have to worry. As for Manfred, give him the benefit of the doubt. He sounds like a clever, diligent, ambitious type. He'll do fine, if not in his own business, then working for someone else. The employment picture has never been better because the government is hiring, the army also needs civilian help and Jewish business is booming. Demand is high for all sorts of supplies for the huge army bases set up in our land. We now even have Jewish pig farmers. And guess who else is reaping in the coin? Malka. Not with dressmaking so much but with condoms. She and her ex-husband sell their little packets as fast as they can put them together. After all, the troops have to have their "distractions," for, as Mr. Churchill says, we're in for a long, tough war. Thank heavens he's now at the helm instead of that namby-pamby Mr. Chamberlain.

   I haven't heard any news about Auntie and Uncle, have you? Not since that one brief and cryptic postcard which was many weeks en route and probably old news. I think we should continue writing even if the chances of our letters reaching their destination are slim. The Red Cross still delivers mail in enemy territory. Oh, how thrilled they would be to hear about the baby.

I've reserved Malka. She's going to measure you for the wedding dress as soon as you get here and I'm paying. No arguments. It's out of the question that you marry in your socialist rags. Malka is so clever she'll be able to design a dress that hides that bulge in your tummy if you're already showing.

Until soon, dear Donkey. Dear pregnant Donkey!

Your loving sister,

Eva

Chapter 17
A Wedding

TWO HOURS LATE, the bus from Afula finally arrived, lurching to a stop and belching out its sweaty passengers, some of whom couldn't wait for the doorway to clear so they scrambled out the windows. My sister emerged, dazed, dishevelled, wrung-out looking, followed by a skinny fellow who didn't seem in much better shape. Liesel took several shallow breaths, as if testing the air.

"The bus had a breakdown just ten miles past Afula. Stranded on a dusty stretch of road without a fleck of shade. And when we got going again, the driver drove like a maniac. My stomach flew in all directions. But here you are, Evaleh. God in heaven, look at you!"

She lunged forward, clutched me and we rocked and moaned together. *Here you are! Here you are!* As we held each other close, I was aware of a foreign presence—her hard-as-a-drum belly—pressing against my midriff. She felt different from how I remembered in other ways too—her arms muscled, her shoulders solid, the sharpness of bone under the skin. Back in Breslau she'd been plump, with Rubenesque curves and a sunny, heart-shaped face. Now, despite the bulge beneath her shorts, she was lean, her khaki shirt drooping loosely over her shoulders. Her hair had been cropped severely, as if someone had put a bowl on her head and attacked her dark locks with a blunt instrument. But none of this could blot out Liesel's natural good looks: her lustrous dark eyes, lovely mouth, the gentle symmetry of her features. With skin sun bronzed as if steeped in strong tea, her teeth shone dazzling white in contrast when she smiled. She stepped back to survey me, put her hand to her mouth, and laughed.

"You look like a pampered poodle. No, forgive me. Like something out of a Paris magazine. Very chic. I'm just not used to . . . If you hadn't waved, I wouldn't have known you. Lipstick. And red nails. And those shoes! How can you walk? My little Mouse, all grown up."

I could tell she didn't quite approve, and I in the meantime started to plot getting her out of that hideous kibbutz uniform into something more flattering. Someone cleared his throat beside us. The thin, wiry man stretched out his hand to me. He too looked as if his clothes were several sizes too big: baggy trousers, belt cinched tight, the excess tongue of leather dangling.

"Don't they feed you in that workers' paradise of yours?"

One corner of his mouth lifted in a wry smile.

"I'm looking forward to the Tel Aviv ice cream Liesel's told me about."

Small head, narrow face, owlish glasses, observant eyes. And because he regarded me so seriously, I broke out into nervous laughter. That finally wrenched a real smile out of him. His teeth weren't just crooked and crowded but discoloured, something Liesel hadn't mentioned in her letters. He seemed self-conscious of them, for he shut his mouth again very quickly. *Brother-in-law.* I tried the phrase out in my mind.

"You don't look like a poodle. You're very fine," he said with a grave, admiring nod, taking in my flowered summer frock and white leather handbag. His eyes lingered on the handbag and widened a little with respect, as if he hadn't seen such a luxury in a very long time and was impressed. The bag was second hand, a rescued and repaired item from one of Malka's clients, but still it made me proud.

"Lemonade first. You both look parched. Let's go to that kiosk. Afterwards we'll take your bags to the hostel and then . . ."

I was right about the thirst. They both tipped their heads back and guzzled their fizzy drinks, sputtering, coughing, and gulping some more to the last drop.

"Nectar fit for the gods," Manfred declared. I liked him already.

I chattered merrily about all the wonderful treats to come as we headed down the sizzling hot streets in the late afternoon traffic. Manfred, carrying their two small rucksacks on his shoulders, swivelled his head this way and that to admire the landmarks I pointed out.

"Here is the Great Synagogue, whose doors I never darken, but it's a fine building don't you agree? Classic elegance. Reminds me a bit of the Storch. Down that road is where Bialik, the poet, used to live. There's Café Sheleg. They serve coffee like in Vienna with mounds of whipped cream. I'll take you to Sapir's as well for *Sachertorte* and we can go to the Galina where they have music—two pianos, imagine, two!—almost every evening."

Liesel said nothing, her eyes casting only cursory, indifferent glances at Tel Aviv's wonders, although her brow knit in a puzzled, disapproving frown when we passed a sidewalk café with the usual afternoon crowd of chess players, newspaper readers, debaters, and gossip hounds. I could read her mind. *How do they have the time for such loafing?* At every blast of a horn and screech of brakes— and there were many—she winced as if stung. At one point, she bolted forward into the road, almost got clipped by a bicycle rounding a corner and jumped back in fright. Could a year in the remote kibbutz really make her so overwhelmed by city traffic? At Magen David Circus, we stopped so that Manfred could read the announcements on an advertising pillar. He expressed delight at the array of films, concerts, dances, and lectures. Liesel leaned back against the concrete pillar and crossed her arms in an attitude of weary resignation. She seemed determined to despise the city, but maybe she was just overwhelmed and exhausted?

"It's hot," she muttered.

"It can't be hotter here than in your Galilee swamp," I couldn't resist saying.

She just closed her eyes and looked as if she might faint and I felt a surge of guilt and concern. Should we have taken the bus to the hostel? But after their long journey in stifling vehicles she'd seemed so relieved to be back on her own two feet and in the outdoor air, even if it was just the dusty air of Tel Aviv. Manfred sprinkled a few drops of water from his canteen onto his hand and dabbed the back of Liesel's neck. Then he straightened her rumpled shirt collar, which had got tucked under.

We finally got to the kibbutz movement hostel, which consisted of dormitory rooms on the second floor of a narrow building. There were separate sections for women and men with two rows of iron cots in each. The women's section was no more salubrious than the men's: haversacks, rumpled clothes, and messy piles of blankets and linen. The baking hot room reeked of Flit, nevertheless, flies buzzed around the ceiling and swarmed a dirty plate someone had left on one of the beds. As we bumped past the bed in question, the loose flies scattered, amid noises of offended fury, but stragglers remained behind, half drowned in an oily puddle of melted butter. No one was around, as if no one could bear staying in such a miserable place a moment longer than necessary. Yet Liesel flung herself on the nearest empty mattress and told us to go off without her. She wasn't interested in supper. If she got hungry, she said, there were rusks in the haversack she could nibble and tea in the communal kitchen down below. "Go, go, enjoy yourselves," she said, her arm covering her eyes. Manfred settled deeper on the edge of the mattress. Of course, he wouldn't leave her. With delicate gestures, he unbuckled her sandals, pulled them off one by one, and gently massaged Liesel's feet. My plans for an evening of entertainment would come to nothing. A childish ache of disappointment welled up inside me, along with a gloomy foreboding about the visit, which I'd so looked forward to and whose every detail I'd set out in my mind.

"She just needs to rest a while," Manfred said with an apologetic smile. I noticed his teeth again. Bent inwards at the top and crammed together in his too-narrow jaw at the bottom, they gave him the look of a man under constant pressure. Duncan had beautiful teeth, I couldn't help remembering. The thought was a thrust of pain in my chest.

THE NEXT MORNING Liesel had fully recovered. I brought her to the seaside early, while the air was still fresh and the sun's rays relatively gentle. We perched on the low concrete wall overlooking the beach—the same spot on the wall on which I'd often sat with Duncan when we just wanted to talk and enjoy the scene.

"Isn't this wonderful?" I asked, spreading my arms wide to indicate the frolickers on the sand down below and the deep blue roll of the waves. "The air! Isn't it perfect?" I exhaled with a loud sigh. Liesel couldn't possibly find fault with the sea. It never disappointed. It wafted salty breezes and sang its soothing song and dazzled our eyes with its azure light. Liesel nodded, conceding.

"The Kinneret is better for swimming, but this certainly is pleasant."

"The sea here is excellent for swimming! Look at all the people in the water. Mothers with their tots. Look at that one dipping her baby's toes into the waves. The salt gives you buoyancy and has medicinal qualities too. And so refreshing. Did you bring your suit? We should all three of us go for a swim. In the late afternoon perhaps, when Manfred has finished poking around the camera shops. And then I'd like to take you to the San Remo Hotel . . ."

"Before we get into the day's agenda," Liesel interrupted, "I want to talk about something. Papa."

"What about him?"

"It would be nice if you two had a chat before the wedding. It would be nice . . ." Liesel turned to look me squarely in the eye, "if you would go and see him and make your peace."

"*I* should go to *him*! He's the one who made war. He should come to *me*."

Liesel sighed and looked down into her lap.

"I can bring you over there to help break the ice and you don't even have to apologize. Just say some civil words and show you are willing to put the quarrel behind you."

"Listen to yourself. Here you go again. You've always expected me to soothe his ruffled feathers, no matter how much he's to blame. You want me to go to him all meek and humble and absorb the poison from his evil tongue. No I won't. Never again."

"As if you ever did!" Liesel snorted. "I want there to be a bit of harmony on my wedding day. Is that so much to ask?"

Her hands now went to the bump in her belly, massaging tenderly as if trying to communicate her position to the new life beneath the layers of taut skin and muscle. For the first time since our reunion, I realized I didn't just have Papa and Manfred as rivals for her affections. Now there would be a further element, the greatest rival of all: this child. If my needs in any way conflicted with those of the baby, mine would come a distant second. Of course they would. And rightly so. It would be immature of me not to accept this reality. Yet a speck of jealousy drifted through my heart, along with a procession of old resentments.

"With Duncan out of the picture," Liesel continued, "It makes no sense for you and Papa to still be *broygez*."

"It never made sense. It was Papa's doing, not mine."

She sighed again. Papa was Papa. How else would he behave?

"He's ready to forgive you, I know. He hinted as much when I explained the situation. All it would take would be the smallest gesture on your part."

The "situation." They'd discussed it. The fact that I was an unattached woman again, no longer entangled with a "goy." Possibly redeemable if I would renounce such escapades forever. Perhaps Manfred had been part of the discussion too and all three had come up with an agreement over the terms of the truce. A mischievous, cantankerous notion popped into my mind and out of mouth.

"As a matter of fact," I said in an offhand way, "I thought it would be nice to invite Duncan to the wedding. I was going to ask if you'd mind."

Liesel's jaw dropped.

"You can't be serious."

"Why not? You've never met him and you should. He's very nice. And he's fun."

"Eva, for God's sake, you told me it was over!"

"Yes it is. But we're friends. We're old friends now. There'd be no harm in our seeing each other again."

"If you want to crawl back to him, that's your business. But it's out of the question he comes to my wedding."

We stared at one another in silence, Liesel's face full of anger and hurt, and, because I couldn't bear it, I looked away first.

"All right. It was just an idea. But I'll never apologize for having been with Duncan. I won't try to make myself kosher in Papa's eyes."

"So we'll have a wedding in which the two main family members aren't on speaking terms! What fun that will be."

"You talked this out with Papa before you talked to me. *I'm* the one who has to bend. Always! You never stood up to him. I was always alone with his wrath."

She looked as if I'd slapped her.

"What are you talking about? I always stood up for you. How many times . . . I couldn't count . . . Remember when he wanted to lock you up in the closet for eating *treif* and I fell on my knees in front of him so he wouldn't?"

"But you wanted *me* to fall on my knees. In your heart you blamed *me*."

Always she counselled caution rather than revolt. I'd run to her howling and she'd soothe me, yes, but then explain in an infuriating older-sister way what I'd done to provoke his rage and what I could have done to avoid it.

"My God, Eva, you crept into my bed almost every night. Even when you got older. We were like this."

She lifted her hand, forefinger and index finger entwined. "I thought we still were. I want us to still be."

Blinking back her tears, she looked away from me, towards the harsh light of the now blazing sun.

I ducked my head and gripped the rough concrete wall beneath my fingers, knowing I was already giving way, but wanting to exact my price. I wanted Liesel to squirm just a bit.

"You could have such a nice wedding without Papa. Why invite that horrible tyrant? He'll find a way to spoil your day, no matter what I do or don't do. Is it about money? I'll pay for everything. I'd be much more generous than he ever would."

"Oh stop, stop, Eva. What are you saying? Papa will be my baby's grandfather. We have so little family here and Manfred has no one at all. I want to hold what's left of us together. Can't you understand?"

I turned from her pleading eyes to look at a group of schoolchildren on the beach. They were playing tug of war: two teams pulling against each other—wild laughter and cheers—while the teacher stood in the middle and watched the progress of the rope over a line drawn in the sand. A happy, wholesome scene.

"All right. For your sake I'll humble myself," I muttered. "I won't go to his flat. Sorry, that's too much. But at the wedding, I'll make the first move and I'll be sweet and civil. We won't have *broygez* at your wedding, if I can help it."

THERE WERE CERTAIN practicalities we hadn't thought through until the last minute. A Jewish wedding required at least two Jewish male witnesses who were not family members. Where were they to come from? Papa, we learned, intended to bring only himself. He had no cronies, it seemed, or didn't see it necessary to invite them. The ceremony was to be held on the morning of a weekday. Malka's boyfriend, Amnon, promised to slip away from his work for an hour, but no one else she could think of had the time.

"Don't worry," she assured us. "The rabbi will just collect witnesses off the street or hangers-on at the synagogue. They'll be happy to come for a glass of schnapps."

On the appointed day, swathed in our stylish cotton dresses, Malka and I linked arms and made our way through the steaming streets, past the vegetable market, towards the warren of alleys with the hole-in-the-wall *shul* that Papa frequented. Men paused in their labours to admire us. Though sweat trickled down our faces over our carefully applied makeup, I felt as if, indeed, we'd both stepped out of the pages of a fashion magazine. We arrived in a small courtyard with weeds pushing through cracks in the buckling concrete. A few people, including Papa, clustered in the small pool of shade by the side of the synagogue, waiting. The *chuppah*, a white, fringed canopy on four poles, rested against the building wall in readiness. There was also a trestle table on which stood a couple of bottles, small glasses, a loaf of challah covered by a cloth, and a cardboard box. Frustrated flies buzzed around the box, so I guessed there was cake inside. Papa's eyes met mine for the briefest moment and then he turned to say something to a stooped, scraggly-bearded man in a shabby black frock coat—one of the recruited witnesses—who looked as if he spent his days dozing on park benches. There were more ancient relics like him, along with two barefoot Yemenite youths in cloth caps, probably called out of the line of porters that hung about the bus depot. The youths did, in fact, possess shoes, but they were wearing them over their hands like boxing gloves and throwing playful punches at each other amid guffaws. Pulling Malka with me, I marched across the broken concrete of the yard. It was hard to step with dignity in high heels over the uneven ground, but I did my best.

"Hello Papa," I said in the loudest, most insolent voice I could muster. "This is my friend Malka."

Malka offered her most charming smile. Papa nodded and raised his hand in a hat-tipping gesture, very proper, reserved and cold as an Arctic gale. I felt the grin slide from my face, but refused to budge even after Malka walked back across the courtyard entrance to look out for Amnon. The bearded relic Papa had been talking to looked up at Papa, mimicked his scowl, tugged at his beard in a gesture of sympathy and scuttled away. I was determined to take the high ground, to conquer Papa's boorish behaviour and win the unspoken contest between us.

"Isn't this a wonderful occasion?"

I waved my hands in an expansive gesture, as if this shabby courtyard were the ballroom of a fine hotel. The corner of Papa's lip lifted in a sardonic smirk.

"I always thought red nail polish makes a woman look as if she dipped her hands in blood."

My fingers curled into my palms, hiding themselves from his gaze.

"Can't you be civil, Papa? For Liesel's sake?"

His hard eyes swept over me, top to bottom—took me in and spat me out.

"For Liesel's sake I've consented to see you again. But that changes nothing. You spurn the Almighty. You cut yourself off from all of Israel. In these times! And you expect me to make polite small talk?"

So much for Papa being ready to meet me halfway. I managed to wheel around before he could turn his back on me, and I did my best to blot him out of my line of vision as I waited for the ceremony to start. By then I wanted the whole affair over with. I was relieved when Liesel, Manfred, and the rabbi emerged through a side door into the courtyard. The sun poured down its punishing fire. We all crowded together in the fast-diminishing shady tract of the yard, with Manfred and Liesel under the *chuppah*, which was held aloft by Amnon, one of the old men and the two Oriental boys, who'd mercifully put their scuffed shoes on their feet. The boys smirked, the grey-beards worked their lips as if practising their prayers and Amnon kept patting the back of his head with one hand to make sure the skullcap he'd been given to wear was still anchored to his bald pate.

Despite Malka's best efforts, Liesel looked odd, for the wedding gown seemed to be wearing her, rather than vice versa, imprisoning her in a stiff, lacy sheath, with puffy sleeves whose cuffs bit into her muscled biceps. Her face beneath her gauzy veil looked pinched. On her feet were a pair of Malka's satin pumps that I knew were too tight and in which Liesel could barely stay erect. Somehow she'd managed to circle her groom the requisite seven times without toppling over, but now she shifted her weight uneasily from foot to foot. Her brown, work-roughened hands clutched a small bouquet of white roses against her midriff, squeezing the life out of the hapless blooms. Meanwhile, Manfred seemed scrawny as a stork in a shirt that hung baggily over his thin frame. Even the white skullcap seemed too big for him, and perched tentatively at the front of his pinhead, like a bird about to take flight. The rabbi began to mumble and Papa barked out the "Amens" just a hair's-breath instant before anyone else could so that a rumbling dissonant chorus punctuated the rabbi's verses.

Something began to bubble inside me. All the absurdity of the moment expanded beneath my ribs like a shaken, fizzing, frothing soda. Malka pinched my side, but that only made matters worse. I shook with suppressed laughter. Liesel's head turned towards me, her mouth opened in dismay. I was about to step backwards so as to ease my way out of her line of vision, but through her gauzy veil I felt her eyes lock on mine and I saw her lips quiver. She too began to shake. Suddenly the same current of hilarity swept through us both. We were like a single stretched wire, zinging and vibrating in sympathy. It was terrible, painful, and also pure delight. Beneath the thin veil, my sister's cheeks glowed red, while the veil itself trembled as if alive. Manfred's face grew more serious as Liesel's composure became more precarious and he put his hand on her arm, pulling her close so that she could steady herself against the unwavering stake of his body. Papa remained thin-lipped and poker stiff, his gaze metallic, as if by act of silent will he could banish our girlish silliness. The rabbi hesitated. The ceremony demanded that the couple share a cup of wine, once, and then a second time after a second set of blessings. How could she drink in such a state? How could she stop her treacherous mouth from spraying its contents onto Manfred's shirt? I squeezed my eyes shut against such thoughts that threatened to undo me completely. I kept my eyes shut tight as the rabbi resumed his chanting. When I opened them again, the danger had passed, the bride had regained her composure and the rites proceeded without mishap: the reading aloud of the marriage contract, the seven blessings, the placing the ring on Liesel's forefinger. At last, Manfred lifted Liesel's veil, removed his glasses, carefully folded them into his shirt pocket, and only then, with the naked, vulnerable, slightly bewildered eyes of the short-sighted, did he face his wife again and deliver a tender kiss. Still gazing at Liesel, he stepped back and under the rabbi's instruction felt with his foot for the empty wine glass that he was supposed to stamp upon as tradition required. A chorus of relieved *mazel tov*'s greeted the feeble crunch. I felt a pang of envy along with joy. My sister looked radiant.

The rabbi recited the blessing over bread. Malka took it upon herself to dole out the contents of the cardboard box—slices of sticky cake with a gluey poppyseed filling—which she arranged on a plate and brought around to the guests. Papa drew back when Malka approached, as if her hands with the crimson nails made the offering unclean. He stiffened his shoulders, cleared his throat, and I knew he was going to make a speech. His grating voice rang through the courtyard.

"My daughter has married according to the law of Moses and Israel. I give thanks to the Holy One, Blessed be He."

"Amen!" chorused the bearded relics, although, as their mouths were stuffed with cake, the word came out muffled.

I braced myself for a harangue, laced with Talmudic quotations, about the duties of a faithful daughter of Israel. I expected allusions to my own less-than-stellar behaviour. Glancing across to Liesel, I saw her bow her head, resigned to being lectured, or perhaps out of embarrassment. The gust of hilarity that had swept us up a few minutes ago had blown itself out and a familiar dreariness dripped through my veins. I knew that whatever came out of Papa's mouth would be the opposite of good cheer and grace, and yet I wasn't prepared for what came next.

"We are instructed to rejoice with the bride and groom, and so we must, so we will. As is it written, '*Eilu devarim* . . . these are the obligations without measure . . .'"

"Amen!" the bearded ones interjected. Their eyes gleamed with anticipation of multiple toasts to the blessed couple that would bring forth the bottle of schnapps.

"Yet there is heaviness in my heart," my father boomed. "Evil is afoot."

A collective gasp greeted these words, followed by a hush. We all stared at Papa. My nails dug into my palms. What was Old Sour-Face up to?

"Evil has devoured the land of my birth, the land I fought for as a front-line soldier."

Papa had started his speech in his awkward Hebrew, but now that he had arrived at the point—the desecrated Fatherland—he switched to German. Only about half the small assembly could follow what he was saying. Amnon, several of the grey-beards and the Yemenite youths cocked their heads with varying expressions of bewilderment as Papa warmed to his subject.

"All we hold dear is in ruins. The wicked have become mighty, the righteous are trampled. A new Haman has arisen who leads the *Volk* to turn against their Jewish brothers. "

Papa had begun to shout. He unleashed his wrath into the courtyard, gazing beyond our heads to address himself to an imaginary audience in the shadows. Malka and Amnon exchanged glances and shrugged. The ancients tugged at their scraggly beards with impatience. The youths gazed enthralled, enjoying the war-like sound of Papa's speech. Liesel studied her borrowed satin shoes with a suppressed smile and Manfred, gripping her hand, stared dreamily into space. They were both too happy, now that their new life as a married couple had begun, to care about Papa's ravings. But the rabbi was another story. Papa's words had drained the blood from his face.

"*Herr* Salomon," the rabbi hissed. "For heaven's sake, stop. This is a *simcha*, as you yourself said. This is not the time for gloomy talk."

He pulled Papa's sleeve, but it did no good. Papa's passion was roused, the fiery lake of anger within him had risen to the surface and his voice was a roar. And though his wrath had nothing to do with me for a change, still it crushed my heart. I'd been right about the old man and Liesel wrong. Why couldn't she see that? Her equanimity during this tirade bothered me more than anything.

"The evil one gobbles territories. Who will stop him? The British are weak. They prefer to persecute us here in our Holy Land . . . calamity without measure . . . brother against brother . . . twenty-five years ago I did my duty on the front . . ."

Papa's forefinger jabbed the air as if to stab at the heart of the evil ones he invoked. Spit flecked his lower lip. His eyes glowed as in a trance.

"*Herr* Salomon, please!"

Papa rose up on his toes, his hands flew into the air, his mouth opened for another searing declaration.

"It is a SIN!" the rabbi thundered.

Papa's ramrod straight body suddenly slumped like a puppet whose strings have been cut. "Forgive me," he muttered to the rabbi. "*Ach*, these times . . ."

We drank a final toast to the happy couple and the gathering dispersed.

In the evening Liesel, Manfred, Malka, Amnon, and I dined at the San Remo in an atmosphere of relaxed merriment. But though I pretended gaiety, I regretted my choice of venue, for everything in the room—the potted palm, the supercilious waiter, the delicious, dusky sounds produced by the saxophone player—all of it reminded me of Duncan: his aching absence. As I shuffled around the dance floor with Manfred (who knew his steps and how to hold me at a comfortable distance), my glittery smile masked my pain. When we'd returned to the table and during a pause in the conversation, I raised the topic of Papa's scandalous wedding speech. I wanted a bit of collective outrage to soothe my soul. But Liesel shushed me in a chiding way. There was no need to rehash that embarrassment. Before they went off for their wedding night to the room that I'd paid for at *Frau* Kleiner's Pension, Liesel squeezed me tight to her bosom and thanked me for being such a darling, wonderful sister. Manfred shook my hand with great vigour, at a loss for words, but clearly moved. I should have been completely satisfied, for in the end we'd done most of the things I'd planned and my guests considered both the visit and the wedding—despite its awkward moments—a grand success. Yet walking home a few steps behind Malka and Amnon, bitterness, loneliness, and restlessness enveloped me. My thoughts drifted once more to that new division at the General Post Office in Jerusalem.

Chapter 18
Malaria

Tel Aviv, Oct. 4, 1940
Dear Liesel,

Manfred wrote to say you're both very sick. How dreadful. How I wish you were here where a doctor could see you and where I could nurse you back to health, instead of stuck in the wilds of that wretched settlement. It's some consolation to know you have the quinine sulphate. Manfred said that although the kibbutz ran out of its own supply, it was able to purchase tablets from the police station at the crossroads. You see? What would we do without the British police? He says the pills are very bitter and that you pull a pitiful face every time he asks you to swallow one. He also says that as invalids you are both entitled to the rare treat of boiled chicken, which neither of you can keep down. His letter was interrupted by his need to run outside and heave. At least you're well past the morning sickness phase of your pregnancy. At least that. Take honey with your pills, Liesel dear, but take them. Rest, get better and then get out of there.

Just to see what might happen, I've applied to the General Post Office in Jerusalem. No answer yet. I wrote Manfred that he should also consider Jerusalem as a possibility. As headquarters of the government and the military, it may offer even more opportunities than Tel Aviv these days for a man of his talents. .

You've probably heard about the bombing raid on our city. We had quite a shock, but I've not been hurt, nor has Papa, for the explosions weren't in our part of town. It was all over in minutes, the Italian planes retreating quickly to their bases before the RAF could respond. But what destruction in the little shanty town on Trumpeldor Street! The houses there are just wood and tin shacks and a whole row went up in flames. The casualties are bad—more than 100 have died in different areas of the city. The bombs didn't spare the Arabs either. Seven, including five children, were killed in a nearby village. We've been assured that proper air defences have been set up now and all has been quiet since, so you mustn't worry about me. Your job is to close your eyelids, have sweet dreams and get better fast.

Your Eva

Tel Aviv, Oct. 21, 1940
Liesel dear,

I just received the news from Manfred. I'm so very, very sorry. And worried, of course, though he says you're out of danger and well taken care of at the hospital in Tiberias. Thank God they had enough of your type of blood for the transfusion. But the baby! Oh how terribly sad. It's so very understandable you're depressed. I can't bear to think of you lying there weak and devastated and Manfred still so ill himself. I've received a leave of absence from work and will be on my way by Friday. I know there's not much I can do, but I have to come.

Much love,
Your Eva

Oct. 25, 1940, Tiberias Post Office Telegraph Service

RECOVERING WELL. RETURNING TO EIN RACHEL. DON'T COME. NOWHERE TO PUT YOU. LOVE LIESEL

Ein Rachel, Nov. 15, 1940
Dear Eva,

I'm utterly emptied, but alive and gaining strength with the help of rest and the bitter tablets. I haven't had a fever all week. The hospital was awful, though the doctors and nurses seemed to know what they were doing. But in hospital you are enveloped by sickness—your own and everyone else's. The groans, howls, coughing and retching and the stinks of putrid things, barely covered up by an acrid disinfectant. Manfred brought me back to our hut on Thursday. A relief to be here, even though our home is nothing more than a wooden crate with a rusted metal roof. It's our crate. Our four walls. The comrades come by after their long day of

*labour to say a few kind words and to try to cheer me up. There's
nothing to say. Mother Nature gives, Mother Nature takes away.
Ruthless, efficient. My illness had affected the baby's development
so it was just as well that my womb expelled the child. Anyway,
Manfred was right. This isn't a good time to bring new life into
the world, with Germany unstoppable in Europe and the Italians
becoming so bold on the African front.*

*I've nothing to complain about. The woman in the bed next to
mine in the hospital was a jaundice-afflicted Arab matron who'd
survived 21 pregnancies. Less than half of them resulted in live,
healthy babies. She looked like a wrinkled, worn-out sack, but was
only fortytwo. We communicated with our hands, facial expressions
and animal noises. Curled up under the sheet, my face to the wall, I
tried to ignore Mrs. Moussa's insistent grunts but finally I turned and
there she was: seated on the edge of her bed, hungry for contact.
She slapped her cheek and dropped her jaw in amazement when
she realized I was 22 and had never been pregnant before. Her first
was at age 16—a son. Having delivered that gift to her husband,
her place in the universe was assured even though afterwards she
had three miscarriages in a row. Proudly, she mimed all the essential
numbers of her life, fingers splayed in the air. She patted the sagging
flesh beneath her white hospital gown—the area of her womb—
and, with a sigh of resignation (or perhaps relief), indicated she was
finished, she could have no more. But she'd done her duty, thanks be
to Allah. Though she expressed pity for my condition, I didn't doubt
she felt superior as a woman of such a fertile race, while I, the weak
Jew, had been broken by my first. We are aliens to one another, our
two peoples, and sometimes I wonder how we can ever co-exist
comfortably in this narrow piece of land. But I leave such questions
for those with bigger brains and braver hearts than mine.*

*Since Manfred's still recuperating, he's been put to work
mending fishing nets, which doesn't require much physical strength.
As soon as I'm up and about, I'll be given the simple job of sorting
and folding clothes in the laundry. "From each, according to his
abilities; to each, according to his needs," as our kibbutz motto
declares. For the moment, I spend the day on my back, watching
spiders crawl across the roof beams and counting the blotches of
rust in the ceiling. I dreamt of my foetus. I saw it quite clearly: a
tiny, wizened, emaciated thing with huge, staring eyes. It opened*

*its thin lips and whimpered as the hospital orderly swept it into the
dustpan. I woke up with the shakes. The laundry is right next door
to the Children's House, which makes me uneasy. Manfred says the
sound of children's laughter will do me good. What does he know?*

Tired now. Must stop.

Your Liesel

Ein Rachel, Dec. 11, 1940 ,
Dear Eva,

*Manfred has left the kibbutz. He's in Jerusalem. Officially, he's
merely visiting an acquaintance from Hamburg who's opened a
camera shop near Zion Square, but I know, and everyone else does
too, that the purpose of his trip is to find paid work. He did not
ask permission from the kibbutz general assembly. Just hopped
on a bus departing from Tiberias, where he'd gone for a check-up
visit to the doctor. He left a letter with me to give to the secretary
arguing that, since he wasn't up to a proper work-day yet anyway,
his absence wouldn't be missed and he'd be one less mouth to feed
this week. The issue of what to do about us came up at the Saturday
night meeting. They expected me to explain our intentions, which
I couldn't. I asked them to leave me alone and walked out. Later I
heard that they've postponed any decisions about us in deference to
my still delicate health. What they mean is they think I've gone a bit
mad and are waiting for me to come to my senses. That's nonsense.
I'm not insane. I'm simply not interested in talk right now. All
conversations get on my nerves. People talk for the sake of hearing
themselves, or gaining praise, or digging information out of each
other, or putting one another down. Let me do my work in peace is
all I ask. I sort and fold. I sew on buttons and repair the seams. That
should be enough. Before supper I visit Becka to sing her a lullaby,
The "Sandman Song." Do you remember how I used to sing it for
you? The fever still attacks me out of the blue, but not as ferociously
as when I first got infected. I should close now. I'm tired.*

Your Liesel

Chapter 19
Unfriendly Bombs

I WAS IN a small space. A cramped and airless space with the brooms, the tin pail, the string mop that coiled its damp tendrils around my bare feet. Locked in the under-the-stairs closet at the back of our Breslau flat. Banished by Papa once again for a misdeed. My only company, the dying flame of Mama's memorial candle, a tiny blue eye, that blinked, wavered, and was suddenly snuffed out. Suffocating darkness poured down my throat. My hands groped at nothingness. My feeble cries fell into the void. And then a rattling noise jolted me awake on my sofa in Malka's workshop.

It was the middle of the night. Outside a winter storm raged, with gusts of wind shaking the balcony door in its frame while rain slashed against the shutters. Just a dream, just the wind. I was about to huddle back under the covers when I heard the noise again. Not the window panes or the shutters. A distinct rap of knuckles against the front door. Who's there, I whispered stupidly into the dark. Nothing stirred next door in Malka's bedroom, so I slipped on my flannel robe, felt for my slippers. "Who's there?" I quavered again when I stood in the hall, straining to hear.

"Eva," a man's voice murmured.

I ripped open the door. There he was, a big, hulking shape in a trench coat in the gloom of the landing. He was drenched. Wetness emanated from his clothes along with the stale smell of liquor. I was too stunned to say a word, so I stood aside to let him in, and he shuffled past me into the kitchen and dropped heavily onto one of the chairs—his usual spot on the balcony side of the table. For a few moments I remained frozen, uncertain, and it was the same for him, it seemed, for he didn't speak. Just slumped, sniffed, and sighed. Finally I slid past him and turned on the overhead light.

"Don't do that," he groaned, shielding his face with his hands. He was hatless, the hair on his bare head plastered against his skull and dripping. There was a bright red trickle of blood on his cheek and a dark stain on his coat collar.

"Duncan! You've been hurt."

He lowered his hands, squinting at me out of his right eye while the left stayed shut tight, sunk into puffy flesh. Blood oozed from a small cut above the brow and dribbled down the side of his wet face. He wiped his cheek, looked at the blood on his hand, and then dug around in the pocket of his coat, looking for a handkerchief, which he didn't find.

"S'nothing. A scratch. Turn off that damn light. Be a love."

"What happened?"

Another sigh. Both eyes shut now, his brow furrowed as if he was trying to remember. His face wore at least a full day's stubble.

"Little argy-bargy with some army blokes in a bar. Aussie bastards."

I grabbed a clean dish rag from under the sink, soaked it in cold water, and tried to attend to the cut myself, but Duncan took the cloth from me with a grunt that was halfway between gratitude and irritation before pressing it against the injured eye.

"Like I said, it's nothing. Will you turn off that blasted light?"

I did as I was told and lowered myself onto an empty chair across from where he sat. Neither of us spoke. Through the darkness, I saw him shift to lean his elbow against the table and his head against his hand, perhaps intending to sleep, perhaps wanting me to disappear, a dry kitchen, a haven from the rain, being all that he required for the moment. Anger bloomed in my chest.

"Do you think you could pull yourself together just for a second to tell me what you're doing here?"

"Sorry, Eva. Sorry. I'll leave. Just give me a minute."

"It's the middle of the night," I began, loudly, then lowered my voice, remembering Malka in her bed next door.

"I haven't seen you for months. You waltz in here drunk. Out of the blue. Without a please or thank you. You deserve what the Aussies gave you."

"You're right, Eva," he said, suddenly sounding quite sober. "I'm leaving."

He started to rise, but I threw myself against him to force him back down, and he let me do so without resistance. My hands were wet from having pushed his coat. He must have been soaked to the skin.

"You're not leaving until you explain yourself. What are you doing in Tel Aviv? What's going on? It's not like you to go off on a tear."

"Oh Eva," he groaned, and buried his face with his hands.

"Tell me."

But he wouldn't. He started to speak, but seized up, his fists clenched on his thighs, his chin tucked against his chest. I couldn't stand it anymore—my cold feet and his sitting there like a tense, miserable lump in the chair. Something bad had happened, I knew that much. Something he was ashamed to tell me about. So I ordered him to take off his coat, which he did, slowly, woodenly. I took the sodden thing to hang over the bathtub, brought a blanket from my sofa to drape over his shoulders. There was still dead silence from Malka's room, for which I was grateful. My anger had softened, replaced by flutters of concern. A cup of tea was in order. But to make tea would have definitely required the light and much noise besides to get the Primus going, so I just sat down again and lit cigarettes for us both. He took a deep drag of the one I handed him, then abruptly flung it away from himself into the sink. I heard the hiss as it went out.

"Mum's dead," he said.

"What?"

"My mother's been killed. Mum of all people."

"Oh Duncan."

I reached out to touch his arm.

"How?"

He went silent again.

"Was it a bomb?"

I thought of the night back in September, when explosions shook our city, when buildings that an instant before had been homes with set tables, cozy beds, and bookshelves, were transformed into rubble and smoke.

"Worse than a bomb. A German hit-and-run plane strafed the High Street in Slough. Attacks against the trading estate you can understand, because there's munitions factories now. There's plants making airplane parts and so on. But Mum doesn't work in one of those."

He caught himself.

"Didn't work there. Past tense. She was at Mars Bars."

His voice had gone eerily matter of fact, detached.

"They're still making chocolate on the estate. Horlicks and chocolate and weapons. Chocolate is a kind of weapon, I suppose. Helps morale. Soldiers get a Mars Bar in their kits. Actually I was glad to hear she was at Mars 'cause I thought she'd be safer than in munitions."

He made a funny noise, a choked attempt at a laugh.

"Anyway, she wasn't at work on the estate. She was getting groceries. On the bleeding High Street, for Chrissake. Out of nowhere, lone fighter plane swoops down, shoots up everything in sight, and disappears before anti-aircraft crew can do a thing. What's to shoot at on the High Street besides civilians, tell me? Women like Mum getting supper!"

"When was this?" I asked, not because it mattered, but just to keep him talking.

"Month ago. Say, could I get a drop to drink? Doesn't Malka keep brandy in the cupboard?"

"Yes, but . . ."

"I'll buy her another. A full bottle. First thing in the morning. Be a dear girl."

"I'd have to switch on the light to find it."

"No matter."

I decided to risk tea as well, filling the kettle, priming and lighting the three-legged beast with as little clatter as possible. Mercifully the thing behaved, for a change. Only after I'd poured two glasses with strong, scalding tea did I fish out the bottle Duncan wanted so badly. He poured a generous splash of Malka's brandy into his glass and slurped. With my grey blanket over his shoulders, his battered, forlorn face and his hands wrapped around the warm glass, he looked as if he'd been hauled out of a shipwreck. Wet sand trailed along the floor from the front door to where he sat. I wondered whether to suggest he take off his shoes and dry his feet, but it seemed more important to get him talking again.

"Your mother died a month ago . . . ?" I began gently.

"Killed," he corrected me.

"Yes. I'm so sorry, Duncan. Did you . . . have you just heard the news now?"

"Got a telegram first, but it wasn't real. Just a few words. That doesn't sink in. But then a letter came from Dad."

He dug into his trousers' pocket and pulled out a damp, creased envelope, bearing the war-time censor's mark and the image of King George in his military uniform gazing serenely from the corner. Duncan smoothed the envelope against the table.

"Do you want to read it to me?"

Duncan shook his head. "Told you the gist already. Rest is about the funeral and such."

We sipped in silence for a while. We heard a dull thump from behind the wall—Malka turning over in her sleep. Duncan winced and stiffened.

"She won't come out. She's sound asleep."

He seemed relieved, not wanting to be seen by Malka or anyone else in his vulnerable state. It was only all right with me. The thought warmed my insides even more than did the tea. I wanted to reach across the table again, but held back for fear of upsetting the terribly delicate balance between his need to grieve and the revulsion he would feel about breaking down. He'd always spoken fondly of his mother. He'd waited to the last minute to tell her about joining the Palestine Police, knowing she wouldn't be able to hide her tears. He was her youngest, the one who shared her love of music and, when still a small boy, the coziness of their private world of make-believe. She liked to weave stories about knights who rescued princesses from lonely towers. I'd never seen a snapshot of Mrs. Rees, but knew she was almost as short as me. "Little Mum" he'd started calling her affectionately, teasingly, when, at age thirteen, he shot up a head higher and could start looking down. I had in my mind an image of a petite, pink-cheeked, dreamy-eyed woman reading her sick boy fairy tales in bed in a whisper so that Dad, who didn't approve of coddling the lad, didn't overhear. I saw her at the piano too, slowly picking out the notes for "Für Elise" with her stubby fingers, smiling with simple happiness at each note she got right. She wrote to him every week. She was always making plans for his return at the end of his contract with the Force, ignoring his hints that he intended to stay on afterwards. Of course I didn't know much about her at all. Though Duncan had liked to talk about his mother, it was just stories, mere scraps. Now she was gone and I'd never meet her. We had something new in common, Duncan and I: both of us motherless.

"It must be very hard," I murmured. "You two were so close."

Duncan straightened up abruptly, making the chair scrape against the floor.

"War's about sacrifice. One has to plough on. It was bloody awkward at first, walking into the canteen and the lads going quiet when they saw me. A moment later, the talk starting up again, everyone trying to sound so normal. No one knowing what to say after they've said they're sorry. But the mates have been good, really. Bertie offered to personally plant a grenade up Hitler's arse for my benefit. We all look out for one another. We're family and the billet is home. More home than anywhere else right now. So I hunkered down to prepare for a second crack at the sergeant's exam and the lads covered for me, taking duties off my hands to give me extra time for studies. I was doing all right. Bucking up. Then Dad's letter came and everything's sort of been scraping up against me since. The exam was supposed to be yesterday, but I didn't show. Went AWOL with a couple of Aussies I met in a Jerusalem bar and next thing I know I'm alone on the Tel Aviv beach in the rain. End of promotion story. Cripes I've blown it."

He twisted the empty tea glass in its metal holder and gazed down in misery at his dirty shoes.

"There will be another chance to write the exam. Surely your officers will understand . . . the circumstances . . ."

Duncan shook his head back and forth, an emphatic "no."

"I've shown that I crack under pressure. Not sergeant material. Even if I wrote ten bloody exams, it wouldn't matter. They'll say I'm pudding inside and I couldn't blame them."

He poured another helping of brandy, gulping it down, neat this time.

"But Duncan, you lost your mother. They ought to take that into account. Just this one slip-up against all your hard work and service!"

It was incomprehensible to me how he idealized the Palestine Police as he did—calling it family, home, and the finest organization of its kind in the world— and yet accept without question that the officers would treat him so shabbily. He was always speaking of loyalty to the Force, but where was the reciprocal attitude towards the rank and file? In the past he'd sometimes grumbled about how any toff from an upper-crust family automatically moved up to an officer position, while ordinary men like him, without a fancy education, were lucky to make sergeant. Yet if I hinted at criticism of his beloved police, he took it as a personal offence. He wasn't listening to me now anyway. He was on another tack, talking about how he'd lost his policeman's cap during the night's adventures. This was almost as bad as going AWOL.

"I've blown it," he said once more. "I'll just have to turn myself in at the district station soon as day breaks. Face the music. The lock-up."

"It's not fair!" I protested.

Duncan looked straight at me, as if seeing me properly for the first time that evening and a gentle smile spread over his lips.

"You're a brick to have let me in, Eva. Another girl would have slammed the door in my face. I must look like a drowned rat. I came because . . . I needed a friend. Couldn't stand to be alone any longer. I'd been walking around for hours. On the streets, on the beach, my feet sinking into the sand. Brought some of it in here with me. Sorry."

We both looked at the trail of wet sand that led from the front door into the kitchen. I waved my hand dismissively.

"I'm glad . . ." I hesitated. "I'm glad you came to me."

I didn't even try to hide my surrender any more, the confession that must have been written all over my face, how I'd been yearning for him since the day of our rupture.

"I kept thinking, here I am on a bloody beach in Palestine, and Mum's dead. It's not right that I'm here when they're getting the hell bombed out of them back in Old Blighty. I should either be with them or shooting at the Jerries."

"Your mother was surely glad you were in Palestine. And proud of you."

"She fretted about the rest of us and she gets herself killed. On the High Street. In broad daylight. What am I saying, I should be with them? There's no 'them' anymore. Just Dad. I can't quite picture it—nobody in the house but Dad. And the cat."

I rose and put my arms around his shoulders, my cheek against the top of his damp head, and he leaned forward to sink against me, his face pressing against my breasts as if he wanted to bury himself there. He didn't weep, not exactly, but I felt his anguish struggling to find air through his hard sighs. I had to brace my legs to stay upright because of the weight of his leaning body. By and by he must have realized the awkwardness of my stance for he pulled away with a muffled "sorry" and straightened up, embarrassed, trying to recover the brave front that had crumbled. I turned off the overhead light. I found his hand in the dark and led him out of the kitchen, manoeuvring my way around the sewing machine, seeking the sofa, my bed. He shuffled behind me, quiet and humble, clutching my hand as if it were a lifeline.

"We don't . . . have to do anything," he whispered. "It would be good just to hold you and feel you near."

But I'd already made up my mind otherwise. I pulled his shirt out of his trousers and slid my hands up his bare, still damp chest. How quickly his heat rose and his heart began to race. We groped and grasped one another, suppressing our moans so that Malka wouldn't hear. Our bodies spoke of loneliness, longing, fear of loss, and the need to banish the ghost of death that hovered at the edges of the darkness in the narrow room. Afterwards, we lay entangled and silent for a long time, both of us waiting, it seemed, for the other to put into words what this encounter might mean for the future. The first glimmers of daylight began to intrude, creeping across the hall floor from the window in the kitchen, bringing the front door into relief and drawing the dressmaker's dummy out of the shadows. Announcing the end of our private time together. I could see his face again too, the battered eye. It looked awful, all swollen and raw—but he shook his head for me not to worry. Quickly he dressed, but before he left he sat at the edge of the sofa to kiss me very tenderly and tentatively, in places that he didn't usually kiss: my eyelids, my forehead, the tips of my fingers, the rims of my ears, as if he were cautiously searching for something he'd lost. Each touch an apology of sorts, for what he'd taken and for what he wasn't sure he'd be able to give. I couldn't bear it, all that sweetness and sadness pouring out of him, the huge question looming over us: the last chapter or a new beginning?

A WEEK LATER, as I was walking down the pedestrian promenade of Rothschild Boulevard, I heard the whistled first bar of Beethoven's *Fifth*. Once again, he'd managed to sneak up on cat's feet behind me. He stood before me now, with his hands behind his back, smiling and all spiffy in his well-brushed blue serge uniform, fully restored, except for the bruised eye. A new cap was on his head, pulled firmly over his brow; his shoes gleamed with polish. Even his eye wasn't so bad, more comical than pitiful now, and somewhat obscured by the shadow that fell over the top of his face from the visor of his cap. From behind his back he produced a new bottle of Stock brandy for Malka and a small jar of imported strawberry jam for me. Both items would be hard to come by because of wartime scarcity. The jam was an Australian brand, compliments of the Aussie bastards. Duncan had been reprimanded, but not charged, he told me. The extenuating circumstances had been taken into account after all. Now he was in Tel Aviv for just an hour, a detour he'd managed after his appearance at a disciplinary hearing for the Australians at the Sarafand Army Base. They'd got off easy too, thanks to his testimony. He insisted they were just larking about and his face got in the way of a flailing arm. The captain hearing the case had smirked skeptically, but was satisfied.

The trees of the promenade still dripped from a recent downpour, but the clouds had dispersed and we found a dry bench in the sunshine. Duncan's face was pale and resolute, a hint of sorrow in his eyes still, but mostly a grave calm. He thanked me for my kindness during the night when he'd arrived on my doorstep "like death warmed over." My heart sank to hear him speak with such formality and distance.

"I wasn't just acting out of kindness, Duncan."

And then he finally said what I'd hoped he would say, though it threw me in a quandary.

"You could find a good job in Jerusalem if you wanted, Eva. I could put a word in for you somewhere if you want."

I looked down. I ground a bottle cap into the sand with the toe of my shoe.

"What are you suggesting?"

He took my hand, stroked my palm with his thumb. "I've missed our times together, Eva. A lot. I'm not in a position to promise anything . . . not just now . . ." His face coloured. "So I suppose I have no right to ask you to disrupt your life here."

He stopped speaking and gazed down at me, waiting for me to fill in the gap. Both a "yes" and a "no" danced upon the tip of my tongue. Manfred was trying to persuade Liesel to move to Jerusalem, and if they did, that would be another inducement—and excuse—but I didn't mention any of this to Duncan. I tried to read the layers of warmth, hope, and hesitation in his eyes.

"I need to think," was all I said, though I'd already decided.

Chapter 20
Holy City

Jerusalem, May 7, 1941
Dear Liesel,

   Now that I'm quite settled in my new city, job and abode—my new life!—all that's missing is you. Come quickly. Please don't delay any longer. I know you still have recurring bouts of the fever, but surely you'd get better medical attention in the city, and the drier climate here would do you good.

   Of course, Manfred must be first in line to embrace you when you step off the bus at the station, but I'll be right behind, eager to throw my arms around your neck. From what Manfred tells me, and from what I've seen with my own eyes, he's doing well at the Vishniak Photo Studio and Camera Shop on Princess Mary Road. An excellent location, right in the centre of town. Since it's very close to where I work, I look in sometimes and, if lucky, am able to say hello to my brother-in-law as he emerges from the depths of the darkroom at the back of the shop, blinking like a startled cat and reeking like a chemical factory. Vishniak seems satisfied, so I don't doubt Manfred will be taken on permanently. Manfred is staying with the Vishniaks and they will have room for both of you. They live in a spacious flat in one of the better districts and it's not too far from where I now am.

   Jerusalem is a world unto itself: a mosaic of distinct neighbourhoods, some crowded and crammed together, others scattered over the hills with big stretches of rock and thistle fields in between. The Old City—mostly Arab—stands apart, enclosed within its ancient, fortress walls. I try not to judge with European eyes and yet . . . even the small Jewish Quarter looks dirty, impoverished and foreign to me. The new city has shabby parts too: clusters of narrow lanes, stone stairways and courtyards, and around each corner you find another tiny synagogue, each with its own style and traditions, but always the men bleat the same well-worn prayers.

Even the modern parts of the city are rather staid compared to Tel Aviv. There is something austere, reserved, sleepy and yet intense here. You're always aware it's The Holy City. From morning to night, religion makes its claims: calls of the muezzins, chant of Jewish prayer, clanging of all manner of church bells—Latin, Greek, Anglican, Lutheran and whatnot. Still we do have some fine cafés, and plenty of good music. What's also wonderful are the views beyond the built-up areas. For example, looking east, you see a great wilderness of barren hills that descend to the Dead Sea. Past that are the mountains of Transjordan. The Jerusalem air is so dry, so crystalline, you can see those distant mountains with the naked eye. In the late afternoon they float on the horizon like a mirage of camel humps.

And now about my new job. I've been employed by the Jerusalem Postal Censor, which is located on the second floor of the General Post Office in the heart of town. It's no small honour to be hired to such a position of trust. I had to swear an oath of allegiance to the Crown with my hand on the Hebrew Bible, which made me smile inwardly at the irony. A copy of Schiller's William Tell is more holy book to me than Moses's creed. Never mind. I swore to be loyal to His Majesty, and I meant it.

The Postal Censor is a big division, employing about 300 full- and part-time staff. Every piece of mail that enters and exits the country undergoes inspection. Not a word—whether intended or inadvertent—that could assist or give comfort to the enemy may escape the censor's indelible pencil. Our motto: "Loose lips sink ships." There are reference lists of forbidden phrases and suspicious subjects. We're the koshering division of the daily mail, so to speak. Incoming letters get scrutinized too, for information that might be useful to British or Allied intelligence and for violations against trading with the enemy. On top of that, we receive bags of intercepted mail from captured enemy ships. The mail must be examined, but the mail must move. We can't sit on it too long. So the second floor is a busy place. Long tables with baskets of letters, with sorters filling the baskets, with readers, their heads tucked down, their pencils at the ready. The examiners in the English section are mostly British housewives, proud to be earning their first-ever salaries and to be making a contribution to the war effort. An assortment of Jewish ladies and a few gentlemen tackle the

Hebrew and Yiddish-language correspondence. The Arabic language
section is all male and consists of retired teachers and clerks along
with some students. So there you have it—the three main groups of
the country represented at their separate tables. But the Censorship
Division handles every other language under the sun as well, with
full-time readers of German, Russian and Polish and part-time
linguists for the whole gamut of other European, Middle Eastern and
Asiatic tongues. Mrs. Khoury, an Arab lady who's befriended me,
knows French very well, along with English, for she was educated at
a posh girls' school in Beirut. She comes in for several hours a few
times a week to offer her services. The staff gets to mingle during
two tea-time breaks, observed religiously throughout the post office
at 11:00 a.m. and 3:00 p.m. and that's how Katy Khoury and I met,
sharing a chuckle over the British national obsession.

In addition to the examining rooms and the library on espionage
and cryptology, there's a comprehensive filing system for the pearls
of information netted from the seas of innocuous words, and that's
where I come in. My job is to type copies of suspect communications
as well as index cards on every name and topic mentioned. These
become part of our big cross-referencing catalogue. On top of
that, I type the reports compiled by the Chief Examiners of every
section. My fingers clickety-clack for hours on end. Tedious labour.
Nevertheless I can't help a naughty thrill at reading other people's
mail, peeking into their lives and secrets—their affairs, scandals,
illnesses, money problems, business rivalries and family arguments.
We're not supposed to talk about these juicy tidbits, but we do,
in whispers, when the section heads are out of range. We all know
about the scion of a distinguished Arab family who is a homosexual
and has a lover in Cairo. (Since he's subject to blackmail, we have
a file and index cards on them both.) One of the Yiddish-language
readers tells about a poor demented soul from a Hasidic sect who
writes a letter addressed to God every week before the Sabbath
asking for 10 pounds to save him from starvation. But you mustn't
think it's only gossip that keeps me interested. Like everyone else
here, I'm always on the lookout for that gold nugget of information
that would allow us to catch a spy or foil a Nazi plot.

The building we work in, the General Post Office, is the finest
of its kind in the Middle East, stretching over an entire city block.
It's solid as a bunker, but graceful in design. The first time I walked

through the big, arched doorway on Jaffa Road and into the great
echoing hall, I felt I'd arrived at the heart of the British Empire.
Nervous about my interview with the Chief of the Reference
Section, I took hesitant steps across the floor tiles, trying not to be
overwhelmed by all that grandeur: the walls and counters of dove
grey marble, the oak panelling behind the stamp wickets, the brass
grills. I don't believe Buckingham Palace could have impressed me as
much. And that made me even more jittery about the interview. But
Mr. Watson, the Chief, soon put me at ease. He's a big, loose-limbed,
florid-faced fellow with a soft paunch and a kind smile. There were
curious objects on his desk and scattered over the window shelf
behind him—pottery shards, lumpy glass beads and dull bits of
metal that turned out to be ancient coins. He caught me glancing at
a clay handle—attached to nothing—lying atop a stack of papers
and he launched into a tangent about this thing. Roman era. Found
in a dig in the Silwan Valley. The archaeology of the Holy Land is his
passion. He seemed much more interested in telling me about that
old piece of clay than carrying on with the interview, but he stopped
himself in mid-flow with an embarrassed cough and went back to his
questions and finally sent me for the typing and shorthand test. I'm
happy to say I passed with flying colours.

My princely salary of eight pounds a month allows me to rent a
whole room of my own—a real room at last, with a door that shuts,
a window that looks out onto beautiful Jerusalem vistas and space
for what feels like the ultimate in luxury—a proper bed, a table,
two chairs and a wardrobe. I'm in a third-floor flat in a building on
King George V Avenue, in the home of a Mrs. Rajinsky, a widow.
There's one other boarder, an odd, shy young man who works at a
bookshop and who keeps to himself.

Duncan comes to fetch me almost every Saturday night, if not
for a concert or a film then for an evening at Fink's Bar, a favourite
among soldiers on leave because of the drinks, of course, but also
because of the piano in the corner, available for the use of anyone
who can bang out a tune. It doesn't take long before the whole
room erupts into an impromptu sing-along. "Waltzing Matilda."
"Wild Irish Rose." I can now entertain you with the anthems and
popular ditties from every part of the Empire.

Oh Liesel. Please don't scold me or send me any more warnings.
Once you meet Duncan, I know you'll like him and forgive us for

*getting back together. You can only disapprove of the abstract
"British policeman." The real human being will win you over.*

*As I look up from my table out the window, I see the top half of
the tower on the YMCA glowing fiery gold in the last rays of the sun.
The bells of the chapel at Terra Sancta College ring out their deep-
throated "dong, dong." I need a walk before it gets too dark. I'll go
east towards the railway station, which is on high ground and offers
grand views of the ancient walls and Mount Zion and the Valley
of Hinnom. Just think, soon you and I will take this evening stroll
together, arm in arm. The light at this hour is magical. Don't delay.*

    Your Eva

Chapter 21
Interregnum

STRANGE AS IT seems to say so now, the war years were the best of times—for me, for the land. For me it was simple. A good job, decent pay and everyone I loved near me at last, while the person I could happily live without ever seeing again was at a safe distance in Tel Aviv. Though it was not so many miles from the coast to Jerusalem, the journey was uncomfortable and inconvenient and Papa had lost his taste for travel since the days when he could crisscross Silesia on the Fatherland's superb railway system. Now he preferred to stay close to home in his dingy den by the bus station and a five-minute walk from the *shul* with the weedy courtyard. Good riddance!

As for the country, the war was a boon. Old animosities were set aside (a few exceptions notwithstanding), as Britons, Jews, and Arabs pulled together in the common cause. Haj Amin Al Husseini, the banished Mufti and arch-enemy of the Jews, still managed to pull a few strings from his exile headquarters in Berlin. A tiny band of Jewish zealots broke away from the other band of zealots to continue the struggle against His Majesty's Government. But these were pinpricks in an otherwise unified front. The halt to Jewish immigration from Europe had calmed Arab anxieties, while the *Yishuv* focused on the fight against Hitler. For the first time in years, the country found peace.

During wartime the land prospered too, became a bustling supply centre and staging ground for the battles of the African desert. Yes, we had shortages and rationing of some goods, but nothing like what Britain had to endure and not remotely like the suffering of our brethren in Europe, of which we heard only whispers. Meanwhile, virtually all of us had work—with the government or the military or in a factory that filled orders for the huge Allied forces camps that had sprouted on the coastal plain. Palestine produced much of what those forces needed—from land mines to uniforms, jerry cans, bandages, bully beef, orange juice, beer. The cities catered to the many layers of military bureaucracy and provided recreation for soldiers on leave. You could stand in Jerusalem's Zion Square and watch a diverse parade of fighting men—Australians with their broad-brimmed floppy hats, Sikhs in turbans, Tommies in berets, navy men in sailor suits—along with Jewish and Arab citizens going about their daily affairs.

The war was everything and it was everywhere. Yet, save for one hair-raising period—the battles were comfortably far away.

For a few months, Duncan brooded anew about his inability to join the fight abroad. He nursed dreams of revenge against the Germans, longed to shoot an enemy plane out of the sky. Some nights, while lying on his back beside me in my bed, a glass of Haig's whisky coursing through his veins, he hatched fantastical schemes which involved a new identity with forged papers, a clandestine journey to Alexandria, a deck-hand job on a ship bound for Canada, enlistment in a far-off colonial recruitment centre. But at last these ravings petered out and, when they did, Duncan focused his attention on getting his sergeant's stripes. He volunteered for special assignments, buckled down to his Arabic studies, spit polished his shoes, and practised his shot at the firing range. By a lucky confluence of incidents, he was able to nab the man who'd murdered the son of a leading Arab textile merchant. This brought him to the attention of the brass and he landed the promotion. As a second British sergeant, he got his foot on the first rung of the Criminal Investigation Department—junior assistant to a British Inspector.

He never talked about his mum. Mother and death and the beating Britain was taking in general and the personal reason he wanted to take his vengeance on Hitler were all taboo. Also, I learned to avoid any allusion to the night he'd arrived at Lilienblum Street, broken in grief. I tried to shun the topic of Slough and family altogether. One time, joking around, I reminded him that our counterparts in the Military Censor would be reading his letters home. I warned him against the sin of "loose lips."

"I don't write letters much," he said, turning his head away from me. "Got no one much to write to."

A grey sadness filmed his eyes. Pain leaked out from that place to which it had been banished. If only he could bury his face in my bosom and allow me to comfort him as he had that one time. But as soon as I reached out my arms, he stiffened, caught himself, put on his self-mocking Fierce Policeman's Stare. Grief was sent packing into that utterly private box where it belonged.

MY ROOM ON King George V Avenue belonged to me alone, but also to me and Duncan together. On moonless nights, with Jerusalem under blackout and the bedside lamp extinguished, the room became dark as an underground cave and all its contours vanished and the world outside did not exist. We became as sightless animals, relying on our other senses: sounds, smells, and above all our sense of touch. I would hear him undress and stretch out on the bed. I would feel him listening with keen, aroused attention to the rustle of my own clothes. Blindly, we would reach for one another, search with our mouths and hands, sometimes bump clumsily and gasp in pain and joy. The thick darkness pressed against us, another presence, another skin. Blindness added piquancy. Movements I couldn't anticipate overwhelmed me. We had to tell what we wanted. We had to guide one another. *Here. Yes. Please. Now.* The blacker things outside, the more intense our inner lights burned. Vows could be said in such darkness—*love . . . forever . . . never leave . . . always with you*—words that hung in the air, true and substantial, and yet disconnected from the mouth of the speaker and so belonging only to this special place and time and not to be examined in the morning light.

Afterwards, the glowing tips of our cigarettes made graceful arabesques in the dark and the room held the scent of smoke and Duncan's seed. When no special duty or emergency required that Duncan return to his billet, he stayed over, falling asleep beside me in the bed that, although a single, was still luxuriously wider than Malka's sofa. Early in the morning, before he returned to his station, we took breakfast at the table I'd covered with an embroidered cloth, decorated with a vase of wildflowers and laid with plates of bread, cheese, and jam and sometimes a soft-boiled egg.

"The King David couldn't compete," he'd say, tickling my leg with the toe of his stocking foot.

Through the window we could see the southern corner of the King David Hotel illuminated in the eastern light. We could see the stone tower of the YMCA and farther on, David's Tower, Mount Zion, and bits of the massive Old City walls. I never tired of that view.

My landlady, Mrs. Rajinsky, professed open-mindedness. With a sniff and a shrug she declared that what I did in private was my business. Who was she to judge? But Mr. Maisel, her other boarder, deserved consideration. "Poor Mr. Maisel," she moaned as she wiped her kitchen counters, lurching from side to side on her stumpy legs, one shorter than the other. I rose to the bait. Why poor Mr. Maisel? Mrs. Rajinsky didn't answer right away. Whenever she was deep in thought her teeth masticated an imaginary piece of gristle while small, querulous squeaks came from deep in her throat. Finally she wheeled around with an accusing glare.

"Mr. Maisel likes his privacy. It was hard enough to persuade him to stay after I rented to you though I promised you'd keep out of his way. But now with this strange man coming by at all hours, bumping into Mr. Maisel in the hallway, occupying the bathroom and . . ." Mrs. Rajinsky paused for effect. She bit down fiercely on the phantom gristle. "And the disturbing noises that travel through the walls! *I'm* not bothered by that sort of business. I was married for twenty-eight years before my husband of blessed memory went to his grave. I've had three children. But poor Mr. Maisel is an innocent. Perhaps a little backward in his development, but a dear sensitive soul. When your visitor comes, Mr. Maisel barricades himself in his room and hardly dares venture into the hall to the lavatory. I'm worried he might one day decide he can't bear it any longer and give notice."

"Sergeant Rees is not a strange man," I retorted. "He is a member of the Palestine Police. What could be more respectable than that? And he pays for his hot water. If Mr. Maisel is not a criminal, he has nothing to fear."

Mrs. Rajinsky would never admit it, but she was somewhat awed when Duncan appeared before her in uniform, the picture of authority in his crisp khaki drill, with the sergeant's stripes on his shirtsleeve, the truncheon hanging from a loop at his side, and the visored cap on his head. Duncan impressed her with his commanding presence and he soothed her with his impeccable courtesy, plus the coins left behind on the kitchen counter as a contribution to the household. Sometimes as well he brought a gift from Spinney's, the English fine foods import shop. All in all, Mrs. Rajinsky accepted his visits, though she felt obliged to utter her oblique reproaches and to let me know her tolerance had its limits.

When I closed the door to my room, Mrs. Rajinsky, Mr. Maisel, and all other annoyances of the world vanished. The room's quiet, simple beauty embraced me. The white tablecloth that I'd embroidered with a border of tulips. The Degas print of ballet dancers on the wall. A vase of deep blue Hebron glass that stood by the window and caught the sunlight in its belly. Legally, my landlady owned most of the furniture, along with the room itself, but I didn't think of it that way. I was queen of my little castle.

The top shelf of the pine wardrobe against one wall held some of Duncan's things: fresh singlets and underwear, a change of socks, a spare toothbrush, and a shaving kit and a small towel. That way, when he stayed overnight with me, he could go straight to his station in the morning, without a stop at the billet to get himself proper. I liked to look at that shelf, to refold the singlets, and bring down the shaving mug and sniff the cake of soap at the bottom. These things spoke of Duncan's imminent return and said that he lived here, at least partially. Also, his cigarette butts mingling with mine in the ashtray, the lingering smell of his whisky and the socks he'd left behind for me to darn. But what made the room *our* home, more than anything else, was the amazing apparatus in the grey leather case that sat on my bedside table. A few months after I'd moved to Jerusalem, Duncan arrived at my door one evening with a small, square valise in his hand and my heart sank, thinking he was off on another out-of-town mission. Then he unclasped and opened the case with the flourish of a magician pulling a bouquet of roses out of a top hat. I gazed in astonishment at the velvet-clad turntable, the shiny chrome needle arm, the detachable crank. The thing in the case was an HMV portable gramophone.

I reached out to touch the turntable. It moved a half circle clockwise under the pressure of my finger.

"Does it work?" I murmured.

"I should hope so or Mr. Kowalski will have some explaining to do."

"Duncan, how could you ever afford such a thing?"

"Oh, I've been saving up. Helps to have the extra two pounds of sergeant's pay."

He shrugged as if this were no great accomplishment but I could tell he was bursting with pride.

Slipping his hand into a compartment under the lid, Duncan produced yet another bit of magic—a recording of Bach's *Suite for Solo Cello, No. 1 in G Major*. Kowalski had thrown it in as part of the sale. Duncan showed me how to wipe the dust off the record with a special cloth, working in a circular motion that followed the pattern of the grooves. Holding the edges of the disc between his fingertips he reverently placed it onto the turntable. He attached the crank, gave it a few turns, lifted the needle arm, and lowered it onto the outer edge of the record, careful as a *mohel* about to circumcise his own son. A crackle of static, and then the plaintive, amber notes of the cello burst into the room. Lying in the dark together, we listened to the Bach again and again, the same nine-minute side, half the night through, drifting off to sleep and waking to the lazy *snick, snick, snick* of the needle in the empty grooves, until I rose on my elbow, lifted the arm, re-cranked the crank, and set the arm back to the beginning.

"You'll wear the record out before morning," Duncan protested drowsily.

I couldn't help myself. It was just too incredible. The power and the freedom of our own private concert. Having a brilliant cellist entertain us at our bidding, as if we were royalty. I kept the volume turned very low so as not to disturb Mrs. Rajinsky and Mr. Maisel, yet every note found its way into my soul. That night I learned how a recording could give me a whole new relationship to music. Of course, a live concert would always be much richer and more gripping. But live music was ephemeral, like travelling on a fast-moving train, the scenery flying by in a blur. A concert left me moved and exhilarated, yes, but unable to remember the fine details. A record allowed me to learn a piece, remember it, hold it close, possess it, and be possessed.

"How long will you leave the gramophone with me?" I asked him in the morning.

The question surprised him.

"I don't intend to take it away."

"But don't you want it in your billet?"

"It never occurred to me to bring it there. I want it here. With you."

"With me! Oh Duncan!"

What a gift to listen to records whenever I wanted! Yet the greater gift was the implication that our lives were now inextricably entwined. The gramophone was something we owned together. And together we slowly built a collection of beloved recordings. Sometimes he bought one, sometimes I did—whoever had saved up enough money. The stack in the orange crate beside my bookshelf steadily grew, and I never kept track of who bought what. They were ours—our brilliant, charming, delightful, infinitely entertaining children.

WE STILL WENT to concerts, of course. At Rehavia High School, at Edison Hall, at the amphitheatre of the Hebrew University, and best of all at the YMCA. The Y was my favourite building in all Jerusalem, and it was just a few steps away from where I lived on King George V Street, near the intersection with Julian's Way. To walk up the Y's flagstone path, between the lines of cypress trees, was to slip inside a better world. A ceramic plaque near the entrance displayed the inspirational words, spoken by Field Marshall Allenby at the opening ceremony in 1933.

> Here is a place whose atmosphere is peace, where political and religious jealousies can be forgotten and international unity fostered and developed.

The building was a mix of styles—neo-Gothic, neo-Moorish, neo-everything. A seraph here, a scimitar there. That was the point: to represent the three Holy Land religions and the best of civilization. I loved to feast my eyes on the graceful stone arches and painted tiles. On concert nights, the six-hundred-seat auditorium would be packed. Military officers and government dignitaries and their wives occupied the front rows and much gold braid, medals, pearls, and ostrich feathers would be on display, though the ladies' gowns were subdued, for it was wartime and ostentation would not do. Every concert would start with the entire assembly on its feet for "God Save the King," accompanied by a naval bugler in white cap and white gloves. Standing at attention as if on parade, Duncan would sing with full heart. *Send him vicTOR-i-ous Happy and GLOR-i-ous*

The insipid melody and pompous words did not improve with the constant repetition. But I would never share such thoughts with Duncan.

After the concert, we'd head to Fink's Bar. Up King George, down Ben Yehuda, into a narrow lane towards the sound of a muffled commotion. Duncan would push open a door, pull aside the blackout curtain and a tumult of voices would roar into our ears, while swirls of cigarette smoke blew into our faces. The crowd sucked us into its boisterous embrace—a madcap throng of soldiers and locals out for some innocent, or not so innocent, fun. There were men who'd come out of the desert with their arms in slings or with half their faces wrapped in bandages and they were usually the ones who put on the biggest displays of jollity. Two bartenders worked furiously behind the zinc counter to fill the glasses for the eager hands reaching out. Bursts of raucous male laughter rose above the chatter, rivalled now and then by a girl's high-pitched squeal. There'd be a tinkle of piano keys, the din would quiet for a moment. And then all would erupt into the drunken chorus. . . . *bluuuuue-birds over/ the white cliffs of Dover*

Anyone who could bang out a tune was welcome to tackle the piano and for a while I tried to push Duncan in that direction, for I was sure he still had it in him. One time, amid cheers, he did sit down on the piano stool and flawlessly played the first few bars of "Danny Boy" but abruptly halted and jumped up again to disappointed groans. His face flushed with suppressed anger. I never did that again.

FOR THE FIRST year after they'd moved from the kibbutz, Liesel and Manfred lived in a room in the Vishniak family home in Rehavia. It was a spacious room by Palestine standards. The Vishniaks and their two children, a boy aged ten and a girl aged eight, were courteous and considerate, and everyone was too busy to get in one another's way. And yet, it was someone else's home. Though Liesel didn't care—a fatalism had invaded her since that time when her malaria-ridden body had expelled the foetus in her womb—Manfred chafed. He couldn't feel at ease without a roof of his own. He worked hard at Vishniak's Photography Studio and Camera Shop. Liesel brought in some income as a maid, pounding carpets and scrubbing sheets for some of the well-heeled doctors and civil servants in the neighbourhood. The work was drudgery—how I knew it—yet it couldn't have been as hard as on the kibbutz. Nevertheless, my sister drooped during that first year. Though the fever didn't return, illness clung to her—colds, headaches, an attack of boils, stomach ailments. Whether at work or leisure, she still dressed like a flagrant socialist: no make-up, no jewellery, only the plainest shirtwaist dress and dowdy shoes. She and Manfred saved every mil, allowed themselves no luxuries. My brother-in-law buried himself in the darkroom and the studio. Wedding photos. Bar mitzvah portraits. Soldiers coming in to pose in uniform before a painted scene of palm trees and camels. Business was brisk and slowly the savings grew.

In January of 1942, Manfred signed a lease for a tiny rooftop flat on Hillel Street in the centre of town. There wasn't much to it. A concrete block structure, exposed to the raging wind and rains of winter and the baking sun of summer. Two small rooms, a galley kitchen, a lavatory, and shower, leaks in the roof and water pressure problems year-round. Other tenants of the four-storey building used the roof as a storage area for spare bed frames, bicycle parts, jerry cans, flower pots, and pieces of furniture they lacked space for but couldn't bear to part with. The odds and ends lay scattered about or covered with canvas tarpaulins anchored with stones. All this, in addition to a row of water tanks, gave a crowded, junkyard atmosphere to the open area surrounding the rooftop flat. When Manfred showed it to Liesel and me the first time, with Dr. Eisenberg, the landlord, standing behind us and impatiently tapping the rolled up, still-to-be-signed lease against his palm, my brother-in-law broke into a sweat, though it was a cold winter's day. He begged Liesel to consider the potential, how they would make it cozy and pretty, with geraniums before the door and pictures on the walls to hide the peeling paint. He needn't have strained himself. Liesel leaned against the parapet on the east side of the roof, gazing out at all that could be seen: the Old City in the distance, with its crenellated walls, its domes, minarets, towers, and church spires and the green groves on the Mount of Olives beyond. When she turned around, the light in her eyes was brighter than I'd seen in ages. And that was that.

Duncan thought Manfred a decent chap, if a bit dull and morose. Manfred thought Duncan an interesting character, if a bit superficial and arrogant. Liesel found Duncan's courtesies pleasant and touching, but his opinions narrow. Duncan thought Liesel lovely and admirable but rather baffling. When the four of us got together, it was usually at Liesel's and Manfred's where, in better weather, we could sit outside on wicker stools on the rooftop "plaza." By the spring of 1942 they had indeed decorated their little haven with pots of geraniums and had pushed the neighbours' possessions into one big pile beside the water tanks, making less of an eyesore. Duncan and Manfred played endless games of chess, while Liesel and I nattered as we peeled potatoes or sorted lentils for a simple supper. We all steered clear of contentious subjects and got along, but we were never an entirely comfortable foursome and always a small sigh of relief floated up from my chest when Duncan and I were once more alone.

Every so often, Liesel would ask an uncomfortable question about the arrangement between Duncan and me. Where was it going? What about the future? *Nu?* I gave the answers that I thought would conform to her sense of reality. No point in discussing a future until the war was over, I said. Only then would we be able to think about what kind of life we wanted to have and where we wanted to live: in Palestine, England or elsewhere. Until the war ended, Duncan had to stay with the Palestine Police, while afterwards, he might consider a different career. Moreover, until the war was settled, the whole question of Palestine—what kind of state it would become, the competing claims of Arab and Jew—remained up in the air. Everyone's future was on shaky ground, not just ours. As I spoke, these things became truer and more obvious. Why would anyone live beyond the moment in such times? But Liesel persisted in remaining obtuse.

"I don't see how that makes such a difference," she pressed. "Will you share your life with him, or not?"

"And what would you think if I said yes?"

"I think you'd be making a mistake."

"Well then, you should be happy to know it's still undecided."

THIS PARTICULAR EXCHANGE occurred during the summer of 1942, when the desert war was going badly. Axis forces under Field Marshal Rommel's command smashed through British defences, causing one defeat after another. Strategic positions were lost at Gazala, Bir Hacheim, Sullum, and the port of Tobruk, which was nicknamed the Libyan "Verdun." Of course, in the news these weren't defeats at all. They were fall-backs, re-groupings or tactical retreats. And, still, the enemy advanced closer. Past the Egyptian border to attack British fortifications near the last seaport before the Nile Delta. Now, a new battle raged. The "Big One." The "Decisive One." But the language of the newspapers was hardly decisive, speaking of "a fluid situation," "changing positions," and "fierce rear-guard actions." Fluid indeed. Our world seemed built on shifting sands. Duncan pooh-poohed the dangers, but Manfred became increasingly glum, a mood that spread first from him to Liesel, then to me.

One Sunday afternoon in early July, my friend from work, Katy Khoury and her husband, Sami, invited all of us—Manfred and Liesel, Duncan and me—for tea in the garden of their villa in the prosperous suburb of Katamon. The scene was idyllic in the shade of carob and fig trees, with an arbour of honeysuckle and masses of bougainvillea along the garden wall. We sat around a low table of hammered brass, laden with dishes of salted almonds, dried figs, biscuits, and flaky pastries soaked in honey. Despite the recent cut in rations, there was sugar for the tea—a whole small bowl full—which the Khourys must have saved specially to offer their guests. Katy Khoury poured, stirred, and served around the china cups and plates with the easy grace of a natural-born hostess. I'd always admired her fine looks: her golden-brown skin, gazelle eyes, and lustrous black hair, with just a touch of grey, done up in a French roll. She dressed with simple elegance. Today she wore a black skirt and a frilled white blouse and the little gold cross that dangled below the hollow of her throat. The Khourys were Christians. But not the kind to hold a grudge against the Jews for the murder of Christ, she'd once hastened to assure me.

It was that dreamy hour of the late afternoon, when the dry heat of the day was at its most intense, but the long shadows held the promise of evening's cool to come. The conversation began in safe waters—inquiries about our hosts' recent visit to Bethlehem and about the progress of their three daughters in school. We spoke English, of course, the common language among the six of us. At her mother's firm command, the eldest girl, Christina, stepped forward, folded her hands prettily in front of her and recited a Lafontaine poem in opaque, Arabic-accented French, while the younger two peeked and tittered from behind the bushes. Christina had fine, delicate features, and a husky voice, like her mother. We all applauded heartily at the end, and Duncan begged the girl to tell what the poem was about. This was too much for the poor child, who stood tongue-tied and blushing, her eyes appealing to her father for rescue. Beaming broadly he obliged. The Lafontaine parable was about an industrious ant who prepares for winter while the short-sighted cricket wastes his summer with carefree song and is caught unawares. When all three girls had scampered back into the house amid hoots of relief, we fell into a conversational lull. Manfred gazed at the garden wall and Liesel at the hands in her lap. Neither had finished the pastries on their plates.

"Has anyone seen the new film at the Rex?" Katy asked, looking around the circle, treating us all to her dazzling smile. "Now what is it called? The Devil . . . the Devil . . ."

Duncan jumped to the rescue. "*The Devil and Miss Jones*. We haven't been. Not yet. But it does sound like fun. Doesn't it, Manfred? Have you seen the write-up? Hello there, Manfred. You still with us?"

Manfred turned around at the sharp sound of Duncan's voice. He shook his head.

"We are all crickets. It's a country of crickets. And of people who play cricket while the storm approaches."

Liesel gave a little gasp. No one else said a word. Manfred continued, speaking in quiet, measured tones like a schoolteacher presenting an equation.

"There has been no proper preparation for the defence of Palestine in the event that—how do you say it—worse comes to worst. And it certainly looks as if it will come to that. Soldiers, civilians—every single man, woman, and child should be mobilized by now to put up a massive resistance. At the very least, all Jews of fighting age should be recruited and trained for the Home Guard. Instead, Westminster hems and haws and the military authorities here present a deaf ear. Oh no, the Jews mustn't receive arms. Wouldn't do. Let's have another sherry and watch the cricket match. In the meantime, the barbarians are at the gate."

"Good God, man, what a way to talk!" Duncan shot Manfred a contemptuous look. "Pure rot. Complete nonsense. It's atrocious to raise false alarms, to say nothing of how unkind to our hosts."

Duncan gave the Khourys a gallant smile that apologized for Manfred's rudeness.

"It is quite all right," said Sami Khoury, with a gracious wave of his hand to Manfred. "Please feel free to speak. You are among friends."

"I'm sorry that it's a not pleasant topic for afternoon tea. But I simply can't sit around and pretend we aren't on the brink of disaster. The Germans are just fifty miles from Alexandria. They run circles around the British. Now Mersa Matruh has fallen . . ."

"More rot!" Duncan broke in. "Rumours. German propaganda. Of course they want to spread panic, so that's what they claim. Your kind of talk plays right into their hands. I hope the rest of you don't take this fellow too seriously." Duncan looked around our little circle with a tight smile. "Our military has things well under control. We've had some setbacks, I'll grant you, but . . ."

"Setbacks! It's a rout. Rommel has outfoxed and out-muscled the British. Everyone knows this is the truth and to pretend otherwise for the sake of putting on a brave face won't help. We have to be clear-eyed about what's ahead. El Alamein is the next domino. If Rommel takes El Alamein, the road is clear to Alexandria, Cairo, the Suez, Gaza, Jerusalem. We must prepare."

Manfred spoke in a dry, matter-of-fact voice, but the eyes behind his glasses held dark, anxious glimmers. When he finished speaking, he pressed his lips together and sighed heavily through his nose.

"Alexandria?" Liesel said with a bewildered look on her face as if waking up from a dream.

"The Germans won't reach Alexandria, so you can just put that worry out of your mind, my dear," Duncan said, cheery and confident. "General Auchinleck knows exactly what he's doing. He's holding them off with delaying tactics until reinforcements come. Meanwhile the R.A.F is pounding the Axis supply lines from the air. The longer those supply lines, the more vulnerable they are. And without supplies the enemy can't maintain its fighting strength. So our fall-back behind the Egyptian border—what Manfred is calling a surrender—was a trap. Stretch the enemy resources, wear them down, cut them off."

"There is German propaganda and there is British propaganda," Manfred said with a disdainful shrug. "I'm not so convinced about those reinforcements. They should have arrived before now. It is absolutely in British interests to hold the Middle East, but they're taking their time to wake up to the dangers. The generals have been asleep."

"What do you know about military strategy, mate? You've never so much as touched a gun barrel in your life. I happen to know a tad more about these matters and I assure you it's all in hand. Our soldiers are doing a hard enough job. They don't need hysteria from the civilians. Next thing you'll be starting a run on the banks."

Duncan's tone was still hearty, but two bright red patches of anger burned on his cheeks when he'd finished his little speech. I knew that face. I knew he considered my brother-in-law a hapless sort at the best of times. He gave Manfred a cold stare. Manfred was not cowed. In fact, his tone now contained a note of pity for Duncan's naiveté.

"I'm not a strategist, but I have an inkling of what's going on. It's not quite what they serve up in our newspapers. Our very censored newspapers."

Manfred glanced at me, and I looked away quickly. To my regret, I'd confided in him what I'd overheard from a murmured conversation as I was passing Mr. Watson's office the day before. British officials in Cairo were burning their files. Bonfires of records in the courtyards. A massive retreat on the way. Something like that. The same story circulated from ear to ear in the second-floor lunch room. Of course, it was merely a rumour and rumours must not be repeated, but, chilled to the depths of my soul, I had to share the story with someone. I felt I could count on Manfred to keep it to himself and to be calm and level-headed, which he had been, taking in my words with a sigh and gripping my shoulder to give me courage. Now I saw he too had been chilled to the depths.

"Of course, not all is lost," Manfred was saying. "One has to hope. But part of hope is being prepared. We should be digging trenches. We should be filling sandbags. We should be . . ." Manfred burst into a fit of coughing, as if the words for all the things that must be done were crowded together in his throat and choking him.

"Please, can we speak of something else?" Liesel interjected.

"Hear, hear!" Duncan boomed.

My sister squeezed her hands together in her lap. She too gave Katy Khoury a look of apology.

Mrs. Khoury lifted up the glass dish of biscuits and waved it around. "But no one is eating. Please! Our maid Sula made these with our own carob paste. You would never know they aren't chocolate. You must eat or Sula will be very sad.

Now, Sami, do tell the story about the funny lady who came to your pharmacy last week." She telegraphed a look of appeal to her husband.

"Just a minute, if you please, my dear," said Mr. Khoury. "I must say something to our friend."

Mr. Khoury had been leaning forward while following the interchange between Duncan and Manfred and I'd seen him take a sharp breath several times as if he meant to interject. Now he beamed, for he finally had his chance. His round, sunny face shone with perspiration. He turned to Manfred.

"You see, if the Germans do manage to march into Palestine, civilian resistance would be pointless. What would you do? Throw stones? They will answer with bombs. We can only surrender. We have unfortunately much experience with foreign armies in this country. All one can do when the battle is lost is submit and survive. And in the meantime . . ." He took the plate of biscuits from his wife's hand to offer it around. "In the meantime we must maintain our strength."

Manfred crossed his arms over his chest. His expression was bleak.

"Yes, you and your family would survive. I don't doubt it and I don't begrudge you the better fate. But what about us? What does submission to Germany mean for the Jews? Massacre. Yes, yes, don't shake your head. The World Jewish Congress says a million have been killed in eastern Europe already."

Mr. Khoury gave a doubting smile. He didn't say so, but we could read his thoughts. *Jewish propaganda.*

"You must not be so gloomy. One of these days the war will come to an end," he said. "All wars do. There will be peace and people will wonder why did we ever go to war. Then you and most of the other Jews of Palestine will return to your homes in Europe."

Manfred burst into a bitter laugh. "Wishful thinking on your part."

"But you are not one of those extreme Zionists. And I know you cannot feel at home here."

"Europe is finished for the Jews. Germany for sure. This is the last station. Like it or not, we are here to stay. You can try to throw us out. It will do no good."

"Of course, we like it," Katy rushed in. "We have many Jewish friends, don't we Sami? Please, you have not even touched the pastries, Mr. Glatt. You must make me happy and eat a little bit. And now we must leave politics alone. Really we must."

Sami told his story about the mad missionary Englishwoman who came into his shop convinced that "Our Lord Jesus" had sent her there for a special brand of medicinal tea. She brought a cup of tea to the top of the Mount of Olives every day to soothe "Our Lord's" digestion as He prepared for His Return. Apparently Lord Jesus had also advised her on the price to pay, for she insisted on haggling over the little tin of tea leaves and drove a devil of a bargain. We speculated on what happened to those cups of tea: whether she drank them herself, or whether one of the sisters from the nearby Carmelite convent tipped them out on the sly so that the mad lady could preserve her cherished delusion.

Somehow we navigated through the rest of the afternoon without more conversational torpedoes. Duncan ate the lion's share of the sweets. He apologized that he had to return to the station for night duty. We all said our goodbyes with some relief.

AS DUNCAN PREDICTED, the Allied forces held firm at El Alamein and the Axis lost the initiative, though the desert war dragged on for many months. Both sides dug in, conducting manoeuvres and raids, rather than knock-out battles. We knew the soldiers had to suffer terribly in that parched wilderness under a merciless sun. *The Palestine Post* allowed that the desert heat made things "most uncomfortable." But all Palestine breathed a sigh of relief that the crisis had passed. Even Manfred stopped talking about mass mobilization and burrowed back into the business of the studio and the darkroom. Wedding photos, family portraits, school graduations, soldiers posing for their girls back home.

Jerusalem, July 24, 1943
Dear Aunt Ida,

This letter won't reach you. If I persist in pushing it through the slot of the post box, it will return to me in a few days or weeks stamped "Undeliverable." Only the simplest, most innocuous messages, compressed into 25 words on a Red Cross form, are allowed for messages into enemy territory. Nowadays these too disappear into mailbags that go nowhere. But I want to, I need to, pretend.

We are well. The big news is that Liesel is pregnant again. It's early days still, but her doctor says all looks normal and, if she takes care, there's no need to fear another unfortunate event like the last one. She hasn't had a bout of fever for several years. But she must avoid being bitten by mosquitoes, for the body weakens with each recurrence of the disease. Jerusalem is much safer than the wilds of the Galilee, yet the tiny beasts still find places to breed. Pregnancy becomes Liesel. Despite the morning bouts of retching into the toilet, she has roses in her cheeks and sparkle in her eyes. I haven't seen her look so animated and hopeful since her wedding day. She continues to work daily, cleaning houses, but once her belly swells, she'll stay home and rest. Manfred buzzes around her like an anxious bee. Drapes her in mosquito netting at night. Massages her feet. Brings home choice figs from the market, which he peels with loving fingers and can barely restrain himself from spooning into her mouth. She laughs and tells him she's not made of glass, but he persists.

Papa and I are still estranged. We haven't seen each other since the wedding and all I know about his welfare is what I've heard from Liesel. She's tried to get him to visit Jerusalem, but he doesn't like to travel, so if she wants to see him, she must make the journey to Tel Aviv. He scrapes together a living with his peddling business, hoards every mil, allows himself nothing. While others felt deprived when rationing started, Papa was quite in his element. He was already slicing his cheese paper-thin and making do with only a film of margarine. Liesel thinks he'll start visiting when the baby is born. I have my doubts. He's more cantankerous and stuck in his ways than ever. This sort of talk can't be nice for you to hear, so I'm sorry. But truthfully, he's as dead to me as I am to him.

Now what can I tell you about myself that you would want to hear? I must think. It would pain you to know about Duncan. You'd be ever so much kinder than Papa, but beneath your strained smile, I'd see an acre of distress. When you imagine me with a man, he looks like a young Uncle Otto—dark-eyed, chubby-faced, a nose that curves slightly down towards the lips and hints of its ancient heritage. So let's leave Duncan aside. At work I've become one of the German-language readers, ploughing through correspondence, translating suspicious bits into English. Ninety-nine percent of what comes before my eyes seems innocent. Most letters sound the same, instantly forgettable. But we must try to read between the lines. Is this nickname a code word? Is this allusion to a private joke a cryptic message from one spy to another? Where have I seen that odd phrase before? Every such question leads back to the reference catalogue where we've documented all anomalies— anything that remotely could be considered a clue. It's like working on a hugely complex jigsaw puzzle and immensely satisfying when even the tiniest piece falls into place (rarely happens). Mr. Watson is quite pleased with my work. Last week, he introduced me to the big chief, Mr. Edwin Samuel, son of the first high commissioner to

Palestine. Mr. Samuel's distinguished looks and way of speaking are so thoroughly English, you would never guess he's one of us. I feel privileged to work in a government where a Jew can rise to such a level.

Where are you now dear Auntie? Still sharing a flat with that other couple? It must seem to you like a mouse hole after your lovely home in the garden district of Breslau. Every so often, our newspapers serve up a shocking story of massacres that we can't bring ourselves to believe. Hide in your mouse hole just a bit longer. The war is going in the right direction. Surely the end is just around the corner and then . . . And then, one day when we meet again, I'll show you this letter and you'll know I did not forget you.

Your loving niece,

Eva

Chapter 22
War Ends, War Begins

ANOTHER YEAR PASSED. On all fronts the tide of war turned against Germany. Victory was no longer in question. The only question was, *When?* With each Allied advance and bombing raid, it seemed the Germans couldn't hold out any longer, yet they did, for months and months more, trapped in the relentless machine they'd created, faithful to their Führer to almost the last gasp. In tones of barely muted glee, *The Palestine Post* reported on German cities reduced to rubble, fireballs consuming famous landmarks, civilians staggering among the ruins. Our home town, Breslau, became a site of the last stand against the Allies, subjected to merciless siege and bombardment. One brilliant morning at the beginning of May, I was visiting my sister at her rooftop flat. While little Ari napped in his mosquito-net-draped crib inside, Liesel and I sat outside under the blue Levantine heavens and devoured the newspapers. We read about the ongoing battles against "Fortress Breslau." About house-to-house fighting in streets we'd once walked. About familiar squares, markets, parks, bridges, and promenades turned to scorched earth and buildings crumbled into dust. It seemed not a single habitable structure was left standing. We looked at one another and I read my own thoughts in Liesel's stunned and troubled eyes. How could this happen to the town that had once been our home? And where in all this spectacular devastation were auntie and uncle?

On May 7, 1945, a few days after "Fortress Breslau" fell to its knees, after five years, eight months, and five days of fighting, Germany offered unconditional surrender. May 8 was declared a holiday throughout the Allied world. Celebrations in our city began with a ceremony outside the King David Hotel—the hoisting of the Union Jack, flanked on either side by the Stars and Stripes and the Red Hammer-and-Sickle of the Soviet Union. The brass band of the Palestine Police played "God Save the King" and now, finally, the anthem sounded both rousing and magisterial to my ears. His Excellency, the High Commissioner, wearing his resplendent plumed helmet, stood in stiff salute as the anthem played, with rows of senior military officers alongside doing the same. And so did Duncan, fingertips to forehead, standing motionless next to me amid the throng of spectators. When the last trumpet notes faded away and the last drum roll ended, we joined in the frantic cheers. Our whoops mingled with the bells of the YMCA carillon and never had those bells clanged with such conviction. Duncan put his hands around my waist, lifting me high in the air.

"It's over, Eva!" he said, his voice choked. "The war in Europe is really over. We've won, we've won, we've won!"

We joined the crowds that surged through the streets into the heart of town, a joyous mix of civilians and soldiers, flags, pennants, and bunting. Windows, balconies, shop fronts, and lampposts declared victory with freshly printed V-E signs. Cars, buses, and lorries honked their horns, bicycle bells tinkled, revellers paraded, arm in arm. Wine flowed from the Carmel Mizrachi wine store on Ben Yehuda Street, which served free drinks to passing servicemen out of three huge barrels set out on the pavement. Soldiers grabbed girls and kissed them and the girls kissed them back and gave them flowers and there were flowers in buttonholes, on caps, behind ears, in hair and underfoot. Cafés and bars overflowed. Music poured out of windows. There were odd, hilarious and touching scenes too as the day wore on and alcohol dripped deeper into veins. Men in uniform staggered about, babbling their favourite filthy ditties. *Hi, ho Kathusalem, Harlot of Jerusalem.* Some fellows tried to get a donkey to drink beer, pushing the bottle towards the beast's muzzle and earning an outraged display of bared yellow teeth. A young soldier plopped down on the curb, put his head in his hands, and burst into tears. Squatting beside him, Duncan draped an arm over the weeping man's shoulder, asked if he was all right.

"Wish I were home already," the soldier blubbered. "What a time I'd be having in Old Blighty now."

Duncan squeezed the fellow's shoulder. "It won't be long, mate. You'll be on your way soon."

I heard the wistful note in Duncan's otherwise hearty voice. The soldier's homesickness was catching. My heart sank as I wondered whether Duncan would want to return to the mother country now that the seas were free of menace and borders open once more. He hadn't mentioned anything of the sort, but would the pull of "Blighty" become too strong to resist with so many others flocking home and a new England rising out of the rubble? I pushed the question away. Today was for celebrations only.

"Let's go to my sister's," I suggested, and was pleased when Duncan readily agreed.

WE CLIMBED FOUR flights of stairs, then an additional narrow set, pushed open a heavy door, and stepped onto the sun-baked surface of the roof. Liesel, Manfred and their landlord, Dr. Eisenberg, who had living quarters and a practice on the ground floor, were seated on wicker stools in front of a makeshift table of orange crates on which stood a bottle of cognac and glasses. Little Ari, wearing nothing but a cloth diaper hanging low on his hips and a floppy hat on his gossamer-haired head, danced on his father's knees while Manfred held him around the waist. The child burbled when he saw me. His plump arms churned the air.

"Come to *Doda*," I beckoned, and I plucked him from Manfred's hands, held him to my chest and whirled him around.

"His diaper is soaked," Liesel warned. "But it's water from the bucket we've been playing in, not pee-pee. At least, not when I last checked."

"So wet, wet, wet," I sang, patting my nephew's behind, which made the child squeal and kick in a frenzy of delight. Then it was Uncle Duncan's turn. But the child pulled back, for Duncan was only an occasional visitor on the roof and so something of a stranger. Ari seemed particularly bothered by Duncan's moustache, this strange, bristly, animal thing in the middle of a human face.

"I won't hurt you, little man," Duncan said, leaning down with his long hands outstretched. The child broke into a howl.

"Ha! He doesn't trust British promises," Dr. Eisenberg quipped.

Liesel came forward to take the boy from me. She bounced him in her bare brown arms, pressed her cheek to his, and cooed something soothing in their secret language until he quieted. But the boy wasn't quite ready to end his moment at centre stage.

"*Aba!*" he demanded from his perch on Liesel's arm. "*Aba! Aba! Aba!*"

Manfred jumped up as if yanked, smiling without restraint, a smile both helpless and proud that exposed his crowded teeth to full view.

"Hoppa! Hoppa!"

He swung his son up and down, then sat him on his shoulders, the chubby legs straddling *Aba's* neck and the tiny fists held in a firm grip. And didn't the boy just feel top cock seated at such a height? Shooting Duncan a look of sheer triumph, Ari crowed in jubilation. We all laughed.

Finally, Manfred set my nephew down to return to his game of splash-splash in the bucket by Liesel's feet and fetched extra chairs and glasses for Duncan and me. The five of us settled into our private festivities, toasting victory with the cognac Dr. Eisenberg had so generously contributed, while on rooftops and balconies all around us and in the tumultuous streets below, others were doing the same. Just before the evening light began to fade, we heard the drone of an aircraft and we all reflexively froze for a moment. No air raids had occurred in Palestine for ages, yet I still had the impulse to throw myself flat onto the roof's surface. Liesel's hand moved protectively towards Ari's head. The moment passed. We looked up to see a lone airplane high overhead, describing loops in the sky, creating a message with plumes of white vapour. Cryptic figures took shape but quickly became bloated puffs of cloud before melting away. We tilted our heads back, attempted to read. What language? And were these alphabetical letters at all, or some other kind of symbol?

"What would make most sense is a 'V' for Victory," Manfred said, pinching his chin between thumb and forefinger. "But frankly, I don't see it."

"I see a camel caravan." Liesel giggled. "With monkeys and peacocks following behind."

Not to be outdone, I announced that I could discern a marching band of tubas and drums and baton-twirling majorettes. Duncan smiled and added flourishes to my vision—horns, bagpipes, a platoon of Black Watch Highlanders in full regalia.

We all looked expectantly at Dr. Eisenberg. A sardonic smile spread over his lips. Devilry gleamed in his deep-set eyes. "I see a pair of scissors in the heavens," he grunted. "Yes, heavenly scissors, with which to cut the British administration's cursed White Paper to shreds."

An awkward silence followed these words. Up to now we'd been chit-chatting about the parades and parties around the country marking this splendid day, a day we'd been longing for all these years. But Dr. Eisenberg had strong views and was used to expressing them. He had a huge bone to pick with the British. His tongue had been loosened by the cognac, but even without it I suspect, he would have tossed out this challenging remark. He couldn't resist putting Duncan on the spot as representative of the Occupying Power.

"After everything that has happened in Europe, how can the British government continue to block Jewish immigration?" Eisenberg blared. "The survivors of the camps must be free to come. We must have our state. We must have it now. Has the world learned nothing?"

"Please, Dr. Eisenberg," Liesel said. "Today is a day of thanks. We have so much to be grateful for." Her eyes, fixed imploringly on Manfred, said, *Do something*.

"Yes," Manfred agreed. "Thanks and remembrance. The British have paid a very high price to vanquish Hitler."

"They didn't do it for our sake," Eisenberg bristled. "They look out for their interests. We have to look out for ours."

"No politics. Not today," I pleaded.

Duncan had already gone stiff and icy with offence. "We went to war to defend freedom, not interests," he hissed. "The fact that there are any Jewish survivors at all is mainly because of British sacrifices."

"You have your freedom. We do not. We love freedom no less than you and we will fight no less than you did to gain it."

The two men stared at each other: Duncan straight-backed and tall on his wicker stool, Dr. Eisenberg, squat and thick as a bull dog. The doctor was much older than the rest of us. He had a large head on a very short neck, and short, thin legs, but a broad chest that gave an impression of great power. After the silent stand-off that seemed to last forever, Manfred leaped to his feet to pour another round of drinks for us all.

"To Dr. Eisenberg, who delivered our beautiful son and who has taken care of my dear wife and who brought this excellent cognac for our enjoyment today."

"Hear! Hear! And to His Majesty, the King, and all his loyal subjects," Duncan added, before tossing the cognac down his throat and causing Eisenberg to pause before swallowing his.

Shortly afterwards, the two of us decamped.

We drifted back to Ben Yehuda Street, headquarters of the revelry, where the cheers, tooting, and high jinks had continued unabated. At the bottom of the street, under a lamppost, a gang of rumpled, capless Tommies tottered against one another, belting out the dirty song in earnest now.

Hi, ho Kathusalem
The harlot of Jerusalem
Prostitute of ill repute
The daughter of the rabbi . . .
It was a fact, she had a crack
With hair so black, it could contract
To fit the tool, of any fool
Who fucked in all Jerusalem

A foul-mouthed, juvenile, witless, offensive song that normally was sung late at night in barracks and bars where no ladies dare set foot. Now, here they were, shameless drunken soldiers in the centre of the Holy City with the good citizens milling about—men, women, and children too. Unable to resist, Duncan drifted closer and joined in a couple of scurrilous verses, so relieved was he to be away from Dr. Eisenberg, whom he couldn't abide, and relieved too of the burden of good British manners. And even I sang along, despite the ugly lyrics, because no one was paying attention anyway, no one's ears were scorched, all were too happy and giddy, the raucous victory hour absolving all. We were at peace, at peace, at peace!

THE FOLLOWING DAY saw more parties, parades, and thanks-giving services throughout the country but there were also some events of a very different nature. The singing and *hora* dancing in Zion Square gave way in the early afternoon to bull horns, placards, and organized rows of marchers—a mass demonstration. Jewish leaders and chief rabbis stood at the head of the great column followed by demobilized Jewish soldiers, youth, workers and women's groups, and so on —a cross section of the *Yishuv*. They marched up Ben Yehuda and along King George V, cheered on by thousands of spectators who lined both sides of the streets. "Free immigration!" the placards cried out. "Down with the White Paper!" "We have a right to settle the Homeland!" Demonstrators and spectators poured into the courtyard of the Jewish Agency Building which was draped with the Zionist colours, bordered on both sides with black to signify mourning for the murdered Jews of Europe. I was part of the determined crowd in the courtyard that afternoon. Beside me stood Liesel and next to her Manfred, with a dazed Ari planted firmly on his shoulders. The boy must witness history.

Dignitaries awaited us on the balcony of the Jewish National Fund Building. Mr. Ben Zvi, President of the National Council, spoke. He congratulated the victorious armies of the United Nations. He praised the thirty thousand Jewish men and women in the Forces. He reiterated the Jewish demand to rebuild its homeland in Palestine. To live as free people among the other nations of the world. The gathering ended with the singing of Hatikvah, but I was unable to contribute to the sea of voices for mine was thick with tears.

Later the same evening, a mass demonstration of Arabs poured out of Jaffa Gate and down the main street of town. They carried their own placards, chanted their own slogans, voiced demands diametrically opposed to ours.

NOT A WEEK went by before ominous posters—printed in Hebrew, Arabic, and English—appeared on billboards and walls about the city.

WARNING!
1. The Government of Oppression should WITHOUT ANY DELAY evacuate children, women, civilian persons and officials from all its offices, buildings, dwelling places, etc., throughout the country.
2. The civilian population, Hebrews, Arabs, and others are asked, for their own sake, to abstain from now until the warning is recalled, from visiting or nearing all Government offices, properties, courts, transportation sites, etc.

YOU HAVE BEEN WARNED!

The poster was signed by the "Irgun Zvai Leumi in the Land of Israel"—the hard-line Revisionists who had tamed their passions only until victory over Hitler seemed assured and had re-emerged from their dens like ravenous beasts after a season of hibernation.

I took in these words as I stood on the corner of Mamilla and Princess Mary Road, gazing up at the billboard on which the poster had been plastered. This corner was one of my favourite places. I always stopped here on my way to and from work to scan the announcements. Every inch of the billboard's surface would be bristling with notices of concerts, films, dances, and other events, and it gave me a lift to dream about the pleasures that awaited in the halls and theatres. The Irgun's warning had been brazenly pasted right in the middle, blocking out an ad for something on at Edison Hall. Pedestrians walked briskly by. No one besides me seemed to give a hoot about what the Revisionists had to say. By now, people were used to such grandiose messages from the dissidents, and besides, what were citizens of Palestine to do? We had to go to the railway stations, the courts, the post offices, and the hundreds of other government agencies for our jobs and our services. Still, everyone knew that the angry youth of the Irgun and the even more fanatical Stern Gang, didn't just spew words. They performed deeds. Well before the end of the war, they had resumed their acts of sabotage and murder.

I thought of the morning, months earlier, when Duncan came to my room, white-lipped, shaken, filthy with dust. He'd been playing cards with some mates at the Police Headquarters billet the night before, when he heard gunfire nearby. Everyone grabbed a firearm and ran across the courtyard. They pelted towards the sound of shots and shouting that came from the second-floor offices of the Criminal Investigation Department in the main building of the compound. Just before Duncan reached the stone steps to the front entrance, a massive blast threw him backwards. Another explosion followed. He lay on the ground with his hands over his head until the earth stopped trembling and an eerie silence had settled over the darkness. He rose to his knees. He wasn't hurt, not in any serious way, but he heard a groan nearby. Feeling his way through scattered rubble, he found one of the mates spread-eagled on the cold cobblestones. He'd been struck in the head by flying debris. All sorts of pandemonium had broken loose by then—shouts, whistle blasts, alarm bells, sirens, men running hither and thither. Duncan managed to get the wounded man onto his feet and supported him as they shuffled back to the safety and relative calm of the billet. The rest of the night he joined the crews digging through the rubble and collecting evidence. The casualty figures hadn't yet been confirmed, but it appeared five coppers were dead and another six wounded. He'd come by just to let me know he was alive and intact. I tried to get him to stop for a cup of tea at least, but he was restless to check on the man with the head injury, who'd been taken to the government hospital. If Duncan had reached the entrance to the main building a few seconds earlier, if he had been at the front of the group running across the courtyard instead of at the back, if he hadn't taken an extra moment to check the loading mechanism of his pistol . . . I clung to Duncan as he stood in the doorway to my room, the "ifs" curdling my blood.

The following days, the story of what had happened emerged. A team of Irgun men disguised as police officers had penetrated headquarters security, climbed through the second-floor windows, and released their mayhem. All but one got away. The Jewish press denounced the "outrage" by a "crazed group of malcontents." The head of the police demanded that the *Yishuv* do everything in its power to isolate the "evildoers" and deliver them to justice. There were a few days of curfew imposed through the Jewish parts of the city. Then life returned to normal and neither the British authorities nor the *Yishuv* wanted to dwell on that awful night at police headquarters. The shadowy figures who conducted the raids were misguided youth traumatized by the plight of their brethren in Europe, some people reasoned. "They do the Jewish cause no good!" others lamented. All the street-corner philosophers—those for and against the armed struggle— had predicted that when the war in Europe was truly over the real fireworks in Palestine would begin. And so it was. And so I needn't have been surprised by the Warning poster.

As I lingered, a police motorcycle puttered to a halt beside me and a constable hopped to the pavement. He wore goggles, which he pushed up to the top of his forehead, and leather boots that reached almost to his knees. The face was vaguely familiar from evenings at Finks.

"Good morning, Miss."

He gave a curt nod. His eyes narrowed, trying to place me.

"I'm a friend of Sergeant Duncan Rees," I said.

"Ah yes. Miss . . ."

"Salomon."

"Yes, of course."

I saw him struggling to remember the night that came flooding back to me. Near closing time at Finks. The last drinks had been poured and the crowd had thinned. Duncan, this fellow and other off-duty lads, all rip-roaring, had got it into their heads to entertain the die-hards in the room with their version of Palestine animals: donkey brays, camel grunts, jackal yelps, and hyena howls. A circus bedlam filled the air, a cacophony one had to be drunk to appreciate—

which I was not. They tossed in imitations of the local human species too—Jewish "Oy, yoy, yoys" and Arab "*yallas.*" The motorcycle copper before me now had no recollection. Or perhaps he did, for the bemused smile on his face faded and his manner became briskly professional.

"Excuse me, please," he said, stepping past me towards the billboard. From a sheath on his belt, he drew a broad knife, slipped the blade under the edge of the Irgun poster and, with quick, efficient movements, excised the offending notice, leaving a neat rectangle of bare board in its place. He folded up the sheet and stuffed it into the saddle bag hanging off the side of his motorcycle. I assumed there were dozens of similarly removed sheets in the bag—kept as evidence or for statistical purposes—and that the copper would spend his day at this task.

"Did you happen to catch sight of the rascal who put this up?" he asked.

I shook my head. "I'm sorry. No."

"No, of course not. No one ever does."

One corner of his mouth curled upwards in a sarcastic smirk.

"They go postering very early in the morning before anyone else is about," I offered.

"And how would you know that?" the copper shot back.

"I don't for a fact," I stammered. "I just assumed . . . I mean . . . how else . . . ?"

"Indeed. How else do they get away with it unless all their fellow citizens are asleep or blind? Amazing how soundly the town sleeps on certain mornings. Good day, Miss Salomon."

With that he jumped back onto his motorcycle, kicked the starter pedal, and roared away.

Chapter 23
Evening Encounter

I WAS TAKING a shortcut home from Liesel's flat one evening through Mamilla Cemetery, the ancient Muslim burial ground, which had once been outside town limits, but now found itself smack in the heart of modern Jerusalem. In Europe, such a place would be bounded by high walls, but here the walls were low and crumbling and invited trespass. I liked to wander through Mamilla, a wide, wild expanse of sloping ground, where olive and pistachio trees spread their gnarled branches over broken mausoleums of long-ago sheikhs. Tipsy headstones leaned this way and that. Rocks, weeds, thistles, bushes, and barren soil filled the spaces between the far-apart graves. In the daytime, an Arab herder might meander through with his goats. Children played hide-and-seek around the headstones and flung pebbles into the murky water of Mamilla Pool, a reservoir dating back to Roman times. Liesel called Mamilla our Garden of Eden, because the cemetery truly had an air of paradise on a still Sabbath morning, when we strolled with Ari beneath the shade of the silvery leaves.

Now, at dusk, the twisted trees flattened into silhouettes and only the hectoring caw of a crow disturbed the peace. I watched where I stepped along the dusty path, avoiding the stones and goat turds. Hearing the crack of a branch, I looked up startled and stopped in my tracks. A dark, indistinct figure approached. As it neared, I saw a woman in a long grey dress, her head wrapped in a tight, black scarf. The head covering was Jewish, not Arab. It was odd for a religious Jewess to be out on her own in the cemetery at dusk, but nothing to cause me alarm, so I continued to walk forward. I said "good evening" in Hebrew and was about to pass, when the woman plucked at my sleeve.

"*Giveret*! Stop a moment. I have something to show you. Something you would like very much."

She had a deep, husky voice but young features, though I couldn't see her all that clearly in the fading light. A cloth bag lay slung over one shoulder out of which she drew a flat, rectangular object. She held it out for me to take into my hands. A gramophone record! I squinted down at the writing on the paper sleeve: selections from Schubert's song cycle, *Die schöne Müllerin*, sung by the famous tenor, Richard Tauber, and accompanied by an orchestra conducted by Henry Geehl.

"Where did you get this?" I asked.

"You may have it for one and a half pounds. An excellent price, wouldn't you agree? In the shop it would cost two pounds at least."

The offer of a gramophone record on a cemetery path at the close of day wasn't as strange as it might seem. Peddlers—Jewish and Arab—roamed all over Jerusalem with their carts and satchels of goods, selling shoelaces, soap, razor blades, sweets, clothing, cigarettes, books, scissors, foodstuffs. My own father was a peddler of sorts, though he schlepped his batteries and light bulbs around to electrical shops rather than accosting individuals on the street. During the war-time rationing, shady characters had lurked in alleys to offer packets of coffee, sugar, and butter at black-market prices. I slid the record half way out of its cover to get a closer look.

"How do I know it's not damaged? I can't see properly in this light. I can't even read the label. It might not be the same as what's written on the sleeve."

"*Giveret*! One daughter of Israel doesn't cheat another. The record is in perfect condition and it is the right one. Don't you love Schubert? And Mr. Tauber is first class, wouldn't you say?"

As a matter of fact, Duncan and I were big fans of Richard Tauber and had two other recordings of his. We admired his warm, lyrical voice but also sympathized with his life's journey. Because of his Jewish ancestry, Tauber had been driven out of Germany and his native Austria to eventually find refuge in England, where he became a huge success. I was severely tempted to buy the record on the spot. But that would be foolish. One daughter of Israel certainly could cheat another. It happened all the time.

"Let's find a street lamp so that I can take a better look," I proposed. "It's almost dark. We shouldn't stay here anyway."

"Tell you what," the woman countered. "Take the record home with you. Try it out. Don't pay me a mil until tomorrow. We'll meet here again at this time and talk. That's how much I trust you. Maybe by tomorrow, you'll trust me a little too."

The offer was too strange. I tried to read her expression but, with the light so dim, the nuances of her face were lost in shadow. Something about her voice bothered me as well. The accent. She was dressed in the severe garb of the Ashkenazi Hasidic Jewesses of Mea Shearim. But she spoke Hebrew like an Oriental, with certain sounds coming from deep inside her throat.

"You've stolen this, haven't you? You're a thief. No, I can't take it."

I pushed the record back into her hands. She gave a low chuckle.

"So honest and upright. A woman of conviction. Very impressive. What if I were to say to you, this is not about something so trivial as a record or making a sale? It's about an opportunity for you to serve your country."

I took a step backwards.

"Who are you?"

She laughed again, more heartily this time.

"I am a proud Hebrew. A patriot, shall we say. Not a common thief. I don't know where the record came from originally, but the one who gave it to me to give to you has a noble mission in mind. We don't want your money. Something else entirely."

"What are you talking about?"

"Information. You work for the British government. In the General Post Office. A great, final struggle is underway between our people and the British occupiers. The battles will be fought by our brave young soldiers, but ordinary folk like you can do much to help. With very little trouble to yourself, you could be our eyes and ears at the Post Office and make a contribution to the cause."

I couldn't speak. Her words, which seemed to have come out of a second-rate spy thriller, scattered my thoughts. So I just stared at the strange figure in the long grey dress and the black scarf. A strange gleam sparked her dark eyes. They held mine; steady, patient, brazen. Beyond her shoulders the branches of the olive trees thrust their branches into the gathering dusk. The crow scolded above our heads.

"I have no information to give," I said at last. "I'm just a typist, not someone with an important position."

"Oh, allow us be the judges of what is important, Miss Salomon."

Her voice had become a purr. She knew my name. A chill ran down my spine, but I told myself not to panic, for she was hardly any bigger than I was and not likely to do me physical harm. She was just a girl with an overblown sense of her own importance, playing a preposterous game. *Stand your ground.*

"I took an oath of loyalty when I joined the government. I don't consider the British my enemy and I'm not interested in helping your insane struggle. Now if you'll excuse me, I'll be off."

She stayed exactly where she was, blocking my way, so I walked around her, stumbling over some stones until my feet regained the path. I heard the crunch of her footsteps right behind. I was glad to be wearing my sturdier shoes, the ones with only an inch of high heel.

"The British are the oppressors, Miss Salomon. Unless you've renounced your own people, the British are your enemy too."

She was almost on top of me, her voice harsh and accusing in my ear. I quickened my pace until we emerged from under the trees into open space, where I could see the way forward more clearly. The path forked, one branch of it winding around boulders and headstones towards Mamilla Pool, the other leading up the slope towards the safety of King George V Street. The sky had turned deep indigo, with a sprinkling of stars, but the street lamps up ahead cast reassuring pools of light. I wheeled around to face my pursuer again.

"You can follow me if you like, but you're putting yourself in danger. I'll report you to the police. In fact, I have a friend who's a sergeant in the Palestine Police."

"Oh ho!" she exclaimed, glee in her voice as if she'd caught me in a trap. "Your friend the sergeant! Your boyfriend! The one who gets you between the sheets. That's why you're so loyal to the British cause. But how do you know he's faithful to you? He has many opportunities to be with other women. You're just his whore."

My hand rose in the air to strike her, and it was her turn to take a step backwards.

"You know nothing about us."

"I know enough."

My heart pounding, I waited for her to continue, but she seemed suddenly uncertain and just stood in silence, grinning at me, her teeth faintly gleaming. Perhaps I'd called her bluff.

"You're right. I am loyal to my boyfriend and he'll be very interested to hear all about my encounter with a suspicious character. I don't know your name but I can give him a reasonable description. You'd better hide yourself well."

The smile on her face disappeared.

"I wouldn't do that if I were you, Eva Salomon. There is no mercy for an informer. None at all."

She made her forefinger and thumb into a pistol shape, aimed it at my forehead, and expelled a puff of air from between pursed lips. *Pffft*. Gunshot.

"You spurn a chance to serve your country. That alone is bad. But much worse is to cling to this oppressor of the Hebrew people. If you know what's good for you, leave him. At once. You belong with one of your own."

"Allow me to be the judge of what's good for me," I sneered. "My private life is no one's business but mine alone."

"Oh my. What grand words." She shook her head as if to pity my boundless stupidity. "A traitor to the Land of Israel is most certainly our business."

She turned around to return back the way we'd come, but stopped suddenly to fling a parting shot.

"Think about it, Eva Salomon. You have been warned."

A moment later the shadows of the olive grove had swallowed her up.

MY HALF-EATEN SUPPER sat on the table—a glass jar of yogurt, with the spoon still in it, my bread and butter torn into bits on the plate. With a cigarette between my fingers, I paced the floor. There were so many questions I should have asked the girl. Burning with those questions, I had the impulse to run outside, down the street, and back to the cemetery to search her out behind the headstones and trees and in the sunken hollows in the ground. How did she know so much about me? How long had I been spied on? Why me, of all people to approach in her quest for someone to become a mole? Who was the "we" she represented? Exactly what mischief did they have in mind? Or was she just a crazed loner? An odious crank like the one from before the war who'd left a poison-pen letter at my door?

My warning to the girl that I could give a credible description of her to the police was pure bluster. Her face shifted constantly in my mind, so that one moment it was round and pale as the moon, the next moment, thin, dark, and foxy. She was slightly taller than me. Stockier. But no, that could have been the effect of the shapeless dress. Duncan had once showed me a "Wanted" notice for Jewish terrorists that was distributed to police stations around the country. The descriptions below the photos were scrupulously precise and somewhat repulsive—estimations of height and weight, remarks on body build, eye colour, complexion, shape of nose (normal, small, or long and hooked) and "Peculiarities" that included bad teeth, thick lips, flat feet, and so on. Yes, I could remember the words on a handbill I'd glanced at months ago. But I couldn't summon a single distinguishing feature about the girl on the path. Only her voice. But how to adequately describe it? Low and hoarse, brash, with a youthful brightness. Yet tinged with a bitter edge, a cynicism that suggested someone who'd seen hardship and disappointment. Hardly the stuff of objective evidence. And perhaps I was making all this up to fill the vacuum of my confusion.

Should I tell Mr. Watson about the encounter? The oath of allegiance I'd sworn when I came into the employ of the Censorship Division obligated me to be loyal to His Majesty, the King, by not divulging information to unauthorized parties. Even now that the war was over and the Division had closed down, I was not allowed to speak in detail about the work we'd done or the secrets we'd uncovered. The obligation might even last a lifetime—whether we remained his Majesty's employees or not—Mr. Edwin Samuel had told the staff when he addressed us for the last time to thank us for a job well done. My lips must be sealed on wartime secrets. That part was clear. But did I have to tell about an attempt to recruit me as a spy in a post office that was no longer the nerve centre of a war effort?

Mr. Watson was a financial officer now, and I his secretary, typing humdrum reports on postal revenues and expenses. As I'd said to the girl, quite truthfully, we had no information of any interest. My relationship with my manager was formal, scrupulously professional. He knew nothing concerning my private life other than what I'd mentioned about my sister and her family. Or if he knew, he didn't let on. And I only knew the bare bones of his—that he was married to a woman called Polly, that he had a son in the primary school at St. George's, and that he was interested in the archaeology of ancient Palestine. If we had any casual conversation at all it was usually about the scraps and shards he'd collected during his rambles around historic sites. To tell Mr. Watson about the encounter in the cemetery would be to pull back that curtain of privacy between us in a way we'd both find awkward. It would raise questions in his mind about who I associated with, why I'd attracted the attention of shady characters. He'd feel obliged to probe. Besides, the more I thought about the girl's request, the more convinced I became that she—*they*—weren't interested in my workplace at all but in my connection to Duncan. That was the plum they were after—someone who could spy on the police.

I should tell Duncan. I didn't relish the thought. We'd end up talking about all that now divided the *Yishuv* and the British authorities—a discussion that went round in circles and left us both sour and tense. When we'd first met, I'd demanded to know whose side he was on. These days, in subtle ways, he asked me the same question. He'd want to know what the girl looked like and I couldn't tell him. I'd rebuffed her approach. Wasn't that enough? Beneath the surface of all this chatter in my head I also heard an ominous whisper, *No mercy for informers. None at all.*

THE NEXT DAY, I searched the faces of passersby as I joined the Friday afternoon throngs on Jaffa Road. My eyes sought out the religious women in tightly knotted head scarves, who lumbered along with their bulging string shopping bags clutched in each hand. My scrutiny also took in the olive-skinned Oriental girls, who gathered around the soda kiosk, laughing, gesturing. They all seemed to have husky voices. They all pronounced certain vowels deep inside their throats. I continued along Jaffa Road to Agrippa Street and into the maze of alleys that made up the Machane Yehuda Market. I saw scores of pious matrons from all over the Jewish city, haggling, poking at the tomatoes, and peppers, adding to the general clamour, as they prepared for the Sabbath. The ones from the Hasidic quarters were easy to spot because their dress was more drab and severe than anyone else's. Thick stockings on their legs despite the heat. Down-at-heel slippers on their feet. Pasty, weary faces, the result of being married off at puberty and giving birth more than a dozen times. Unthinkable that the brash girl from the cemetery would be among these careworn wives.

Nor was there anything of her to be found in the ancient Muslim cemetery to which I eventually returned, retracing my steps along the dusty paths from the eastern to the western edges. I even forced myself to walk through at dusk. I heard the whisper of the breeze through the leathery olive leaves. I heard the boisterous chorus of crows. *A murder of crows.* I remembered the phrase from a jocular column in *The Palestine Post* on oddities of the English language. No one blocked my way again or followed behind. No spectres popped out of the sunken mausoleums. The long-buried sheikhs remained in the ground where they belonged. She *was* just a crank, I told myself, just like that anonymous letter writer of long ago. To be ignored. Forgotten. As days passed, it seemed less urgent to speak to Duncan about the strange encounter. He didn't tell me everything either. He spoke less and less about his work these days because so much of it now concerned the "Jewish Troubles." So the passage of time frayed at my memory of what had happened in the cemetery until it became a grey, wispy presence, like an old spider's web stuck in an unreachable corner of the ceiling. Now and then it felt like unfinished business I ought to attend to. And then I'd push the thought away.

Chapter 24
King David Hotel

THE REPORT WITH tricky tables and footnotes required cross-referencing information from handwritten notes against data in a densely printed document. A tedious business, but I'd promised Mr. Watson I'd get it done before end of morning, so I stayed at my post after everyone else had gone for lunch. The fan overhead click-clicked its monotonous song, stirring the air but giving no relief from the thick July heat. I tore a blotched page off the typewriter carriage. *Damn this machine. Damn!* The ribbon buckled when it was supposed to unwind smoothly. The carriage was prone to jump ahead if my thumb hit the space bar just a tad too hard. Why hadn't the repairman come? *Take a breath. Begin again.* I inserted another page, along with a sheet of carbon and copy paper, wiped my sweaty fingers on my handkerchief. Somewhere in the distance a siren wailed and became a mosquito I was determined to ignore.

"Eva!"

I jerked in my chair. Mary Griffin, who used to work with me in the censorship service, stood in the doorway with her beige handbag over her shoulder and a straw sun hat on her head. Her cheeks were red and her lips pursed. She looked as she used to when she'd convinced herself a coded message lay embedded in someone's unremarkable letter to his uncle.

"Something's going on," Mary said. "Didn't you hear? The explosion!"

"When? Where?"

I hadn't heard a thing. Only the mosquito siren.

"Twenty minutes ago. My pen almost flew out of my hand, I was so startled. Come on. There's sure to be an announcement in the cafeteria."

"I'll come soon. Would you save me a seat? I need to finish up."

Mary shook her head. "Everyone's down there already, waiting for news. I just came back up to fetch my things in case we're evacuated."

Her determination to get me up, cemented my resolve to stay put. There were too many disruptive incidents these days, too many emergency announcements. What had happened to the plucky spirit of "Keep calm and carry on"? I told her to go ahead without me, for I wanted to finish what I was doing.

"Bloody nuisance having to look over one's shoulder all the time," she grumped. "But we *must* put security first."

With a last reproachful glance, she marched off down the hall. I turned back to the lists in my handwritten notes—statistics on postage stamp sales and numbers of telephone calls and telegrams. My fingers tapped. Some moments passed, I'm not sure how many, and then a thunderous roar flung my hands up in the air. The roar did not belong to this world. It went on forever, filling every crevice and corner with its black sound. And did the building shake or was it just the trembling of my whole body? After a long silence, several sirens began to howl at once. I knew in the pit of my stomach this wasn't just another incident. Something awful had happened, something that would make all the other acts of violence of recent months seem like child's play. On shaky legs I rose and made my way down the hall.

The second-floor cafeteria swarmed with excited, gesturing, yammering people. They stood in huddles or milled about aimlessly. Some were streaming out the door but the exit below was apparently blocked, so they boiled back into the room. Others crowded around the windows, shouting out commentary over their shoulders.

"There's another ambulance. It's heading for Mamilla Road."

"No, not Mamilla. Julian's Way!"

I saw Mr. Watson staring morosely at the halfeaten sandwich in his hand. He was one of the few people still seated and trying, unsuccessfully, to maintain a semblance of normality. A man clambered up onto one of the tables, cupped his hands around his mouth and shouted for attention. The room stilled at once. A senior official came forward.

"Ladies and gentlemen, I regret to have to inform you that the offices in the southern wing of the King David Hotel have apparently been the target of a terrorist action."

A collective gasp greeted these words. The southern wing of the King David housed the Government Secretariat, the command centre of the Mandatory administration. This wing was also the headquarters of British Forces in Palestine and Transjordan. An attack at that level seemed impossible, beyond audacious.

Our official continued, in a calm, but hesitant voice, as if reading a notice that he himself could not quite make sense of. We were not to panic. We were all to leave the building immediately in a quiet and self-controlled manner. All work was suspended for the day until the police had conducted a thorough search for suspicious objects. Go directly home. Listen to the wireless for bulletins. Do not, under any circumstances, interfere with the rescue operations.

The excited, almost holiday mood in the room vanished. We'd had bomb scares before, but this was on another scale. A hush came upon us as we all—British, Arab, and Jewish staff of the General Post Office—filed out of the cafeteria, down the stairs, and across the shiny floor of the main hall. The high-ceilinged room that I admired daily for its palatial air, for the richly patterned marble on the counters and walls, now echoed with the sombre tramp of our footsteps.

Once outside, my thoughts immediately turned to Duncan. Something terrible had happened and Duncan would be amid the action. In the rescue, in the chase, in the chaos. If only by some magic I could see what he was doing, call him to my side. An agitated crowd filled Jaffa Road, with all the civil servants from the nearby government buildings, the clerks from Barclay's Bank, the shopkeepers and shoppers and café patrons and the guests from Hotel Fast. Rumours buzzed through the air. Two explosions. No three! No ten! Terrible casualties. The King David in ruins. Some people were heading in that direction despite the orders for everyone to go home. I too headed towards Julian's Way, drawn by the need to find Duncan and by a more primitive impulse—to behold with my own eyes the site of the disaster.

The King David Hotel sprawled at the top of a long, sloping hill. Well before I saw the smoke, I could smell the bitter odour. I could see shards of glass sprayed over the sidewalk and glittering in the noonday sun. Military vehicles blocked the road, but there were gaps between them and people were craning their necks and holding their hands against their mouths. I dodged past a couple of distracted soldiers, scrambled over some rubble, and placed myself behind a cedar tree on the grounds of the YMCA, where I had a good view. And then I too held my hand to my mouth.

The whole six-storey southwest corner of the King David was gone. Collapsed as if smashed by a giant fist. Broken girders, splintered wood, and shreds of masonry poked out of the chasm. Sections of floor hung down like ripped cloth. Black smoke billowed from huge piles of wreckage. My eyes took all this in and then they registered the real horror. Dust-covered figures staggered about with dark lines of blood etched on their faces. A man clutching his head screamed, "My sister, my sister, she's in there." Rescue workers scrambled over the mountain of debris with picks and shovels. There were shouts, moans, sirens, the gabble of commands bellowed through bull-horns. Two men with a stretcher, bearing a bloodied, quivering mass of flesh, passed close to where I stood. My stomach convulsed and I spewed the remnants of my breakfast onto the cedar roots at my feet. A soldier wearing the cap of the Argyll and Sutherland Highlanders appeared beside me and took my arm.

"You all right, Miss? Yes? Just a bit shaken? Well then, come along."

I pulled away from him and asked if he'd seen any policemen about.

"You want to give evidence?"

"No. I have a friend . . . I'm looking for someone."

"You have to leave here, Miss. You'll be in the way."

He spoke gently, with the soft burr of a Scots accent, but maintained a firm grip on my arm as he led me back to the other side of the police cordon. "A gawker," he said of me to one of the officers. A few minutes later a truck with a bullhorn rolled slowly up Julian's Way announcing a curfew for the entire city. All civilians, except for doctors, nurses, rescue workers, and others with special permission, were to leave the streets immediately or face arrest. A daytime curfew! Highly unusual, but these were extraordinary times.

LATER, FROM MY window, I could see the glimmer of search lights illuminating a patch of night sky beyond the rooftops. The streets were so deathly still I could hear the tap of picks and faint shouts from the site of the disaster several blocks away. Where was Duncan? Why hadn't he come? Was he among the searchers working around the clock to extract shattered bodies from the wreckage? Had he been hit by falling debris? Had he been at the Secretariat at the time of the explosion? As a C.I.D. officer, he often went to the King David for briefings or as part of a security detail for some dignitary. In my room, I waited, chain smoked, leaped to my feet to peer outside whenever a vehicle passed below. As the evening wore on, I couldn't dispel the hideous thought that his luck had run out. This time he'd been hurt. Surely if he was unharmed he would have found a spare moment to let me know, as he'd done that time the Russian Compound was bombed. I finally sank into a fitful sleep, but woke every couple of hours in the grip of a terrible foreboding.

At five a.m. the next morning the curfew was lifted. I drank a hasty cup of coffee and ran back to the King David, but a much more secure cordon of soldiers and vehicles now barred the way. At Yossi's, the neighbourhood grocer, I bought a newspaper and, leaning against a lamppost, scanned the list of dead, wounded, and missing. An appallingly long list, encompassing many inches of newsprint. The Postmaster General, Mr. Gerald Kennedy, was among the missing. Our own Mr. Kennedy! To my great relief Duncan was not on the list. There was still much confusion about the casualty numbers. But I was calmed by the daylight and the movement of Jerusalem citizens going about their business and the sober statement of facts in the newspaper. The likelihood Duncan had been caught up in this explosion now seemed more remote. Could I allow myself to ask about his welfare at police headquarters? Would he think it amiss? If only I could slip into the building and discreetly pose my question. I hurried downtown to Jaffa Road and the Russian Compound. Overnight the place had been transformed. Barbed wire surrounded the perimeter. Soldiers with Sten guns stood guard. I couldn't enter the courtyard without stating my business. The sentry would have to check with a higher-up, who'd want to interrogate me further. And all this trouble I was causing would just infuriate Duncan. So I gave up and went along the street towards my place of work, the General Post Office. Things had changed here too. Armed soldiers blocking the doorway asked to see identity cards and the contents of briefcases, parcels, and bags. They paid special attention to anyone with a Jewish name or face. When my turn came, the soldier, who was quite young—a new recruit perhaps—thrust his big paw into my handbag and groped around among my face-powder cases and lipstick tubes. I smiled. He reddened slightly, but did not smile back.

All morning the atmosphere at our workplace crackled with tension. Voices in the halls. Constant footsteps. High traffic to the Ladies Room. Mid-morning, as I pushed open the heavy wooden door to the Ladies, the excited chatter I'd heard on my approach came to a dead halt. Four women, all Britons, turned their heads. Their expressions went from startled to strange. Mary Griffin, speaking in a falsely bright tone, said something innocuous about the weather. That it was hot.

"Yes," I agreed. "It's July."

Poor Britons, I thought, as I entered a toilet stall. They couldn't rely on their favourite smokescreen subject during the long Palestinian summer. For a good half of the year the weather was always the same, hot and dry—perhaps the only thing in the country that was utterly predictable. From behind the closed stall door, I heard the sound of water in the sinks and the rustle of clothing, but no more conversation. Soon afterwards, they all left and I was alone in the empty, white-tiled room.

Even the normally jovial Mr. Watson looked pale and distracted that day. When I tapped at his open door to bring him the completed revenue report, I found him with his hands folded on the desk, his eyes closed, and I wondered if I'd interrupted him in prayer. I stammered an apology which he dismissed with a wave as he took the typed pages, muttering his approval. "Yes quite correct, all in order." But he'd merely glanced at the top sheet. And then abruptly he jumped to his feet.

"Wait, Miss Salomon. Let me show you something."

He picked up a file folder that had been lying on the window sill behind him and came around to my side of the desk. He opened the folder so that I could view his latest treasure.

"Isn't it lovely. I found it at an Oriental curio shop on Suleiman Road. It's just a copy, of course. Not a real antique. In fact, it's probably just an illustration rescued from some book that was falling apart. Still the colours are very nice, don't you think?"

We were looking at a stylized map of the world in the form of a flower with three petals, each of which represented a continent—Europe, Asia, and Africa. In a circle in the centre was the Holy City, Jerusalem, pictured as an idealized medieval European town in miniature with narrow, red-roofed buildings, embraced by greenery. The entire "flower" was set in a sea of wavy lines, on which rode a sailing ship and mermaids. Falling off the map in the left-hand corner was a blob called America.

"That's how they saw the world in Renaissance times," Mr. Watson said, still gazing reverently at the illustration. "A beautifully ordered place. And Jerusalem was the centrepiece, the precious heart of the rose. No other town could compete. It's been loved for thousands of years. Too much loved, perhaps."

He chuckled sadly. Then he noticed that my eyes had shifted from the map to his face and he grew flustered, snapping the file folder shut, raking his fingers through the thin strands of dark hair plastered across the bald part of his head.

"Ahem. Well. I mustn't keep you, Miss Salomon. You must get back to your work. We all have much to do. Ah, by the way, you know about the assembly at noon? In the main lobby downstairs. To pay our respects to those who fell in yesterday's . . ."

He groped for the right word to describe what had happened at the King David. Most people called it an "outrage" but Mr. Watson didn't care for such drastic expressions. He left his sentence incomplete and went on to the next.

"It's the least we can do."

He waved me out of his office with a weak attempt at a smile.

The entire staff had gathered for the assembly. The wicket clerks, the sorters, the parcel department, the telegraph and telephone girls, the administrators and supervisors. We filled the ground-floor hall, standing in a semi-circle in front of the closed wickets and facing the mezzanine stairs, where the assistant postmaster general gave us an update on the situation. The death toll now stood at 41, but this was considered to be an optimistic number because of those who'd not yet been pulled from the wreckage and the many who lay in hospital in critical condition. Our own chief, Mr. Kennedy, was among the dead. All of us had heard the whispered story of how his body had to be scraped off a wall of the YMCA after being flung right across the street by the force of the explosion. Of course the assistant P.G. said nothing about that piece of horror. He said we must pray for Mr. Kennedy and his family and for all the other victims and for the brave rescuers and for our police and military. There could be no doubt that this was the work of Jewish extremists. The Irgun had taken responsibility. It was the worst act of terrorism our country had ever seen. Hopefully the perpetrators would swiftly be caught and those who felt the least sympathy for their cause would come to their senses. Please God this would be the last of such heinous crimes. And now, the assistant postmaster said, we would bow our heads in fifteen minutes of silence. Throughout the civil service, right across the country, all employees of His Majesty's Government would be doing the same.

Normally such commemorations involved a single minute of silence or, at most, two. Fifteen minutes of public silence seemed excessive, almost sadistic. But of course, not a whisper of protest escaped anyone's lips. We stood together in the lobby—the same crowd that had been so wide-eyed and animated in the cafeteria just twenty-four hours before—hushed and painfully self-conscious, at least I was, as the long minutes ticked by. Though I wanted to focus on the victims as we'd been asked to do, my thoughts flew elsewhere. To Duncan. Worms of doubt gnawed deep. He hadn't come. He didn't care.

I stared at the dove-grey marble floor between my shoes, felt my stomach rumble, was aware of the small movements of the others and their suppressed sighs. I looked up once and saw the backs of bowed heads and quickly cast my eyes downwards again. The ceremony was meant, in part, to bring us all together, but I sensed a coldness seeping out of the pores of the British and Arab staff. I felt them overwhelmed by a hidden pressure—embraced by some, feebly resisted by others, perhaps—to ostracize their Jewish colleagues. An unmistakable and depressingly familiar miasma of hostility was in the air.

WHEN I RETURNED home that evening, my landlady, Mrs. Rajinsky, pounced upon me in the hall with the words, "There's no electricity."

She said this with a bitter satisfaction, like one pleased to see her pessimistic view of the world confirmed.

"They've done it on purpose," she added. "To punish us. They must punish us all for the crimes of a few madmen."

There was no point in responding to such nonsense, so I merely shrugged and went into the kitchen. On the counter I noticed candles stuck onto plates with melted wax, in readiness for the darkness to come. Though the sun had set, there was still enough daylight to see what I was doing. As I opened the ice box to find some food, I heard my landlady's heavy tread behind me.

"You see? It's good I didn't buy that electric refrigerator, as you suggested. We still have ice. That is, as long as the ice factory stays open. Who knows what they'll close down next. Insane times, we live in. If you're going to light the Primus, Miss Salomon, do it soon, and put enough water in the kettle for me and Mr. Maisel too. He just got home. We could all eat supper in my room if you like, to save on the candles. No? You're not so keen? Well, I can give you one of these, but not more than one. I've run short. And you better be careful, because it has to last until morning. I'm not putting a candle in the WC, by the way. We can all do our business in the dark. We know well enough what it looks like."

At that point, to my relief, a loud knock came at the door. Mrs. Rajinsky hurried down the hall, her slippers slap-slapping against the tiles. I heard her exclaim in dismay and the stern rumble of a male voice. Three Tommies wearing the maroon berets of the Sixth Airborne Division entered our flat, bunching up around Mrs. Rajinsky in the narrow corridor. The one whose voice I'd heard identified himself as Sergeant Michaels.

"You were here yesterday!" Mrs. Rajinsky protested. "I mean, the police were here. They came to snoop around the whole neighbourhood directly after the explosions. Whatever they were looking for, they didn't find it."

"Sorry, Ma'am. We won't be long. Just another routine check to make sure we didn't miss anything."

"The electricity is off!" Mrs. Rajinsky's tone was accusing.

"Yes Ma'am. Very inconvenient. Who else lives here with you? Is there a sitting room we can use?"

While Sergeant Michaels spoke, the other two soldiers banged on all the doors along the hall and pushed them open. They poked their heads into my room, Maisel's room, Mrs. Rajinsky's, the lavatory, and the bathroom. A flustered Mr. Maisel, barefoot and with his shirt hanging half out of his trousers, emerged. We filed into Mrs. Rajinsky's room, which was the largest in the flat and had a sofa and chairs in addition to her bed. No one sat down. Sergeant Michaels examined our identity cards by the light of his electric torch, then passed them on to one of his men, who appeared to be checking our names against a list. The third soldier stood in the doorway as if to guard against any of us attempting to bolt. Daylight was fading fast. The sergeant shone his torch up and down Mr. Maisel, revealing the young man's hair standing out in tufts, the glint of his round glasses, the awkwardness of his half-tucked shirt at his thick waist, and the whiteness of his bare, pudgy feet. I could tell by the odour that Mr. Maisel was in a sweat.

"You, sir! Where were you yesterday between nine a.m. and twelve p.m.?" the sergeant demanded.

"He was at Steimatzky's, like always," Mrs. Rajinsky said.

"I'll beg you not to interfere with the questions, Ma'am. Let him answer for himself."

Maisel stammered that he had indeed been at his workplace, Steimatzky's bookstore, where he ran the small lending library at the back of the shop. Yes, he'd been there all morning and even after the commotion caused by the explosions and, yes, there were people who could confirm this. No, he'd not seen nor heard anything of interest at any point during the day that could help with the investigation. The sergeant took similar statements from me and Mrs. Rajinsky, and then it was time for the search, which was done one room at a time with the room owner present. I brought my candle from the kitchen and set it on the table, but the soldiers also used their torches. They poked under my bed, lifted the mattress, opened the cover of the gramophone, opened the wardrobe, and felt around behind the clothes. The sergeant's assistant found Duncan's shaving kit—the razor, brush, and soap mug—and brought these things out for the sergeant to see.

"I have a friend," I said. "He visits."

"And who is this friend?"

I wasn't sure what to say and as I hesitated, Mrs. Rajinsky who'd slipped away from the guard soldier and was standing in my doorway chirped, "He's a policeman. A British policeman. A sergeant, just like you."

Wheeling around, Sergeant Michaels roared at her to get back into her room. He asked me his question again. So then I had no choice but to give Duncan's name, his rank, his police number, and where he was billeted. That wasn't all the sergeant wanted to know. He asked how long we'd been friends and how often Duncan visited and whether he was the only one who visited, or whether there were other British policemen and soldiers who came to my room. I dug my nails into my palms and kept my voice as even as I could. I was glad of the dusk, which hid the flush of my cheeks and the expressions on the soldiers' faces. All my answers were written down in the assistant's notebook. When they were finished with me, the sergeant and his assistant spent a long time behind closed doors with Mr. Maisel. Mrs. Rajinsky, and I waited, in the kitchen, by candlelight, with the third soldier standing near. We heard the thumps and scrapes of furniture being moved around in Mr. Maisel's' room and the murmur of voices.

"He's a shy boy, a nervous type, but he has nothing to hide. They'll frighten him into saying something he shouldn't," Mrs. Rajinsky fretted. "Why are they taking so long. It's ridiculous."

At last, all three returned to the corridor. The soldiers were done. They had nothing more to ask of us and apparently no reason to detain the bookshop clerk. The whole episode had only lasted about fifteen minutes, but total darkness had fallen by now. They were already clattering off to the next flat, their torch beams bouncing along the walls of the stairwell.

"Tell the government to turn the electricity back on," Mrs. Rajinsky shouted after them.

None of the soldiers bothered to answer.

THERE WAS NOTHING to do but lie in the dark. To wait, to hope, to listen for the sound of his whistling at the front door. The shutters of my window stood open, letting in a breath of air and revealing the night sky with its profusion of stars. The door to my room stood slightly ajar too, so that I could hear if he came. *Tap, tap, tap.* The rescue men were digging still. There'd been terrible stories. About severed limbs in the rubble. About a piece of flesh tossed by the explosion into one of the nearby trees. About people buried alive and the diggers frantic, but unable to reach them. Parts of the bombed building were so unstable that chunks of concrete still came tumbling down onto those wielding the picks, creating more casualties. *Tap, tap, tap.* The pathetic, desperate picks had come closer. They knocked against the wall of my room, broke through. Their sharp points hovered above my sleeping body and were about to dig into my skull.

I started awake. Had I dreamt the knock? No, it was real. My legs swung out of bed. My bare feet flew across the cool tiles as I hurried through the dark to rip open the front door. A tall figure filled the doorway, intact, alive. With a small cry of joy, I crushed myself against him, feeling the soft cotton of his shirt against my cheek, and the hard-muscle chest underneath. His arms wrapped around me and he grunted softly. Then I noticed the reek of liquor on his breath.

"Where have you been?" I whispered, when we'd moved into my room and I'd closed the door behind us. I couldn't help the hiss of reproach in my voice.

He groped for a chair in the dark and sat down heavily without answering, slumped in his seat. I found the other chair and sat down across from him.

"You've been out drinking?"

"And if so? What's it to you?"

"I've been worrying about you for two days. There are so many rumours about who got hurt and about booby traps laid for the police. I thought you would come to see me as soon as you had a free moment. The police precinct is like an armed fortress now, so I'm locked out, but it's nothing for you to walk across the street to the GPO. You could have sent word at least. You could have . . ."

I stopped in midstream. It was an old complaint and it had gotten me nowhere in the past. Already I was regretting my words. And the fact that I'd spoken too loudly, for I thought I heard a movement in Mrs. Rajinsky's room and held my breath to listen for her step. I heard nothing more save the thump of my own heart.

"What a splendid welcome," Duncan muttered. "Guess I should have stayed with the lads at Finks."

"Go back then, if that's how you feel."

It didn't help that I couldn't see his face. After several moments of silence, I heard him sigh. He reached across the table and found my clenched fist, covering it with his big, warm hand.

"There's been a lot going on, Eva. Can't tell you much, but it's not been pretty."

The bitter edge had left his voice. Now he just sounded weary, dispirited.

"Oh Duncan, I'm sorry. Look, it's silly that we're sitting in the dark. I have a candle right here."

I felt for the box of matches, was about to strike a light, but he gripped my arm to restrain me.

"Don't. Not yet. Stay where you are."

He rose to his feet, went to the wardrobe, and rummaged about the shelves until he found what he wanted—the mickey of Scotch he'd stowed away. There was only about a third of it left, not enough to do much damage. I heard the clink of glass and the splash of liquid as he poured himself a drink.

"Want some? Oh, come on. Have a nip."

I said what I always said to his offer of whisky.

"No thanks. It tastes like petrol."

"How would you know? Have you been drinking petrol, Missy?" He chuckled. We were back on familiar ground. "Suit yourself. More for me. So when did you lose the electricity? It's just this part of the street that's still without power, by the way. I saw lights on in the rest of the neighbourhood. Your landlady must be fit to be tied."

So I told him about the search party and how Mrs. Rajinsky had held the soldiers responsible for the power outage, glad that I had something amusing to tell. I waited for him to laugh, but he didn't and he also didn't ask about what the soldiers said when they'd searched my room. His thoughts had gone elsewhere. I stopped talking, fiddled with the box of matches which made a soft clicking sound as I rolled it over and over on the table.

"Are you all right, Duncan?" I whispered.

"Right as rain."

More silence. I lit a cigarette, offered him one and we both hid from one another through the business of smoking—the sucking in, the breathing out, the flicking of the ashes into the ashtray. Whenever the tip of his cigarette glowed red, I got a glimpse of his lips, his moustache and the faint gleam of his eyes and then all was extinguished again.

"Talk to me, Duncan. Say something. Anything. I can't bear it when you're here, but not here."

"I've been taking evidence," he finally told me. "We set up an interview station at the Y and questioned eyewitnesses all day yesterday. Today I went around to the hospitals to talk to more survivors. Then I had to cross-check the statements, record the missing, look for clues and leads, sift through the jumble of stories. I've been at it non-stop."

"Oh," I breathed. But I was relieved. Better to be taking statements than to be clambering through the unstable, blood-soaked wreckage with the rescue teams. He sensed my thought and brought his glass down hard against the table.

"Been a long two days, I can tell you. Not exactly fun and games, getting people to describe what they'd been through."

"Sh! Keep your voice down. Oh Duncan, it's awful what happened, just awful."

"Mass murder's what it is."

The words smacked me in the face. Where had I heard them before and why had the statement unsettled me? I tried to remember and to digest the bitterness in Duncan's voice, a bitterness I felt was obscurely directed at me.

"A terrible crime, yes . . . but . . ."

Duncan's head snapped upwards. "But what? What sort of 'but' can there be?"

"No. Nothing."

"Come on. Something's on your mind, Missy. Tell me." He was the investigator now, calm but insistent and I knew better than to avoid the question. He'd dig around until he'd extracted the truth. I pressed my fingers to my temples as I tried to think.

"Mass murder is what the Nazis did. One has to be careful of one's language or the phrases lose their meaning, don't you see?" I pleaded. "The bombing of the King David was a horrible terrorist act, but to call it mass murder . . . it's not the right term."

I remembered now that I'd read the phrase in this morning's *Palestine Post*. An unnamed British official had been quoted, venting his anger but also, it seemed to me, deliberately using loaded expressions to hurl at the Jewish community.

"Oh, forgive me for not choosing my words," he spat. "Some fellows pack milk churns with sticks of dynamite, plant them in a hotel filled with civilians and blast the place to smithereens. Men and women killed. British, Arabs and fellow Jews. And the injuries, you can't imagine . . . !"

He paused. I heard him suck in his breath.

"No regard for human life—not a smidgen," he continued. "But I should find a nice term for the act, a diplomatic term that doesn't wound any local sensibilities."

"The Irgun say they phoned in warnings to evacuate the building and that their warnings were ignored. I'm not defending what happened. No one is. It's completely unforgivable. But perhaps they didn't mean . . ."

"You *are* defending them. That's exactly what you're doing. Oh, they didn't *mean* to hurt anyone, the poor sods. Just wanted to make a bit of noise with their hundred sticks of dynamite."

"Duncan, I can't stand this anymore. I'm lighting the candle."

The flame leaped high, revealing Duncan in his khaki drill, the whisky bottle beside him on the table, his lips set and his jaw thrust forward. He wasn't looking at me. He was looking past me at the dancing shadows on the wall.

"Tell you one thing. We'll get the filthy scum," he said through gritted teeth. "We'll get 'em this time. We won't leave off until we've caught every one of those vermin and seen 'em hang. Except hanging's too good for them. String 'em up by the feet and use their heads for footballs, is what we should do."

I'd never heard him speak with such venom and it frightened me.

"Yes," I said carefully. "And the whole *Yishuv* would be glad if those responsible were put behind bars, although . . ."

Duncan interrupted me with a sharp laugh."

"The whole bloody *Yishuv*, from Ben Gurion on down, is protecting those rats."

"How can you say that? Ben Gurion condemned the bombing. All the leaders of the *Yishuv* denounced the crime in the strongest language possible."

"Sure they condemn it," Duncan sneered, "To cover their arses and win world sympathy. They say one thing and do another. A clever game."

There was something ugly and all too familiar about this accusation of treachery. Duncan might as well have spoken of the proverbial stab in the back, the Jew as fifth column. I jumped up and began to pace, unable to sit still for another instant. My back-and-forth movements made the candle flame flicker and the shadows jerk so that the whole room seemed to be shaking.

"You can't think . . . It's not fair. We're all against the extremists. And you said it yourself. Jews were killed too. At this very moment Jews all over town are sitting *shiva* for the loved ones they lost. Everyone says the extremists harm our cause. I'll show you what it says in *The Palestine Post*."

"*The Palestine Post* is a Zionist rag."

He spat the word "Zionist" out of his mouth like a shred of foul meat. I stopped in my tracks. His unabashed revulsion made my knees wobble so that I had to grasp the back of my chair for balance. Though the *Post* was Jewish-owned, I'd never thought of it as an advocate of Jewish interests alone. The paper was written in English and so it had always been a little piece of England in my mind. And its tone was never shrill, not like that of some of the Hebrew papers. To me, the *Post* was calm, objective, professional, my companion and my Bible ever since I'd begun to read it in the first months after I'd stepped off the boat. My mind zigged and zagged and finally came to rest on Duncan's words "the whole *Yishuv*."

"Are you accusing me too? Am I also to blame for this horror? And if I tell you it makes me sick to the depths of my soul, will you think I'm just playing a treacherous game?"

He sat with his arms folded across his chest and his head bowed and I wondered with sinking heart whether we'd finally arrived at a point of no return. Why didn't he jump up to take me in his arms and reassure me I was his beloved, his dear Thumbelina? I clung to the chair back and listened to the thud of my heart.

"Of course I don't mean you," Duncan finally said. "And I know there are lots of decent, ordinary Jewish citizens who are appalled at the terrorists. But tell me, why is it so hard for us to get information? You know how small this place is. No one can fart without it being known from one end of town to the other. A shifty-eyed terrorist hides in a basement and the neighbours aren't aware? I've talked to a lot of Jews. They wail denunciations of the barbarity and then lock up their lips."

I sank back into my chair. I almost felt inclined to ask for a shot of his awful-tasting liquor. How could I explain what was understood by virtually every Jew in Palestine, no matter what his political leanings? Fear was part of the equation, of course. *No mercy for informants. None at all.* But even stronger than fear was the aversion to betraying one's own. You didn't turn your own flesh and blood over to the lords of the land to be hanged. And we were all flesh and blood, especially now, after the horrible losses of the war and the boatloads of desperate survivors of the camps being brutally turned away from Palestine's shores. I was sure Ben Gurion was sincere in his fury over the King David debacle. But even if he knew exactly who had carried those dynamite-filled milk churns into the King David and where the men were hiding, he couldn't give such information to the police. To do so would be to risk revolt within the Jewish community and hand the terrorists the greater victory of sympathy for their cause. I couldn't say any of this to Duncan. Not in the mood he was in now.

I leaned across to touch him and found one of his hands, clenched into a fist, on the table. I fitted my fingers between his large knuckles, let them nestle there, the cold sweat of my skin mingling with his. Somewhere outside a tomcat moaned, giving voice to his lust in a long, low-toned, masculine lament, which was answered finally by the female he was wooing. The two feral creatures wailed in perfect counterpoint, with dramatic pauses and resumptions, and then came a murderous screech, followed by an infantile yelp. Duncan's eyes scrunched up and his shoulders shook, little gasps and mews escaping from his lips, which alarmed me until I realized he was laughing, not weeping. I started to giggle too. I hushed him because of Mrs. Rajinsky next door which set us both off even more. Like the days when we sat close together at a concert and shared a joke during intermission over some little thing. A refined-looking man in front of us absentmindedly digging earwax from his ear—something banal like that—could launch us into an explosion of shared hilarity. Now I tittered until a sob caught in my throat. Duncan's fist uncurled and he enclosed my hand in his, held it tight.

"The cats are the real lords of the city," he said. "They'll be prowling the ruins here long after the rest of us are gone."

"Maybe they deserve Jerusalem more than we do."

Duncan rose, pulled me to my feet, bent to kiss me in a long, hopeful, hungry kiss, while his hands became busy under my nightgown. I felt the urgent press of his body and the answering ache in mine as he hoisted me up onto his shoulder and carried me to bed. It was our best, our only, answer to the clashing words and impossible questions.

We had just finished and disentangled with great sighs when the power came back on, evident because of the ceiling light glaring down into our upturned faces. We both groaned, shielded our eyes and laughed again and I hopped up to flick off the switch that I'd inadvertently left in the on position. Returned to bed, nestled against his shoulder, I felt him slipping away from me into sleep while my mind raced in relentless loops. I hadn't been as open with him as I should have. He would find out and accuse me of treachery.

"Duncan," I whispered. "Are you awake?"

"Now I am," he muttered. "Yes?"

"Nothing. Just . . ."

"Spit it out."

So I told him how the soldiers found his shaving things and that I'd been forced to reveal his name and how sorry I was to put him in an awkward position. Through the darkness I could feel him taking all this in. To my surprise, he wasn't concerned. It wouldn't be news to anyone that mattered at C.I.D., he assured me. They were aware of our liaison. It had been quietly, if not so happily, tolerated. There might be some brusque words between army brass and the Force over the matter. The military men liked to pretend they were the ones who ran a tight ship while the Force was full of weak spots, when it was the other way around, of course. His superiors would play the thing down, as they should, Duncan said.

They knew he could be trusted not to let his private life interfere with his duties. So far, no one had ever made a fuss.

So far. His words didn't put me entirely at ease. I snuggled up against him and waited for what else he might say, but he fell silent again, tense and lost in thought. To bring him back to me, I decided to put on some music that had soothed us through many a difficult night lately: Chopin's *Nocturnes.* I adjusted the volume to barely audible and slipped back into bed. The dreamy melodies were like massaging fingers along my spine. Halfway through the first nocturne I heard my own deep breathing between the notes.

"If you had information, would you give it to us?"

Duncan's question jerked me awake.

"What?"

"You know, a tip about someone you thought was suspicious."

I twisted myself around to get a look at him, but the room was so black I saw nothing but the outline of his profile: forehead, straight nose, jutting chin.

"I don't have any tips. Why would I?"

"The telephone and telegraph exchange is just one floor above where you work. We know it's got spies. One or more of those girls have been listening into calls at police headquarters and passing on warnings to the terrorists. There have been leaks and we're pretty sure those leaks are coming from the third floor of the post office."

"I don't work at the exchange. I don't know any of those girls."

"Yes. I suppose you don't."

His voice was disappointed.

"But you could find out."

"What do you mean?"

"You could befriend those girls. It can't be that hard. They're very young some of them and they must get bored after repeating the same words and plugging wires in and out all day long. They must be dying to chat. You would run into them in the Ladies and in the lunch room, wouldn't you? All you'd need to do would be to strike up a casual conversation. Exchange gossip, find out their political views. Next thing you know, you're a confidant. And even if you're not that close, well, you might pick up something. You worked in censorship. You're used to deciphering codes and secret messages. Think it over."

I was so astounded, I couldn't speak. Duncan's voice had become a bit louder as he outlined his plan. His hand gestured in the dark.

"You want me to become a spy?"

"Not to do anything that would put you at risk, of course. Nothing dramatic. Just asking that you keep your ears to the ground. Even the smallest tip can be helpful sometimes. And of course, we'd treat anything you said in the strictest confidence."

"You're raving."

He grunted.

"I suppose so. Never mind. Let's sleep. It's late and tomorrow's a workday."

He pulled me to lay down with him in the nestling position we'd always liked best, both of us on our sides, his long body curled around my short one, his chin resting against my head. Within seconds, he was asleep and his arm, draped heavily across my waist, pinned me to the mattress. I slipped out from under this imprisoning embrace and sat up. *Think it over.* Was he just testing my loyalties or making a serious proposal? I allowed myself to drift down the road of fantasy. Spying would be interesting. It would indeed be a bit like the heady days in the Censorship Division, give zest to my otherwise routine job in Finance. If I became a spy for the police, Duncan and I would be allies. I'd be supporting his work in a new, direct way. The discussions of possible evidence would bring us closer together. The subtle, unspoken rifts that had arisen between us since war's end would disappear. And if I found out something useful, it would reflect very well on him with his superiors and with his mates. All these years, he'd wanted to keep his job and our togetherness completely separate. Now he was finally inviting me into his sacrosanct world—a backdoor entry, to be sure, but a real one. This was what it would take to cleave to him completely.

And it was utterly out of the question.

While Duncan snored, I played the Chopin again. We both loved this piece. Many a night, after a day of high tension, Duncan had lain on his back beside me, letting the cascades of exquisite notes wash away his stress. Holding hands in the dark, we would ride the brilliant sound to another world of beauty and peace. We'd become as one soul. But not this night. This night he was absent and I was alone.

PART III

Chapter 25
Snatched

I STOOD BEFORE the billboard on the corner of Mamilla and Princess Mary roads, in broad daylight, doing nothing that could give offence to a soul. It was a cool January day, but cloudless, with the sky scrubbed clean by the winter wind. And it was late afternoon on a Friday, that magical hour in Jerusalem, when the light softens, the shadows lengthen, and the pre-Sabbath ferment begins to still. At this hour, the chiselled stones of the city, all the houses and walls, turn from harsh white into pastel shades of pink, mauve, and amber.

My string bag of groceries from the Machane Yehuda Market lay at my feet. My trilby hat sat at a jaunty angle on my head. I had bought that hat just days earlier at the milliner's on Ben Yehuda Street to lift my battered heart. For a few minutes, after the shop girl showed me how to tilt it just so, part of my face coquettishly hidden and the brim reaching skywards, I did indeed forget. The mirror showed a pretty woman, not as fresh-faced as she was a few years earlier, perhaps, but still charming. Still able to make men swivel around for a second look. If only *he* could be one of those men.

So I lingered in front of the billboard and whenever I heard footsteps or a vehicle passing by, I glanced out of the corner of my eye with an absurd, pathetic, self-defeating hope that it could be *him* in the turret of that armoured car, *his* face under the peaked cap. After so many weeks of having accepted the inevitable, I still searched for his face among all those groups of uniformed men who patrolled our city. A glimpse of a badge with the entwined double "P" could make me weak at the knees.

My rakish trilby. My fawn-toned jacket with a contrasting gold scarf knotted at my throat against the evening chill. My high-heeled shoes. A line from some American film flashed through my mind. "All dressed up and nowhere to go." Nowhere but to my spinster room with the furnishings that seemed now to consist of sharp angles only, dullness and maddening irritations, such as the wardrobe door that refused to stay closed. I'd slam it shut and two minutes later, it would slowly creak open, revealing the empty space on the top shelf that had once held Duncan's things and that I couldn't bring myself to fill with my own.

If it were any other Friday, I could have gone to Liesel and Manfred's. But they were away. The three of them had left earlier in the afternoon for Tel Aviv.

Manfred had received an exciting new commission to photograph buildings for an architect's prospectus. They'd decided to make it a bit of holiday too, a celebration of Ari's third birthday, a chance to show him the seaside and to give Papa time with his grandson. They'd be staying at Pension Kleiner, an unheard of extravagance, but that's how wealthy Manfred was feeling because of his new commission.

Yes, I might have gone to see my sister, though she would have greeted me with a face I couldn't bear. That expression of suffocating sisterly concern. That silent (and sometimes not-so-silent) plea for me to forget him, find a solid, decent *Yecke* and settle down. *Gott im Himmel,* she'd exclaim, what do you see in that man? The question made me furious because it was perfectly sensible and every answer was beside the point. Having finally given him up, I wanted him more than ever. I searched for his face in the posters of the film stars smiling or scowling down out of the cluttered billboard. James Mason. Stuart Granger. They didn't look anything like him, but I re-created them in his image as I fantasized us together in a fast-paced, modern, neon-lit city in some part of the world untouched by war.

It was a calm hour on an ordinary Friday afternoon. The common folk were going about their end-of-week business. But this is a country where appearances deceive. Tremors rumble beneath the surface. Any moment an explosion can rip apart the quiet. As happened that evening a couple of months back when Duncan was out drinking with some mates at the Trocadero on Jaffa Road—an area well patrolled by police and soldiers—and a light flashed and something went bang in his ears. When the dust settled, the bloke across the table, who'd been about to deliver the punch line to his joke about the priest, the pastor, the rabbi, and the whore, lay twitching on the floor. Duncan fell to his knees beside him, but seconds later the fellow was gone. Then shouts, screams, crash of furniture, smoke, flames, sirens, and a relentless thudding in Duncan's ears. The dead man was Duffy Pike, a swarthy Cornish man, a good boxer who'd almost won the coveted Cafferata Shield a year back. Of the men who'd been drinking with Duncan, one got a piece of shrapnel in his gut, another lost an eye, and then there was Pike, dead. Duncan survived with only a few scratches, a piece of luck that made him instantly famous in barracks and billets around town and earned him many a gift whisky for days afterwards. But he didn't come away quite as Scot-free as it appeared. He'd gone half deaf. Sounds were muted, except for that noise that still thumped in his right ear. When I played Chopin for him on our gramophone a few nights later, Duncan had to ask me to turn up the volume, but he still lost the low notes so he told me to turn the machine right off. He lay beside me pretending to be asleep, but I knew he wasn't.

The explosion in the café had been a grenade, tossed into the open door by a youth on a motorcycle, who'd roared away down the street while snipers on a nearby rooftop fired diversionary shots. I hated to let Duncan out of my sight after that incident. I begged to go with him the next time he went out with his mates. It was right after the funeral for Duffy Pike. We all crowded into Finks—a bunch of the lads from the Force and soldiers who'd been near the Trocadero that day and had come running. While armed sentries stood watch, toasts were drunk to the dead man and rounds bought for Duncan, who must have been born with a horseshoe up his ass, so they said. Closing time arrived. The other patrons had cleared out. An officer with gold braid on his cap motioned to the bartender to keep pouring. The talk around our table had gone vengeful and ugly. Loud grumbling about how the Force's hands were tied, how fair play didn't work with "these people." I was just returning from the Ladies when I heard the man at Duncan's elbow say, "If a Jew-boy was on fire, I wouldn't piss on him to save his life." The others hooted in approval. I waited for Duncan to make some kind of mitigating comment, but he didn't. I caught his eye and he looked back at me stonily. But that was all right. There was no point in contradicting a drunk man, I reasoned. They were all too deep in their cups. Duncan came home with me and fell onto my bed, pinning me underneath his dead weight so that I had to struggle to pry myself free. Next morning, when I mentioned the comment about pissing on a Jew-boy, Duncan's jaw tightened. We stared at one another in appalled silence and at that moment we both knew it was over. Really. Finally. Irrevocably. We made it official the next time he came by, but that was just a formality. Ten years of my life clumped out the front door and down the building stairwell.

We'd done the right thing I said to myself as I looked up at Charles Boyer, who winked down from the billboard poster. I was an addict. I just needed time to cleanse the poison of love from my veins.

Some people were still about on Mamilla Road. Jews rushing home to light candles for the Sabbath. An Arab family out for an evening stroll. As the Arabs neared, I anticipated unpleasantness. Two men walked in the front—a younger and an older—both in European suit jackets over traditional robes and their heads adorned with black-and-white checkered keffiyehs. They leaned close together, deep in conversation, their guttural syllables rushing by my ears. They shot me unfathomable glances and then they paid me no more notice as they waited on the corner with their hands behind their backs. Three women followed, finely decked out too, in black dresses with colourful embroidery along the front and sides. A flock of children, of varying ages, boiled around them. The women stopped to point and giggle at the poster of an Arabic film. I had the impulse to move away, escape. But for that very reason, I stood my ground. *I was here first.* It's what everyone thinks these days; it's the sentiment that hums like a bass chord throughout the country. So I stayed where I was. I greeted the women in their own language and they raised their eyebrows and said "Salaam" back, but without smiling. This was about as civil as things got between our two peoples in these times of trial and terror. The children stared at my hat in a mixture of astonishment and mockery but they didn't go so far as to jeer. Two of the younger ones had strayed into Mamilla cemetery and were called back by the anxious mothers, perhaps fearing malevolent spirits among the sunken graves. The men crossed the street and the flock moved on, leaving me with a vague sense of triumph. And wasn't it just because of this childish emotion that I lingered on the corner even longer?

Shifting from foot to foot, I lit a cigarette, continued to scan the notices. About a lecture on the Hasmonean era. About the importance of shutting water taps properly. About a rental flat in Security Zone A. At the top right-hand corner of the billboard, a tattered note asked for any information whatsoever on the whereabouts of a Mr. and Mrs. Kuchinsky, last seen July 5, 1944 being deported from the Gare de Bobigny. The shameful helplessness beneath such words made people cringe. We all knew someone who'd vanished into the black maw of deportation. Those of us who had run out of prayers wrote notes. Or pushed their dark thoughts away, as I did now by re-examining the announcement of the Mozart concert with the Jerusalem String Quartet at Rehavia High School. *Eine kleine Nachtmusik* and other delights. I would buy a ticket. I would enjoy a concert again, even if I had to sit by myself. *And perhaps, among all the backs of heads in front of me, I would recognize a certain pair of stick-out ears and a sand-coloured slick of hair, pressed down against his skull from that heavy cap that he cradled in his lap. And he would turn without my having to make a noise, and he would let out a soft whistle of delight.*

As I drifted away into seductive reverie, an automobile screeched to a halt on the corner, a door clicked open, footsteps scuffed on the pavement. I woke from my dream the same instant a pair of arms seized me from behind and a strong hand gripped my face. It squeezed so hard I couldn't breathe and I thought my jaw would crack. Did a squeak of alarm leak through the lips that were squashed against the rough palm? Did my feet do a little dance of resistance on the pavement before they left the ground? The billboard whirled. I was heaved forward like a bag of straw and other arms caught and hauled me in and flung me onto the floor of the vehicle. A heavy foot pushed against my back, another rested on my head. When I tried to move, the feet pinning me to the floor pressed harder, grinding my nose against cold metal. So I lay still like a small animal that knows its last defence is to shrink into itself and play dead.

"*Sa! Sa!*" a hoarse male voice yelled in Hebrew. *Drive!*

Chapter 26
Captive

I SAW NO faces, heard only grunts, and felt ruthless, determined hands pushing and pulling at my limbs as if they were weeds to be ripped out of the ground. The hands bound my wrists and ankles with cords that burned into my skin. Someone flung me like a sack over his shoulder and carried me downwards into a dark place. The last thing those hands did was to tie a rag around my mouth so tightly it wrenched apart my lips and teeth and made my head ring. Then I heard feet pound back up a set of steps, a door slam, and the bolt of a lock click into place. How many feet were there? I couldn't tell. As suddenly as they'd crashed into my life, my captors vanished. Inky darkness blotted out my eyes. Silence stuffed my ears. I was alone, bound like an animal made ready for slaughter with a gag in my mouth. My tongue lapped helplessly against the stiff cloth.

I was on my side in a foetal position. My cheek lay against damp, hard-packed dirt that smelled rank, of sewage, of cat's piss, making me desperate for air. But when I tried to lift my head, pain shot down my spine because of how my hands were tied behind my back. Desperation ballooned in my chest. My heart became a runaway train. I twitched, struggled, but the ropes only bit deeper into my flesh, the gag pressed harder against the corners of my mouth and the base of my tongue. The darkness exploded into a million wriggling dots that swept me into oblivion.

When I came to, I was exactly as before only now the rag was slimy wet with my own saliva and the dampness of the floor had seeped into my clothes. I waited. I expected that any moment the cellar door would bang open and my kidnappers would be upon me with their threats and demands. I dreaded that moment, yet as the emptiness stretched out, I began to long for their coming. Whether I dreaded or longed didn't matter. No one came.

I was afraid to move. But I had to move. Rocking myself gently, pushing with my toes, I managed to roll over on my back. This was progress. Bracing my weight on my fists, my bottom, and my heels, I wriggled along like an inchworm. The sand and protrusions of the floor scraped my knuckles, snagged at the wool of my skirt. But at last I arrived somewhere—at a wall. And this wall allowed me to push myself up into a sitting position and to rest my head. I gasped with the effort, straining against the gag. The wall was uneven: rough-hewn stone with mortar in between. Though my eyes had adjusted to the dark, all I could discern in the gloom was the vague shape of a pillar. Otherwise nothing. For the first time since I arrived where they'd dumped me, I had a clear thought. I was in a cellar of some sort, perhaps underneath someone's house. With that clarity came a stampede of questions. Who had done this? What did they want of me? Were they coming back, or had they left me here to be buried alive? Why me? The questions galloped around my mind with no answers. Again I shook with panic. My trapped voice gurgled in my throat. *Stop, stop, stop*, I screamed to myself. *Think!*

What would Duncan tell you to do? He would say, Steady there, that's a girl, be calm. He would say: Take deep breaths and count to ten. Listen to me. One steamboat, two steamboat, three steamboat. . . . *Become aware of where you are.* But I'm nowhere, my panic answered. I'm like Joseph cast to the bottom of a pit. Peer into the darkness, the Duncan voice murmured. If there's a wall, there must be other walls. If this is a cellar, there must be a door. There were steps that led down here, and the same steps lead back up. *Find them.*

Once again I inched my way along the rough floor, exploring the space with my body, feet going first as my head dangled behind. Every inch seemed a mile. The darkness refused to resolve into shapes. For all I knew, I was moving away from the cellar steps instead of towards them. What a mistake to have left the wall. *Now you're back in the black void, helpless and aching. Don't panic. Steady. Listen. Wasn't there a sound? Just the hammer of my heart. But no! Something more.*

I held my breath and strained to listen and it seemed I heard a murmur coming from the direction in which I'd been going. I wriggled forward, driven by the hunger to hear. Pausing to catch my breath I heard it again: faint, so faint it could have been a dream. But the murmur was real and as I moved closer became the sound of faraway voices singing. The voices pulled me towards them, reeled me in. After what seemed a long time, my feet struck up against something hard. I lifted them and groped with the toes of my shoes. The hard thing had shape, an edge. It was a step. Exhausted by my efforts, I flopped onto my side, and for a few moments I could barely keep myself from retching as my lungs sucked for breath against the barrier in my mouth. When I stopped gasping, I stilled and listened, all my being focused on sound. I knew this song. I knew it well. The awareness made me dizzy with joy. The voices were singing "*Lekhah Dodi,*" the traditional song to welcome the Sabbath and that pictured the spirit of the Sabbath as a bride.

Come my beloved
let us meet the bride
let us welcome the presence of the Sabbath

Only the ghost of the melody came to my ears, not the words, but the words weren't necessary because they'd been stored in the deep vault of childhood memory.

Observe and remember in a single word
He caused us to hear, the one and only Lord
To welcome the Sabbath, let us progress
For that is the source from which to bless

Of all the hymns of the Jewish liturgy, this was the one—perhaps the only one—that had made a permanent dwelling in my heart. Tears pricked my eyes as I became a child again, leaning against the wooden rail of the women's gallery at the Weisse Storch Synagogue, gazing down upon the rows of men in their prayer shawls.

Arise now, shake off the dust
Don your robes of glory, my people, you must

The cantor would stand on the dais, wearing the hat I'd always craved for myself for it was black velvet in the shape of a plush crown with a tasselled pompom, and it made the person who wore it look so very tall. Beneath the magnificent hat was a wizened monkey face with glasses, but when the cantor sang he became a winged angel. His tenor voice soared to the ceiling, to heaven itself, people liked to say. He stretched out the words, embellishing each with exotic vocalizations that became pure, throbbing gold.

Rouse yourselves, rouse yourselves,
your light is coming . . .

Through all my years in Jerusalem I'd never been tempted to attend a synagogue service, though I had peeked into windows of some of the historic ones out of curiosity. They were musty, shabby places that left me cold. But on Friday evenings in summertime when Duncan and I strolled about, letting our feet take us into tumbledown older quarters of the Jewish town, we both liked to listen to the hymns that poured out of doorways. I would hum along with *"Lekhah Dodi"* and translate the verses at Duncan's prodding. He found the words quaint, while to me they carried the oppressive weight of religion, especially the call to "observe and remember the Sabbath." But the melody! It sprang free of commandments, floated on the caressing breezes of a Jerusalem evening, took me back to a happy corner of childhood I hadn't realized existed.

> *Come in peace, her husband's crown*
> *Both in happiness and jubilation*
> *Amidst the faithful of the treasured nation . . .*

The congregation would sing eight verses facing the Ark, the carved wooded cupboard that held the Torah scrolls. But at the last verse, the ninth, the tempo slowed and everyone turned around to face the western wall of the synagogue, direction of the setting sun, bowing low as the spirit of Sabbath entered, a spirit we drew towards us with song.

> *Enter O Bride, enter O Bride*

The faraway singing now came to an end. It was replaced by faint muttering, punctuated every so often by a thin yelp that I knew was a shouted "Amen." There had to be a synagogue nearby, crammed with Jews reciting the Friday evening service. And if they were only welcoming the Sabbath now, then not much time had passed since my abduction from my spot in front of the billboard. An hour at the most. It hardly seemed possible, but must be so. The version of *Lekhah Dodi* they sang was Ashkenazi. Perhaps I was in an Orthodox quarter of the city where the men had side curls and wore black hats and long black coats. The synagogue had to be close by, perhaps just across a courtyard from the door that led to my cellar. In half an hour, the service over, the courtyard would fill with congregants, at least for a few minutes before they all dispersed home for their Sabbath evening meals. If only I could make my presence known!

I writhed around to reposition myself so that I was facing the direction in which I'd come, my back to the steps. I could touch the bottom step, explore its blunt edge with my fingertips. Pushing with my heels, heaving with my elbows, kicking and panting, I manoeuvred myself into a sitting position on the bottom step. The cords had loosened slightly so that my ankles were no longer crossed, and this gave me traction. I heaved and panted up another step. My skirt rode up awkwardly beneath my thighs and I cursed its slippery lining. What had possessed me when I'd dressed in the morning to don this fine, but cumbersome suit when I had nowhere particular to go? Only the mad hope of catching Duncan's eye on the street, even though he'd vanished from the streets and I hadn't seen him since the day we'd said goodbye.

Keep going! Keep going! I struggled upwards, backwards. Another step. Another. Trembling, out of breath, I cranked my head around as far as I could, hoping to catch sight of a door. My famished eyes beheld a glimmer. A faint gleam of light had squeezed through a gap and sent thin, golden fingers into the gloom. And yes, I could see the shadowy outline of the door as well as the top of the steps that were still far above my head. It was a yellowish, artificial light. Beyond the door was a courtyard, I decided, with a lamp post whose lamp had turned on before the start of the Sabbath. If I could heave myself upwards some more, I'd soon be bathed in its miraculous glow. I was going to get myself up to the door, and when there, I would bang against it with the back of my head. Bang and bang and bang, so that the black-robed creatures who'd arrived in the courtyard from the synagogue after the service would hear me, break the lock, exclaim in wonder, and pity at my plight and gather me into their arms. The thought sustained me as I heaved myself up another step. And another. I was at least halfway up when my bottom slid on the lining of my skirt. My feet lost their grip, my body lurched and I tumbled—bump, bump, bump, all the way down—the cement floor crashing against the side of my head. For a split second, the darkness went white.

For a long time, I didn't try to move, huddled into myself, retreating into blank shock. My face throbbed with pain. But at last I did stretch out my legs and roll over to wriggle back to the steps and though my body ached, it seemed to have survived the fall fairly intact. I wasn't in the mood for gratitude. Where was Duncan? An insane anger against him ricocheted around in my mind, for he was supposed to be my protector. All those times he'd made a show of holding doors open for me and walking on the outside of the sidewalk, the perfect gentleman. What a farce, for it was because of him—it must be because of him—I'd been thrown into this hellhole. He knew I'd be in danger, so how could he have walked away from me with that lame excuse that I'd be safer without him? He knew. He didn't care. But the news of my death would finally reach him in the form of a brief, matter-of-fact paragraph in *The Palestine Post*, and he would know what he had done. I ground my teeth in anger, biting down hard against the hateful, saliva-soaked rag in my mouth. My tongue lurched about like a snared fish and the tip of it touched something and, to my astonishment, I made a discovery. I discovered that I'd made a tiny hole.

Once more my hopes lifted. The rag was fallible. It could be shredded if I worked at it with enough determination. The teeth on the right side of my jaw, the side that had been spared the blow when I'd fallen, chewed frantically.

Precious time was running out. In a few minutes the evening service would be over. If I could chew the rag in half before that happened I'd be able to free my voice when the worshippers spilled out of the synagogue doors. I became a fevered rodent, gnawing at the cloth. The fibres gave way so slowly. The rhythm of the far-off voices told me they were reciting the Mourner's Kaddish now, the last prayer before the end of the service. And then they burst into *Yigdal*, the closing hymn. Based upon the 13 principles of faith articulated by Maimonides, it had thirteen short verses, sung to a triumphant, rollicking tune. At the Storch Synagogue, a newly bar mitzvahed boy would lead *Yigdal*, singing the first verse alone while the whole congregation chimed in on the second, and so on, responsively, until the finale. Liesel and I always had looked forward to *Yigdal*, which heralded freedom, the end of the service. Now I wanted them to continue singing as long as possible, at least until I'd chewed my gag in two.

Exalted be the living God . . . He is one, there is no unity like his Oneness.

I gnashed my teeth against the cloth. My dread mounted as the verses unrolled.

By the end of days, He will send our Messiah . . . In his great mercy, He will revive the dead/ Blessed for ever . . . His name.

It was over. The area outside the door to my prison filled with a tide of people, just as I'd expected—chattering voices, children's shouts. Something even thumped against the cellar door, perhaps someone stumbling. I screamed against the rag and the inhuman noise I made seemed huge. But it was not. It was a stifled mewing. The voices died away. The footsteps faded. The silence of the grave returned as I gazed up at that thin, mocking glimmer from beneath the door.

How long would my captors leave me here, bound and drowning in the darkness? Did they mean for me to die a slow and agonized death? When would anyone notice I was missing? When would a search for me begin? Not soon. Liesel and Manfred were away in Tel Aviv, for at least a week. (*Oh, why hadn't I gone with them?*) It was the Sabbath, and I was not expected at work until Monday. Mrs. Rajinsky might wonder that I hadn't come home, but she'd think I'd gone to stay with Liesel. And even if she were concerned, would she approach the police? Likely not. She didn't trust the police. No one did these days. No one thought they looked out for Jewish interests. I was buried alive, left to rot in this foul cellar along with the mouse carcasses and the cat feces, my stink to finally mingle with theirs. As these thoughts ran through my mind, my teeth had continued to chew and finally broke through the last thread, allowing me to spit the disgusting rag out of my mouth. My voice freed, I howled and howled for help.

The people in the houses were blessing their wine and challah. They were sitting down to the festive Sabbath meal. They were listening with rapt attention as their *Rebbe* gave a lesson on the weekly portion of the Torah. They were becoming a bit tipsy and singing joyous hymns about the sanctity of the seventh day. They had no ears for the trussed, bleating creature locked in a cellar. I wept and called. I shouted for Duncan, for Liesel, for Manfred, for Mr. Watson, for Papa, for the men who'd brought me here. Help, help, help. Shrieking at the darkness, my voice hoarse with the strain.

After an eternity, a key rattled in the lock above, the cellar door creaked open. A blinding flash of torchlight stung my eyes. There was a muttered curse as the door banged shut again and heavy footsteps clumped down the stairs. They stood above me, their torch trained upon my face making them invisible to me while I was like an insect under a microscope to them. My captors, my saviours, had come.

Chapter 27
The Trial

"EVA SALOMON. YOU stand accused of high treason and you have been brought to justice by the Fighters for the Freedom of Israel. Do you know who we are?"

I knew only too well, but I couldn't say. They had removed my gag, replaced it with a blindfold, but still I couldn't utter a word for my dry tongue stuck to the roof of my mouth and no sound reached my throat. They weren't expecting or wanting an answer anyway. The voice continued, for the sake of my enlightenment.

"We are those whom the British oppressor calls the Stern Gang. We are indeed the followers of that blazing star, Avraham Stern, gunned down in cold blood by the oppressor. We are his avengers. More important, we are the liberators of the Land of Israel. We are dedicated to the conquest of the Homeland from foreign rule. We use every means at our disposal. Cunning and courage and force of arms. We strike down the British tyrant and all who betray the cause."

The voice was high and smooth, calm and compelling and unearthly in the pit blackness of the cellar and against my sightless eyes. It was a male voice, an extraordinary one, for its power was not in some gruff masculine timbre but in its control over every modulation. It went on with the manifesto in cadences like drum rolls. *Cause of the just . . . spirit of the Maccabees . . . die or conquer the mountain . . .* I listened intently, almost fiercely, to every word, but they were all disconnected, without meaning.

I was seated on a chair now. In what seemed at that moment an act of immense mercy, they had lifted me off the cellar floor and placed me onto a chair with rungs, against which my aching back found support. I gasped, but my relief was short-lived. I had an impression of other chairs. Perhaps a table. The one with the high, authoritative voice sat facing me, I assumed, while his lieutenants sat to the left and the right. A match struck and I smelled smoke, but though the darkness became a tiny bit warmer from the light of a candle flame, I still saw nothing.

"Read the charges," Smooth Voice commanded.

A paper rustled. Now came a hoarse, adolescent voice, perhaps belonging to the one who'd yelled "*Sa! Sa!*" in the kidnapping vehicle. He did as his captain ordered. He reeled through the list of my crimes, his tone ever more sneering and triumphant.

" . . . collaboration with the Oppressor of the People of Israel . . . liaison with a member of the colonizer's police force . . . comfort to the enemy . . . betrayer of the People of Israel . . ."

On and on the accusations continued against Eva Salomon: the Collaborator, the Traitor, the Polluter of the People and the Land. Finally the reading of the charges ended and there was an awful silence.

"The accused may speak."

"I'm not that person," I croaked.

"Are you Eva Salomon of Number 42 King George V Street?"

My head drooped as I agreed that I was.

"Do you deny the liaison between yourself and Sergeant Duncan Rees of the C.I.D., the vicious arm of the colonial police, the department that pursues, imprisons, and tortures the Fighters for the Freedom of Israel?"

"Yes . . . no."

I searched for words, but none came. I could feel their loathing wash towards me in waves.

"You have a chance to redeem yourself," Smooth Voice said at last. "We'd like to meet this man, Rees. We'd like to have a word with him. When is your next rendezvous? "

The sharp question penetrated my confusion.

"But he's gone," I said.

"Gone where?"

"From me. From my life. I was for a long time . . . his girlfriend." I had to stop to catch my breath. "But not anymore. We broke it off."

"You're lying. When will he be back to your room? What have you arranged?"

"Nothing. Never. It's the truth. It's been finished between us for months. I haven't seen him for . . . at least two months."

My mind scrambled to think of the date of that November day, when he'd stood in my room for the last time, stiff and resolute and sad, and wished me luck and shook my hand, holding it tight for a long moment and then letting go. We'd both agreed it was for the best. We couldn't go on. Even when we didn't argue, the unspoken accusations sat heavy in the air. We had come to a point where we both dreaded an encounter with the other. It was November 3, a Sunday, and he was off-duty, wearing his wide-belted trench coat and grey fedora. He'd come by early, planning to go to the service at St. George's because of a visiting choir from Damascus, he told me. He'd planned out his goodbye to me so that he'd have somewhere to go afterwards. Now the date, November 3, was clear in my mind and I wanted to say it out loud into the darkness of the cellar as evidence. But the man with the commanding voice spoke first.

"So where has he been posted? What are his current duties?"

"I don't know."

"Has he gone underground? Has he changed his appearance in any way?"

"I don't know."

"Lying!"

A chair scraped, a shadow rose and fell—the candle flame flickering—and steps came towards me. The man's voice was close, purring in my ear. His warm, tobacco-tainted breath bathed my face.

"Why do you protect the British bastard? He has another whore in Jaffa he goes to when he's tired of you. She's a juicy girl, ten years younger than you, very pretty."

He kept on in this vein about the girl in Jaffa, giving her a name—Leilah—drawing a picture of her luscious body, describing scenes with her and Duncan fornicating against an alley wall. I knew it was a ruse, yet the lurid pictures he painted snaked their way into my mind.

"Avenge yourself. Save yourself. Help us," he barked.

"I can't."

"Can't? Or won't?"

"I know nothing. I'm nobody. I type reports for the Finance Division of the Department of Posts, Telegraphs and Telephones. That's all I am. And he never told me things, even when we were together. When he went away, he didn't tell me where or what he did. He's not coming back. You can search in my room. He used to keep some things there, but they're gone. The shelf is empty."

Where did I find the courage for this outpouring? Terror made me speak. Each word gave strength for the next and I was afraid to stop talking because of what would happen when I did. But then my words ran out and, panting for breath, I stopped.

There was silence in the room. The man was behind my chair now. I sensed him taking in my words, considering.

"All right then, suit yourself," he said coldly as he walked back towards the candle flame. More scraping of chairs, shuffling of feet.

From a distant part of the room, came the mutter of their voices in conference. I caught the sense of urgency and excitement among the lieutenants answered by the cool authority of the commander. There seemed to be some disagreement. The hoarse one burst out, so that I could clearly hear: "She'll make trouble." I also heard the words, "Death sentence." My heart went cold. I trembled against my bindings. A spurt of hot liquid shot out of my anus into my knickers and its foul smell reached my nostrils. The stench took away the last of my courage, enveloped me in profound despair as I sat in my own sticky mess and waited for the verdict. When at last they returned, the smooth-toned commander spoke.

"Eva Salomon, you stand convicted of all charges. Whether or not you are still the consort of Sergeant Duncan Rees is immaterial. You spread your legs for an enemy of the People of Israel. However, the death sentence is commuted. Death is too good for you. You should live with the burden of your shame."

An "oh!" escaped my lips at the word "commuted." I would not have to plead for my life. I would not have to reach down into the empty pit of my soul to find words to convince them to have mercy. This realization gave me almost as much relief as knowing that my life would be spared. I wanted to thank him so I asked his name.

He gave a short laugh.

"You may call me Shimshon. Like the man in the Bible who brought down the Philistines. Except that I will never be undone by any treacherous Delilah. Don't be too pleased with yourself. You are still a traitor and must be punished. You said before that you are a nobody. That's part of the problem, Eva, the Nobody. Every Jew must be a Somebody. Every Jew must stand tall. But you, craven creature! You stoop lowest of the low. You lick the boots of the oppressor. And other parts besides."

Ugly snickers followed these words.

"Eva Salomon, you stand convicted of fornication with an oppressor, of giving comfort to the enemy, of betraying the People of Israel. You will be taught a lesson. But we are honourable fighting Hebrews and we'll not do to you what *goyim* soldiers would do. We won't defile ourselves or you. Not any more than you've already defiled yourself. Remember that, because it's part of the lesson. This trial is now over."

I heard the thump of a fist on the table.

"All right boys. Get on with it."

I heard a chair scrape once more and a pair of footsteps march across the floor and up the stone steps. The door creaked open, slammed shut. While all this happened, the others remained quiet, waiting for their captain to leave. A long pause ensued, filled with the pounding of my blood in my ears as I held my breath and struggled to find my next words. How to address the boys in the dark, how to appeal to their better natures? I quaked with fear but also desperate hope, for I couldn't allow myself to fathom what the captain meant by "get on with it." I opened my mouth. A "please" had formed on my lips. A lightning blow to the side of my face knocked it away. As my head flew sideways, my whole being reared up in astonishment. How could this be? Such callous brutality! How could a human hand and arm become so disconnected from all that was human? These thoughts lasted only an instant. The second blow flung me from the chair onto the cement floor and, by that time, my state of outraged wonder had been replaced by animal fear. Shimshon's men were all around me. In front and behind and on top of me. They were fists and shod feet connecting with the soft pulp of my body. Along with the blows, they delivered grunts and low curses and also, I believe, at least one gob of spit.

Chapter 28
Dumped

I OPENED MY eyes to the toss of branches above my head and a glimmer of moon behind a shroud of clouds. Gingerly I touched my face, crusted with dirt, sticky with blood, and realized my hands were free, my feet too. Yet I was afraid to move and lay rigid, in case they were near, waiting to pounce again. That last kick had been the most savage, connecting with my tailbone, a searing shock that knocked me senseless. I listened now. To the creak of branches in the wind. To the far-off rumble of an engine. The smell of outdoor things came to my nostrils: rain-moistened earth, trampled weeds, and something more pungent—goat droppings perhaps—all blessedly fresh and alive. I inhaled deeply and paid the price. A knife thrust of pain in my ribs. What had they done to me? What would they do next? *Get away, get away, before they come back.*

Heart hammering, I rolled onto my knees, staggered to my feet, and looked about. A thicket of dark twisted trunks. A lozenge of stone leaning sideways. A path. I took a few staggering steps, saw more of those odd black shapes looming up out of the earth. I was in Mamilla Cemetery, not far from the site of my abduction. Through the trees I could see the light of the lamp standards on Mamilla Road and a hint of buildings beyond. My soiled knickers clung like a rude hand to my backside. I tugged them off and flung them into the bushes. I tottered on my high-heeled shoes along the uneven ground, tripping over roots and feeling my way around the graves. When I reached the street at last, I removed my shoes and half limped, half ran, on shredded nylon stockings along the rough, damp pavement. Not a soul was about, the windows of the houses were shuttered and dark, all the good citizens of Jerusalem deep asleep in their beds. This gave me some heart, for a conviction had taken hold in my mind: no one must see me in the state I was in. No one must ask, What happened? As I hobbled through the empty streets, every step was a stab of pain, yet I moved fast, so desperate was I to get home, home, home, no place like home.

Up the slope of Mamilla Road, along King George V, past Terra Sancta College and the rock-strewn empty lot, to the building that beckoned on the corner. My battered body arrived on the landing in front of Mrs. Rajinsky's flat. My string bag of groceries was long gone. My handbag too. The trilby hat had vanished as well, knocked off my head when my abductors had seized me. But I did have the house key because I'd absentmindedly stuffed it into the pocket of my jacket that morning instead of into its usual place in the side compartment of my bag. The miracle of this small, ordinary, wonderful object between my fingers made them shake as I fitted the key into the lock. Without turning on any lights, I crept down the hall to the bathroom, gulped cold water from the tap, and splashed some on my face. The left side of my face felt swollen and raw, throbbed and stung. In the lavatory, I cleaned my bottom as best I could. In my room—my dear and precious room—I tugged off my filthy clothes and eased my aching body into bed. *Don't think, don't think.* Near dawn, a black veil fell over my eyes and I sank into the blessed well of sleep.

When I awoke, bright spears of daylight pierced through the gaps in the window blinds. Pots crashed and dishes clattered in the kitchen. A rattle and splash came from the other side of the flat: Mr. Maisel in the lavatory. These ordinary sounds, reminders of the presence of two other people, assaulted my soul and made me cower deeper under the covers. It hurt to move, hurt to breathe. Best was to lie still and disappear, if not into sleep exactly, then into a numb, vegetable state. I closed my eyes and ears, let the hours slide by until the urgent need to relieve myself drove me out of bed. I wanted to slip down the hall, as unnoticed as a fleck of dust, but Mr. Maisel chose that moment to step out of his room, dressed for a Sabbath hike in the hills with a cloth cap on his head and a rucksack on his back. His soft face went as pale as a bar of soap when he saw me, a startled rabbit look, which I must have reflected back to him, the two of us staring at each other like apparitions in a mirror. *Please, Mr. Maisel. Don't speak.* He started to stammer something, but I shook my head and lurched into the lavatory before he could get his words out. Holding myself still, I heard his steps down the hall and the front door close behind him and I exhaled in relief at the strange timidity that made the bookstore clerk shun awkward encounters. We were two of a kind now.

When I lowered myself onto the toilet seat, I whimpered with the pain. To empty my bowels was to feel the jab of hot irons against the base of my spine. I remembered how old Mrs. Mandelmann used to gasp and strain and suffer on the toilet and how my pity had been mixed with disgust. My captors had aimed their boots so cleverly, sending me into a place of ugly humiliation.

MRS. RAJINSKY'S HAND flew to her mouth at the sight of me.

"God in heaven, what happened to you?" she shrieked. I dug my nails into my palms to keep myself from shaking.

"It's all right," I mumbled, wrapping my arms tighter around my chest, tucking my head deeper into the collar of my housecoat.

"You look like you were attacked by wild beasts." She peered more intently.

"I fell down some stairs."

"Is anything broken? Should I call a doctor? Oh, but it's Shabbat. I don't know who I could find to come on Shabbat. We could walk to the hospital on the Street of the Prophets. It's a long walk, but I don't mind. You shouldn't go alone. You really should have someone look at you."

"No, no. It's nothing. Looks much worse than it is. I just need to rest."

"How did this happen? Where? But of course, you always insist on such high heels. A little bit of heel is elegant, but yours are stilts, Miss Salomon. Quite impractical. I'm sorry to mention this again when you're in such a state, but I've often thought it's just a matter of time before you take a tumble. You're sure nothing is broken? Well, I suppose the shock is the worst."

Somehow I managed to get back into the safety of my room without further well-meaning interference from Mrs. Rajinsky. She could be nosy, but at least had the blessed talent of answering her own questions. This made it easier to maintain my silence.

My door had no lock, but I braced the back of a chair under the knob, a trick Duncan had shown me and that we'd always used to ensure our privacy together. Then I summoned the courage to open the wardrobe. The mirror on the back of the door showed me the face that had alarmed my landlady and Mr. Maisel. The whole left side was a mess of purple bruises and raw, weeping patches. The right side was fairly intact, but my nose was a swollen mushroom in the middle. I was a bizarre Picasso painting, a thought that pulled my lips briefly into a lopsided smile until pure revulsion returned. Quickly I closed the wardrobe door again. In the bathroom I'd made myself a cold compress with a wet washcloth which I laid on my sore face. I swallowed two aspirins and returned to bed. My cave, my refuge, beneath the blankets. I stayed there until I was sure that both Mrs. Rajinsky and Mr. Maisel had left the flat and only then did I venture into the kitchen for some food. All that day I remained in bed, the blinds closed and the room sunk into a grey gloom. I shrank from the noises of the street—children's shouts, people greeting one another with "*Shabbat shalom*," the occasional rumble of a military truck. I longed for the darkness and silence of night. I longed to put hours, many hours, between myself and the incident in the cellar. In the evening, when Mrs. Rajinsky tapped on my door, I didn't answer. She should think me asleep. But she didn't go away, for I could sense her listening intently on the other side. Her insistent knock came again.

"Is there anything I can get for you, Miss Salomon?"

"No thank you," I finally mumbled.

"Would you like me to contact your sister? I can cross over to Yossi's and use his phone and call her landlord and he can run upstairs and give her the message. But no, of course. You told me. She's away. Let me know if you want something. I'm glad to help. We have to help one another in these hard times."

At last she took herself off.

Now I was glad that Liesel had gone to Tel Aviv. A few seconds of Mrs. Rajinsky were unsettling enough. Despite my effort to smother them, strange thoughts swirled through my mind and the only one that gave some comfort was my resolution to avoid human contact. There was no reason, no logic. I just had to hide. *I'm not ready, I'm not ready,* I pleaded with the dark walls. Pain was my companion throughout those hours and days. When I drew breath, a knife twisted in my side. When I attempted to sit, a nail pieced the bone at the bottom of my spine. My face was aflame. I whimpered with self-pity, but, when I look back now, I realize the misery of my body was a welcome distraction from the torments of my mind. I didn't want to think about the men in the shadows. Nevertheless, they came, with their accusations, their matter-of-fact statement of my crimes, their back-and-forth discussions of what to do with me, their earnest explanations of their goals and their contempt for my anguished cries.

The one who had called himself Shimshon was more thoughtful than the others, more mature, more cunning. It was he who decided that my life should be spared and that it would be enough to teach me a lesson, written into my body with their feet. *Observe and remember.* He dearly wanted to teach me. He wanted me to understand. The others egged one another on in boastful, adolescent excitement, but Shimshon brought them into line like a lead wolf with his snarling pack. His intentions were subtle and driven by a relentless zeal.

Even now, when I close my eyes, I can hear him quite clearly, crooning in my ear with that soft, insidious voice. A high and almost musical voice, that could hardly be called masculine—not in the usual sense—but is pure and compelling and thrills as it terrifies.

Eva Salomon, why do you tremble, wretched thing? I'll tell you why. Because you have nothing inside, no spine of ideology. Those fired by virtue and justice cannot fail. They tremble not, though they stand before the might of Pharaoh. But what do you believe in, beyond your miserable skin?

Though he was hidden from my eyes, a picture of him rose in my mind. I clothed him in a black uniform with a wide leather belt and peaked cap low on his forehead. I would have licked his boots if he'd let me, crawled on my knees to beg for mercy. For I was exactly the creature he said I was.

Chapter 29
In My Room

THE HOURS MELTED, one into the other, day and night, time a blur. I kept the blinds closed, but even so preferred the deeper darkness of the blanket over my head. Yet I'd jerk awake, struggling for air, heart pounding, chest aflame. When hunger gnawed and when I was sure my landlady and Maisel had gone to bed, I crept out of my den to the kitchen. Grab a few provisions—bread and butter, a jar of yogurt. Scurry back to safety with the hoard. I chewed with the good side of my jaw, while the battered side of my face ached at every movement. The food stilled my hunger but all tasted pallid and a grey lassitude lay upon me. Outside, winter rain rattled the window panes. A gaggle of children squawked as they trooped off to school. The church bells of Terra Sancta Monastery clanged. In the street below, the Arab egg man called out to all the housewives in the kitchens of the neighbourhood, "*Frishe Ay-YER!*" he sang in his mangled Yiddish. The city was working. The city was living, while I paced, smoked, stared at a crack in the wall.

How to let them know at the post office that I couldn't come to work? All my years as a loyal public servant, I'd hardly missed a day, so Mr. Watson would wonder as the hours passed without a call or a note of explanation. I imagined his frown of annoyance at the sight of my neat desk and empty chair with the grey wool cardigan left hanging over the back. There were Monday morning letters to be dictated and typed. He would have to ask for a clerk from another division to take my place. Most inconvenient. Would he send someone around to inquire about me? Would he go to so much bother? How long would he wait before he became alarmed? My head swam with inchoate noise, rumbles, and shrieks, like an orchestra tuning up endlessly, with no conductor's baton to bring calm and coherence.

Sometimes I'd drift off into sweet oblivion, only to wake in a spasm of terror and then the darkness of the room would press down with dead weight. Craving the light, I switched on the lamp only to be distressed by the long shadows that writhed along the walls. Clothes lay tumbled on the floor. A plate of soggy bread crusts defaced the table, along with the overflowing ashtray. The embroidered cloth had grey streaks from the ash I'd carelessly allowed to drop. My room, my precious haven. I couldn't imagine ever leaving it. And yet it was not the room of before. Every object now mocked with its silence and ugliness. The smell of stale smoke and unwashed linen crawled up my nose, made me yank up the blinds and lean out of the window to gulp the night air. An unearthly scream sent me to the floor with my arms over my head. Did the scream come from my own throat, or was it a cat prowling the black streets? I could barely tell if I was awake or asleep.

Where was Duncan? Why had he forsaken me? Why had he not shielded me from my tormentors with his muscled body, his bully club, his pistol, his trained eye and swift hand and all the other trappings of an officer of the Palestine Police? I hurled these questions towards the blinking stars. Why didn't he come now to enfold me in his arms? After our breakup, I couldn't help but scan the faces of the men in blue serge on patrol, and I would brace myself for the encounter I thought inevitable, for Jerusalem is just a handful of zigzag streets, especially the downtown core where we both worked. But I never saw him. Now it occurred to me that he might have left town for another posting. The thought filled my chest with rage and just as quickly deflated into a desperate ache. I tried to will the tender Duncan into the room, tried to recall his face, but I saw nothing beneath the policeman's cap with the sharp, shiny visor. When I whispered his name, I heard that other voice, like harsh wind in my ears, of the man who called himself Shimshon.

He denounces us as terrorists, but what is he, your noble British policeman? Has he never used the whip or the club on human flesh? What do you know about what he does behind the cloak he calls "duty?"

Seeking solace in music, I put on a record that used to lift my spirits— Chopin *Études*—but immediately cringed. What had once sounded light and airy became a clamour, a meaningless chaos of notes. I yanked the record arm off the spinning disc so that the needle scratched across the surface with a loud *zirrrp*. Never before had I violated one of our records like that. *Our records!* Not anymore. Duncan had left them all behind. When I'd said we should divide them up equally, he'd said no, he wanted me to have them, and this had planted in me a desperate seed of hope. *Surely he left the records as a message. Surely he'd come back some day.* Now I had the impulse to throw every one of the useless discs out the window and hear them shatter on the pavement below. The only thing that stopped me was the fear of causing a disturbance that would bring Mrs. Rajinsky to my door.

Mrs. Rajinsky! I needed a better story to keep her from digging at me for an explanation. In my more lucid moments, I concocted a tale, rehearsing it, ironing out the logic until I felt I had it right. I was ready for her when she cornered me again during one of my sorties to the lavatory.

"Yes, like I said. It was a fall. A stupid accident. My foot slipped when I was coming down the mezzanine steps to the main hall of the post office. My arms were full of files that I was taking for storage to the basement. The steps had just been washed. One of my heels was wobbly. Silly me. I was overdue for a visit to the cobbler."

Words poured out of my lopsided mouth in a rapid stream. I could almost believe my own concoction.

"I toppled sideways and, boom, boom, went down, the papers from the file folders flying in all directions. Clerks jumped from behind their counters to catch me but it happened too fast. When I opened my eyes, I was looking up at the plaster mouldings of the ceiling. It's quite a beautiful ceiling, by the way. I'd never noticed it before."

My landlady gave me a round-eyed look of exaggerated pity. Since Duncan had vanished from my life, she often subjected me to that look. *What bad luck, but perhaps you brought it upon yourself.*

"I'm much better, Mrs. Rajinsky. It hardly hurts anymore, just looks a fright. Yes. All right. I'll put on some Ozonol. Can't do any harm. You'll understand if I hide this ugly face until it heals? I'm a *Schrecken für die Kinder.* Ha, ha. A face to make babies cry. Thank you for your kindness, Mrs. Rajinsky. And now I'll just go back to my room. No, I don't need company. Really not."

MORE TIME SLID by in fog. Mrs. Rajinsky intruded again one morning with a loud knock and the announcement a letter had arrived from my sister. At my insistence, she consented to slip it under my door, groaning mightily at the effort of having to bend her knees. The letter lay on the floor for long minutes before I could summon the courage to pick it up, for everything seemed fateful to me during those strange underworld days of my seclusion. But it turned out to be good news. Manfred had received another commission, so they would be staying away at least another week. I wouldn't have to face Liesel just yet. This respite gave me the courage to scribble a quick note to my employer about being down with the flu and not wanting to bring my germs to the office. I think I used the word "contamination." Holding my door open a crack, I called to Maisel as he was passing in the hall and bade him deliver my note to the General Post Office, which was on his way to Steimatzky's on Jaffa Road. I also thrust a handful of bills towards him for a few supplies from the grocery store.

"Just leave them in the kitchen. And keep the change."

He looked down at the money in his hand and then at my face and then averted his eyes and mumbled some good wishes for my recovery before bolting towards the front door.

Exhausted by these efforts, I sank back into my bed.

ONE AFTERNOON I awoke from a stupor to sirens and bullhorns announcing a curfew. *What now?* Through a gap in the blinds I peered down at the police car inching along King George V Avenue as the crackle of static and the thin, distorted words floated in the air. *High alert . . . dusk to dawn . . . only authorized traffic . . .* People poured out of the houses, hurrying to the shops to buy provisions before everything closed up tight and the armoured behemoths took over the city. I saw Mr. Maisel carrying two jerry cans towards the corner where the horse-drawn wagon with the big, cylindrical tank—the kerosene truck—had come to a stop. No doubt Mrs. Rajinsky had recruited him for the errand. For the first time since the beating, I wanted to be outside as well. The busyness of the street stirred me to restlessness and the four walls that had been my sanctuary closed in. Everyone would be so preoccupied with their own needs they'd pay me no attention, I reasoned. I put on my coat and wrapped my head in a wool shawl, arranging it carefully over the injured side of my face. Still very sore about the ribs, I stepped with care, clutching the banister in the stairwell as I descended, one tentative foot at a time. The brightness of the street made me gasp. I stood still and counted to ten, pulling myself together.

There was hardly an ounce of space to move in Yossi's tiny grocery store as his customers—all in bulky coats or jackets—tried to elbow their way to the counter and clamoured for his attention. Hovering outside the door, waiting for my turn between the waves of traffic, I caught snatches of conversation about the incident that had caused the curfew. Something unprecedented. Audacious. People shook their heads. They sounded worried, but their voices also betrayed a hint of admiration. A dark sense of foreboding came over me, but I willed myself to stay at my post. At last, during a lull, when Yossi was alone at his counter, scribbling numbers into his account book, I slipped inside, pulling my shawl snug to hide the worst of my unsightly mug.

"Hello, *Giveret* Salomon. Good to see you again. I hear you had an accident. *Oy yoy*, life is full of peril. May the One on High send you healing. Blessed be His name."

Of course, there were no secrets in the neighbourhood. Nevertheless, I tucked my shawl more tightly into the top of my collar to cover the bad side of my face. I asked for Dubek cigarettes, half a loaf of bread, cottage cheese, jam, tomatoes. Yossi fetched things from the shelves and bins. He wore a brown jacket, a scarf and a stocking cap, for the shop held a chill despite the kerosene heater in the corner. On one of the shelves was the last of a stack of newspapers and I caught a glimpse of a banner headline. The word "kidnapped" in bold black letters kicked me in the chest. Yossi saw my glance and clucked his tongue against his teeth.

"Don't worry, *Giveret*. The British soldiers will swarm like lice for a few days but this will pass. The People of Israel will prevail. God's justice will prevail."

I swallowed hard. Against my better judgment I had to ask, "What happened?"

"You don't know?"

Yossi's bushy eyebrows almost disappeared into the tangled mop of hair poking out of his cap.

"You didn't hear about the kidnappings?"

Once again that word sent a shudder down my spine. I shook my head.

"Here. Read!" he said, thrusting a newspaper under my nose. But I was already too dizzy to read, and I didn't want all the details. The bare bones would be enough.

"Just tell me," I murmured.

"It's because of the death sentence against Dov Gruener. The British want to hang him. Not because he took part in that raid on the police station in Ramat Gan. No, no, no."

Yossi's forefinger waved back and forth in the air.

"Not for the raid. And not for the gunfight that killed the Arab constable. And by the way, there were lots of bullets flying. Who knows which one killed the constable? But even if Gruener's did, that's not why the British are dead set on hanging him. So why? Tell me."

He paused for me to appreciate his question and smiled at my silence. He leaned over the counter towards me, his eyes filled with a glow that urged me to share in the triumph he was about to reveal.

"Because of Gruener's chutzpah in court. He said it was an illegal court. He called them all illegal—their judges, their lawyers, their police, their government. It is the duty of citizens to fight an illegal regime, he said. Threw their justice back into their faces."

"What about the kidnapping?" I asked in a small voice.

"Ah that was brilliant chutzpah too. Our fighters kidnapped a judge and an army major and are holding them captive until the death sentence is commuted. In broad daylight they grabbed them. Walked into a court in Tel Aviv for the judge and grabbed the major from his flat in Jerusalem. Brave boys and there was a girl among them too. They show they can take who they want, when they want. They are hiding the captives in some hole somewhere. They show they are the masters, not the British."

When a new flurry of customers arrived to distract Yossi's attention, I asked to use his phone. It rang and rang in Mr. Watson's office and finally someone picked up. Mary Griffin.

"Oh it's you," she said. "We were wondering whether you'd dropped off the face of the earth."

There was impatience in her voice, along with distraction. She didn't sound as if she herself had been wondering all that much.

"The government is closing early because of the curfew. Everyone on the floor has gone home already. I was just about to lock up. What was that? There's a lot of noise in the background. Are you calling from a bar?"

Hunched over the counter, my hand cupped around my mouth, I muttered my explanations as people milled and jostled, grabbing packages off the shelves. "Bad flu still . . . nothing to cause alarm but . . . need a few days more . . . please tell Mr. Watson . . ."

"Yes, yes. Will do. Cheerio."

The line went dead at the other end. I hoped that with all the to do about the kidnappings, my continued absence wouldn't be so noticeable.

I scurried back home with my small bag of provisions. When I stepped into my room the rank smells of my self-imposed confinement again assaulted me— the stale cigarette smoke, the fumes from my little heater, the dirty underthings. I shut the window and lowered the blinds anyway, and tried to wrap myself up in grey light and silence. But it was no use. Shimshon came through the keyhole. Though I covered my head with my shawl, I saw his black uniform and heard his soft, purring voice.

Against an illegal regime there is no other recourse but a war of liberation, fought with every available weapon and with every available means. We are small in numbers, but the Lions of Judah. With an outstretched arm and a strong hand, we take what we want: an army major from his flat, a judge in his wig and gown from his courtroom. Go ahead, cover your head with your pillow. I'm still here.

I WAITED FOR Sergeant Michaels to come back and search the building for signs of terrorists or witnesses or any kind of information an honest citizen might be willing to provide. An intelligent man trained to ferret out evidence (just like Duncan!), he'd immediately know something was amiss when he walked into my room. His lie-detecting senses would snap to attention. My fabrication about the fall wouldn't fool him. I could tell him everything, I would have *no choice* but to tell him the truth. It was a risk, but an opportunity too. Though nowhere as important as a British judge or a major, nevertheless I was a citizen of Palestine under British protection and with all the rights to British justice and compassion. Beneath the stern mask of the hardened soldier surely lay a kind heart. Moved by my story, Sergeant Michaels would get word to Duncan, who'd come back from whatever corner of the country to which he'd been posted and take me into his arms. Yes, behind the closed door of my room, alone with Sergeant Michaels, I could be completely anonymous, tell all, as to a priest. I had no evidence to give that could lead to anyone's capture, but if my plight could awaken a soldier's sympathy and reach Duncan's ears . . . oh, if only Duncan could be here, gripping my shoulders and pouring his deep-blue gaze into my eyes, I could feel safe again.

Sergeant Michaels became my hope. I rehearsed my testimony to myself, fretting about the answers to the obvious questions. *How many were there? Can you give any details of their appearance? Can you guess at their ages? What exactly did they say?*

My fingers splayed against the table to steady myself, I tried to carve out a coherent narrative from the swamp of my mind. There were three. Four at the most. Their leader was older but the others were boys and they could barely control their frantic excitement. They knew my name and Duncan's, though that didn't necessarily mean much. Jerusalem is a village, with eyes in every chink of the walls. They'd wanted to use me as bait to catch Duncan and were disappointed in my answers. They didn't know we'd broken up. So their intelligence was flawed. Were they really that cunning? Or maybe they'd set a trap, deliberately let me go so that word of my beating would reach Duncan and he'd return to my room in a blind fury. Maybe they were keeping watch in the scrub behind the building. Sergeant Michaels would be able to sort through my confusion and give me the answer. He would understand what had happened much better than me.

In a state of fevered expectation, I waited for the sergeant and his men as the barking voices in the bullhorns did a final round of announcements in our neighbourhood. When they'd left, the streets settled down into curfew silence. Mrs. Rajinsky muttered to herself on the other side of the wall. I lit the lamp and waited some more. But Sergeant Michaels let me down. He and his soldiers never came. Later I learned, they'd focused their attention on a completely different part of the city.

Chapter **30**
Operation Polly

THE FACE IN the mirror had started to look human again. My bruises faded from pulsing scarlet to aubergine to greenish yellow. Scabs had grown over the scrapes. With a thick layer of powder I could be relatively presentable, or so I told myself as I argued with the reflection in the mirror. The pain around my ribs had abated somewhat too, manageable with liberal doses of aspirin. On a bright February morning, when an eastern wind had wiped the sky clean of clouds, I dressed in my navy blue suit and my cream-coloured blouse. I arranged a paisley scarf around my neck to hide the lingering evidence of rough hands around my throat. Lipstick, mascara, rouge. From a distance at least, I passed muster. I donned my trench coat and took the package I'd prepared—the tweed jacket and skirt I'd worn the day of my abduction—loosely bundled in newspaper—under my arm.

When I stepped out onto the street, I breathed in the blessed smells of an ordinary winter's day in Jerusalem—muddy lanes, rain-washed pines, almond blossoms, donkey turds from a passing peddler's cart. The chirping finches in the oleander bush gave me courage and I crossed over to the grocery shop.

Yossi was alone, hunched over the day's edition of *Hatzofeh*, spread out on the counter. He barely looked up when I entered.

"What do you need, *Giveret*?"

His head still bowed, the forefinger of his left hand moved down a line of newsprint while his free hand paddled the air. The gesture invited me to consider his cornucopia of wares—the picked-over shelves of dusty tins and packages, a clod of sheep cheese on a piece of waxed paper, olives half submerged in a bucket of murky oil. The sour smell of the cheese made my stomach quiver, but I willed it back into submission.

"Dubek's please."

"Ah, Jewish cigarettes!" Yossi looked up and smiled, revealing tobacco-stained teeth. "Not so sweet as Camels, but made in our own land. You've become a patriot."

I shrugged. "They're cheaper and I'm not feeling rich."

"Yes, of course. But if you like the foreign brand, you better buy them now. Soon they'll all be gone, with the British evacuation."

"What nonsense!"

"Why nonsense? I'm only saying what's true. Yesterday a dozen British housewives stormed in. Cleaned me out of my best biscuits and sardines. All over the city they are buying, buying, buying. Food. Clothes. Cigarettes. Whatever they can get their hands on. It's like Christmas again. They're buying things to take home because noble Britannia still has shortages. You still have to stand in line there, even for a scrap of sausage. "

He grinned at the thought of Britannia's deprivations.

"Yes, I know. There's rationing in Britain. What does that have to do with the British here?"

"The evacuation, *Giveret* Salomon, the evacuation! Don't you know?"

Yossi shook his head at my ignorance. He told me what I'd missed during my days in my burrow. The High Commissioner had postponed Dov Gruener's hanging, which led to the release of Judge Windham and Major Collins. As brazenly as the two men had been plucked out of their daily pursuits by their abductors, they were returned to the streets, the judge in good spirits and unharmed, the major less so. He had a broken arm and burns to his face from the chloroform used in his capture. The British authorities had conducted massive searches for the kidnappers—to no avail. And now the administration had ordered all non-essential British civilians to leave the country within forty-eight hours. Operation Polly, it was called. All British wives and children and private citizens and even some low-level civil servants had to pack their bags and get out in a hurry. The government couldn't afford body- guards for everyone. The terrorists' reach had proven too great.

"Forty-eight hours. How is that possible?"

Yossi shone his nicotine smile again.

"Where is will, is a way," he proclaimed in Polish-accented English.

"But this is terrible."

He heaved his shoulders and spread his palms in a great shrug.

"Why terrible? Less business when they go, but we will survive. We don't need them."

He leaned over the counter, lowered his voice.

"First their women, then the rest. It's just a matter of time. The British—may they perish—are hanging on by their fingernails. They make a big noise about law and order, but this proves they are running scared. Have you seen what it looks like downtown? No? Well, you're in for a surprise. The mighty British have made themselves a ghetto. Ha, ha. Once the Jews had to hide behind walls. Now it's them. Those British housewives who came to my shop yesterday? They came with soldiers to stand guard. Yes, even for Yossi's they need an armed escort. It's the beginning of the end. Remember when Mr. Churchill said that in the war? If Winston Churchill were still in government, we might be in trouble. But that turncoat Bevin? Pah, Bevin! May his name be erased! A hollow tooth. Him we can beat."

I wasn't used to hearing Yossi express such brazen anti-British sentiments. Maybe he'd thought these things in private but he'd held his tongue. Or maybe the tide of public opinion had turned and he was just swept along. Bitter resentments and stubborn dreams throughout the populace were giving sustenance to the men in the shadows. I tried to fathom the upheaval of Operation Polly: the frantic packing, the tearful goodbyes. Schools with British children or British teachers would close. Shops would lose faithful customers. Servants would be discharged. What was Yossi thinking? I knew the British. They would not simply pull up stakes and abandon the mandate in Palestine. They had made a promise. They had their interests. They would never let a bunch of Jews chase them out. With their women gone they could come down on the populace with a heavier hand. But I also now knew the power of the other side, the zealots. There'd be no end to the tit-for-tat violence. Action and reaction would continue until we were all engulfed in chaos.

"Come, *Giveret*. Take a packet of Camels too."

He took a stub of pencil from behind his ear, licked it, and marked my purchases on a page of his ragged notebook.

"I haven't been to work for a while." I swallowed hard against the tightening of my throat. "I'll pay as soon as I can."

"What? You need to explain? You think I don't trust you?" He looked genuinely offended. "Haven't you been coming to my shop for years? You're a fine lady. Take more cigarettes. Take anything you want. Don't be shy."

IN THE LANE behind Yossi's shop, I threw my newspaper-wrapped bundle into a trash can. My damaged jacket and skirt might have been resuscitated. A clever seamstress could have fixed the tears and pulled threads and removed the grit that had become embedded in the fibres. But the garments that had once been my delight now filled me with loathing. That I'd spent two months savings on the suit, that it was almost brand new, didn't matter. I couldn't wait to be rid of the thing. I would have burned it if I could have done so without attracting notice. I placed the lid back on the bin and hurried out of the alley like a criminal escaping the scene of the crime. And then, instead of taking my usual route to town down Mamilla Road, I made a huge detour, walking almost the whole length of King George V Avenue. Past Terra Sancta Monastery, past the Yeshurun synagogue, and the Jewish Agency buildings. The route took me along the western edge of the cemetery but by sticking to the opposite side of the street, I could avoid looking down the slope at the scattered graves and the twisted limbs of the olive trees. Down Ben Yehuda Street to Zion Square. And then I got the shock that Yossi's words should have prepared me for.

The city had changed profoundly in my absence. The normal bustle of a workday morning was gone. None of the usual milling about, shouts and greetings, peddler cries and car horns. Instead, a funereal quiet had fallen upon the streets. To go east from Ben Yehuda Street was like travelling from one country to another. Massive coils of concertina wire obstructed the way, separating a cluster of government buildings, but also businesses, banks, and some residences, from the rest of town. The only way into this fortified zone was through an opening in the middle of Jaffa Road. Armed sentries stood at either side of this gate, inspecting the vehicles and pedestrians queued up to pass through. Grim-faced bystanders gathered on the curbs, stared at the menacing coils, shook their heads, but said little. I waited my turn in the queue, peering anxiously around the shoulders of those in front of me to see how things were progressing up ahead. I saw the maroon berets of the Sixth Airborne Division soldiers, the muzzles of their guns. All the shops on the wrong side of the fence were shuttered. The kiosk where I used to buy a pretzel and a glass of soda was gone. The broad sidewalks were empty, swept clean of litter, loiterers and the newsboys and shoeshine boys who used to vie for civil servant trade in front of the General Post Office. And what about the camera shop on Princess Mary Road where Manfred worked? That too was behind the hills of barbed wire.

"Welcome to Bevingrad," someone shouted in Hebrew. "Here's the New Jerusalem of Foreign Secretary Ernest Bevin."

I recognized a young Jewish clerk from the parcel department. He was addressing no one in particular and everyone round about—his fellow sufferers in the queue and the blank-faced Tommies up front. Heads nodded. A few people chuckled. I gathered that the "Bevingrad" coinage was no longer brand new.

The gate inspections proceeded at a snail's pace. And when my turn finally came, the soldier told me my identity card was no longer enough. I now needed a special pass for Security Zone C. This required a letter from my employer and a trip to the police station.

"But I can't get to my employer if you don't let me in."

"Sorry Miss. Not my problem. Move along."

A little up the road beyond the barriers I spied Mary Griffin and screamed her name. She settled the matter quickly, efficiently, but with her usual irritating forbearance. Passes had already been prepared for everyone on our floor. A pity I hadn't been there last Monday, when they'd all been handed out.

As she escorted me past another line of sentries by the entrance of the General Post Office, Mary informed me this would be her last day at work. She was among those being evacuated and she couldn't wait to get out of this wretchedly violent country, she said. Despite her eagerness to return home to England, Mary looked pale and shaken, preoccupied by all the personal turmoil that the evacuation implied.

"Who will take your place?" I asked.

She shrugged. Gave a tight-lipped smile. "I suppose they'll have to rely more on the locals now. Glad you're feeling better. You are all right aren't you?"

Abruptly, she turned to stare at me with an intense, appalled interest. Her eyes peered closely, trying to penetrate the mystery of the disfigurements beneath my makeup. I wanted to bolt right then, run back through the gate, through the streets and home, to disappear again into the safety of my room. It took all my nerve to continue up the stairs to the Finance Division.

When Mr. Watson saw me, his affable smile faded into a more uncertain expression. Flustered, he rose to his feet as if to come around from behind his desk to greet me, but changed his mind and sat down again. The chair creaked beneath his weight.

"Miss Salomon. Are you really well again? Do please take a seat."

He wiped his brow with his handkerchief, blinked a few times before regaining composure. He asked me about my flu and I repeated the lines I'd rehearsed. Yes, the flu. But there was also this silly accident. My landlady had been mopping the landing in front of our flat just as I rushed out the door one morning and I'd slipped on the soapy tiles to tumble down the stairs. My body and dignity took a bruising, but that was the worst of it, I assured him. His eyes drifted away from my face as I spoke, and I had the feeling he was only half listening. When I finished, he nodded and seemed relieved that I was able to explain myself.

"Dreadful luck. But you're on the mend. That's the important thing. You'll be needed more than ever now with all the . . . ah . . . changes."

He cleared his throat. He tapped his thick, blunt fingers together. He spoke of reorganizations and transition time and the division soon being back to its well-oiled self. Not to worry. Then he detailed my day's work to be done. First priority, a report on revenue losses due to new security procedures in post offices around the country, next, various letters to insurance companies, staff bulletins, and so on, and he motioned for me to take away the stack of hand-written drafts that filled the wooden "out" tray on his desk.

Through the open door we heard high-pitched cries of "goodbye" in the hall as Mary took leave of one of her colleagues.

"We'll all have to pull a bit harder these days," he said, his eyes suddenly losing focus, turning dark and sad.

On the windowsill behind him stood the photo of his wife and young son on the veranda of their home in the German Colony, one of Jerusalem's finer neighbourhoods. Framed on either side by lush bougainvillea, mother and son squinted into the sunshine, their faces brimming with suppressed laughter, as if they'd just exchanged a joke about the person behind the camera. The woman was pretty in a robust sort of way, while the boy had a winning, impish look. The photo was from another time, before the neighbourhood, where most British civil servants lived, had become one of the main three closed-off security zones. My thoughts flew to the evacuation. Had Mr. Watson's wife and son left already? He caught me gazing at the photo and gave a half smile.

"Operation Polly. That's my wife's name. Polly. Pure coincidence. She's just one of thousands. But it's made some of the others look up to her anyway. They're all quite upset about the order. 'This Polly is not going quietly,' she told me."

He chuckled.

"Closest she's ever come to open insurrection. She had half a mind to lead a column of placard-waving ladies up to the High Commissioner's residence. We've been here for so many years, you see. We consider Palestine our home. My son was born here, in the government hospital on the Mount of Olives. Well, I managed to persuade my Polly in the end, so they won't have to haul her off to the train station in irons. It's only for a while, only until things settle down. She must leave for the sake of the boy. For him it's a big adventure, of course, the long train journey to Alexandria and the ship to Liverpool. Converted troop carrier. Not exactly luxury accommodations, but Polly will make the best of it. She always does. She's a rock."

This was the most he'd ever told me about his family. He put on a brave face, but I could see he was distraught. He'd picked up a shard of pottery that he kept on his desk as a paperweight and rolled it around in his hands. It was a fragment from the lip of a large jug, the broken edges worn smooth over time, and smoothed some more now by his restless fingers. It was fitting that a man like him—well-meaning, easy-going, the type who avoided quarrels—would have a rock for a wife. He'd be a soft touch for hawkers in the souk. His wife, though, would know how to drive a bargain and manage a household despite the limitations of the Orient. He seemed quite lost without her.

"Will you be all right, sir?" I allowed myself to ask.

"Oh yes, yes. Of course. This evacuation business is just temporary. Polly and Raymond will be back here in a couple of months after the army gets the situation under control again."

He continued to fondle his pottery shard, which was a faded rust colour and probably of no value whatsoever, a piece of common rubble, Roman-era or not. Much of Jerusalem was like one huge midden. Was his house in the German Colony also cluttered with the bits and pieces he'd collected during his archaeological rambles? Did his wife scold every time he came home with his pockets full? He'd once told me that each ordinary shard represented stubborn endurance and immutable testimony, and so, even if one could find none of its companion pieces, it still told an amazing story all on its own. When he'd told me all this, his face had brightened with an open, childlike joy, very different from the weary sadness he wore now.

"Well, Miss Salomon, good to have you back. The GPO wasn't the same without you."

I was being dismissed. And there was no reason to linger. I had my instructions, his drafts. Yet I delayed, gazing down at the stack of papers in my lap, wishing he could intuit that I too had changed. I too carried a burden inside me. If only he could see into my troubled soul, without my having to spell out the details.

"I'm afraid I might be a bit slow today," was all I said as I squeezed my trembling hands together.

"I'm sure you'll have your sea legs back in no time."

He smiled and nodded and still I didn't rise. If he'd asked me what was wrong, I'm sure I would have burst into tears. But he didn't. His face clouded over, a look of discomfort, and then he became stubbornly distant as he waited for me to pull myself together. He had his own concerns. The clock on his desk ticked quietly.

"I'm sorry," I stammered, finally getting up to leave. He didn't ask what I was sorry about. He bent down to a file on his desk, pretending to be suddenly absorbed. I was sure that the moment I left he would go to the windowsill and run his hands over his collection of fragments.

In my office, I lowered myself carefully onto the wooden swivel chair, gnashing my teeth at the shock of pain. I rolled a sandwich of white paper, carbon, and copy sheet into the typewriter carriage and held my hands above the keys. They shook as if palsied. I rubbed them together and pressed them between my thighs and still I couldn't get them to stop trembling. Duncan's story came to me. About how his hands had turned to jelly when, as a schoolboy, he was about to perform at his first piano recital. He played anyway, botched the piece, ran offstage without taking a bow and never played again. Duncan could hold a pistol in his outstretched arm with such steadiness that the weapon and the arm holding it seemed to be made of the same cold metal. But he could not, to this day, bring himself to touch a piano. I'd never understood the contradiction until now. There was nothing logical about it. The human body simply has a mind of its own. I went into the Ladies for a fag.

Returning to my desk, I tried again. Closed my eyes and thought of a piece of music, a Mendelssohn hymn based on Psalm 55.

> *Hör mein Bitten, Herr, neige dich zu mir . . .*
> *Hear my plea, O Lord, incline Yourself to me . . .*

I ran it several times in my mind until it became embedded there, the same bars over and over again like a scratched record on which the needle keeps skipping back to the start. The fingers that I splayed over the typewriter keys shook less. Slowly and with mistakes that required many new beginnings, I made a dent in the pile of drafts. To make up for lost time I stayed at my desk through the lunch hour, not wanting to face my colleagues in the cafeteria anyway. By the end of the day, my back and bottom ached, while the muscles of my arms shivered. Yet it felt good to put my mind to something so wonderfully dull as expense tables.

Chapter 31
Liesel's Return

THOUGH MY SISTER had been home from Tel Aviv almost a week, I'd postponed a visit, just as I'd held off returning to work for as long as possible. I was afraid that her horror would undo me even more than I'd already become undone, so I'd waited for the chaos on my face to subside. But as I sat at my desk, defeated by yet another day of blotched pages and sins of absent-mindedness, a demon panic rising in my chest, I ached to see Liesel. I longed for the comfort of her arms. Rather than stay late to finish the backlog on my desk, I fled the office. I ran, ran, despite the shrieking pain between my ribs, out the front entrance of the General Post Office, past the guard posts, away from the barbed wire security zone, through the city centre, straight to her building on Hillel Street.

And the first thing that greeted me when I'd climbed the four flights of stairs and stepped onto the rooftop—panting, almost blind from my exertions—was a gun. It was pointed at my head. Its grey metal held a vicious gleam.

"Boom!" a gleeful voice yelled.

I screamed.

In the cellar, when my assailants had let loose with their fists and feet, I'd hardly made a sound. I'd peeped and gasped, groaned and shrunk into quivering silence. Now a shrill, unearthly noise spilled out of my lungs and filled the air around the little concrete-block flat on the roof. Liesel flew out the door, her arms outstretched, but not to me. She stooped to Ari who was on his backside, with his face tilted to the heavens and his mouth twisted in a pretzel shape. He howled and howled, even after Liesel picked him up and pressed him close. On the ground beside him lay the "gun"—a dented soup spoon that he normally used for making splashy-splashy in the washtub water.

"I didn't kill *Doda*. It wasn't me," the child blubbered into Liesel's bosom.

"Of course you didn't my chick. Look, *Doda* is here and she's perfectly fine. She was playing a game."

Liesel lifted her chin from her son's mop of curls to give me a chiding look that let me know what she thought of such games.

"Come give your nephew a kiss."

But Ari wasn't ready for kisses from me. He wrenched his face away.

"*Doda* is a *golem*."

The next ten minutes Liesel fussed over Ari indoors, settling him down with a cup of cocoa and a piece of bread and jam, while I paced beside the roof parapet with a cigarette clutched between my fingers. The February sky was grey and gloomy, threatening rain, and the wind made me shiver, but I hesitated to go in, unable to summon the cheeriness to make friends with my nephew again. Only when I heard them both calling, did I squash out my cigarette against the wall and step inside. Ari was dancing around on his cot, singing out his new name for me—"*Doda-Golem, Doda-Golem*"—until he caught sight of my strained smile, at which point he went round-eyed and quiet. His intense stare seemed to penetrate to the depths of my soul. Luckily I was able to break that unnerving gaze with a toffee I dug out from the bottom of my coat pocket. Blissfully engaged in unwrapping the sweet from its shiny gold paper, he forgot I was a *golem*, forgot about me altogether. But I was still unnerved. I said I needed another cigarette. Since Manfred didn't like me to smoke in the flat, I had an excuse to go back out. Liesel followed.

"What's the matter with you today?"

She peered more intently and, noticing the odd blotches beneath my makeup, her expression changed from mild reproach to alarm mixed with pained fascination. It was the same expression I'd encountered on everyone's face the last few weeks—that automatic human reaction to disfigurement. My own reaction was involuntary too—a wall of resistance. The tale I'd told everyone rushed to my lips without my bidding.

"I had a fall. I know I look grotesque, but I'm quite fine. That's why I stayed away until now. Didn't want to upset you for no reason. Or the boy. Sorry. I suppose I should have waited a bit longer. Or maybe I should wear a veil, like the Arab women."

A numb calm had come over me as I spoke, so that my fingers could strike a match and bring it to the end of my cigarette without trembling. I exhaled a stream of smoke. Liesel chewed the inside of her cheek while regarding me in doubting silence and I braced myself for more questions. To my surprise, she just shook her head and uttered a small, exasperated cluck.

"You worry too much about your looks. That's no reason to shun your own family. I've been dying to talk to you since we got back. What an awful three weeks it's been—first the disaster of our so-called holiday and now this mess about the shop. But you have no idea what happened, do you? Come, let's sit for a moment until his Royal Highness demands our attention again. He's busy tearing the remaining eye off his bunny rabbit and drooling toffee spit over his pillow. You really shouldn't give him so much candy, but never mind. Maybe he'll fall asleep. Let's sit."

With a sigh she plunked down on the up-ended orange crate against the north side of the house, where we were sheltered from the wind, and I took my place beside her on the wicker stool. I lowered myself with care, sat forward slightly because of the pain that still shot up from my tailbone. Liesel was wearing Manfred's jacket which she'd hastily thrown over her shoulders as she'd come outdoors. Her grease-stained apron stuck out from underneath, along with a loose brown dress that hung over her knees. She smelled faintly of onions, for she'd been making soup before I'd arrived. She, who was usually so unruffled, now raked her oniony hands through her short-cropped hair and looked at me with worried, distracted eyes.

"Where to begin? Everything's a mess. Like I said, it wasn't much of a holiday in the last days because of the curfews, the cordon and the massive searches. Tel Aviv was at a standstill. Shortages of milk and bread because the delivery trucks were delayed. The army herded Jewish men, including Papa and Manfred, into a schoolyard, where they had to wait their turn to be questioned. It took hours and I didn't know where they were being held. But never mind. That's not the worst. We get back to Jerusalem and find that Vishniak has been evicted from his shop along with all the other shop owners and residents on the wrong side of the barbed wire. You must have seen how it looks. *You* can get into the security zone. Shutters down everywhere. Soldiers strutting about. The eviction orders came from one day to the next. Vishniak just had a few hours to salvage what he could—the cameras, the tripods, the film—everything ripped off the shelves and crammed into his flat. Now he and Manfred are running around looking for another location to start over. But who knows what they'll find with so many in the same boat? Who knows when Vishniak will be able to afford to pay Manfred his salary again? Well, we just have to get through this. Maybe the British will have a change of heart and reopen those areas for business. They can't just deprive so many people of a livelihood. What do you think?"

She looked at me, hopeful, appealing, as if my opinion might be the proverbial word in God's ear.

"I don't know what to say," I said.

"But you know the British so much better than we do. You're always defending them. Tell me something nice about the government. Doesn't have to be true. Just to cheer me up. Or tell me a funny story, Evaleh. I'm tired of feeling gloomy."

She broke into a smile that brought out the radiant beauty of her face. Despite the upheaval in her life, she was resolved to be brave, strong, accepting of fate, and this resolve to endure, along with her need for me to become her ally in adversity, just evoked in me a trembling helplessness and irritation.

"Manfred will manage," I said with a shrug. "He always does. He's a clever fellow. As for funny stories, sorry but I'm not feeling terribly funny today. As for the British, why would they reopen the zone? They're under attack and have every right to protect themselves."

My callous words—which seemed to come from a stranger's mouth and which I regretted immediately stung my sister. She sucked her bottom lip in brooding thought for a moment, gazing out over the city. A woman on the rooftop across the way was taking in her laundry in advance of the approaching rain.

"Oh *you're* all right, aren't you? You have a nice, secure job at the General Post Office. Our troubles are just an inconvenience to you."

"As a matter of fact, my job isn't so secure."

I told her about having missed three weeks of work and of the mess I'd made of the day's typing. I'd slipped up with a phone message too, failing to jot down the details of an appointment properly, so that Mr. Watson, noticing something amiss, had to ask me for clarification. Thank God he did, otherwise he might have been late for the meeting. I said I'd been sore, jittery, unable to sleep, unable to concentrate. The worst of it was, I couldn't see that tomorrow would be any better. Considering all this, I deserved the sack. Even Mr. Watson's good nature had its limits. As I spoke, I was conscious of the agitated quaver in my voice, the nervous jiggle of my knee. Liesel had gone still, watching me.

"But I knew something was wrong as soon as you came. A child playing soldier makes you scream like you've seen a headless ghost. And now you're jumpy as a cat on hot coals. You haven't told me the whole truth, have you? About the stairs? Did you really fall? Did someone hurt you. Don't look away Evaleh. Tell me everything. I'm your sister and weren't we always like this?"

Liesel twined her index and middle finger together—the secret sign between us from our childhood, when she would try to comfort me behind Papa's back as he gave me a dressing down. The sight of her honest, work-reddened fingers raised in our old pledge of solidarity wrenched something loose in me.

"Oh Evaleh, my darling, don't cry."

The arms I'd been longing for wrapped around me now and pulled me close. The soft bosom and the shoulder I needed, at last. Tears spilled down my face, seeped under my scabs. It hurt to be embraced and rocked because my body was still so sore. But that was nothing. The ache in my heart was so much greater.

"*Zo, zo, zo*," Liesel murmured—the little nonsense words she used to sing to me and now to Ari when he took a tumble. "Poor Mouse. I know what must have happened. It's that man, isn't it? After all this time and everything he's done to you, you can't let him go. You've seen him again. And now he's raised his hand to you. Like a drunken Cossack, he beat you. Men like him are all charm on the outside and brutes underneath. And still you hang onto to him, your fine English policeman with his badges and his bully club. It's a sickness, Eva, to cling to such a man. He never deserved you and you must never let him near you again."

I gasped and stiffened. Her arms had become heavy, crushing. I tore myself free.

"No, no, no. You're completely wrong. It wasn't Duncan. He wouldn't . . . he's not like that. And anyway I haven't seen him for ages. It was Jews that hurt me. Jews! Do you understand?"

And so I finally told her the story, the bare bones of it, not all the details, which I couldn't bring myself to speak out loud. But what I said was enough to make Liesel fall into stunned silence.

"But why did you lie to me?" she asked when she found her voice again.

"I don't know. I've been so . . . upside down. Nothing I do or say comes out right."

I'd started to pace back and forth in front of her, my eyes on my feet and my hands clutched together while Liesel remained seated, wrapped in a cloud of confusion and dismay.

"But didn't you tell them you'd broken off with him? That you don't see him anymore?"

"Yes, I did. And it didn't make a difference. Or yes, it did, because it's for that they spared my life. But I'm still a traitor, a whore in their eyes. I'd consorted with the enemy. I deserved to be punished."

At that point I caught sight of a little half-naked figure. Ari, clad only in his underwear, holding his bunny by one ear, watching me with wondering eyes. Liesel must have seen him at the same moment for she leaped from her seat and swept him up. What was he doing out of bed, she scolded. He'd catch his death of a cold coming outside without his jacket and shoes. She rushed him indoors to settle him back in his cot. Or perhaps to get him dressed. I wasn't sure. I just had the sense from the speed of her movements that it wasn't only the cold wind she wanted to protect him from. *Doda* with her strange pacing and smeared makeup had indeed become a *golem*. And maybe Liesel too needed relief from my pained presence. As I waited for her return, the rain began, a few spatters first and then the slashing downpour. I huddled beneath the tin awning over the door, hugging myself against the wind, mesmerized by the fury of the elements until Liesel begged me to come back inside.

"We have to do something," she said when we were sitting at the table over a glass of tea and Ari was playing quietly on the floor with his empty film canister collection. I had washed my face and reapplied my powder, lipstick, and mascara.

"What do you mean?" I asked.

"We can't let those despicable people get away with this. The pigs! How cruel. Oh Eva, to hurt you of all people!"

She spoke in an undertone because of the child, though there was no mistaking the outrage in her voice. And she moved closer as if she wanted to enfold me again, but I pulled back not wanting to break down a second time. My tears had frightened me. I feared that if I started again, I wouldn't stop. A huge wave of grief lay just beneath the surface, threatening to sweep me away. And I regretted having spoken, for the relief I'd imagined from spilling out my story hadn't come. Instead, I felt uneasy at the pity in Liesel's eyes and guilty for the sorrow I'd brought upon her.

"We must report them. To the Jewish Agency. Ben Gurion hates those madmen. We can rely on him to do the right thing."

My sister nodded her head vigorously, agreeing with herself.

"Don't be ridiculous."

I pictured us approaching some harried, rumpled official in the Agency corridor, and his look of astonishment that we'd want to bother the chief with such a trifling matter.

"Why ridiculous? A terrible crime has been committed by fanatics who are out of control. They must be brought to justice. They must be forced to see the harm they've done. Oh Evaleh! I wish we'd never gone to Tel Aviv. This would never have happened if we hadn't left you alone for so long. What a stupid, cursed idea it was to go. And you know, I wasn't so keen on that trip in the first place because it wasn't cheap and the weather was miserable, but Manfred was adamant. I relented only because I thought it would be good for Papa and Ari to spend some time together. What exactly did they do to you? Where did they hurt you? Show me."

I shook my head but she insisted and I could see that I wouldn't get away from there until I'd done what she'd asked, so I did. I lifted my blouse, so she could see the swathes of bruising on my sides and back. By now the marks had faded to a subdued violet. Nevertheless, Liesel cried out at the sight.

"Oh the devils! The swine. Oh Evaleh."

"Shush! You're shouting."

Ari's head was raised, his face startled. I'd quickly pulled my blouse back down, but had he caught sight of something that three-year-old eyes must never behold? To even come close to exposing him so was a violation, a betrayal. I distracted him by puffing out my cheeks and pushing the air between my lips to make a squeaky noise, one of my repertoire of tricks. The barely healed scrapes on my face stung with the stretching of my skin. A small price to pay. Now Ari felt compelled—for the love of fun, or because of the shock he'd endured?—to display his own tricks. He scrambled to his feet and careened around the room with his arms outstretched, making airplane noises. An airplane that had lost its pilot, was flying in zigzags, crashing against the sofa, the table, our legs, the walls while being shot at by the enemy and screeching in pain and ecstasy at the sound of the exquisite explosions that filled the flat. Liesel and I watched in numb silence, which seemed to give the little airplane more fuel.

At last Liesel rose and uttered a quiet, but firm, "Enough!"

When he was back on the floor, merely commander of his army of canisters and bottle caps once more, I urged Liesel to return to the kitchen and finish making supper. Manfred would be home soon, famished after his long day of crisscrossing town in search of new premises for the photo shop. I was ready to leave right then, but Liesel implored me to stay.

Rain streamed down the windows. Gusts of wind rattled the tin awning over the door. The kerosene heater in the corner emitted faint heat along with wisps of smoke and noxious fumes, which required at least one window of the flat to be half open. I sat like a lifeless doll at the table, while Liesel crashed around with her pots. Manfred arrived, his cap and coat soggy, his glasses fogging up as he stepped inside and swept up his jubilant son. Manfred—solid and reassuring in his grey trousers, his white shirt with the pencils and notepad in the pocket, and his small, grave, thoughtful eyes behind his wire-rimmed glasses. I told myself, "Everything is normal. I'm with my family. We're going to have barley soup and bread and omelette and talk about this and that and urge Ari to eat a little more egg. Otherwise he'll never grow muscles like his *Aba's*."

Yet I felt I was looking at them from the other side of a pane of glass.

ACROSS FROM WHERE we sat at the table, Ari lay peacefully asleep in his mosquito-net-draped cot. The netting wasn't strictly necessary during the winter months, but intimate knowledge of malaria had made Liesel and Manfred hyper cautious, at least where their child was concerned. So billows of gauze, suspended by a piece of wire from the ceiling, enveloped Ari's cot all year round. We'd finished the meal and Liesel had served tea. Manfred told about his day's pursuits. He'd found two possibilities for the relocation of Vishniak's photography business: a room on the second floor of a building on Agrippa Street close to the market versus a ground-floor shop at the western end of Jaffa Road. Agrippa Street had the advantage of being fairly central, but it was a very small room, and out of sight of foot traffic. The Jaffa Road location was almost at the outskirts of town, but larger, cheaper and at street level. Neither property was ideal. Methodically, Manfred reviewed the details for us, sketching diagrams on his notepad. I listened with half an ear, and I think Liesel did too, though earlier in the day nothing had loomed larger in her mind than the loss of the premises on Princess Mary Road. I excused myself to use the lavatory. I sat on the edge of the toilet seat in a daze of indecision, thinking I should go home, unable to summon the requisite energy.

When I emerged from the lavatory, I could see by Manfred's appalled expression that Liesel had told him all. She'd blabbed even though I'd hissed at her earlier, "No. Don't. Not tonight. He's got enough on his mind." Now they both watched me intently as I returned to the table. The room felt small and crowded, the kerosene fumes exceptionally pungent. I gazed past the two of them at the tent of mosquito netting over Ari's cot. I wished I was in there with him. After another moment's hesitation, I sank back down on my chair.

Manfred contemplated me with sorrowful eyes. He shook his head.

"Unbelievable. But why do I say that? These are terrible times and people are driven to extreme actions. I half expected something might happen to you because of Duncan and I was relieved when it was over between the two of you. I'm so sorry about this Eva."

"Well, it's not entirely your fault," I said, with a stupid grin.

Neither of them smiled at the joke.

"I've told her she must report this to the Jewish Agency," Liesel said.

To my relief, Manfred was on my side. He couldn't see the point of raising a public stink. Liesel lifted her hands in a supplicating gesture.

"But the Agency should do something about the crazies in our midst. They should find those boys and punish them."

"What can the Jewish Agency do? The terrorists are beyond its control." Manfred shook his head again. "And what boys are you talking about? Eva doesn't have names. She didn't see their faces."

"Well, there should at least be an article in *Ha'aretz* denouncing such travesties. An article that expresses the complete and utter revulsion of the *Yishuv* for a senseless, brutal crime."

Liesel's face was full of innocent anguish, the conviction that if only one approached the right authority, the wrong could be righted. Of course, that authority had to be a Jewish one. Even she, in her longing that my assailants be brought to justice, didn't suggest going to the British. Things had gone too far for that. The wall between the *Yishuv* and the British had grown too high.

"I don't want my story in the newspaper," I said. But they were arguing with each other, not listening to me.

"When people hear what's being done in the name of the *Yishuv*, they will bring those lowlifes to justice. Someone must know who they are." Liesel leaned across the table to gaze insistently at Manfred, convinced of her own logic.

"How do we know it was a genuine cell of the Stern Gang that attacked her? It could have been amateurs. Some hangers-on who are trying to catch the attention of the real terrorists or impress one another."

"So what do we do? Absolutely nothing? I can't believe you'd suggest that." Liesel clutched her head. "You're always the one urging *me* to make noise. Not to be so easy going. The other day when I came home with a tiny speck of mould on the bread, you pushed me to take the loaf back to the grocer. You said we mustn't let ourselves get taken advantage of by a swindler. A speck of bread mould rouses your sense of injustice, but this kind of outrage you'd take lying down?"

Manfred sighed. He raised his glass of lemon tea, held it to the light, as if the answer to Liesel's accusation lay in the pale yellow liquid. He set the glass down again, the tea untouched, no doubt gone cold.

"There are all kinds of outrages happening daily . . ." he began, but Liesel interrupted him.

"Yes, but by Jews! Against one of their own!"

"What's so new about that? They mean business, those fanatics. Haven't you seen their warnings? 'Death to traitors and informers.' "

"My sister is no informer or traitor. What has she done? Who has she hurt? Look at her! She's a tiny, defenceless woman, beaten up by Jewish scum."

Manfred glanced at me—a quick, pained, guilty look—as if he'd had a hand in the beating himself.

"I wish I'd been there to stop it," he muttered to me, before turning back to Liesel.

"People get roughed up. And worse. I heard a story—who knows if it's true—about a man who was shot because he prevented his adolescent children from joining a terrorist cell. If you think our papers are so eager to report such incidents . . . or that they can even begin to get to the bottom of them in times like these . . ."

I'd been staring at my own cold tea through all this, but now I couldn't hold back any longer.

"I don't want to speak to a newspaper. I don't want people to know. The thing happened. It's in the past. I want to forget. And anyway, Manfred's right. No one's interested."

"But they should be interested," Liesel wailed.

Manfred clenched his teeth. "If I could get hold of the scum, I'd wring their necks myself. I mean it. Don't laugh."

For I'd broken into a nervous giggle at the thought of my mild, restrained, neatly dressed brother-in-law mustering up the fierceness to get into a brawl.

There was a pause during which we all listened to the groan of the wind, the drum of the rain and our own thoughts. The light above the table flickered as if the electricity were about to go out, causing Liesel to suck in her breath, but nothing happened. We were spared a blackout. Manfred drank his cold tea, tilting his head back to catch the last drops, for he did not favour waste. He was very much like my father in that way. I imagined them together at Papa's table, both ploughing through a plate of slop, manfully chewing and swallowing every bite. Now he put the glass down gently and cleared his throat.

"Suppose we could get a newspaper to write about this incident?" he said to Liesel, "Would that be a good thing? No it wouldn't and I'll tell you why. As Eva points out, she would find it upsetting. She would be exposed. People would say, 'There is the woman who got thrashed for taking up with a British policeman.' And, by the way, that's exactly what the terrorists want. They want to make an example of her. They want her battered face in the public eye. It would demonstrate their reach and serve as a warning to others. No, Eva's right, the best for her is to heal and get on with her life. You're lucky they didn't do more damage," he said, turning to me with a thin smile. "You're tougher than you think. Not so easily broken. But what's this about fearing for your job?"

I told him about my shaking hands, the various blunders of my recent days back at work. We discussed whether I should confide in Mr. Watson, and Manfred, after much careful consideration of the pros and cons, counselled no.

"Mr. Watson will pity you, to be sure, but pity is not the best feeling a man should have towards his secretary. He shouldn't feel anything for her at all. And you mentioned his wife is gone? Of course! With the evacuation. No, no, you must be very careful to keep your distance at this time when he will be especially lonely and vulnerable. Otherwise you invite complications that will definitely lead to loss of your job. He must see you as an efficient tool. Nothing else. Tomorrow you'll do better with your work. The next day, better still. Don't look back, look forward and you will prevail. You're a smart and brave girl. I have every confidence in you."

I was grateful for Manfred's calm, soothing presence, his very sound and sensible advice. He put into words what my instincts had told me about being guarded with my story. He was steady and solid as a rock. Once again, I could see why my sister had been drawn to him.

"She can't shake off a case of nerves just like that," Liesel protested. "Plus she's sore all over because of what those brutes did to her. And she can't sleep. She's always had trouble sleeping. At home, I sometimes would wake up at night and find her at the window, fluttery as a moth."

Liesel leaned across the table to put her hand on my arm. "Poor Mouse. What can we do for you?"

"Dr. Eisenberg can give her something to help her sleep. You should see him in the morning, Eva. But don't tell him what happened. It's not necessary and I doubt he'll probe. He's a busy man."

"And in the meantime, she must stay here tonight," Liesel said with the eagerness of having finally lighted on the one little thing she could do for me. Her hand pressed more firmly down on my arm. She gazed into my eyes more intently, as if she wanted to pour herself into me, all her love and concern. Seeing me waver strengthened her resolve to keep me under their roof.

"It's much too miserable a night for you to go home. I'll make up your bed on the sofa. Don't worry about disturbing Ari. Once he's down, he's out cold until morning. And we'll close our bedroom door so you'll have privacy. If you need to smoke, just stand by the door with it open a crack. Yes, Manfred, let her do that. I insist. A little wisp of cigarette smoke won't kill us. The kerosene heater makes a thousand times more stink."

My sister bustled about with sheets, blankets, a pillow, a fresh towel, and the loan of one of her nightgowns. I didn't relish going out in the dark and the rain. A wave of fatigue washed over me and the sofa beckoned. The thought of my sister and brother-in-law next door, and my nephew sleeping peacefully in his cot across the room, gave me comfort. I reasoned that when insomnia pounced, I could toss and turn here just as well as I did at home. But once the lights were out and all of us settled, I soon lost consciousness, falling into the profoundest sleep I'd experienced since my ordeal in the cellar.

WHEN I OPENED my eyes, Ari was gazing down at me, his bunny pressed to his cheek, his forefinger against his lips.

"Shh," he said in a stage whisper. "*Doda's* sleeping."

And he broke into a mischievous giggle.

The room was bright with daylight, for it was past seven a.m.—late by Palestinian standards. I jerked to a sitting position just as the front door flew open and Liesel, wearing her overcoat, stomped inside, muttering curses. Manfred pulled her into the kitchen, where they exchanged some words in hushed tones so that I couldn't make out what they were saying. But I could tell she was agitated and that he was trying to calm her.

"We'll discuss this later. I'm late," I heard him say.

He emerged from the kitchen, threw me a tight-lipped smile, hoisted Ari and gave him a goodbye-for-the-day toss in the air.

"There's never enough time," he said, as he gently put his son back down, his hands lingering around the boy's waist, reluctant to let go.

"Did you have a good night's rest? Yes? I'm glad. You see? You'll get through this. *Ein breirah.* Or how do the British say? 'Muddle through.'" He smiled sheepishly, patted my shoulder. "You're welcome to stay here any time."

When he'd gone and I'd dressed and Liesel and I were having a bite of breakfast, I asked my sister what was bothering her. For my sister could never hide her emotions. Every change of mood was plainly written on her face. This morning she was in a state of high indignation, though she tried to pretend otherwise. I had to coax and cajole, but finally—smacking her hand against the table—she blurted out that Dr. Eisenberg was not the man she'd thought him to be. He was a callous and narrow-minded bully.

"I could have told you that myself. I never liked him. But what brought you to that conclusion all of a sudden? You were talking to him earlier this morning, weren't you? That's where you were before I was up. Downstairs with Dr. Eisenberg. What did he say to get on your nerves? Wait a minute! You didn't tell him about me? Yes! You did! Don't try to pretend with me. You're a useless liar. Oh Liesel, you shouldn't have. He's the last person I'd want to tell. His views are uncompromising. He supports the Revisionists."

"I'm so sorry. I could kick myself. You're right. I shouldn't have shot my mouth off, and I wasn't planning to. I just happened to meet him in the lobby after I'd gone to buy some extra milk and I asked him about sleeping medication for you. And then he asked if you were suffering from hysteria. Just the way he asked got under my skin. I wanted him to know what you'd suffered. I wanted him to know that the outlaws he thinks are such heroes can be the vilest of brutes."

She bit her knuckle. Her face contorted in apology.

"Well, what did he say?"

It took her a while to spit it out. Finally, choking with fury, she did.

Dr. Eisenberg told Liesel he didn't believe the followers of Avraham Stern had beaten me up. He refused to acknowledge that idealistic Jews would do such a thing. But if they did, he added—and I can picture the cold, sardonic smile which accompanied these words—if they did, well then, I must have deserved what they'd dealt out.

Chapter 32
Goldschmidt Bombing

THE BRUISES FADED, the scabs fell away. The skin of my face was almost good as new again. Elsewhere on my body too, the marks my assailants had made became mere shadows, their traces erased by the healthy processes of nature. The pain in my ribs and at my tailbone took longer to heal. A sudden movement, a sharp intake of breath could still make me wince. But with each passing day, those hurts diminished too. Strangely, this stirred in me a vague unease. I felt compelled to press my fingertips into my side, searching for the tender spots as if hunting for something lost. *There you are, there, you little devil!* All this healing seemed just too relentless, happening without my conscious effort and almost against my will. When I gazed into the mirror I was not as relieved as I should have been. I saw the powdered cheeks and red lips of a mannequin and peeking out from under this mask, a pair of frightened, bewildered eyes. What had the blows felt like at the moment of contact? I wanted their shape and colour, their ragged edges and blinding sensation. When I tried to remember, I saw a rag doll jerk this way and that along a rough cement floor. I heard the scuffle of feet and grunts. The doll made no noise beyond impotent gasps, offered no resistance and merely absorbed what came. Had I even felt pain at the time? Yes, of course. I must have. But I couldn't make the pain come alive enough to connect with it now. And this troubled me profoundly, though I knew I was mad to think so. It was like watching a film with the sound turned off. Something essential was missing.

Whole hours could go by without my time in the cellar coming to mind. I gazed at the spring fashions in the shops on Ben Yehuda. I breathed in the scent of ground coffee beans from Café Atara. I took walks past the outer reaches of Rehavia to the Valley of the Cross to see the cyclamens in the fields and the ancient monastery, standing timeless and undisturbed amid its cedars. Everything was normal again, except for my unease. It would ambush me in the oddest ways. I'd catch sight of a billboard in the distance, and suddenly I couldn't breathe. I'd glimpse a hat like the trilby I'd lost on another women's head and I would hear Shimshon's sneering voice at my side, *"That woman thinks she's safe, but you and I know she is not."*

He would come to me at odd moments—during the workday, during an evening walk—to pour his poison into my ear.

"We are not afraid of the word 'terrorist.' On the contrary, we claim it proudly. What justifies our terror, Miss Eva-the-Dwarf? Pure and simple: the justice of the cause."

On and on he would go, an intense, monotonous tirade vibrating through me like the metallic, high-pitched note of a tuning fork. His words appalled me, yet I could see their logic and couldn't help but wonder sometimes whether Eisenberg was right: that I deserved what they'd dealt out. To still that voice and the doubts and to get me through the nights, I had little yellow pills, prescribed by a doctor. Not Eisenberg. I would never darken his door again, and neither would Liesel. She found us all a new physician on Rambam Street: quiet, dry-voiced, efficient Dr. Panofsky, who was abrupt in manner, but had layers of kindness beneath his outer reserve. With the help of his pills, I'd fall into a leaden, dreamless void, my being washed entirely away until shortly before the first light, when I'd flutter my eyelids open, surprised to still be present on this earth. Too groggy to rise, I'd drift off again, and then the dreams did come with a vengeance.

I WAS MANAGING at work. Just. I got through the day by dint of sheer plodding and long hours. I buried myself in the monotony of statistical charts and the properly formatted letter.

Dear Mr.__ ... (double space, paragraph indent) ... It has come to my attention, etc ... (far-right indent) I remain your obedient servant ... etc.

When Mr. Watson called me to his office for dictation, I entered with a formal nod, bowed my head over the steno pad on my knee, focused on the symbols that issued from my pen and made my face expressionless. Manfred's warning that my superior might be tempted to view me differently now that his wife was away, filled me with sick apprehension. Indeed, he sometimes sent a wistful glance in my direction—nothing bold or overtly suggestive—but a hint of appeal in those eyes nonetheless, an unwelcome intensity. I'd see him gazing at the photo of his wife and son on the windowsill, and then he'd turn around suddenly to smile at me, bashful, apologetic, sad. A smile that begged for my sympathy and that offered to transgress the formal boundaries between us that had been absolute over the years. Maybe he just wanted someone to talk to, but even that would have been too much for me to handle. So I dressed more cautiously in sober greys and browns, toned down my lipstick. I tried to make myself into an efficient, detached automaton of a secretary. Also, I avoided the lunch room and the daily huddles of colleagues around the tea cart, the chit chat. I worried about kindly meant but unnerving questions: How I was managing? Was I all better from that awful tumble on the stairs? I avoided people even though I knew everyone was too preoccupied with the challenge of living in a city that had become a tinderbox to pay much attention to me.

I managed. I coped. The effort was exhausting. When I was desperate for a break at work, I smoked by the window of the Ladies Rest Room, from where I had a good view of police headquarters in the Russian Compound across Jaffa Road. The whole area was an enclave within an enclave, with barbed wire thickets, pillboxes, armed sentries, and concrete obstructions called dragon's teeth placed on the driveways to prevent unauthorized vehicles from storming the entrance gates. Over it all brooded the massive and empty Russian cathedral, a relic of czarist ambitions in the Holy Land. I watched the comings and goings, the smart salutes, the officers striding towards HQ offices, or the central prison, or the billet. Was I still pining? Yes and no. It seemed years, not months, since I'd last seen Duncan. The image of his face had faded. The desire for his embrace was utterly gone, for I couldn't imagine pleasure at any man's touch. I'd become protective of my body, maintaining a physical distance between myself and the rest of human-kind—even Liesel—and even though the soreness between my ribs had finally dwindled to a mere twinge.

But I wanted to *tell* him. Not because I thought there was anything he could do. Neither he nor the entire Palestine Police Force would be able to make me feel any safer on the streets of Jerusalem. Nor because I wanted him to feel badly. My motivation for telling was something else. It was for the sake of connection with the person I'd been before the incident—the girl who loved to walk out in her fine wool suit with the gold scarf and the trilby hat. For the sake of remembering what it was to feel alive and attached through his caring. It seemed preposterous that Duncan might be just a few hundred yards away from me, marching across the dusty courtyard of the compound. What if I ran downstairs, across the street, called his name? Why, surely he'd hurry over to my side of the barbed wire fence. That's all I'd have to do, I said to myself. Yet I didn't budge from my spot at the window.

ON THE FIRST *Shabbat* of March a yellow haze hung over the city: once again the sultry breath of *khamsin*. It was a foretaste of summer, blunting the memory of the winter rains. The leaden heat made me jittery and unsociable, but Liesel was expecting me, so I trotted up towards Hillel Street to pay her a visit. When I approached the building, I saw Mrs. Eisenberg shaking out the doormat of their ground-floor flat onto the street. She stopped what she was doing to stare at me intently. Small, shrewd, knowing eyes behind the thick lenses of her glasses.

"I heard you had some trouble, Miss Salomon. Are you quite well again?" she sang in her high-pitched, forceful manner.

Dismayed to have her poking into this darkest corner of my life, I merely nodded and was about to hurry past, but she blocked my way.

"If you ever need someone to talk to, come to me. Don't be shy."

Her voice dripped pity. I felt reduced to a pathetic rag in need of starching by someone with her strength of will. At that moment, I hated her almost as much as I hated her husband, but it was not the energizing, pleasurable kind of hatred. Something much heavier, more burdensome. I rushed up the steps without giving her the courtesy of another glance. When I told Liesel of my encounter, she burst out in indignation.

"You should have told that interfering witch you've never felt better. And that, anyway, you've got a loving sister to talk to if you need someone."

Liesel cocked her head to one side. She took me in. She smiled warmly.

"You really do look fine. Your face is all better. You don't need so much make-up anymore. And you're quite elegant in that grey frock. Like something out of a Paris magazine, my elegant little sister. It's lovely to see you looking your old self again. Watch out! The Zion Square Romeos will be after you in no time."

I murmured my thanks, attempting to appear pleased, and then we lapsed into companionable silence. We sat outside on the rooftop, under the awning over the door of the little flat. Liesel peeled potatoes, while I darned Manfred's socks—I was ever so much better at it than my sister—each of us lost in our own thoughts. Manfred and Ari were inside, having their afternoon siesta. Liesel hummed *Leise zieht durch mein Gemüt* under her breath, the exquisite ode to spring with the words penned by Heine and the melody by Mendelssohn. I envied the peace and fullness of her life, its humble normalcy despite the day-to-day worries. Liesel and Manfred, like the other couples all around us, were sturdy as a team of oxen, sharing the yoke, putting one foot in front of the other, doing their bit for the renewal of the land and the people—a people so desperately in need of rebirth. And yet, even now—especially now!—this simple, noble destiny seemed impossible for me. *The pretty face is a sham*, I wanted to scream. *It doesn't belong to me. I'm a shattered vessel, so don't expect me to rise like a phoenix out of this trauma.*

The temperature on the roof had risen to a fiery intensity. The sky, gone from yellow to grey, pressed down upon the city with leviathan weight. Liesel fanned herself with a folded newspaper. Her cheeks were flushed and her eyes glassy.

"Why don't you lie down too?" I suggested.

"There's no air inside. Out here at least there's the illusion of a breeze."

Everything glared—the stone buildings, the metal flashings, the listless white sheets on wash lines, while the heat beat down on my head. I lay aside the sewing basket, closed my eyes, let my chin drop to my chest. From below came the faint clamour of children's voices in the public park beside Mamilla cemetery. From their hiding place in a shady recess under the eaves, came the coo of doves. The threads between here and nowhere gently pulled apart, allowing me to float away.

A violent *rat-tat-tat, rat-tat-tat,* yanked my head upright. Liesel and I stared at one another. Again, we heard that staccato sound, followed by a series of single pops. Where was it coming from? Hard to tell, but it seemed uncomfortably close by. The shots stopped and the city seemed to lapse back into its dreamy mid-afternoon doze, but a cold foreboding clutched my breast. I saw my sister open her mouth to give voice to the warning that sat frozen on my own tongue and at that very moment a gigantic blast ripped away her words and the air shook and the concrete of the rooftop trembled beneath our feet. We remained immobile in our chairs through the long moment of deathly silence that always follows such explosions, during which time stands still and all the glittering rooftops of the city seem suspended in the air as if they've become part of heavenly Jerusalem at the end of days. Nothing stirred or whispered. And then, the shouts, sirens, gunshots, slamming doors, bullhorn announcements. All so familiar, as Liesel's first remark neatly expressed.

"Not again!"

I found myself at the southwest corner of the roof, gazing over the parapet at plumes of smoke that billowed upwards only a few blocks away. Liesel was beside me and she called a one-word question to someone on the street below.

"Where?"

But no one knew as yet for sure.

Then Manfred was out on the roof beside us, with the boy held tight against his shoulder, urging us to get back inside. Now. Now! For God's sake, don't be stupid, for who knew if there might not be another explosion. But Liesel and I couldn't budge. We were riveted to the spot, craning our necks and squinting through the smoky haze, fascination overcoming fear. We all agreed—and shouting spectators on nearby rooftops said the same—that the target had to have been somewhere on King George V Avenue. Confirmation came soon enough, hollered from street corner to balcony to rooftop. The British officers' club in the fenced-off security zone across from the Yeshurun Synagogue had been bombed.

"Terrible," people screamed. But there was awe in their voices. They were dazzled and strangely exultant as much as horrified, it seemed to me. And I was no different, carried away by the noise and drama as armoured cars rumbled through the side streets and soldiers poured into Mamilla Cemetery, poking into the bushes with their bayonets. Then the bullhorn shouts became more emphatic.

"Everyone inside. Military orders!"

Warning shots rang out. Manfred herded us quickly into the flat and shut the door.

We sat around the table and waited and tried to distract Ari with games of Broken Telephone but the boy was restless and so were we. There was nothing to do but endure the stifling heat in the low-ceilinged room. The little flat was a cooking pot under the fierce *khamsin* sun, while we inside its simmering contents. After a while, in defiance of the curfew, Manfred took Ari in his arms and they slipped downstairs to gather news and then Liesel and I followed, to the cooler landings, where other tenants had gathered. Some people crowded into Dr. Eisenberg's apartment, for he had a wireless set tuned to the Palestine Broadcasting Service, which issued special bulletins at times like these, but my sister and I kept our distance, getting the news through word of mouth.

We learned that the assailants, disguised in stolen British army uniforms, had sprayed the officer's club with diversionary gunfire, while a truck loaded with explosives ploughed through the barbed wire barricade. The driver leaped free. The mammoth bomb went off, pounding one whole corner of the building into rubble. At least a dozen were dead and many more injured, with civilians caught in the crossfire among the casualties. There had been simultaneous assaults in other cities, but the action in Jerusalem had been the most brazen and spectacular, having wreaked the most havoc and made a mockery of the latest security zone defences. Soldiers and police would be digging through the wreckage throughout the night. Meanwhile a massive manhunt was underway in the surrounding neighbourhoods. In the PBS emergency broadcast, General Gage vowed he'd spare no effort to catch the perpetrators. Martial law was declared and would remain in effect until, in the general's words, "terrorism is eradicated." All affected areas—ours included—would be under curfew until further notice. The collective wisdom held that this was an Irgun operation, for the Sternists could never pull off anything that huge, though maybe they had helped.

Up and down the stairwell, people spoke their minds.

"They're combing every inch of the area. They'll be knocking on our doors soon," said Chaim, the schoolteacher, as he slumped his shoulders and hung his head in a sigh of resignation.

"I hope they find the bastards," said Shulamit, his pregnant wife, standing in their doorway and rubbing her curved belly.

"They won't. It was a brilliant operation."

This declared by Dr. Eisenberg, who'd planted himself on his landing, feet apart, chest out, hands slightly curled like a wrestler ready to take on opponents.

"An operation? An outrage? And we all pay for the work of dirty zealots," shrilled Shulamit.

"Yes, the British impose collective punishment," Eisenberg said with grim satisfaction. "But it will backfire. The people won't stand for it much longer."

The chatter in the stairwell ended abruptly with the arrival of a small search party of soldiers whose captain ordered us all back into our flats to await our turn for their inspection. We could hear their boots stamp up the stairs as they progressed, storey by storey, and the occasional gruff shout of command. At last they were on the roof, three privates and their officer, red-faced and sweating from their exertions of poking under beds and prying into cupboards. Liesel offered them glasses of water. Not because she was trying to curry favour or make a point ("*See! We Jews are decent human beings, despite all the nasty things said about us.*"), but because my sister just *is* decent and generally assumes the same about others until knocked on the head by contradictory evidence.

The captain brushed aside her offer with a staccato "thank you, Ma'am, we have our own," and a cold, suspicious look, as if no gesture we could make would be trustworthy. There was none of the humour and kindness I was used to seeing among the British soldiers once you penetrated their mask of formality. I had the sense a line had been crossed, although that feeling had come to me with every new "outrage" and its aftermath of stern government actions. Nevertheless, this time really was different. They rifled through Manfred and Liesel's small store of possessions—clothes, dishes, Manfred's precious collection of camera equipment—with a vindictive roughness. My brother-in-law controlled himself, but I could see a muscle in his jaw twitch as one of the soldiers ripped a close-up lens out of its leather case, rolled it around in his meaty hands and plunked it down hard on the table. Another of the soldiers examining the bathroom poked his bayonet into the bucket in which Ari's shitty diapers were soaking. He pulled a disgusted face—what did he think soiled diapers smelled like?—and wiped the blade clean on the hand towel beside the sink. In short, the soldiers didn't bother with the usual veneer of politeness, for they were in a nasty mood. The ugly feeling spread from them to us like a virus, so that we felt no real relief when they'd gone, only the bitter aftertaste of their hostile presence. We still weren't allowed to leave the building. An indefinite curfew lay over the whole area.

Later in the evening, when Liesel tried to fill a kettle, nothing came out of the faucet except a brown spit and a hiss of air. Without warning the plumbing had gone dead. Not a drop of water was to be had.

"*Zum Kotzen!*" she shrieked as she slammed the kettle down against the counter.

Fortunately, Manfred kept a stash of milk bottles filled with drinking water in a corner of the kitchen for precisely this kind of contingency and usually Liesel took the sudden shutdowns that often befell our city in her stride. Not this evening.

"They've done it on purpose. Collective punishment. What are we supposed to do? Die of thirst?"

It sickened me to hear her latch onto Eisenberg's refrain, but there was no use contradicting her while her nerves were so frayed. Her hair lay plastered against her forehead. There were damp circles in the cloth of her dress under her arms. Her eyes sparked like a viper about to strike—which was so unlike my normally stoic and sunny sister. Meanwhile Manfred had gone grey with migraine and Ari whimpered miserably for that other glass of lemonade his Ima had promised him if he'd consent to go to bed. We all finally did—me on the narrow sofa, Manfred, Liesel, and Ari in the other room, for they'd moved his cot at the boy's request to be closer to *Ima* and *Aba*.

In the darkness and the stillness, the flat became even more of an oven. The heat swam out of the walls, thick and viscous, clinging to every surface, clogging my pores. The thin cotton of Liesel's nightgown weighed against my skin. The unflushable toilet added to the stale smells in the flat. Of course, I couldn't sleep. I lay on my back, listening to the restless movements and sighs from the other room, considering whether to go out for a smoke. I resisted for I had only three cigarettes left in my packet and the night was young. By and by, Shimshon stood before me in his belted black jacket and pillbox cap, a vision that was neither dream, nor hallucination, nor conscious thought, but something hovering in between all three. When he spoke, his voice was a soft purr: calm, confident, rational, and unrelenting.

As you see, Dwarfling, all the King's horses and all the King's men are helpless before the Fighters for the Freedom of Israel. An Empire is shattering, and it is Jews— do you understand? Jews!—who are bringing it down. Our secret weapon? White-hot conviction—more powerful than Bren guns and armoured cars.

I closed my eyes to shut him out, but it did no good. Shimshon made himself at home on one of the chairs, tipping the back against the wall and resting his booted feet on the table. He flicked open a penknife and pared his nails. He even downed the last of the lemonade in the jug that we'd been saving for Ari's breakfast. *What do you want of me?* I asked in my heart, though I knew. He wanted me to realize the supremacy of his world view and the inferiority of my own.

Let's put aside for a moment our three thousand years of history with this country.
Can there be any doubt in your mind of our absolute moral right to the Land—the
whole of the land, mind you, on both sides of the Jordan—after the death camps
of Europe? To which your own beloved aunt and uncle were schlepped, by the way,
in a filthy, airless cattle car—a hundred men, women, and children stuffed into a
compartment fit perhaps for a dozen livestock, without light, food or water and only
a couple of buckets to hold their stinking wastes.

Having heard all I could bear, I stumbled off the sofa and out the door
to the relative freedom and fresh air of the rooftop. A wilderness of rooftops
stretched out around me. Down below, armoured cars equipped with Bren guns
that poked out of the cabs like long snouts lumbered up and down the streets.
Beyond the rooftops, in the circle of dark hills that surrounded our city, villagers
with daggers beneath their robes and blind fury in their hearts were just waiting
for their moment to strike. And above the hills, the profusion of brilliant stars
winked their meaningless Morse code. And above the stars stretched the cold,
indifferent void.

THE WATER FLOWED once more from the taps the next morning, but
that was about the only thing that was back to normal. Manfred came upstairs
from Eisenberg's where he'd heard the details of martial law as announced by
the cool, crisp, oh-so-civilized British voice on the wireless. The Jewish districts
of the city were under heightened surveillance and closed off by military patrols
from the rest of town. Both public and private transportation were suspended,
which meant the flow of goods to shops came to a standstill. Banks and post
offices were shut, the use of telephones restricted. Manfred and I rushed out
to see what foodstuffs could still be bought and found ourselves jostling with
the swarms of other shoppers, clamouring for the day-old bread and whatever
else was left on the grocery shelves. A few earnest citizens shouted above the
melee, "Jews! No hoarding!" But their cries were largely ignored. Meanwhile, the
soldiers of the Sixth Airborne in their maroon berets yelled at people to move
along whenever a little cluster formed in the street. Loitering, gathering together,
street-corner philosophizing was now forbidden. Much of the Jewish city was
more or less under siege.

When my brother-in-law and I trooped back up the long flights of stairs with
our pathetic gleanings, we found Liesel in the kitchen, triumphantly mixing up
the ingredients for a cake. She had got her hands on half a dozen eggs. Manfred
and I were suitably astounded. With a pleased grin, Liesel told of how she and
other housewives of the neighbouring flats had gone door to door, bartering
their supplies: extra onions for some potatoes, a bottle of milk, for a few eggs.

Whoever had too much of something gave it away in exchange for an item she lacked. Thus, Liesel could afford the luxury of baking a cake, though it wasn't even *Shabbat*, but rather the start of the work week. A very unusual work week, however, in which very little work would get done because of the extensive closures and restrictions, so all the more reason for a treat. Manfred kissed her lovingly on her flour-powdered cheek and a tender look passed between them. Newly energized, he went to their bedroom to gather up some papers—floor plans and photos of the premises he'd been viewing—which he intended to bring over to Vishniak's place in Rehavia so that they could put their heads together and the day wouldn't be a total waste after all. Liesel continued to stir her batter, the big ceramic bowl balanced on her hip, her face gleaming with sweat and the contentment of vigorous, wholesome activity. Ari was visiting his girlfriend in the flat one floor below.

Having hung around with my sister long enough, I was about to take my leave, thinking to return home. I didn't really want to go back to my empty room, but what else was there to do with the General Post Office closed until further notice? Just then, Shulamit from downstairs appeared at the door to deliver Ari to his parents along with a piece of bad news. All of us in this building and the neighbouring ones had to abandon whatever we were doing immediately. We had to report for questioning to the girls' school in Rehavia, which had been commandeered by the military authorities and remade, temporarily, into an inspection station. We were to take our identity papers and file outside promptly in an orderly fashion to Ben Yehuda Street, where soldiers were waiting to accompany us to the school. Anyone who delayed or resisted would be arrested and charged under the emergency measures.

"What sort of questioning?" Liesel asked.

"What do you think?" Shulamit answered, throwing her hands in the air.

Corroborating her story, the bullhorns had started to croak and bark outside. "By order of the General Officer Commanding . . ."

With an air of mourning, Liesel covered the mixing bowl with a cloth to protect it from the flies. Together, we put shoes on Ari's feet and a floppy sunhat on his head. Manfred thought to bring a canteen of water. We joined the exodus of cursing, grumbling, last-minute-searching, foot-shuffling, door slamming residents that emerged from the building into the dusty glare of Hillel Street, there to be herded by stern-faced Tommies into the long column that had formed on Ben Yehuda. I saw more than one mock Hitler salute directed at the soldiers and heard muttered taunts of "Gestapo!" The mass of people began to move forward, urged to step smartly by armed soldiers blowing whistles and waving us along.

"Take your time, friends!" someone boomed over the din and I recognized Dr. Eisenberg's gravelly voice. "Make them wait. We aren't sheep. We're a free people in our own homeland."

Men, women, children—old and young—we trudged up the hill and past the bombed-out officers' club, where heavy equipment and rescue crews were still picking through the rubble, past the cordoned off Jewish Agency compound, that seemed to be under a separate siege. Down side streets of Rehavia and into the heavily guarded schoolyard. There we sat for hours, on the dusty clay of the tennis courts, beneath the punishing sun—for there was little shade—or we milled about aimlessly while we waited our turn for questioning.

"Look at their faces, how they hate us," said an elderly woman, holding her hand against her panting breast. Her own tone dripped contempt.

I did look at the soldiers for there wasn't much else to do. One fellow stood close by, a freckle-faced youth, the rims of his ears as scarlet as his beret and his lips flaky with heat blisters. We shared a similar kind of skin: the fair, delicate European variety that couldn't stand up to much punishment from the sun. Our eyes met for an instant and I saw the soldier's hand tighten on his rifle. What did he see? Another one of "them?" An abstract entity called the "locals" whom he had to regard with utmost wariness? He seemed both on edge and profoundly bored. I didn't envy him the job. I imagined this wasn't what he'd signed up for when he'd shipped overseas to maintain Britain's benevolent rule over the natives in the Holy Land. The ungrateful natives!

After about an hour, a water truck pulled into the yard to be swarmed by a thirsty mob and the soldiers fired in the air to make us stand back while they filled buckets and organized us back into little herds of thirty or so, each with an appointed leader to supervise the distribution. I brought a tin cupful of water to Liesel who sat with Ari between her legs, holding a sheet of newspaper over his head in a pathetic attempt to give him shade. Manfred had already been taken off into the school where the interviews were being held. The child was tomato-faced from heat, like everyone else, but otherwise seemed to be enjoying himself, watching the activity all around with saucer eyes. He was especially enchanted by a group of boys who had organized a boisterous game of "horse and rider" to while away the time. Two teams composed of smaller lads hoisted onto the backs of bigger boys crashed into one another as each tried unseat the "rider" of the opposing team. Several soldiers, blowing whistles, broke up the game and made the youngsters sit back down in a submissive row on the hard, sun-baked earth.

"They want us to look like a beaten people," Liesel fumed. "Like slaves. Like proper Jews. They want to make us suffer. Why else stop a harmless game?"

At last Manfred returned to us, greyfaced and limp, for his migraine had resumed with a vengeance, and he took care of Ari, while Liesel and I were herded into the school with a group of other women and children. One by one, we were sent into the classroom where the questioning took place. Children under ten were allowed to stay with their mothers, but anyone older had to face the interviewers alone. Finally, my turn came. I stood before the broad teacher's desk, where now a military officer sat, flanked by two soldiers with rifles at the ready by their sides. Behind them, near the blackboard, though not exactly leaning against it, stood a sergeant of the Palestine Police, there presumably to offer backup support if needed. Without looking up, the military man examined my identity card and checked my name against a typed list. Next, the routine questions. Address, workplace, what I'd been doing and who I'd been with yesterday between ten a.m. and two p.m., etc.—all spoken in the curt, irritated voice of one who'd already conducted hundreds of such fruitless interviews and was thoroughly unimpressed by my innocence-confirming answers. All the while he regarded me with cold loathing, as if I were an unsightly insect he would have loved to stamp underfoot. I'd never come face to face with such a degree of contempt in a British official before and the experience unnerved me to the point of confusion. Breaking free of that hostile gaze, I glanced across at the policeman and my heart squeezed. Surely this man knew Duncan. Perhaps he was one of the mates in the police billet in the Russian Compound, who'd played cards and exchanged jokes with him and maybe even covered his back in some dark alley. And surely too, he and I had met at Finks during those good old days of linking arms and belting out "It's a Long Way to Tipperary." The growing conviction made me want to fling myself at his feet. However, this sergeant looked right through me, his eyes a glaze of boredom and indifference. The military man's voice ripped through my thoughts.

"I said, Miss, is there anything else you want to tell us? Anything related to yesterday's incident, or any other incident? Speak up."

"I . . . I . . . was a friend of Sergeant Duncan Rees," I stammered, addressing the policeman, whose vacant expression snapped to attentiveness, like a light switched on. The military officer turned around and the two men exchanged glances. The policeman shrugged.

"Duncan Rees of the Palestine Police," I continued, though my throat had gone to dust.

"Yes? And? What about him?"

"I was wondering if he's still in Jerusalem."

"Why do you want to know?"

"I . . . just because . . . I haven't seen him for some time."

"Ah!" the officer snorted, a single syllable that said he knew exactly now what category of female I belonged to and where to place me in his hierarchy of regard. A little sneer raised a corner of his lips as he allowed himself a long pause, during which he was clearly enjoying my embarrassment and trepidation. He turned again to the policeman.

"You know this chap Rees?"

The other, who'd come closer to the desk, gave an affirmative grunt while looking me over with a quick one-two movement of his eyes.

"Heard of the bloke. Heard he's gone. Shipped out."

He opened his mouth to say more, but closed it quickly, as if he'd changed his mind, and scratched vigorously behind his ear.

"Gone where?" I cried. "Out of the country? When?"

The military officer gave a rueful laugh.

"You trying to interrogate us, Miss? You aren't the first. I've had a number of characters in here who answered my questions with questions of their own in the manner typical of your people, but your angle is unique."

"It's not an angle. We knew each other a long time. He wouldn't just leave without . . . unless . . . Has he been injured?"

The policeman's face softened, but he could only shake his head at me and offer a sympathetic shrug.

"You'll have to make inquiries at HQ, Miss."

The military man gave his desk an impatient tap.

"I'm not here to provide a match-making service. Thank you. You can go."

THE *KHAMSIN* LASTED for three more days, during which the city seemed wrapped in a dirty blanket. Even the doves on the railings drooped in silent stupefaction. Martial law remained in place for another week and a half, with seventeen-hour curfews and the isolation of all Tel Aviv and of a chain of neighbourhoods in Jerusalem. Supplies came into the cordoned-off zones through carefully controlled check-points, soldiers handing parcels of food, clothing, and medicine to Jewish volunteers across the barbed wire barriers. Occasionally a truck was allowed in after a thorough search of its wares. There were long queues of grumbling citizens in front of grocery shops and kerosene wagons. Martial law literally stank, for with garbage pickups cancelled, the refuse overflowed from the bins into the lanes—a feast for rats and feral cats. The festival of Purim arrived but there was not much of a holiday mood, as all street processions were banned. In Jerusalem, the military closure was called Operation Hippo and the one in Tel Aviv was Operation Rhino. There were jokes about the British obsession with big game hunting and their nostalgia for large lumbering animals to shoot at since the small, swift ones eluded their grasp. As the searches and investigations continued, many government buildings, including the General Post Office, remained closed and even when it re-opened, stayed out of bounds for Jews for another week except on receipt of special passes that required time-consuming applications. Throughout those idle days, one question looped tenaciously through the turmoil of my thoughts. Where was Duncan?

The question persisted though I argued with myself that it didn't matter where he was. We were finished. No letters. No contact. Clean break. And yet it seemed outrageous that his long, vital body no longer bedded down on a cot in the stone police barracks on Queen Melisande Road. That he was nowhere I could imagine. Only now did I feel the full impact of the cruel decree. So I had to know: Was he really gone from Jerusalem? From the country? And, if so, where?

Chapter **33**
B.I. Morton

THE POLICEWOMAN USHERED me into a hut near the entrance of the Russian Compound and proceeded to pat me down. Brisk, thorough and professional, her cool hands felt along my sides, my belly, my buttocks, my breasts. She made me take off my blouse so that she could poke a finger under my brassiere. She made me take off my shoes. Satisfied at last that I carried no concealed weapons, she ordered me to walk in front of her across the broad parade ground to the imposing grey-stone building that once was a hostel for Russian pilgrims and now housed police headquarters. The whole time that she accompanied me, she kept her expression blank as a sheet of cardboard. A neutrality that blotted me out. We proceeded down a cool, gloomy corridor, filled with sounds of purposeful activity—clack of typewriters and urgent, muffled voices from behind closed doors. A shiver passed through me, realizing I'd entered the Central Intelligence Department, nerve centre of the Palestine Police, and the organization Duncan had so often talked about with a pride bordering on awe. He'd also told me of the beastly chill that these thick-walled buildings harboured in winter. In the early years of his career, he'd often had to stand guard here, stiff with the tedium of the watch, like the constable we'd passed in the lobby.

The policewoman delivered me to a small office with a desk, behind which sat British Inspector Reginald Morton. He was lean, spare and swarthy, with keen, intelligent eyes behind his glasses and he too exuded efficiency, but something more as well—a hint of warmth.

"Do sit down, Miss Salomon," B.I. Morton said with a courteous gesture.

He assumed the poise of the patient listener, hands folded in front on the desk, a small encouraging smile on his lips, suggesting competence, self-discipline, and high principles. He had a face that inspired a spark of hope. The bands inside my chest loosened a notch and the drumming in my ears softened.

B.I. Morton wanted to know all about my connection to Duncan—how we'd met, how long we'd known one another, who we'd associated with, what my family and friends thought of our being together. I found myself speaking frankly and without holding back the quaver of emotion in my voice, confident that he wasn't about to mock me as did that awful officer at the girls' school screening station. I told him everything up to the moment of our separation and stressed we'd parted on good terms. When I'd finished spilling out my story, I leaned forward and asked again the question that had brought me here. My eyes sought the inspector's. I didn't say these words aloud, but they welled up in my heart. *Help me! Please!*

B.I. Morton pushed away from his desk and tilted back just a hair's breadth in his chair, while regarding me thoughtfully.

"Isn't there something else you want to tell me, Miss Salomon?" he said softly. "I sense you have something more on your mind."

Even before the words were out of his mouth, the floor started to wobble beneath my feet and my vision went black around the edges. *Perhaps I could . . . perhaps I should.* The "more" he was alluding to rose up like a tide in my chest. And then condensed into a fist in my throat. I licked my paper-dry lips and shook my head.

"Would you care for a glass of water, Miss Salomon?"

He got up to pour me the glass himself from a ceramic jug on the filing cabinet in the corner.

"There you go. Take your time. When you're ready, please continue and tell me everything."

What did he know? What did he intuit? And if he already had an inkling, wouldn't it be best to come clean with the ugly details, which would surely arouse his sympathy and make him more willing to contact Duncan on my behalf? B.I. Morton had blue eyes. Not quite the same as Duncan's. Not that fiery, laughing, heart-breaking shade of blue. The eyes behind Morton's glasses were paler, quieter, the subdued blue of a winter sky. He looked calm, authoritative, encouraging, and patient. But as I hesitated I discerned a change, a slight hardening of his jaw, an intensity of focus that I recognized. Hunger for Information. I'd seen that expression before—on Duncan, on some of his mates. Had he really guessed I had more to tell or was he just using one of his police investigator tricks to fish out of me whatever he could. A serpent hissing started up in my ears, warning that once I began, there would be no turning back, and I'd have to bear the consequences. That subdued, almost-healed tender spot at my tailbone came alive and began to ache.

"No, there's nothing else. Really, nothing. Please, sir, I was hoping you could tell me about Sergeant Rees' whereabouts. That's the only reason I came to see you."

His disappointment was palpable. But he didn't go all hard and cold on me. At least that.

"I can tell you that Sergeant Rees has indeed shipped out. He asked for and received a transfer to another location, which I'm not at liberty to divulge because that would be trespassing on his privacy."

"But why would he go? He loved it here. The work, I mean. He used to say, 'There's no promotion after Palestine.' Is he hurt?"

B.I. Morton hesitated, just for a split second. He was not the type to hesitate for long.

"He's quite safe and sound, I can assure you of that. His circumstances have . . . ah . . . changed."

He cleared his throat—a quiet, embarrassed "harrumph"—before continuing in a firm voice.

"I can't tell you more because, as I said, it's a matter of privacy. You could write him, care of his station and I'm sure your letter would reach him."

The stupid question tumbled out before I could stop myself.

"How could he leave the country without letting me know?"

The inspector's half smile was apologetic, as if he himself had had something to do with the betrayal that now slapped me in the face. But he'd already lifted the receiver of the telephone on his desk to call for someone to escort me out of the building.

"These things happen, Miss," he said in a genuinely sorry tone.

That was that.

THE BLAZE OF noon-day sunshine assaulted my eyes when I stepped out of the vault-like darkness of C.I.D. headquarters. The glare pursued me as I left the security zone, wandered aimlessly up Jaffa Road and found myself face-to-face with a billboard full of notices in front of the Egged bus station. All these innocent posters about films and concerts and the black-bordered funeral announcements mocked me as I stood frozen, unable to read a word, drowning in meaningless messages about a life beyond my grasp. And I fell into Shimshon's ambush. Before I could escape, his serpent voice was in my head.

We drove him out of the country, that brave boyfriend of yours. He left for safer harbours, while you took the blows that should have come to him. With him gone, you're even more of a nobody than you were before.

"Leave me alone!" I cried out aloud. A woman passing by shot me an odd look over her shoulder and moved closer to the curb to give me a wide berth.

When I tried to light a cigarette, the matches, one after another snapped between my shaking fingers. Even if I could have forced my feet to take me back towards the security zone and the chain of pass inspections, back to my desk at the GPO, I knew my hands would be useless today and my mind a swamp. So

I trotted off up Jaffa Road in the opposite direction. Without asking to use a phone at one of the shops and calling the office with an explanation. I simply went AWOL. Irresponsible and cowardly, it went against plain courtesy and the public servant code of conduct, but I couldn't do otherwise. I just could not. Past the bus station, past the Tnuva Dairy offices, I hurried. Past the usual crowds of peddlers, schoolchildren, and housewives with their string grocery bags and swollen feet, making their way from Mekor Baruch to the Machane Yehuda Market.

I arrived at the edge of the civilized world, at the place where the built-up town abruptly ended and the rocks and craggy hills held sway. Green grass and wildflowers coated the slopes, but to my eyes the vista seemed hopeless, desolate. The brave growth of spring would soon be devoured by beasts or blasted by the summer sun. The limestone rocks lay scattered over the hillsides like bleached skulls. On a rise in the distance, the Arab village of Deir Yassin jutted out of the earth, forlorn and silent, ancient and unchanging and as helpless as the land itself. Or was it only me who was helpless? I sank down onto a rock, bent my woozy head to my knees and saw Shimshon in his black shirt, black trousers, peaked cap, and a shoulder patch bearing the Stern Gang's two-fingered salute.

We are the inheritors of this sacred soil. Every stone that you scorn, every scrawny bush, is ours to adore. We will conquer again with our blood and fire.

I covered my ears but his fiery declarations only blazed louder, more insistent, drilled into my head. Then I heard a sharp whistle, almost like a scream, and jerked upwards. A herd of black-haired goats approached. They had strange, wizened, old-men faces. They bobbed and bleated as they tripped along and were followed by a young Arab goatherd, brandishing a stick. He wore a striped tunic, like a nightshirt, tied around his waist by a cord, a checkered headdress and sandals, and his skin was dark as coffee. Would the Biblical Joseph have looked any different? At another time—perhaps even just a year earlier—I might have thought the picture charming, but now I was simply afraid. Maybe he had a knife hidden in the folds of his tunic. Maybe he was one of the Mufti's men. Maybe there were concealed explosives nestled in the thick coats of his animals. Once upon a time, I'd walked through the Arab market of Jaffa all alone, convinced that fear was a choice and that if I chose not to fear, I'd be untouchable. That blithely confident young woman had vanished. Though seeing me in his path, the goatherd didn't change course even a hair's breadth but urged his flock forward faster, so it seemed. Before I could move out of the way I was in the midst of a sea of snorting beasts. Only in the last minute did each of those horned heads swerve to avoid me and the sharp hooves skip past. The young goatherd turned his head to stare—a brief, scalding challenge delivered through coal-black eyes. And then he passed too. The danger was behind me, but still I shook.

And so you should, Shimshon gloated. *Could have been one of the Mufti's men. Or could have been one of mine. We wear a thousand disguises.*

Jerusalem, May 5, 1947

Dear Duncan,

Where could you possibly be? Back in Slough visiting your mother's grave? Or in a new job with the Metropolitan Police in London? Malaya? Tanganyika? Ceylon? Perhaps some place of lush jungles, vibrant colours, smells more pungent and locals more wild and primitive than the Palestinian natives. Some new untamed territory to stoke your adventurer's heart. A man like you can go anywhere he wants. The whole of the British Empire is his oyster. Wherever you end up, you'll have mates that speak your language, drink Haig's Scotch, belt out a familiar, nostalgic song about Old Blighty around a campfire. You'll never have to choose between "here and there." For you there's never really a question of where is home.

In Palestine, in case you're wondering, things have gone from bad to worse. They hung Dov Gruener, one of the Irgun men from last year's attack on the police station of Ramat Gan. You might remember that the execution was postponed after the Irgun kidnapped Judge Windham and Major Collins. Well, the authorities finally did the deed—without warning and in the dead of night, to avoid the usual pleas for mercy and crowds of protesters to whom he's a martyr and a hero. At work we had a pep talk from Mr. Watson, who exhorted us to be extra vigilant, but also to stand together in defiance of the outlaws who want to sow suspicion and hatred among us. "We stand as one," he said, "Christian, Muslim and Jew." His face blazed with earnestness and sweat dripped down his heavy, smoothly shaven cheeks. I felt quite sorry for him in a detached sort of way. In the end, we all sang "God Save the King." It sounded mournful and distorted to my ears, like a record on the wrong speed. But these days everything sounds that way to me.

I'm hanging onto my job by my fingernails. I'm distracted. I make mistakes. I'm late. Precisely now, in these trying times, the public service needs personnel who are 100 percent reliable. I must count on Mr. Watson's patience and good will. And his dislike of confrontation.

I wish I could picture your face, Duncan. I still have the photo you sent me years ago of you standing in front of the rural police station at Kfar Yusef, but it doesn't really help. All that's clear in the photo is your uniform and the black cap with the white metal badge. A brilliant design, that badge. Two entwined capital Ps for "Palestine Police." Two ornate letter Ps joined together in a conjugal embrace. On top of the letters, the image of the crown, bestowing its blessings. Palestine and its police inseparable. Married to the Force.

There's another man in my life now, Duncan. His name is Shimshon. His face has replaced yours in my thoughts and dreams though I can't say his presence is a comfort. Quite the opposite. He wears a dark uniform too, and a cloth cap with a visor. The symbol on his sleeve of two fingers held upright in salute is less elegant than yours, but there's similarity in the fused-together look, the suggestion of undying comradeship. His smile is black, his eyes are white and penetrating, like a photo negative. He follows me everywhere, his footfall just one step behind mine, and his voice is incessant, sometimes an indistinct murmur in my ear, sometimes a spew of words—always distracting, unnerving. He wants me to believe in his cause, and, if nothing else, he's done a good job of searing its tenets into my mind. I can quote whole paragraphs from the underground posters that creep back onto the walls as quickly as the soldiers of the British army tear them down. The leaders of the Yishuv call Shimshon and his brethren nothing more than "a few desperate men." The British call them pure evil. I find myself wondering about Evil, its fascinating mysteries, its compelling force. And how one man's wickedness is another's shining virtue. As a child I pictured the Evil One as a hideous apparition with a monkey face and a goat's beard, leering and salivating and sticking out a black tongue. But Shimshon, when he stands still for a moment, has a terrible beauty that takes my breath away. Like a great gold statue with lightning bolts shooting out of its nostrils and flames from its horns. He fears nothing. His beliefs are razors that could cut yours into shreds.

You see? He has me in his grip. I've been trying to write to you, Duncan, but Shimshon has insinuated himself onto this sheet of paper.

B. I. Morton said my letter would find you wherever you might be, but I don't believe it. Shimshon is cleverer and more determined than the Imperial Postal Service and will find a way to intercept an envelope with your name upon it. He will black out my thoughts with a thick lead censoring pencil. He will replace them with his own.

There are times when I want to run to the Jewish Agency offices and call out to Ben Gurion, to Mrs. Golda Myerson, to anyone in the corridors: "Help me. Do something about Shimshon. He's your enemy too, for he mocks you almost as much as he mocks the British and undermines your painstaking diplomacy to wrench sympathy for a Jewish state from the nations of the world. Surely Mrs. Myerson, a woman like you, with your masculine jaw and maternal eyes, your tightly rolled hair, bluntly clipped nails, plain dress and no-nonsense shoes—all these things that speak of dedication and competence—surely you won't stand by as Shimshon rides roughshod over my soul." But there's no point in such fantasies, for when I imagine her answers, they always fall short. She puts her hand on my shoulder and bids me to be patient. The Jewish state is coming, she says. Unity of the Jewish people is just around the corner and reckless men like Shimshon will have to submit to the will of the legitimate leadership. And in due course, when all the grand matters of state-building have been settled, we can think about what to do about those unpleasant things they did back then. But in the meantime, I must excuse the Secretary of the Jewish Agency. She has a speech to deliver to the national council which is of the utmost urgency.

Will you receive this cry from my heart, Duncan? Or will some C.I.D. officer, after steaming open the envelope, decide that you shouldn't be bothered by the ravings of a madwoman? Can I even bring myself to mail this letter? Could I bear to see it disappear past the cold metal lips of the box in the wall?

Chapter 34
Eviction

A GRIM-FACED MRS. Rajinsky was waiting for me in the corridor when I opened the front door.

Her deep-set eyes glittered with a feverish look of victimhood that made me think she was about to accuse me of being in arrears. I was tired from work and from the long tramp home through hot streets via the roundabout route I took to avoid Mamilla Road. There was that certain billboard I couldn't bear to see. Or better put, I couldn't bear to have the billboard look at me. Despite my fatigue, my landlady's face roused me to battle. Though I always paid the rent on time, every so often, feigning innocence or indignation, she'd insinuate I owed her for hot water or heating fuel. I'd learned to keep meticulous record of all my extras in a notebook. Over the years, I'd come to the conclusion her little sideways attacks were at least partly motivated by disapproval of Duncan. Since his disappearance, Mrs. Rajinsky had left me in peace. But now once again she hovered like a vulture poised to swoop.

"Here you are at last, Miss Salomon. Come into the kitchen. We need to speak."

"I'm up to date with the rent and everything else, to the last mil."

"Won't do you any good," she brayed. She stomped into the kitchen, where I followed, my teeth clenched. She grabbed a sheet of paper from the counter and, wheeling around, shoved it close to my face.

"What's that?"

"An eviction notice."

"What?"

"Yes! You're out on your ear and so is poor Mr. Maisel who never did any harm to anyone and so am . . ."

Mrs. Rajinsky sucked in a long sobbing breath before she continued. "So am I. Along with every last soul in the building. I've lived in this flat for thirteen years. Owned it for almost ten. Scrimped and saved. My only security . . . for my old age. Thieves! Cossacks! Haven't I been driven from pillar to post enough in my life? *Nu?* Haven't I?"

Her upraised palms beseeched the heavens. Her deeply seamed face contorted in woe. She was unhinged, but she had good cause, which I understood after I'd pried the notice out of her fist and read it for myself. By order of the General Officer Commanding, Security Zone B, which encompassed the King David Hotel and the YMCA, along with other important properties, was to be greatly enlarged and therefore many houses in the area were requisitioned. A thick black line delineating the new zone showed that our building was now on the wrong side of the border. We had forty-eight hours to pack up and leave. Mrs. Rajinsky continued to rage and wail, her bitterness directed at those remote, uncompromising powers—the General Officer Commanding and His Excellency the High Commissioner. I felt sorry for her. I even felt a twinge of guilt for having jumped to unflattering conclusions when I'd walked in the door. Then I began to realize my own predicament and had no pity left over for my landlady. I went into my room, closed the door, sank onto the edge of my bed, and gazed about.

I'd lived in this room for seven years, but it seemed much longer. This little space was the first that I could call my own. Since Duncan and I had parted ways, I'd often felt trapped or lonely between these four walls, nevertheless they'd been my sanctuary. What would I do without them to hold me together? The furnishings were simple, unremarkable, but, familiar and comforting. The table under the window with the vase made of azure-hued Hebron glass. The blue and white striped cotton bedspread that I'd bought in the Old City market. The four-shelf pine bookcase which held my German classics and the English novels, some of which I'd read and others that I meant to get to when I had the time and tranquility for reading again. In crates on the top shelf were the gramophone records that I still, deep down, considered "ours." My eyes fell on the pine wardrobe, which also came to me through Duncan, for it had belonged to a police officer who was moving to a Tegart fortress in the north. After I bought it, Duncan and a mate of his staggered up the stairs with the wardrobe braced between them, manoeuvring the wooden beast around corners, sweat pouring down their faces, tossing cheerful insults at one another as they inched forward. Mrs. Rajinsky had stood in the hall with arms crossed over her chest. If they dare scrape her precious walls. I'd had little to put into the wardrobe at first, but over time I stuffed its recesses with clothes, shoes, winter and summer blankets. And then Duncan's shaving kit and singlets. Now, my handbags and straw hats spread across the top shelf where Duncan's things had once been. I'd had the sense to finally fill the gap he'd left behind in my wardrobe. I'd had that much sense at least. Each object in my room belonged exactly where it was. Each was a storehouse of memories. But this was no time to indulge in nostalgia. I had forty-eight hours to find a new haven for myself and my belongings.

Despite the leaden heaviness in my limbs—a sick despair over the task ahead—I forced myself up and out, to Yossi's grocery shop down the street. Though it was after seven p.m., the lights were lit and the shutters raised. If anyone knew of vacant rooms it would be Yossi. I found the narrow store crowded with packing cases and the grocer's fourteen-year-old son behind the counter. The boy's eyes shone with excitement over the changes afoot. He bounced on his heels as he cursed the British. His father had also been served with an eviction notice and was scouring the town this very moment for new premises. I made inquiries at several cafés—all fruitless—and ended the evening at Liesel and Manfred's, the three of us in conference around their rickety dining room table.

"If you don't find anything in time, you'll stay here," Liesel said, gesturing towards the sofa. "There's room on the roof to store all your things, except for the wardrobe. That you'll have to leave behind. Who'd want to schlep it up all those stairs anyway? You'll stay as long as you need. Don't rush into anything. And if it makes you feel better, you can pay us a little rent. We could use the extra, couldn't we Manfred?"

My brother-in-law gave a half-smile that was hard to read. Before he could open his mouth to venture an opinion, Liesel quickly continued.

"Actually, there's lots of space when you count the roof outside. We even sleep out there sometimes on hot summer nights. Other families manage in closer quarters. Others have far less than we do. Where else can you go? To Papa in Tel Aviv?"

"Are you mad?"

"Well then?"

"Let's make a list of the steps you can take," Manfred said. He already had a pencil and scrap of paper at the ready. "Make the rounds of the corner shops and cafés as you've started to do. But also check the billboards. And put your own notice up. I'll ask Dr. Eisenberg if we could give his phone number as a contact."

"She doesn't want to have anything to do with that snake," Liesel spat. "Look! The very suggestion upsets her."

"All right then. The pharmacist on Ben Yehuda Street. We'll ask him. The essential thing is for Eva to put up notices on as many billboards as she can. We'll write up a batch tonight in Hebrew, English and German and first thing in the morning she should go around . . . What's the matter?"

The very word "billboard" brought a wave of nausea to my throat. I shut my eyes, clamped my hands over my ears. I shook my head and mumbled, "I can't, I can't, I can't."

When I opened my eyes, they were both staring at me in alarm. Liesel reached across the table, grabbed my hands and held them tight.

"It's all right, Mouse. There's no rush. You can take your time. You'll be with us in the meantime. With your family."

"There's got to be a room somewhere," said Manfred. "You just have to make a methodical search."

Liesel dropped my hands and wheeled around to face him.

"Hundreds have been made homeless by these evictions. And that's on top of the ones still scrambling for a corner to rest their heads after the British tricks of last month. People are living in shacks, in unfinished cellars. Like rats. I wish the terrorists would blow up Government House and let His Excellency see what it's like to lose your home."

"You don't mean that," Manfred interjected.

"How do you know what I mean?"

I heard a scuffle under the table as she gave him a kick and I saw them exchange a look, or maybe it was a series of looks in which she berated him for his lack of understanding and he answered with baffled self-defence, whereupon she warned him he was on thin ice and he finally acquiesced. But not without a sigh of resignation. He didn't have to put it into words. I knew my very sensible brother-in-law thought it best for all three of us if I found a place of my own and that the sofa in the rooftop flat should be a last resort. And of course he was right.

Trudging back up King George V Street, I remembered my father's horror all those years ago at the thought of being a burden by moving us into his brother's flat. At the time it seemed a petty concern considering everything else that was going on. Now, I felt a belated twinge of sympathy.

THE NEXT MORNING I went to Yossi's to use the phone. I dialed the Finance Division and told the girl on the exchange I wanted to speak to Mr. Watson. Then, wedged into the narrow space between the wall and the counter, the phone receiver pressed to my ear, I listened to the mournful "brrr, brrr, brrr" at the other end, while beside me Yossi and a customer loudly exchanged opinions about Jerusalem's exorbitant rents. The phone was ringing at my desk. I wasn't there to pick it up. When Mr. Watson finally came on, he sounded harried. I began with profuse apologies, but Mr. Watson interrupted me to answer a question of someone who'd come into his office.

"All right, Miss Salomon. Continue. What are you so sorry about?"

I explained my plight. If I wanted to find somewhere to live before the army deadline, I had to begin the search this very moment. Would he mind very much if I only came in this afternoon? There was a long, excruciating silence at the other end of the line when I was done. Mr. Watson coughed.

"I know I've missed a lot this month," I rushed to say. "But this is an emergency."

"Miss Salomon, there have been many emergencies these past weeks and other staff have managed. I'm afraid . . . I think it best . . ."

"All right, I'll be in shortly. But perhaps then I could leave an hour or so early today? After I've done all my work, of course."

"No, that won't be necessary. Your coming in, I mean."

His voice was apologetic but depressingly firm. He'd made up his mind.

"You haven't been yourself lately, Miss Salomon. I think it best you take an extended leave. I'll make sure you are paid for the days you already put in this week, but we'll have to take you off the payroll until you can return, full strength. Take care of your business, all your business, whatever it is. And do get back in touch, say, in a month? No, make that two months."

His voice had risen in strength and cheeriness as he reached this satisfactory conclusion. He'd finally found the right moment and excuse to be rid of me. If I were standing before him with a forlorn expression he would have found it that much harder. The telephone offered a convenient shield. I tried to think of an argument for why he should let me stay, but couldn't, and so just apologized again for my erratic behaviour of late. He interrupted with polite reassurances. He was in a hurry to hang up.

Returned to my room, I stood by the window in a daze and looked about me again at all the things that needed a new home within . . . I made a quick calculation . . . within thirty-two hours, now. The bright morning light spilled across the table and danced over the blue surface of the Hebron vase, pouring a liquid reflection onto the floor. There was something not right about the room. I kept turning my head this way and that, trying to figure it out, wasting precious minutes. At last the simple truth struck me. I wasn't used to being here mid-morning on a weekday. I had that vague, out-of-place, guilty feeling, like a child who'd skipped school. Despite the absurdity, I couldn't rid myself of this feeling. I began to pace.

On the table were the "Want ad" notices in Hebrew, English, and German that Manfred had insisted on writing up for me the evening before. He'd cut sheets of lined paper out of a notebook and meticulously printed the words, "Woman of good family and with secure job urgently seeks room with amenities. References available. Please leave word at the desk of the Eden Hotel on Hillel Street." Manfred had provided a matchbox filled with thumbtacks as well. What could be so difficult about running around to the billboards in the vicinity? There was one by the high school, one at the bus station, and in Zion Square and, of course, the one on Mamilla Road. I could do them all in an hour at the same time that I made inquiries at blocks of flats along the way. That's what Manfred must have been thinking when he wrote out the notices in his neat, precise hand, while I puffed on a cigarette by the rooftop parapet, trying to still the quaking of my limbs. Now as I paced from the window to the door and back, I heard my tormentor cry out with savage glee.

Send away the she-ass who defiled the people's camp! Drive her into the wilderness. She is an abomination and must wander among the thorns.

I sank to my knees onto the hard, tiled floor, fists pressed to my cheeks, while my heart thumped without mercy.

Where are your British heroes, your false gods? Weep and gnash your teeth, Dwarfling!

I remained in that position of abject paralysis for many long minutes. If the earth had swallowed me up, obviating the need for decisive action, I would have wept in gratitude. But no such thing happened. So by and by, I unbent my stiff knees, stood up, looked about and realized what I had to do.

I ripped Manfred's notices into little pieces, flung them into the wastebasket. The "woman of good family" no longer had a secure job anyway. Yes, it had become clear to me what I had to do and clarity gave me strength. Calmly, efficiently, without delay, but free of nervous haste, I set my plan in motion.

Chapter 35
The Plan

IN A LANE off Chancellor Street, I found a man who dealt in used furniture, and he came back to the flat with a donkey cart and a brawny Kurdish porter. We haggled a bit, but soon agreed on a price for the wardrobe. After I hastily flung armfuls of clothing onto the bed, the dealer hoisted the empty wardrobe onto the porter's back, securing the bulky thing with straps around the man's forehead and waist. The Kurd seemed amazingly unfazed though he was doubled over and dwarfed by the load. Guided by the dealer, the porter proceeded out the door of my room into the corridor like a slow-moving tortoise.

"Don't worry about the walls," I said. "They belong to the British now."

The men had a good chuckle about this, but moved cautiously anyway for fear of damaging the dealer's new possession.

Without the wardrobe, the room now looked unbalanced. There was a large pale rectangle on the wall where the thing had stood and the whitewash had darkened around its outline, forming a kind of wardrobe ghost. But that was the only piece of furniture I had to deal with; the rest belonged to Mrs. Rajinsky. Filling several string bags with clothes, shoes and odds and ends, I took the bus to the Machane Yehuda Market where I found rag peddlers who relieved me of everything. By then it was mid-afternoon and I was famished. I bought a roll and some cheese and washed down this simple meal with plain soda I got at a kiosk. Though I'd been going hard since early morning, my body zinged with energy. It was amazing how vigorous I felt in comparison to the weakness of recent weeks. It was as if I'd recovered from a bad case of the grippe.

With the help of tips from several stall owners, I made my way to Mea Shearim, the Ultra Orthodox quarter. It was an older, poorer, more crowded part of town. A maze of lanes, low, ramshackle houses with sagging roofs, courtyards cluttered with lines of laundry, swarms of pale, snot-nosed children, black-coated Hasids and their overworked wives, clothed in long, faded dresses and with kerchiefs tied tightly around their shaven heads. There were stalls and tiny shops exhibiting a jumble of goods behind windows of dusty glass. A bearded cobbler with grey earlocks sat on a stool, hammering at a shoe braced between his knees. No one bothered me, but the area made me uneasy. The tired stone walls pressed close. The slick cobblestones tripped me up. I looked down and saw a cellar window covered with a rusty iron grille and a sickening dread came over me. *Could it have been here?* For a moment my knees swayed, but I squeezed my eyes shut and asked myself, *If so, what then? You are no longer there.*

Quite lost in the labyrinth of alleys, I asked a housewife who was peeling potatoes if she knew a shop owner called Brodsky. She looked me over through narrowed, suspicious eyes. "I'm a customer," I said in bastardized Yiddish. Her expression remained wary and somewhat appalled, as if I were an unclean presence in the sanctuary of her neighbourhood, nevertheless she wiped her hands on her apron and brought me around a few corners to a wooden shed crammed with all kinds of orphaned machine parts and whole items as well: radios, cash registers, electric fans, and more. Brodsky could have stepped out of a Shalom Aleichem story. He was a burly man in a long grey smock smudged with machine oil. He had a forked, rust-coloured beard, flaming red cheeks, and sausage-finger hands. When I told him my mission, he rolled his eyes upwards as if asking for heaven's advice, and, satisfied with the answer, nodded his big head in agreement. He was definitely interested. We made arrangements for the next morning.

As a test of my new state of mind, I went out of my way to walk in front of walls and hoardings that were plastered with notices. And it pleased me to see these were merely flat, innocuous surfaces crowded with words I could read or choose to ignore. They had no life or power on their own. I summoned Shimshon for his commentary; I actually invited him to speak, which he did with his usual fervour.

Never again, the passive Jew, the eternal victim to be mocked and crushed underfoot. Never again, the bent head, the averted eyes, the furtive scurrying along the fringes of other people's realms. I act, therefore I am. I take fate into my hands, raise a pistol, create history. Fear is just a vapour of the mind to be banished. A life hoarded like guilty treasure is no life at all. Only life that is used, spilled, spent, is truly human and vital.

Despite the exalted rhetoric, I relished his words, hugged them to my chest, warmed myself on the energy of Shimshon's assertions and agreed that, at last, we were of one mind.

AT HOME—WHICH was no longer home, but rather a way station of denuded walls and scattered bundles—I lit a candle and opened the cover of my gramophone for the first time in weeks. The familiar needle arm and the felt-clad turntable made me sad, but not overly so. Strolling my fingers over the record collection on the bookcase, I chose one at random—Bronislaw Hubermann playing violin sonatas by Brahms. Curious to see what would happen, I turned up the volume and lay down on the bed. The last time I'd tried to listen to a record, I had to yank up the needle arm after just a few minutes because it had all become disjointed noise. I couldn't enjoy, couldn't concentrate. Now melody flooded the room, filled my heart and I was grateful, so grateful, drinking in every note like a parched wanderer at a desert oasis. After the Brahms, I put on a selection of choral pieces including "O Welche Lust" from Beethoven's *Fidelio* and, though I haven't got much of a voice—not like Liesel—I couldn't help but sing along.

> *O welche Lust in freier Luft*
> *Den Atem einzuheben . . .Oh what joy, to breathe again*
> *In freedom's air . . .*

All evening long and through much of the night, I feasted on an orgy of music: orchestral works, opera highlights, sonatas, suites, nocturnes. Such richness, variety, and colour—a whole universe exploding out of the spinning grooves. Both lovely and painful memories rushed in with the music, and I let them come, for soon enough they would be purged. On the other side of the walls, Mrs. Rajinsky and Mr. Maisel were busy with packing and organizing their little existences. I drifted in and out of sleep, woke to the soft hiccuping of the needle at the end of the disc, cranked up the machine, and put on another. It was just like old times.

In the morning, Brodsky came at the appointed hour, along with his wife—a small, shrewd-eyed woman—since an Orthodox Jew must never be alone in an enclosed space with an unrelated female for fear of the evil impulse. He examined the gramophone, liked what he saw, offered a price. I countered with one much higher. The three of us argued and haggled, a business I never had much stomach for in the past but now quite enjoyed. I made a drama of how hard it was to part with my treasured possession. I talked about my love of music, showed Brodsky my records, and I even shed tears. My performance (and it wasn't entirely a performance) was convincing. Brodsky's eyes grew moist as he studied my record collection. He nodded when I pointed out my special favourites. Turned out he had a weakness for worldly music, couldn't help but hunger for more than just the sanctified tunes of Jewish prayer. Mrs. Brodsky scolded her husband— an outpouring of Yiddish invective, but it did no good. He raised his offer considerably. I countered again, this time throwing my entire collection into the bargain—plus my books—for the fantastic sum of 96 Palestine pounds. Brodsky tore his beard, chewed the edges of his earlocks. His wife screamed. I bawled openly at the thought of what I was losing, told them I'd changed my mind, the sale was off. It was a scene worthy of an opera buffa. At last Brodsky and wife departed, the handcart they'd left at the bottom of the stairs now filled with my gramophone, records, and books, while I was newly rich with a hefty wad of Palestine pound notes.

There wasn't much left to dispose of. I trundled various other bits and pieces to second-hand shops until I'd pretty much cleaned out the room. A small valise, packed with a few necessities and mementos, remained on the floor beside the stripped-bare bed. During the afternoon siesta hour, when the town lay drenched in heat, I walked over to Hillel Street, tiptoed up the stairs, and slid a thick envelope under the door that led to the rooftop flat. I'd debated with myself a long time over what explanation to give, along with the money. In the end, it seemed best to make it brief.

> *Dear Liesel,*
> *I managed to sell a few things I don't need any more and make a tidy sum. This is for you, Manfred and most of all, for little Ari. I still have plenty left over, so you needn't worry.*
> *I love you all,*
> *Your Eva*

Was I fully aware of what I was doing? I'd gone through all the options calmly and rationally and chosen the one that made the most sense. I focused on the immediate—the practical steps of putting my plan into action. But was it me who was driving my actions, or Shimshon? When I'd crept back down the long flights of stairs, I picked up my valise from where I'd left it in the corner of the lobby. Relieved to have done all this unnoticed by anyone, I headed off to the bus station on Jaffa Road.

Just in time for the afternoon bus to Tel Aviv, I bought my ticket and fought my way through the back door with the other last-minute passengers. The bench at the rear offered a small space that a Dwarfling like me could squeeze into once the other occupants made room. No sooner had I settled, than, with a groan of gears and a belch of exhaust, the bus lurched out of the Egged station, rumbled up the road towards Givat Sha'ul, reached the crest at the outskirts of town and began its winding descent through a region of mountain slopes and narrow gorges. Despite the air rushing in through the open windows, the bus steamed with the heat of tightly packed bodies. Some passengers stood in the aisles clinging to the short loops of leather that dangled from the ceiling, laughing as they bumped together, chattering and shouting greetings and questions to acquaintances. Jewish Jerusalem was more a big village than a city. Two lively girls—kibbutzniks on their way back to their settlement in the Emek—sat to the left of me.

"You don't look so well," one of them said, peering at my face. "Are you going to throw up?"

"Just tired," I said.

They rearranged themselves to give me the window spot, for which I was grateful and said so. Before they could pepper me with the usual questions—where did I come from, who did I know that they might know—I shut my eyes and pretended to sleep. Through the veil of my quivering lashes, I watched the scenery rush by. Down, down, down, we jounced, through the rough, sun-scorched ravines, past Arab houses that seemed carved out of the hillsides, past a lone clump of pines that marked a Jewish colony. Leaving Jerusalem is a descent, not just physical but also spiritual according to Jewish tradition and the Hebrew language. But for me it seemed quite the opposite. My spirits rose as we arrived at the flat, cultivated plains, where the air was soft with humidity and warm as thick wool. The girls started up a pioneering song which other passengers took up. The noise around me flattened into a dull clamour, my eyelids shut for real. I surrendered to a muscular oblivion.

When I jerked awake I found that my head had fallen heavily onto the shoulder of the girl next to me. I apologized profusely, but she only laughed.

"You're a *Yecke*, aren't you?"

All too soon we arrived in bustling, clattering Tel Aviv. At the station kiosk, I bought sodas and cakes for the two kibbutzniks and myself. I was running through my gramophone money fast, but it didn't matter. Before our parting, the girls gave me their address at Kibbutz Gesher and said I must visit someday. Then arm in arm, they wandered off to explore the city, for they had a couple of hours to kill before the next bus.

THE CITY HAD mushroomed since I'd visited last. New buildings, new shops, and cafés, more traffic than ever. Whole neighbourhoods had sprung up in my absence. But I wasn't interested in any of that. Valise in hand, I strode through the clanging, dusty streets, taking the shortest route to the sea. The strip of blue beckoned, just beyond a shanty town of rough shacks, home of hard-luck squatters and refugees from the devastation of Europe, people who'd been smuggled into the country in the growing fleet of "sardine can" boats. Ignoring the scampering half-naked children, cooking fires, and barking dogs, I made my way between the huts. And there it was, unchanged and splendid, the wide, gently heaving Mediterranean, aglow under the late afternoon sun. I took off my shoes to squiggle my toes in the soft, burning sand. Not far from the shanty town, the bathing beach began and I headed in that direction, walking north, away from the jumble of packing case walls and tin roofs.

Though it was still fiercely hot at this time of day, people were about, sprawled in deck chairs, strolling with parasols held aloft, splashing around in the shallow waves. I went past the lifeguard tower and the soda kiosk. Past the wild-haired, hard-faced woman—a shanty town resident I presumed—who was poking a stick around in the beach litter and who cast a covetous glance at my small valise. I continued until I was alone with the blazing sea and the stretches of undulating sand. Here I opened my valise, spread out the blanket I'd brought, and assembled my feast: a tin of the best Cadbury's biscuits, a pomegranate, an orange, a packet of Camel cigarettes. From a velvet drawstring bag, I pulled out my recorder and blew a few exploratory notes before laying it down on the blanket. I also had with me a bottle of Haig's I had kept at the bottom of my wardrobe just in case Duncan might someday return for a visit. Also a shaving mug he'd forgotten to take away. Though I wasn't really tempted by the treats, I nibbled away in a mood of defiant celebration, determined to enjoy myself. I poured the shaving mug half full of whisky, chugged down a couple of mouthfuls.

"*Pfui,*" I said aloud to the gulls that had alighted nearby and were watching my every move.

The whisky made the sweat pour down my face and the sun on my head a merciless fire. I regretted not having brought a hat. Why hadn't I started my picnic an hour later? I'd planned to be here for sunset, when the flaming ball in the sky extinguished itself in a last hurrah of crimson streaks and the evening breezes began to stir. I'd arrived at my destination just a bit too early. I drank another gulp from the mug. Immediately, my throat tightened, my stomach lurched, and I heaved a mess of chewed biscuit and pomegranate between my knees. Shimshon arose to berate me. For the past twenty-four hours he'd been merely a quiet shadow at the back of my mind, an almost soothing presence, but now he returned in his most hectoring, mocking, bullying form.

Can't even do a such simple thing right, can you? What a pathetic Dwarfling!

I had to go somewhere he couldn't reach me. I jumped to my feet. Stumbled through the sand to the water's edge. Then farther, up to my ankles, up to my knees, the bottom on my dress swirling around my legs, the ebb and flow sucking at my heels. I paused to look around. Far to the south, the bell tower of St. Peter's Church reared high above Jaffa town, a tiny black finger in the heat haze. Ages ago I used to look out at that tower and imagine Duncan patrolling the lanes of the Arab town and I would long to run, run, all the length of the coast to where he was. Once, so long ago, Duncan and I lay naked in each other's arms in the dunes. Not far from here he taught me to swim. He'd made a plank of his outstretched hands, holding me up until my stiff body finally relaxed enough to float on its own. The sudden memories of our happiness pierced my heart like splinters of glass.

I drifted deeper into the cold, embracing water. The waves heaved, sucked, pulled, seduced. And, with a sudden powerful thrust, knocked my feet from under me. *Let go, let go. Give it up.* Was that me speaking to myself or was it Shimshon? *What does it matter? Give it up.* A wall of water crashed down on my head. I was caught, grasped, flung, squeezed, a puny piece of flotsam, while the sea roared its angry song into my ears. Lungs bursting, I clawed my way upwards towards the glimmering surface. My animal self scrabbled and flailed, but it wasn't just my body that struggled. Heart and soul, my entire being fought to be free of the water's crushing weight and when I burst through the surface, my whole being opened its lips to the sky. One desperate gulp of air before the next wave smacked me in the jaw. I tumbled backwards beneath a rain of pebbles. The tip of one toe touched sliding sand. Then the sea heaved once more to fling me shorewards. I crawled past the sucking current to grab onto terra firma.

Still on my knees, gasping and sputtering, I blinked open my salt-water seared eyes. A woman was down on her haunches in front of me thrusting a stick towards my hands. When she realized I didn't need it, she hooked an elbow under mine and helped me stagger to my feet. It was the wild-haired beach scavenger I'd glimpsed earlier. Her haggard face, the grim set of her mouth, gave the impression of a person who'd been chewed up and spat out by the world many times over. She scowled down at me as I coughed my lungs clear and wiped the grit from my palms.

"What kind of an idiot goes bathing on her own at this hour?"

Her Hebrew was heavily accented. Familiar. Hungarian.

"Someone suicidal I suppose," I said, attempting a smile.

"Pah! I've seen plenty of suicides. Dying is the easiest thing in the world if you really want to. You should have had stones in your pocket."

I took another look at her. She saw my glance stray to the tattoo on her arm. Quickly, she pulled down the rolled-up sleeve of her dress.

"Is that your stuff over there?"

She pointed her stick to my blanket in the sand and my open valise. The gulls were jostling one another as they fought over the remains of my picnic. I nodded and she strode forward with sudden fury waving her stick in the air. The gulls scattered amid angry screeching.

"What a waste!" she scolded as she bent to see what was left in the biscuit tin. The orange was intact. I offered her that, along with the rest of the Haig's and half the cigarettes, all of which she shoved into a cloth bag that hung from a piece of cord tied around her waist in lieu of a belt. She remained standing there, expectant, as I shook out my blanket.

"I saved your life, you know," she said in an accusing tone.

"You did no such thing. I was already on the shore. What chutzpah."

"Well, I would have. I hate the water, but I was ready to pull you out."

Her hard, needy, stubborn eyes bore down on me. After a moment's hesitation, I bent down and dug some money out of the handbag that lay in the valise, steeling myself for a struggle, for I expected her to try to grab all of it away. Instead, after a quick examination of the bills, she tucked them into her brassiere and nodded her thanks.

"I consider this a loan. You'll get it back. Every mil. With interest. I used to be a kindergarten teacher in Budapest. I don't have the heart to be with children anymore. With children you have to smile and laugh, and my face has forgotten how to do that. But I'll do something. I'll be someone again. Soon. By the way, I could have had a bed at the centre for immigrants. It's my choice to sleep rough for the moment. I can't stand any kind of institution, being a number in a crowd or the silly rules. This—" she pointed at her ragged dress "— this is just for now. I'm looking for a job, even if it's just cleaning houses. Next time you see me, I'll be sitting at one of those fancy cafés in Moghrabi Square and *you'll* be bumming cigarettes off *me*."

Her tone was flat, stripped of emotion, as if she were merely stating facts rather than an ambition. Her eyes held a fierce, uncompromising light, but also a deeply guarded darkness.

"I don't doubt you will," I told her.

"Where do you live. Give me an address. I want to pay you back when I can."

I told her it wasn't necessary, but gave her Malka's address and told her go there without delay and to say I sent her. I explained that Malka was from Budapest too and had a soft spot for newcomers down on their luck. She'd be able to help. Then I draped the blanket over my wet shoulders, packed my scattered things into my valise, picked up my shoes. Carrying my valise, the woman accompanied me to the steps leading up to Ha'yarkon Street and waited while I brushed the sand out of my shoes and put them on.

"Don't throw away the life that God gave you," she admonished, as we were about to part.

"You believe in God?"

"On a day a total stranger hands me a gift of 10 Palestine pounds, I do."

She grimaced as if in pain, but then I realized it was the best she could do with a face that had forgotten how to smile.

Chapter 36
Papa Again

DARKNESS HAD CREPT over the city when I began walking southward on Ha'yarkon Street, soaked to the skin and shivering in the evening breeze. My dress clung to my body and the blanket over my shoulders trailed behind, while my shoes, still peppered with grit inside, irritated the soles of my feet. My intention was to call on Malka, but before I got anywhere near her place, I found myself turning onto Frishman Street, where Papa now lived. In front of his building, I put down my valise and looked up into the first-floor window at a room well-lit by yellow light. The window framed the top half of a man, standing sideways and bent over slightly, his arms and shoulders moving in a weary rhythm. I heard the gush of water and the clatter of crockery. Papa in his kitchen, unaware of being watched. The fact that he had to wash his own dishes brought home to me that he was still alone. On impulse, I entered the lobby, climbed the stairs, knocked on the door. I was curious to see his reaction. After the adventures of the afternoon, I suppose I felt invulnerable. How could he hurt me any more than I'd already been hurt? Or maybe I just wanted to hear one of his tirades for old times' sake.

My father's jaw dropped at the sight of me on his threshold. He stared in shock at this bedraggled creature with sodden hair, wrapped in a brown blanket, valise in hand. I must have looked like one of those battered souls who crawled out of the holds of the "misery ships" that sneaked through the British blockade, a refugee from the lands of hunger and ash. But he knew me, of course, despite the gloom in the hall. I saw him mouth my name.

"Well? May I come in?"

Startled by the question, as if a ghost had spoken, he took a step backwards, then recovering his composure, he waved me inside. We stood in the middle of a small room and I babbled a half-baked explanation. About wading through shallow water, straying out too far, being sucked up by a rogue wave. I mentioned the nice stranger who'd come running to my rescue. I steeled myself for the inevitable questions, delivered with Papa's signature sarcasm. What did I want of him? What was I doing with my life? How could I be so clumsy as to fall into the sea? What mischief had I been up to really? But instead, Papa latched onto the detail of the stranger who'd given me a hand. We were beholden to her. We must run after her to ensure she was properly thanked, perhaps offer a small monetary reward. I assured Papa I'd done all that was necessary in this regard. He looked at me askance, as if he didn't believe me.

"I gave her ten pounds."

"Are you out of your mind? Have you become a millionaire all of a sudden? I hope you don't think I can make up the small fortune you just threw away."

Same old Papa. But he was not the same. He'd aged so: dark pouches under his eyes, white hairs on his throat, a tremor in his hands. And I'd caught the stricken look on his face when he'd first laid eyes on me, before he'd had a chance to disguise his feelings.

"I didn't bring a change of clothes. All I want is to dry my dress and then I'll be on my way. Do you have a housecoat I could wear in the meantime?"

A preposterous question. Papa looked at me dumbfounded. Why would an old widower like him, a man who lived alone in a tiny flat and pursued a life of rigid self-discipline, need a housecoat? But now, as I let the blanket drop from my shoulders, he properly registered my scandalous appearance. A glance at my damp bosom made him wince with shame on my behalf. He made a dash through a doorway and I followed him into a smaller room—the place where he slept—which had a cot and a wardrobe. Together we inspected the wardrobe's meagre contents: several suit jackets, long and short-sleeved white shirts, a few pairs of trousers. Papa rubbed his grizzled chin, flummoxed.

"Is there a neighbour we could speak to? A woman who could lend me something?"

"Out of the question!"

He threw up his hands and I understood he wouldn't dream of making the neighbours aware of my predicament. Evidence of those neighbours came through the thin walls and the ceiling: the scrape of chairs, muffled voices, and laughter. Papa had lived in this building for a couple of years, but he probably didn't know any of the people except to say good morning and good evening. He grabbed one of his shirts and thrust it at me.

"Here. Take this. Or whatever you want," he stammered. "A dry blanket perhaps? Yes, a blanket."

He pulled a folded blanket off the shelf and thrust that at me too.

"There should be some warm water left, if you want to wash up." He gestured towards the bathroom. Abruptly a new thought struck him and he glanced at his watch.

"*Ach*! I'm late. I was on my way to *shul* for Talmud study. I go Tuesdays and Thursdays at this time."

With trembling hands, he fumbled around on his desk and gathered together some notes, his reading glasses, a heavy volume.

"Gone a few hours," he mumbled as he bustled about. "If you need supper . . . there's . . . but you'll see. In the kitchen."

His voice trailed off. He patted his pockets, checking to make sure he hadn't forgotten anything.

"May I stay the night then? Is there somewhere . . . ?" I looked around at the cramped, modestly furnished flat, wondering where I could lay my head. There was no sofa in the main room, only an armchair, along with a small table, a couple of straight-backed chairs, his desk, and some bookcases.

"Perhaps there?" I pointed to the lone armchair that stood in front of the shuttered doorway to the balcony. "I can sleep anywhere," I lied.

Papa gave me another blank, stupefied look, as if I'd asked a question that was simply beyond him and, with a vague gesture that could be assent or surrender, he rushed out the door.

In the bathroom, beneath the thin stream that sputtered from the shower head, I scrubbed the saltwater and sand from my body. Washed my under things and hung them over the shower rail. Donned one of Papa's shirts, which came well below my knees, while the sleeves flapped like a scarecrow's until I rolled them up. For respectability's sake, I also put on a pair of his trousers, folded up the legs, and secured the waist with a belt pulled tight and fastened on the last hole. Then, raising the shutters to the balcony, I suspended my wet dress on a hanger over the open entrance. Immediately the hanger began to sway in the breeze. What would the neighbours think to see a woman's dress fluttering like a flag in the respectable Mr. Salomon's apartment? And what would they make of the Chaplinesque figure who was me? It was all so absurd, and I felt so unreal, as if the rough sea had tossed me into the midst of a theatrical farce, that I began to enjoy myself. With nothing else to do, I poked about the flat.

Frishman Street was a better address than the lane near the railway tracks where we'd first lived, and the building was relatively new. But this flat was smaller than the other, so Papa couldn't claim to have come up much in the world. He'd had to part with some of the furniture from our Breslau days: the oak dining room set and the matching buffet with the carved doors and brass handles. On one wall was an etching I remembered from childhood of Breslau's magnificent Gothic town hall circa 1900, with its soaring spires, the equestrian statue of Frederick the Great and the busy vendor stalls all around, along with horse-drawn cabs lined up, waiting for customers. The bookcases in the main room held double rows of books: the usual religious tomes as well as German classics, a travel guide to the Rhineland and a railway schedule for the Breslau-Berlin line from 1936.

Papa still had his handsome rolltop desk and the chair with the upholstered seat—the cloth faded now from a rich wine colour to muddy pink. On top of the desk was the pewter-framed photo of Mama. Her white dress with the high, stiff, ruffled collar and puffy sleeves belonged to an era that now seemed fantastically remote. Her mild smile hadn't changed. Her wide dark eyes still seemed full of sad premonitions. Not much else in the flat was familiar. A modest-sized table where Papa took his meals, the armchair, a brass-bound leather trunk, where he probably kept some winter things. Wooden crates stacked beside the desk—some inventory from his business, no doubt. It was all clean and tidy, Spartan and sad.

Returning to the bedroom, I noticed something I'd overlooked the first time: another framed photo. This one showed a beaming Ari seated on Manfred's shoulders, with Liesel and I posted on either side. The two of us were in our best summer frocks, while the child wore a darling pair of Tyroler style shorts with suspenders that I had bought him for his second birthday. Manfred's eyes were almost blotted out by the glare on his glasses. Behind us was a clump of cypress trees and part of the wall that spanned the St. Simeon Monastery in Katamon. I remembered that day, how the five of us had gone for a celebratory picnic. The long shadow of the man holding the camera slanted across the front of the photo. It was Duncan, but Papa wouldn't have realized that. He must have received proper professional portraits of Ari from Manfred, yet he chose to frame this clumsy shot that showed us all (minus Duncan, of course) together. It was rare for that reason. The shelf holding the photo was directly opposite the head of his bed; perhaps the first thing he would see on rising in the morning. I ran my finger along the stretched-out shadow. I searched for the outline of a face. Then I placed the framed photo back in the same spot as before.

In the kitchen I found some black bread, margarine, and cheese and a kettle for tea. I brought my plate and tea glass onto the balcony, where more crates were stored and I perched on one to devour my meal. I was parched and famished. I hadn't realized just how much until I began to drink and eat. The simple fare tasted divine. Rummaging in my valise, I found the remnants of my pack of Camels—four precious cigarettes left—and lit up.

Why hadn't Papa ever married again? I ruminated upon the question as I smoked. A Jewish religious man, even an impossible one like Papa, always could and should find a wife. Some good soul from his synagogue could have acted as matchmaker and dug up a widow or an overlooked spinster. It went so much against the soul of the religion for him to remain alone and not try for more children. Something kept him from the attempt. Bitterness? Pride? Lack of confidence? I tried to imagine Papa happily married—the man he'd once been before I was born—and couldn't. Perhaps he couldn't either and so he'd condemned himself to perpetual widowerhood through stubborn lack of imagination.

I finished a second cigarette, stabbed it out in a saucer, and suddenly found myself assaulted by the question Papa had neglected to ask when I'd come through the door. What was I doing with my life? These past months, whenever the uncertain future gaped, Shimshon had rushed in to fill the void. But tonight he was strangely absent, not even bothering to mock me for my botched attempt at escape beneath the obliterating sea. So I, too, now sank into a failure of imagination except for one salient point: I was going to live. Life, my future, were simply mine to carry forward, like a heavy package I had no choice but to deliver to its eventual destination. Somehow I would have to manage to scratch out an existence from this harsh and arid land. Perhaps even suck some happiness from its stones. The realization drained the last drop of energy from my body. It had been such a long, insane day. Papa was due back soon and I wanted to settle for the night before he arrived. I washed the dishes, took down my dress, brought in the crate from the balcony, and arranged it as a footstool in front of the armchair. Still wearing my father's shirt and trousers, I curled up under the blanket he'd given me. Within seconds I was gone, plunged into a deeper sleep than I had known for a long time. I didn't hear Papa return, or even feel when he placed a pillow under my head.

AT BREAKFAST TIME next morning I became halfway respectable again in my own dress, which had dried and was not too much worse for wear despite its dowsing in the sea. I made Papa a soft-boiled egg, cooked slightly runny, as I knew he liked it, along with a glass of black tea. I arranged everything nicely on the table—some jam I found at the back of a cupboard, the bread, and slices of yellow cheese. Also matching forks and spoons that I fished out of the dairy cutlery drawer after rummaging among the mismatched items. It was the least I could do—make an effort. Papa glanced at me sideways as I bustled about, but he let me take over his kitchen without a word, while he pored over some accounts at his desk. When I called him to the table he came shuffling over like an obedient old dog following a well-known routine. He sawed a couple of slices of bread from the heavy black loaf. His lips moved as he said the blessing and then handed me my piece.

Nevertheless, it was terribly awkward facing one another across the table, avoiding one another's eyes. I couldn't read him. He was uncomfortable with my presence. Yes, but why exactly? Was it all the bad blood between us, or a desire to start afresh without knowing how? Liesel must have let him know that Duncan—*that man*—was no longer part of my life. Had Papa become more reconciled to my past sins, was he merely resigned, or was he as hostile as ever—merely biting his tongue for the sake of peace and quiet? Or, could he possibly be aware of his own failures—not just mine? Could he even be a little afraid of me—of what I might do next? I couldn't bring myself to ask any such questions out loud. I was grateful for the truce—this seemed enough for now. We sat together at his table, tame and courteous with one another and pretending we had no poisoned history.

In the middle of the table, taking up a good chunk of the available space though it stood flat against the wall, was a wireless set. Papa now switched it on, fiddling with the dials with his pale nervous fingers until he had the tuning and volume just right. We ate while listening to the English language news, broadcast from Jerusalem. The stories of the bitter struggles engulfing the land were deeply distressing, of course, even as filtered through the polished phrases of the Palestine Broadcasting System. Yet I could still enjoy the crisp, authoritative voice of the British announcer, his articulation so calm and steady but with an underlay of breezy good cheer. His tone brought forth apple orchards, windswept downs, Big Ben, Regents Park, Stratford-upon-Avon, and Sir Winston's rousing speeches, along with plucky citizens singing in the Underground during the Blitz. The best of England was contained in that voice—the England I still wanted to believe in.

The announcer told us about the discussions at the United Nations over the partition of Palestine. His Majesty's government had decided to let the UN have a go at this intractable problem. Britain would consider the recommendations, but would not be bound by any decision. There was also a report on the ongoing reaction over the most recent atrocity by Jewish terrorists. The announcer reminded us of the details of that horror: two kidnapped British sergeants hung to death in a Netanya orange grove. Their bodies booby trapped with explosives so that the army captain who cut them down had half his face blown away. In Tel Aviv, enraged soldiers went on a shooting rampage, firing bullets randomly into buses and private cars. In Liverpool, a synagogue and Jewish shops were vandalized. A newspaper editorial was quoted as saying it was a "natural reaction" considering the brutality of the terrorists' crime. The terror toll for the last two weeks of July, the announcer informed us, was sixteen dead and ninety-two injured, most of them police and soldiers. Next came the cricket scores, the football scores. And then the news in Arabic. Papa turned down the volume so that the radio muttered softly—muted hisses and guttural sounds—as we chewed our bread. He restored the full volume for the Hebrew news, delivered in a deep, cultivated baritone by a Mr. Chaim Isaac. It was pretty much a repeat of the English version, except for a report on the football match between Maccabi and Beitar. No doubt the radio always kept Papa company at breakfast and I was glad. It was a relief not to have to try to make conversation. We passed one another the margarine and the jam with quiet pleases and thank yous. We behaved as if this were a morning like any other, as if we'd been doing this for years instead of having been estranged for almost a decade.

Just before the "Morning Melody" program came on, Papa snapped off the radio. The room was suddenly quiet. Papa filled the void.

"Butchers! Heathen, who call themselves Jews. Their hands reek with human blood, but they lust for more. Vicious murderers who set themselves up as the saviours of the people. They bring shame upon our heads and misery into our lives. They make it easier for the British masters to betray us. As for those masters: self-righteous hypocrites. Lord High this and His Excellency that. British justice. Due process," Papa uttered these last two words in English, with pursed lips, as if saying something especially distasteful. "One hundred thousand soldiers in the country but they can't impose their will? Ha! They want an excuse to leave so they can abandon us to the cut-throats, the marauders from the deserts with their galloping camels and blasting pistols and thrusting knives. To do their dirty work, that's what the British want, those polite, cultivated anti-Semites."

Papa thumped the table with his fist.

"They warn about a bloodbath, but that's exactly what they're aiming for . . . get rid of the messy Jews so they can return and be lords again, pashas in checkered headdress . . . best friends with the effendis . . . the bothersome Jews cleared out, slaughtered . . . the flow of Jewish blood makes way for the gush of Arab oil . . . yes, that's the plan. You can't fool me with your royal commissions and learned committees . . ."

Papa jabbed his forefinger towards the silenced radio.

"Your conferences, Parliamentary debates, emissaries, diplomats, inquiries. You have a simple, cold-hearted plan."

Papa was in fine form, just like in the old days back home when he railed against the Nazis, the communists, the Zionists, the misguided community leaders, the muddled masses, and anyone else he could think of, a stance that suggested the only sane person left in the world was himself. I'd mocked him back then. But now, considering the deluge of catastrophic events in the country and the ranting and raving heard daily in the streets—and in my own head— Papa didn't sound so mad.

As abruptly as he'd begun his rant, Papa fell silent, bowing his head over his empty plate.

I made a move to rise.

"I'll wash up and be on my way," I said. "To the Egged station. I'll take the next bus home."

Papa cleared his throat emphatically. His lips were moving and I realized he had to recite his Grace after Meals so I sat down again. Mumble, mumble whisper, sigh, and the near-to-last lines barked out loud, *"He who makes peace in His heavens, may He make peace for us and for all Israel; and let us say, Amen."*

An echoing "Amen" came to my lips but I stifled the automatic impulse. "Amen"—a proclamation of belief—but I didn't believe, so it would be a lie.

Papa finished. He looked up at me, blinked several times and said, quite matter-of-fact, "There's going to be war here."

"You think so?"

"Of course."

He gave me a sharp look, as if wondering how I could possibly be so dense as to not be aware of the obvious. A prickle of annoyance went up the back of my neck.

"Yes. Quite right. We'll have a war. But it won't be me who starts it."

My irony went over his head. He was rubbing his chin with his knuckles, chewing the inside of his mouth. Thinking.

"What will Manfred do? Will he stay in Jerusalem? Does he have plans? What are his plans? He must make plans. To protect the child. Tell him I said so. Tell him," Papa leaned across the table to look me fiercely in the eye, "that I expressly said so."

"What sort of plans? What are you talking about?"

"They should send the child to me. Tel Aviv will be safer than Jerusalem. Anywhere will be safer than that shack on the roof when the bullets fly. The child . . ." His lips trembled. A desperate plea came into his eyes. "The child must not be harmed."

In a flash, I knew what gave him hope and solace these days, a sense of purpose, a hold on life, a stake in the future, along with a terror of the calamities that the future could bring. If he was hoarding his coins it was for one reason. If he made plans for tomorrow, he had one goal in mind. The boy child! The grandson! Little Ari was the sun around which Papa now revolved. The prayers that he mumbled, morning, noon and night, his sighs and wishes were all about the boy. And his having this new, overwhelming, all-encompassing love, meant I didn't matter. The blinding light of Ari blotted out everything else. There wasn't room left in Papa's heart and his head for him to contemplate my sins. Or to contemplate me at all. The peace between us was due to his having other preoccupations. In fact, I'd been completely superseded. It was a bitter pill to swallow. To test my theory, I asked Papa if he had any photos of the child. Immediately he rose, wiped his hands on a kitchen towel, and went over to the oak desk to lift up the roll top. There was little Ari—his mop of curls, his cherub cheeks, his impish grin—

seated like a prince in his grandpa's lap and cradled in his arms. The photo was in a kitschy, ornate brass frame and placed towards the back of the desk between the two rows of pigeon holes. Safe here from dust and from the Evil Eye, which Papa's unquiet mind had absorbed at some level, though he would never in a million years admit to believing in such a thing, for that was an *Ostjude* superstition. The bottom desk drawer produced an album of snapshots, meticulously secured between photo corners, each black sheet covered with onion skin paper. A record of Ari's progress, from the day of his circumcision to his current irrepressible three-year-old self. Papa hovered over me as I flipped through the pages, pleased to show me his treasure, but anxious too in case I might put a greasy thumb where it didn't belong. The photos were familiar. I had copies of many of them myself. And despite my irritation with Papa, they brought a smile to my face.

"So you'll talk to them," he urged again. "About sending the boy here."

"I'll tell them what you said. But . . ."

"They can come too, if they want. I'll make room," Papa pleaded. "You were able to sleep in the armchair. So can I."

"Really Papa, I don't think . . ."

Papa walked away and shook his head, not wanting to hear what I thought on the matter. The discussion was over. The visit was over. He had to get to work. At once. He had an appointment to see a client. Never mind the dishes. Just rinse and leave them in the sink, he told me. They wouldn't run away. He began stuffing a heavy leather briefcase with papers and small packages from one of the big crates beside his desk. As I stood before the door with my packed valise, I had a terrible urge to ask Papa for his blessing. And I think he would have given it to me. He would have performed a hasty mumbling of the ancient words, with his hands twitching against my head and his impatient feet shifting about. No, I couldn't bear that. I couldn't bear to receive what he would only halfheartedly give, out of a sense of duty. I thanked him for his hospitality.

He nodded and muttered, "It's nothing. You're welcome. Safe journey." He reached out to pat my shoulder, while ushering me out the door.

The sun was already beating down on the pavements when I left the building. The air was dense with humidity, but I filled my lungs, relieved to be out of Papa's flat. Away from him. The outside air tasted good. Of freshness, freedom, and a hint of the sea.

Chapter 37
What Malka Knew

MALKA NOW LIVED in a freshly whitewashed building on Mazeh Street, close to Rothschild Boulevard. She was on the top floor and the printed sign on the door said, "Mr. and Mrs. Amnon Levi," and below that, in larger letters, "Malka Levi, Professional Seamstress."

She welcomed me into her flat with open arms, cries of delight, and kisses to both my cheeks.

"Look at you. Slim and lovely as ever. Belle of Jerusalem *and* Tel Aviv."

But she was the one who looked good, I thought, though she'd put on weight since I'd last seen her. Yes, Malka had grown plump, but dressed in a flowing cream-coloured shift of a fine, light material, she wore her fat well. Her hair was perfectly coiffed, her face made up, her nails—short, but well-manicured— glittered with red polish. She had the relaxed, confident, beaming look of someone whose life is unfolding according to plan.

First thing, she toured me around her flat, sumptuous by Palestine standards. She still had her workshop in the main room, with all the tools of her trade— cutting table, ironing board, sewing machine, baskets, and shelves—on one side. And yet there was ample space for a handsome couch, armchairs, a coffee table, and dining set all made of the same blond wood, very modern and tasteful. There were Persian-style carpets. There was a dreamy, pastel drawing of one of Tel Aviv's oldest streets in Neve Tzedek by an up-and-coming local artist, which gave an impression of chic nostalgia. The bedroom was nicely appointed too—a new vanity with a mirror that tilted up and down and the largest armoire I'd ever seen. The kitchen had hot and cold running water, a gas stove, and a good-sized refrigerator. But the "pièce de résistance" was a third room, an almost unheard- of luxury, furnished with a set of bunk beds and littered with a child's clothing. Malka and Amnon had a six-year-old son—that much I knew. He was outside with his playmates, and Malka assured me that the shrillest of the voices coming from the bedlam in the back alley belonged to her Shuki. But who was the second bed for?

"Is someone else on the way who might be moving in?" I asked with a teasing nod towards Malka's belly.

She seemed pleased at the question and laughed.

"Not yet, but we're doing our part to make it happen."

Over biscuits and coffee, laced with a celebratory drop of cognac, and taken on the covered balcony, Malka brought me up to date. Her first husband Kurt had at last agreed to a divorce and bought out her share of the condom business. Amnon, having studied the electrician's trade and acquired his credentials, was busy on construction sites. And despite the unrest, uncertainty, and periods of martial law, Malka's work was in high demand too. She'd even hired a girl to help her out three times a week. Their Shuki was a gangster in the making, Malka vowed, a lusty and charming little Sabra. She promised to call him upstairs to meet me after our coffee.

When it was my turn, I made light of having lost my job and on the spot concocted a tale of my plans to go independent, typing manuscripts for professors in my home as a way to get my foot in the door at the university. I described Brodsky's establishment and the very serviceable Olivetti I'd discovered on a back shelf, making it sound as if I'd already put down a deposit. As for Duncan—gone and forgotten months ago, I said. He could be in Timbuktu for all I cared.

"Oh, that's good to hear," Malka said, visibly relieved. "I wasn't sure."

"Yes, it's so," I said, and bit my lip.

"Really and truly?"

"Yes and no. I can't entirely forget him because I don't know why he left Palestine. We'd agreed there'd be no contact, but we'd parted as friends. Why would he have gone without writing a note at least? They wouldn't tell me what happened at Headquarters when I asked, but they were hiding something."

Malka went quiet, looking down at her lacquered nails. "So he never wrote you?"

"No, he didn't. I told you that already. Why? What are you thinking? What do you suspect?"

Her face flushed and her eyes glittered with anger. "I don't suspect anything. I know."

"How can you know?"

Malka pressed her lips together in thought for several moments, then she seized the cognac bottle and poured a good splash for herself and me into our coffee glasses.

"Drink up," she commanded, tossing back the contents of her glass.

"It's not even noon. I can't start tippling at this hour. Malka, what's going on? What do you know?"

"Not a word until you drink."

Alarmed about what she had to say, and seeing she was adamant, I took a sip. Malka nodded, satisfied.

"All right. Here goes. Five months ago, last March, while I'm alone in the flat, I hear a knock and answer the door. A uniformed policeman is standing there. Your old boyfriend Duncan. By now, we're all used to the police and army snooping around, so I immediately think it's about the security situation. But no, he says it's a personal matter. He assures me that nothing terrible has happened to you, because that's my first question. No, nothing like that, he says. So I invite him in. I give him coffee and some of this very cognac, which he accepts with a charming smile. I'm a good hostess, as you know. If someone's under my roof, I treat him well."

"Malka, get to the point. What did he want?"

"He ums and ahs and tells me he's been in hospital for a month."

"I knew it! He's been hurt. What happened?"

"It was near Haifa. The police were investigating a tip about an arms cache in the basement of a school. Turned out to be booby trapped and the bomb went off when they kicked in one of the doors."

"Has he been maimed? Malka, tell me. You're holding something back."

"He's quite fine now. Don't worry about him. The other man was blown to bits, but Duncan was down the hall, poking into a different closet. Escaped with minor wounds. He took some shrapnel, in his shoulder I think he said, and he's gone rather deaf in one ear. Kept turning his head sideways to hear me when I spoke."

"The hearing problem is from before. From another incident a while back. But you said he was in hospital for a month."

"Yes, well. I suppose the shrapnel went in deep. But it was mostly the shock that laid him low, I think. He didn't say so exactly. He was vague, but I read between the lines."

"Oh, poor Duncan. To see a mate blown up in front of your eyes. How terrible. And it's happened before, too many times. Of course he'd be down. He's been mentally hurt, even if the physical wound has healed."

"He seemed quite fine to me in every way." Malka's manner was crisp, dismissive. She'd been infected by the general anti-British virus, I thought. She couldn't find it in her heart to feel sorry for a member of the Palestine Police, no matter what harm befell him.

"Well, where is he now? Did they ship him home to England? Why did he come to you? And why didn't you tell me about this, Malka? Five months ago! Why didn't you write to me immediately?"

"Sit down. Give me that glass before you break it," Malka said. For I had jumped to my feet and my hands were clenched, one in a fist, the other around the empty cognac glass. "Before you take that accusing tone with me, sit down and listen."

I lowered myself back down onto the edge of the wicker chair.

"Ok. So he tells me about the bomb and the hospital. And I ask him the same question, more or less, as you just asked. Why has he come here? What's this got to do with me? He's got this funny look on his face. And I'm thinking, you and he have had an argument and he wants me to intervene, that's what this is about. He wants me to help him mend fences with you, which, by the way, I wouldn't have done, even if that's what it was about. But it wasn't."

"Malka!"

"All right, I'm getting there. So he hems and haws and finally tells me he's just got married. To a Polish girl he'd met a little while back when he was transferred from Jerusalem to Haifa. She's the daughter of an officer in General Anders' resistance army, who hasn't been able to return home to Poland because of the Russian takeover. She was working as a salesgirl at Spinney's and she must have caught Duncan's eye when he was in there buying supplies for his billet. He got to know her and then, after he was hurt, she visited him every day at the hospital. I suppose he decided he couldn't live without her. Christian girl, of course. Catholic. Duncan went through the motions of conversion, found a priest to marry them. Yes, I must have looked as astonished as you do now when he told me all this. Not because the story was so strange, but why bring this story to me? I hadn't seen him for years. He was telling me because he wanted my advice about whether to tell *you*. He explained that you and he had finally broken up some time ago and he didn't want to interfere with your life. But, since he was leaving the country for good with his new bride, he wondered if he should let you know."

"But he didn't," I cried.

"Obviously not."

"But how . . . when . . . ?"

"He must have thought you and I were closer than we are. That we've been writing one another on a regular basis. He told me he'd always been impressed by my womanly instincts and wanted to know what I would suggest."

"And what did you . . . ?"

"Oh, no. I wasn't going to make it easy for him. And be blamed if it was the wrong thing to do? Are you joking? Yes, I have good instincts and they said, 'Stay out of it.' I told him that. To his face. He had done what he had done and he had to take full responsibility."

"How long could he have known this girl?" I was utterly bewildered, trying to imagine who she was and what would make him take such a rash decision.

"If you're wondering whether he was drinking from two cups, I can't answer. He said he met her after the two of you parted. But can I swear he was telling the truth? How should I know?"

"*I* would have visited him in hospital. *I* would have taken care of him, if I'd known." I said this softly, more to myself than to Malka.

She made a face. "Yes, I suppose you would have. You would have put him first instead of yourself, my impossible little *Yecke*. Just as well you didn't know. Let the Polish girl have him. Let them sail off into the sunset together. They probably deserve each other."

"I never thought he would leave the Palestine Police. Did he say where they were going?"

"Bermuda."

"Bermuda!"

He'd once told me that Bermuda had to be the prettiest, easiest, most peaceful and most boring posting in the entire Empire. I tried to understand who this man was who had about-faced so abruptly. An adventure-lusting creature one day, a yolked, domesticated animal the next. I expressed these thoughts to Malka. She shrugged.

"Adventure is being the hunter. Being the prey is an altogether different matter. He lost his nerve. Went soft. I can't blame him. I do blame him for keeping you dangling all those years."

"Did it not occur to you to write to me after his visit?"

"Oh, I did think of it, Eva, and I planned to, even though I didn't want to mix in. I thought I'd write at least to see how you were doing. But that week all hell broke loose with the Goldschmidt Officers' Club bombing and more waves of terror throughout the country. Tel Aviv under curfew, martial law, the roadblocks, the searches. Amnon was stuck in Petach Tikvah and couldn't reach me. There were arrests without charge. Rumours about revenge attacks, and not all of them rumours. A man just down the street was roughed up by soldiers who got carried away. By the time life got back to normal, you and Duncan had gone right out of my head. If I'd known you were concerned about his welfare . . . Ha! You see? He took very good care of himself. You can rest easy on that score."

Malka offered more cognac, but I waved it away. I lit up a cigarette instead, pulling the smoke deep into my lungs to feel the soothing burn of tobacco. I gave Malka my last Camel. She blew a wobbly smoke ring towards the row of cactus plants that hung from the balcony rail.

"Did he say anything else about the girl?"

Malka smirked.

"I got the impression she's young and naive. Easy pickings. But also very Catholic, I think, so maybe she'll make his life miserable someday. Let's hope."

She raised her glass as if to toast this prospect, but set it down without drinking. She couldn't stomach more alcohol at this hour either.

DURING THE LURCHING, twisting bus ride back to Jerusalem, on the serpentine road through the Seven Sister hills, Shimshon appeared again. His face was everywhere, in each of those sun-bleached, pitted rocks that look like skulls, scattered along the hillsides. And when I closed my eyes against those boulder faces with their rictus grins, Shimshon stood before me in the aisle of the bus. A double bandoleer stuffed with bullets criss-crossed his chest. At his side, a rifle with a gleaming bayonet. His voice rang with triumph, with a bright, bold, feverish blast of trumpets and the relentless roll of drums.

So where was he, your policeman hero, while you and I had our rendezvous in the cellar? In another girl's arms! Didn't I tell you? Ha, ha, lost his nerve! They will all lose their nerves. They'll all go marching home with their sparkly medals and fancy uniforms and their tails between their legs. After we've done with the British, we will drive out the Arabs who have set themselves against us. And after the Arabs, we'll polish off the traitors and informers in our midst. We will eliminate all the servants of betrayal: the whiners, the sycophants, the bleeding hearts, the weak-kneed liberals and the craven appeasers.

As his froth-mouthed tirade drew to a close, a thin, but stubborn cry of protest arose in my heart.

"And what sort of Homeland will it be?" I demanded of the rough hills that a moment ago seemed to echo with righteous diatribes. "What's left after you've finished your attacking, eliminating, and driving out and polishing off? *If* you ever finish."

Chapter 38
Encounter with Eisenberg

"CONSIDER IT RENT," I said to Liesel about the envelope full of pound notes I'd slipped under the door two days earlier. "With no room or job, I had to get rid of things, so I sold the lot and got rich."

"But your gramophone and records? You loved them so."

My sister stood before me on her cluttered rooftop plaza and wrung her hands. More odds and ends had accumulated around the water tanks in recent days—bed frames, cupboards, crates, and trunks, covered with brown canvas tarps that made the heaps look like miniature Seven Sisters hills. Other tenants in the building had friends or relatives with nowhere to go and excess baggage to stow. For this reason alone, I was glad I hadn't come back to her burdened with belongings.

"I can live without a gramophone. It was baggage from the past. Reminded me of Duncan."

My sister cocked her head, a sideways look, uncertain about my lighthearted tone. Had I gone a little mad, or was I newly sane? I wasn't sure myself.

We borrowed one of the bed frames, found a mattress, and set me up in the open air behind the house, snug in a corner of the parapet. The autumn rains were still two months away, so this would do for now. The arrangement would give us all a bit of privacy. Quite romantic to sleep under a canopy of stars, I told Liesel. And inwardly I hoped that Shimshon would be less prone to invade out here in the open. Another advantage: whenever the urge struck, I could smoke.

The same evening that I returned to Jerusalem, I revealed my plan for the future to Liesel and Manfred. They were both impressed. So the very next morning I went to see Brodsky.

To my good fortune, his wife was away, attending at the bedside of a sick relative. The dealer was alone with his shed-full of used goods. I found him seated in the doorway, tinkering with the bowels of a dismantled wireless set while listening to one of my records on the gramophone, which he'd placed on a shelf above his workbench. The intense, beseeching notes of Beethoven's *Violin Sonata No. 9*, the *Kreutzer Sonata*, played by the brilliant Bronislaw Huberman, with Ignaz Friedman on the piano, resonated between the thin board walls and bounced off the assorted machine parts. When Brodsky saw me before him on the pavement, he hastily stood to lift the record arm and switch off the gramophone, looking guilty as a thief.

"You have something else to sell?" he asked.

"This time I've come to buy."

We argued and haggled. I shed crocodile tears, cast wistful glances at the gramophone that I'd been so recently bereft of and that he now—due to my misfortunes—so obviously enjoyed. I twisted my thorns of deprivation into his soft spot of guilt and, finally, I wore him down. He agreed to let me have the Olivetti on credit. It was a battered old dear. The "A" and the "S" letters had been half worn away from years of thumping fingers. The keys were clogged with ancient ink, and the shift key and the space bar immediately stuck when pressed and would only be returned to their resting positions after a firm shake of the whole machine. Brodsky set to work with oil and alcohol-dipped rags, refurbishing as best he could. At last, in triumph, I bore away my prize in its metal carrying case, the heavy load knocking painfully against my thigh. At a stationers on Jaffa Road, I bought a new ribbon and a supply of paper and carbons.

With Manfred's help I constructed an office on the roof terrace, amid the rusting clutter and fluttering laundry. We erected a canvas awning strung between the roof entry and a couple of poles anchored with sandbags. Beneath its shelter, we placed a desk, fashioned out of orange crates and boards, and one of the kitchen table chairs. My new-old typewriter sat in readiness on the makeshift desk, along with my stack of paper, weighed down by a stone. Ari was delighted with the "fort" and wanted one too, so Manfred complied, creating a little den with crates and a towel, into which Ari crawled and pretended no one could ever find him. I did the same with my canvas-topped hidey-hole, my refuge from the sun and other demons. Then, early one morning, on the Street of the Prophets, I caught a bus that bypassed the downtown's barbed-wire security zone and that rumbled past St. George's Cathedral, through Sheikh Jarrah, upwards to the university on Mount Scopus. There I knocked on doors until I found my first client: a Professor Neuman of the Archaeology Department.

A NEW DAY dawned. A new beginning as a private typist, manager of my own hours, beholden to no boss. What I could earn would be a pittance compared with my former salary at the Finance Division, but it would be something. As they said in *Yecke* quarters: better than a gob of spit in a beggar's palm. Yes, but would my hands behave themselves under the pressure to perform once again? Though daylight had barely broken over the eastern hills, I sat down to practise, testing out my fingers and the Olivetti, tap tapping lines that popped into my mind: scraps of songs, poetry, mottoes.

There'll be bluebirds over
The white cliffs of Dover . . .
Underneath the lantern
By the barrack gate
Darling I remember
The way you used to wait . . .

I hummed as my fingers limbered up, as the words shot out and the carriage return zinged its merry refrain. Just as I was getting smug, these poisoned lines insinuated themselves onto the page.

By blood and fire did Judea fall
By blood and fire will Judea rise

It was the motto of the Revisionist fighters and Shimshon's favourite rallying call. My tormentor hovered near me still. I tore the sheet off the typewriter, crumpled it into a ball, but too late. My hands curled into bird claws. My fingers cramped and twitched. Groping for my cigarettes, I found the pack empty. It was barely six in the morning, the town just waking up, with another hour to go before the shop owners rolled up their shutters. This tiny misfortune was enough to make my heartbeat frantic. *Cursed, cursed, cursed*, I thought, as I paced beside the parapet. Any moment, Liesel would emerge from the house with an armful of bedding to air on the wash line. She would see me in this distressed state, know I was still a tangled ball of misery and she would try to console me, but no, no, I couldn't bear her bewildered concern and her loving, but intrusive, touch.

I came to a standstill. I looked out across the rooftops, across the city to the east, where a faint finger of stone caught my eye: the pointed tower of Augusta Victoria on the Mount of Olives already ablaze in the fire of the newly risen sun. And I remembered the kiosk at the Egged bus station on Jaffa Road. That it opened before any of the others. This small, simple fact became a ring buoy flung to a drowning soul. Grabbing my handbag from under my cot, I eased open the heavy door to the stairwell and slipped away unnoticed by Liesel, Manfred and Ari, who had just begun to stir inside the house.

Down the dark stairway I went, stepping softly, quickly, past the silence of the neighbours' flats. I'd almost arrived at the first-floor landing when I heard a door open on the parterre, and instinctively, nervously, guiltily, I froze and crouched. There was a shuffle of feet. Men's voices speaking low. Peeking between the railings I saw Dr. Eisenberg step out into the lobby, along with another man.

The doctor was in shorts, a singlet and slippers, his thick, naked shoulders and chest hair very evident, making him look like a feisty old bear. The other man was a stranger. Tall, younger, with a mop of tousled hair. He was fully dressed, but his shirt was torn at the shoulder and his arm was in a sling.

"Thank you for everything, comrade," the stranger said in a husky voice.

"Nothing to thank," Dr. Eisenberg growled softly. He held out a paper bag. "Here's some medicine and fresh dressings. Take the tablets when you need them for pain. Get someone to change the dressing tonight. But you're sure you don't want to stay here a couple of days? You'd be safe with us. Our back room is very private."

"No. It's not safe. Too much coming and going here. Better I leave."

Dr. Eisenberg moved over to the building entrance, and his head swivelled left and right as he peered up and down the street.

"The patrol has passed. Quick now."

The two men clasped hands briefly and the injured one slipped outside.

"Take care, my son," Eisenberg whispered into the empty air in front of him, for the stranger had already vanished.

The doctor remained standing in the doorway, gazing up the road in the direction that I presumed the other had gone. All this time, I'd made myself as small as possible, pressed against the rails, squatted down, barely breathing, but my teeth chattering in my head. I waited for the doctor to return to his flat. Instead he stayed planted on the threshold of the entrance for an eternity, lost in thought, a bulky silhouette against the morning light.

I must have made some kind of noise, for abruptly Dr. Eisenberg wheeled around, stepped over to the stairway, and looked directly at me as I cowered like a cornered mouse.

"Who's this? Miss Salomon. What are you doing here?"

I could have asked him the same thing. Straightening up, barely able speak, I stammered a far-fetched explanation about how I'd lost my key the other day and had been searching for it through the stairway. I tried to convince him I'd just got down here a moment ago, while he'd been gazing up the street.

He grunted in disbelief. Legs apart, hands on his hips, he stood before me, blocking my escape. He ground his teeth—I saw the slow, circular motions of his jaw—as he contemplated what to do about me.

"What did you see just now?"

I shook my head.

His jaw thrust out. His deeply furrowed brow jutted over his eyes. His big head sank lower into his thick shoulders.

"What did you see?" he said through gritted teeth.

"A wounded man."

"And what did you hear?"

"You . . . you asked him to stay. But he said no, that it isn't safe."

"And who do you think that man was?"

I knew who he was—not specifically, only generally, which was enough. And Eisenberg knew I knew. The story was clear as a bold-lettered warning on a billboard. A wounded fighter from the Underground had been sheltered by the Eisenbergs. The doctor had treated his injuries. That the man belonged to one of the splinter groups could also not be in doubt. Perhaps he was a follower of Avraham Stern and one of the Fighters for the Freedom of Israel, the very same group that had terrorized me in the cellar.

"Well, Miss Salomon? Have you nothing to say?"

Eisenberg sneered as he said this. He contemplated me some more, a cold calculating stare as if gauging whether I was sufficiently frightened, and finally his shoulders relaxed.

"Good!" he said, almost heartily. "You saw nothing. You know nothing. We understand one another. I also saw nothing. You were never here. At this moment, you don't exist."

He chuckled, and as he did so, a crackle of electricity shot through my body, a lick of heat in my chest.

"You're very good at being blind when it suits you, doctor."

He looked as startled as if a wax dummy had spoken.

"Well yes," he said slowly, "And I hope you are too. For your own sake."

"I know something about those comrades of yours. Those brave heroes who would beat up a defenceless woman."

"If you got beaten, you know why you should keep your mouth shut."

He'd gone back into his menacing bulldog pose. But I was standing several stairs above him, looking down. And he seemed just a bit ridiculous now in his singlet, shorts, and slippers—a top-heavy, barrel-chested body on pale, skinny legs. A nasty gargoyle. I held his eyes.

"Do we understand one another?" he asked.

I didn't answer.

"Well?"

"I don't intend to stick my neck out right now. I'm not stupid. But when the time is right, I will say what I need to say."

"There will never be a right time for betraying the cause."

"Call it what you want. I call it the truth. The day will come when people will know about all the deeds done in the name of the struggle, not just the fine ones. And they'll know about a doctor who's a disgrace to his profession."

His head jerked back slightly, as if struck.

"History is on my side, Miss Salomon. *You* are the disgrace and the people will always have better things to think about than the likes of *you*."

His face was stiff with anger, but its cool smugness had drained away, while the hurt in the doctor's eyes told me my words had hit a nerve. He cared intensely about his professional good name. He opened his mouth to say something more, but thought better of it. After another scowling look he finally turned away from me and shuffled back into his flat, the slippers hissing along the tile floor as he went.

FORTIFIED BY AN injection of nicotine, I typed. Professor Neuman's heap of hand-written pages, interspersed with clippings from journals, sat before me on my make-shift desk and held in place by a cratered field stone. The wind flicked at the edges of the pages. The sun beat down on the canvas over my head. A speckled dove came to rest on the parapet beside me but took flight again at the sound of the clacking keys. Gradually I became less anxious about every keystroke, lost myself in the dance of my fingers and the absorbing subject of the professor's research.

It was about Hezekiah's tunnel, the underground passage dug deep beneath ancient Jerusalem in biblical times to prepare for the impending Assyrian siege. Hezekiah, King of Judah, had the tunnel built to conduct water from the Spring of Gihon to the Pool of Siloam, a water supply hidden from Judea's enemies. It was an amazing engineering achievement for the time. A 1,765-foot tunnel cut through solid stone with primitive Iron Age tools. Professor Neuman's manuscript included the relevant texts from the books of Kings and of Chronicles and the inscription describing how two teams of stone cutters, starting at opposite ends, had made their way towards one another, axe-blow by axe-blow, until they met in the middle and the water flowed. There were various theories on how the two teams—working blind so to speak—managed to find each other without much deviation from the course. Professor Neuman discussed all the possibilities, while concluding that the feat was still not fully understood.

I typed the stories, the competing hypotheses, the technical descriptions, the quotes, the footnotes, and the notes for the figures. For a while, as I typed, I was underground in a cold, damp, narrow shaft, listening with all my might for the faint tap, tap, tap of a hammer—a sound like a heartbeat deep within the bowels of the earth. They gave me courage, those brave, indefatigable ancient stone cutters, even though, ultimately, the water tunnel did not save Jerusalem from the Assyrian assault. Ultimately Judea fell.

Now and then, I looked up to rest my eyes with the long view across the rooftops of Jerusalem. The Union Jack fluttered above the Russian Compound. The Old City walls hovered near in the mirage-making light. A puff of smoke in the direction of Sheik Jarrah could have been from a back-yard fire or signalled the detonation of a bomb. These days, and especially during the nights, gunfire and explosions punctuated the hours. The countdown to the UN vote on the partition of Palestine had begun. The Arab Higher Committee warned of a Genghis Khan-style massacre. Rumours went back and forth over whether the British truly intended to leave. The terrorist actions by the rogue groups of the Jewish Underground continued unabated. One way or another, people said, war was coming. And yet, the professors at the university continued to churn out their scholarly research. One was doing a paper on nitrates in the Dead Sea. Another had written a history of cooperative farming. A third was editing essays on the golden age of Jewry in Moorish Al Andalus. A fourth had a theory about the Maccabees to prove. The professors worked with frantic determination to publish before the war began. Many of them wrote in English or German. I had no fear that I wouldn't find manuscripts to type.

EVEN THE CAFÉ philosophers on Ben Yehuda Street, whose gallows humour normally signalled a cheery optimism, did not take the blood-curdling threats of the Arab Higher Committee lightly. Even the wise men of Café Atara warned of desperate struggles ahead, struggles that would draw on the depths of the people's strength. They argued among themselves about the numbers: how many Jewish fighters could rise out of the Underground versus how many men in the combined Arab armies. They whispered rumours about secret weapons, diplomatic coups, American intervention, and Arab militiamen armed to the teeth gathering in the villages nearby. Yes, the street-corner experts agreed, there would be food shortages, water problems, hospital beds filled with the wounded. But of course we would win, they declared. They made hand-wiping gestures or lifted their palms upwards as if raising heavy weights. Absolutely, we would win. No question. Because we had to. We had no choice. *Ein breirah.*

Meanwhile, on the quiet, civil defence committees formed in each neighbourhood of Jewish Jerusalem. Manfred went to a meeting in Dr. Eisenberg's flat that had brought together fellow citizens of all types and political stripes. Greying university professors. A few twitchy hothead youths. Proletarian types from Nachlat Shiva. Several housewives still in their aprons and anxious about the half-cooked suppers they'd left at home. On the edge of despair, my brother-in-law sat in a corner, his mouth shut tight as the others let their tongues wag without restraint. Eisenberg delivered a bombastic speech about the spirit of the nation. A professor interrupted to ask about the rules of order for the meeting. Another raised his hand and begged for the opportunity to explain his analysis of the UN debate. A man in overalls flecked with paint demanded that people talk the plain Hebrew of the land instead of that imported highbrow rot. The youths jiggled their knees and finally one got up to pace like a caged animal, a second collapsed into hysterical laughter and a third yelled at everyone to shut up. The housewives scolded them for their lack of respect. Finally the group did pull itself together well enough to deal with some practicalities. There was talk of sandbags, water cisterns, food stores, guard duty, first-aid training, makeshift bomb shelters, and even of buying, stealing and hiding small arms. Some volunteered for tasks, while others grudgingly accepted assignments they felt were beneath them. Nevertheless, the meeting ended on a more harmonious note than it began. Manfred gave Liesel and me a full report after he returned to the rooftop flat.

"If we have a chance of survival, it will only be because the Arabs are even more inept and divided than we are," Manfred said. He gave us one of his wan, tight-lipped smiles.

IN THE DARK of a moonless night, I shivered under the blankets. Above me, a billion stars blinked their sightless eyes. Down below, a mechanical beast growled in a voice I'd come to know well—the armoured car of the Police Mobile Force, patrolling the otherwise deserted streets of the city. Somewhere in the hills a shot rang out. Though I burrowed deeper into the blankets, I was aware of a looming presence, a black shape that hovered over my bed. The shape stood over me as I lay still, barely breathing. Then it padded away softly to another side of the roof. The stillness weighed down on me until I had to peek out from my blanket den. Though the dark blob by the parapet was barely visible, I knew it was Liesel. In her flannel housecoat, hugging her arms to her chest. I called her name and she came over, stumbling against a bucket, cursing softly, as she made her way towards me. She sat down on the edge of my cot.

"Can't sleep," she said.

"What's the matter?"

But I knew. What sort of terror would rise out of the villages? How could she protect her child? I reminded her of Papa's invitation to send the boy to Tel Aviv. My sister waved away the idea with a flick of her hand.

"He's mad if he thinks I'd allow Ari to leave my sight. And we can't all move in with Papa. Besides, who's to say it's any safer in Tel Aviv? It's right next to the sea the Arabs want to drown us in."

She chewed her knuckles for some moments.

"He wants to get your son in his clutches so he can make a proper little Jew of him," I said, in hopes of making her chuckle. "Stuff him full of prayers and kosher food."

Liesel's attempt at laughter came out as a gasping sigh. I heard her teeth chatter.

"You're cold. You should go back to bed."

"How can you sleep out here? It's freezing!"

But she didn't move. Remained a woeful, shivering lump with her head bowed and her hands tucked into her armpits. I lifted the blankets so that she could crawl in beside me, which she did, unwittingly pushing me to the edge. But what could she do? The space was narrow and she was wider than me.

"I used to sing you to sleep. Remember Eva? *The flowers they are sleeping in milky moonshine . . . sleep, sleep, dear child of mine . . .* No I can't. My voice has gone all froggy."

Indeed, the lines of the familiar lullaby had come out of her throat as a croak.

"It's all right. You don't need to entertain me."

I rested my hand against the top of her head.

"Oh, do *kribbly krabbly* in my hair," she begged. "Remember? How you used to do that? "

My fingertips became a spider, skittering across her scalp, tickling through her coarse black hair. Her breathing softened and her body sank deeper into the straw mattress.

"What I'm most afraid of is that I'll fall to pieces when all hell breaks loose, and the child will see my fear. Already, Ari clings to his father, not just for the usual reasons but because Manfred is calm in a way I can't be. The boy senses my anxiety though I try not to show it. I have to be strong, but the weakness creeps inside. I'm so afraid of failing him. Other mothers can be brave. But me, I'm poisoned with fear. Oh, my little boy! "

"Hush, hush. You're much stronger than you think. I haven't witnessed a single moment when you lost control around Ari. You're just as brave as all the other mothers going quietly about their business while their hearts quake. Hush, it's all right. We're all together. And when the time comes, we'll do what we have to do."

I don't know from what hidden resources I hauled out the reassuring words and the steady, soothing tone. I was going through the motions, but as I did so, I became convinced of what I was saying. We would strengthen one another. Come what may, we would manage to hold it together for the sake of the boy. And strangely, madly, I was almost grateful for the coming crisis that would require us to focus on just getting through from one moment to the next.

"You know what I used to worry about?" Liesel murmured through a stupor of sleepiness. "That you'd marry the Englishman and leave the country with him and I'd never see you again. It's not that I didn't approve . . . I didn't want to lose . . ."

Before she finished her sentence she was asleep, spread eagle on her back. I shoved at her slumbering body until she rolled over onto her side and made room for me too.

Chapter 39
Last Words

March 18, 1948
Dear Duncan,
    Your pretty blue aerogram came to me just before the latest
disruptions in postal service and even though it showed the wrong
address, for I'm now at my sister's flat. How your letter found its
way to Hillel Street in the Jewish enclave of this divided city, instead
of being stamped "return to sender," is a mystery. Maybe someone
from the GPO recognized my name and made inquiries and handed
the thing to a Jewish postman on the other side of the fence. I don't
know which of my former colleagues to thank or how I would get
in touch with my Good Samaritan if I did. Parts of the city have
become like foreign countries. Most government services exist in
name only and can't be reached from the Jewish sector. Streets
I used to walk daily are now forbidden territory to anyone of my
birth, regardless of our former oaths of loyalty to His Majesty. The
decision about where we belong—what side of the fence—has
been made for us. But it's the same for the British and the Arabs.
Since a string of horrific bombs, planted by renegade British soldiers
and police, we have erected our own barricades and checkpoints.
Jewish militiamen openly stand guard. No British or Arab foot may
enter Jewish areas without permission. We all live in ghettos, sealed
off from one another by walls and barbed wire, fear and hate.
Remember you once said the real lords of the land are the feral cats?
Well, that's truer than ever. Only cats, rats and stray dogs meander
past the barriers with impunity.
    So, Duncan. Thank you for your explanations and apologies, but
I already got the story from Malka. Can I forgive you? I don't know.
You're a louse for not getting in touch before you left. You're a
stinking piece of excrement for marrying someone else. Not that
I would have accepted your proposal, but I would have liked the
privilege of first refusal. After ten years of ups and downs with you,

*it was my right, don't you think? And at the very least, you should
have trusted me with the news of your injury and your plans, rather
than slinking away like a rat into a gutter.*

*I imagine you on patrol in a sleepy Bermuda town. Your spit-
polished boots slap the empty pavements while you wait for the
occasional automobile to chug by. A prayer lodges in your heart
for someone to throw stones at a neighbour's dog, or to utter foul
language in public. Please somebody, anybody, commit an offence
that you can ticket! Beneath your Bermuda policeman's helmet,
which looks like an overturned funeral urn, your head is going bald.
At home, the little wife in her apron fries up a mess of bangers
and mash. Or has she converted you to Polish sausage as well as
to the Catholic faith? Evenings you mutter the rosary together.
Sunday finds you on your knees before a priest, your dutiful tongue
stretched out to receive the communion wafer.*

*There! I got the spite out of my system. I'm not writing to vent.
You offered to stay friends, so I'll take you at your word for I can
use a friend right now. Someone who's distant from this powder-
keg country, where the news darts like vipers from the pages of the
morning papers and we await Armageddon or the Messianic age.*

*You say you've been following the events in Palestine with great
concern for our safety. I don't know how much of the real story
gets out to the world press. Officially, Britain still maintains law and
order, and has sworn to do so until the day of the withdrawal on
May 15. But that's pure fiction. You'd be appalled at the chaos the
authorities tolerate and the highly selective policing, especially of
the roads. Any Jewish vehicle heading in or out of Jerusalem must
travel in convoy. Arab snipers lurk in the cliffs above the gullies. As
the convoy snakes round an opportune bend, the attackers let loose
with their rifles and grenades. But you know the drill. You've been
there yourself. Our defenders—the boys and girls of the Haganah—
shoot back as best they can with the motley collection of arms they
managed to smuggle past the British patrols. The Englishman's
old-fashioned prudery and sense of honour is our salvation for, even
now, girls don't get searched. So when the patrol approaches, the
defenders' dismantled guns vanish beneath skirts and brassieres, to
be reassembled afterwards, ready for service. Yet our casualties are
awful. Every convoy that runs the gauntlet of ambush, leaves behind
a trail of toppled vehicles in smoking ruin by the side of the road.*

People say that the Arab militiamen do a war dance around the fallen vehicles and pierce the air with their vibrating howls. Every shipment of flour comes to us at the cost of dead and wounded. When the food trucks arrive, people line Jaffa Road to cheer and bestow the drivers with kisses. Immediately afterwards, there's a stampede to the shops to grab whatever can be bought before the next long spell of waiting and bare shelves. Food rationing will soon begin (kerosene is already rationed), which will at least bring some order to the daily quest to fill one's belly. The Arabs' plan is to disrupt all Jewish lines of communication, besiege our side of the city and starve us into submission—an age-old strategy. British complicity strengthens their hand.

In the mixed Arab-Jewish neighbourhoods battles rage for every house, every rock and thistle. Shots ring out intermittently during the day, and almost non-stop at night. To protect us from stray gunfire, Manfred has built us a blind along the parapet of the roof. He made it out of loose boards, bed frames, sandbags, upended tables, piles of furniture—anything he could get his hands on. It's a child's clumsy approximation of a fort. Of course, these flimsy barriers could never withstand the impact of mortar shells or sniper bullets. But at least we're hidden from view as we enter and exit the flat. Gives the illusion of safety, which is not to be sneezed at. Illusions sustain us as much as do our meagre daily portions of bread. By the way, little Ari is delighted by our circle of "fortress" walls. How wonderful this topsy-turvy construction! Finally the adults are making sense, playing games in earnest! We just have to keep our eyes on him every moment to make sure he doesn't try to climb the "ramparts."

The siege of the city means I have hours of idleness to fill. Before the partition vote, I typed manuscripts for clients at the university on Mount Scopus, but it's too dangerous to go there now. Besides, many professors and students have joined the Haganah, which means work has dried up. Cafés have little to serve and we have no money anyway. Concerts are few and far between. Instead, when I've done with scrounging for supplies in the market and with helping Liesel in the household, I sit at the table and type these thoughts. Manfred sits opposite, sorting through his photo negatives. Liesel tackles a basket of mending and hums. Ari sleeps beneath his cloud of mosquito netting.

I mentioned a string of bombs in the Jewish sector. In early February, an explosion tore through the offices of The Palestine Post. A month later, cleverly disguised British saboteurs targeted the Jewish Agency. But the worst shock happened in between, on February 22, with the bombs on Ben Yehuda Street. As you know, Liesel and Manfred's building is just a few minutes away. Early that morning, as I stood over the kitchen sink to fill the kettle, a massive roar almost flung me off my feet. My sister and brother-in-law burst out of the bedroom, flakes of plaster in their hair, their faces white as the walls. Shards of glass covered Ari's cot. Thank God, for the mosquito net. The child escaped without a scratch. When Manfred and I went out to see what had happened, we found a scene like out of the London Blitz. Eviscerated buildings, mountains of rubble, towers of smoke. Walls teetered, masonry crashed, balconies dangled. Rivers of shattered glass lay underfoot, along with splintered wood and slabs of concrete. Men, women and children still in pyjamas staggered about, smeared with blood and plaster. Dazed and sickened, I went back to Liesel, who'd stayed home with Ari, while Manfred volunteered for a fire brigade struggling to train hoses on what was left of the Amdursky Hotel. Later, I helped serve sandwiches and lemonade to the rescue squads. All this mayhem came from two truck bombs planted on Ben Yehuda Street by British police deserters. The authorities deny the story, but eye-witnesses swear it's true. Which of your old comrades would have done such a thing, Duncan, and if you knew, would you tell? You once confronted me with just such a question, and now I ask it of you, though I know the answer perfectly well. The Palestine Police Force has one mind, one heart. And no mercy whatsoever for informers and traitors.

Meanwhile, our own saboteurs haven't been quiet. The zealots took revenge the very next day with road mines that blew up military transports in the heart of town, killing at least one soldier and injuring many. In short, the situation is not yet all-out war, but very far from peace. All three sides—British, Jewish and Arab—take part in the "actions" against one another. The thud of explosions, clatter of machine guns and wail of sirens have become our daily concert, drowning out the church bells and calls to prayer. Yet despite the horrors, the tension, the food shortages, I'm not sorry to be here instead of outside the country. Despite everything, this is where I belong. I don't mean "nation," "homeland," "the people." These grandiose concepts make me nervous and, besides, everyone has his own definitions. But here on this roof, with Liesel, Manfred and Ari, and in this building, and in the streets all around with their markets and shops and clusters of houses for Jews from different corners of the world—here I plant my feet and refuse to budge. The hardships of the siege haven't yet fazed me. Maybe I've learned a lesson from those feral cats, the lean hunters, the natural inhabitants of the city. Focus on the next meal. On the water allotment and the kerosene queue. On the splendid prize of a half-smoked cigarette in the gutter. I've heard that mad people can experience a kind of sanity during times of crisis. I've seen it with my own eyes. Do you remember the demented, pock-marked wretch who used to accost people in Zion Square, proclaiming he was Elijah the prophet? He would flap his arms and say he was ascending to heaven in the whirlwind. Well, the other day I saw him lining up for kerosene, subdued and sober, clutching his jerry can, maintaining his position with crafty jabs of his elbows, just like everyone else. Necessity made him pull himself together. I can say the same for me. There is magic in "ein breirah," for it clarifies the mind. Also, necessity can embolden the meek. Remember Maisel, the nervous librarian who lived in the back room at Mrs. Rajinsky's? Early one morning I found him in a side street with a satchel of tinned asparagus soup he'd acquired somehow and which he was bartering for other foodstuffs. He persuaded me to part with a clump of dried figs for one of his tins, speaking with the dogged persistence of a seasoned salesman. Gone the fluster, the stammer and the pudginess too. He was leaner and tougher looking than before, having put in duty with the Civil Guard filling sandbags. I quite enjoyed our little exchange.

You might think I'm aloof to the national fervour. Not true. On November 29, night of the U.N.O. partition vote, I was swept away like everyone else. I stood outside the door of Dr. Eisenberg's flat as the neighbours crowded inside to listen to his radio, to hear the vote count, broadcast live from Flushing Meadow in New York. As each representative said "yes" to partition, the walls of our building rocked with cheers. And then, well past midnight, the final tally was announced. We would have our country. After two thousand years of dispersion, the Jewish state would be reborn. Within minutes, the streets filled with deliriously happy crowds, a bit like during V.E. Day, but much more so. Back then it was the relief of the long struggle over, whereas this night, it was all about birth. Once again, chains of hora dancers snaked up Ben Yehuda Street, wine flowed, strangers embraced. With Liesel and Manfred and Ari (hoisted from his bed and enthroned on his Papa's shoulders), I joined the throngs pouring into the courtyard of the Jewish Agency. From a balcony the leaders were addressing the populace.

"I can't see," I shrieked in fury into the din. A small miracle happened. A youth crouched before me and hooked his arms under my legs. And then I too was seated on a pair of strong shoulders, high up, with a splendid view over the sea of heads. I was moved the most by Mrs. Golda Myerson. I don't remember what she said. I couldn't see her clearly either. But I felt I was standing right beside her, aware of the trembling of her body as she struggled to control her thoughts. I was aware of her tightly rolled hair, her plain, horsey features, her sturdy black shoes, her ink-smeared, nicotine-stained fingers grasping the pages of her speech. A wave of love washed over me for this woman who'd worked so hard and had believed in the dream so tirelessly. For her brave, rasping, slightly hectoring voice, distorted by the loudspeakers and swallowed up by the noise of the crowd. I loved Golda. I loved everyone. The greatness of what I was witnessing shook me to the core. The weeping, singing and partying lasted all night. But in another part of town, black flags of mourning drooped from the windows. Crowds of angry Arabs shook their fists. And the very next day, a Jewish business centre was ransacked and the reign of chaos began.

The birds of Jerusalem too have free passage across the enclaves. How I wish I could send an army of doves over the rooftops to the other side. They would flutter down onto the parapets and windowsills in the Old City. They would speak my thoughts in their soft, rippling voices. Coo into the ears of those who want us gone. There must be another way. There must be a way to share the land.

Fantasy! It also helps, along with illusions and the hoarded tins of soup.

I'll cling with all my might to these streets, learn to shoot if I have to. If we win—and we must win, we absolutely must—it will be at the others' expense. Not that the thought troubles me much—I'm no saint. But I don't think I'll ever see another night as I did on November 29th, when it felt as if heaven and earth had joined together at last and the era of redemption had arrived.

Some weeks after the partition vote, during a lull in the unrest, I decided to call on my old friend, Katy Khoury, at her villa in Katamon. We hadn't seen each other for many months. The glue of a common workplace had long ago dissolved, and social events where Jew and Arab could mingle were non-existent. Katy's life revolved around her family, church and community, while mine would be equally alien to her. Perhaps I'd be putting her in an awkward position with her own people by my visit? A depressing thought, reminding me of my schooldays in Germany. I went anyway, not wanting to give into such pressures. I wanted her to know she was still Katy to me, not the enemy. So I ventured out of the Jewish sector into what had become almost out-of-bounds, but not quite, the lines and restrictions still somewhat fluid at that time. I kept to the main streets, Ussishkin, Gaza Road, Salameh Square, walking close to the buildings in case of stray bullets. Past the fine villas of chiselled stone, the Greek Embassy, the Swedish Embassy, the Park Lane Hotel. Past the walled gardens and the glimpses of jasmine and honeysuckle bushes through the gaps between the gates. My heart thumped beneath my ribs, but no one took notice of a little woman in a long beige raincoat and matching kerchief trotting purposefully forward. All was quiet. Normal. A grocery shop open. A bus rumbling by. In the vacant field across from the Khoury's street, a cat sunned itself on a rock. Yet when I arrived at the familiar wrought-iron gates, I saw something was amiss. The garden looked untended: debris lay on the path, weeds poked between the flagstones, a cracked branch hung down from the fig tree, the pale, splintered wood creaking in the breeze. Closed shutters hugged the windows of the house. No one seemed to be at home and my knock at the door sounded hollow, echoing through emptiness. But at last I heard a step, the clack of a bolt. Sami's face appeared in the gap.

"Eva Salomon! What brings you here? Come in. I'm sorry to make you wait."

He shut the door behind me with a loud bang. He led me into the salon with the high, vaulted ceiling that had always given the room a palatial air, but today, because of the shuttered windows, harboured a cold gloom. The salon furniture was covered with dust sheets. Pictures had been removed from the walls. Trunks and boxes stood in the corridor that led to the bedrooms. Sami switched on the chandelier in the salon and hastily pulled a sheet off an armchair so that I could sit down, while he perched on the edge of a covered divan.

"Katy and the children have gone to Bethlehem. We feel safer there. This neighbourhood . . ."

He shook his head. Dark pouches of weariness lay under his eyes. His round and normally smiling face had a grey, trampled look.

"It used to be a neighbourhood. Now it's Jewish houses or Arab houses. Men from the Arab resistance army came here because they'd heard we had Jewish tenants. I told them that was years ago, but they still poked into every corner to see with their own eyes. They decided our house is strategic, so they posted a couple of lookouts on our roof. They come at night, walk in and out as they please. They sow bullets into the darkness and reap bullets in return. Look . . ."

He jumped up, opened the window shutter a crack to show me the shattered pane of glass. He pointed to a gouge in the wall opposite. As I looked around, I saw another—a hole in the plaster the size of my fist.

"The Jewish fighters too are hungry for my house," Sami said. His voice was bitter. "They took over the villa on the other side of the field, home of my friend Khaled. They can't win this war, but they are determined to do as much damage as they can. I sent the family away in a taxi last week. I am packing up my valuables and will join them in Bethlehem. When it's all over, we'll return. Who knows what a mess we will find, but . . ."

He shrugged and shook his head again.

"Holes in the walls are easy to fix. Holes in the flesh, a different story. We'll come back and repair everything. This house is strong. Good solid bones of stone, built by my father twenty years ago. It will still be standing when we return."

He made apologies for not being able to offer me the usual hospitality, but he was in a hurry to finish his packing. Though he didn't say so directly, I also knew he wanted me out of there in case the lookout men came by early. Both for my sake and his own, I had to make haste. We shook hands and he promised to convey my greetings to Katy. When all this madness was over, he said, I must come by with Liesel, Manfred and Ari for a party in the garden.

A couple of weeks later, men from our side blew up the Semiramis Hotel, just a few streets away from the Khoury home. Twenty-six killed, all civilians, including the Spanish vice-consul. No Arab militia leaders had been caught in the explosion, as had been hoped. It was a botched mission by the Haganah, not the dissidents this time. I've heard the explanations and they all sound lame. I'm glad the Khourys are out of there.

Well, yes, the Khourys can get away to Bethlehem. If war engulfs that town, they can go to Lebanon, where they have relatives. We Jews have nowhere to run to and anyway, now it's too late. Our leaders have made it clear: we must stay put in our homes in Jerusalem. Jews who want to flee the city would be branded as defeatists and no one dares own up to such cowardly desires.

I make it sound as if we all, myself included, stick to Jerusalem out of duress. Partially true. Truth is complicated. The official story (from our side) is that morale is excellent. That we calmly line up to receive our necessities. That we bravely go about our daily business. The jostling in the queues, the grumbling in the bare-shelved shops, the bickering—these things The Palestine Post conveniently fails to mention. Nevertheless, it is true that the common resolve hardens with each set-back, with each report of a supply truck ambushed or an acquaintance killed. Our backs are to the wall, but we do have fighters, arms, an organized community, leaders and ordinary folk who have been preparing for this day for years. My Aunt Ida and Uncle Otto were so terribly alone in their ordeal because, though surrounded by other persecuted Jews, none could help the other in any substantial way. Today, in Palestine, it's altogether different because we are facing adversity head-on together. If we have to die, we will be amongst our own, firing back. Even if there's a bloodbath, it will not be a massacre. It will be different. This is the prevailing view, and I believe this too because I must. Amazing how faith blossoms under necessity.

Do I sound brave? Fatalistic might be the better word. Stunned into a state of calm by the overwhelming events beyond my control. But I have my weaker moments. At night, in the oppressive darkness of this tiny flat, listening to muffled gunfire, I hear a voice that sends chills down my spine. Without going into details, let me tell you, I'm very well acquainted with fear. I know its odour: a damp, fetid, pungent smell like the belch of a blocked toilet, like the rot that creeps out of mouldy walls. Fear gets into my nose and under my skin and I become a reeking carcass of terror. And it's not Arab daggers I fear the most. Something else. Something I can't talk about. Another time maybe. Not now. Though it helps me get a grip on myself just to put this much down in black and white.

The Arab militias are firing from Sheikh Jarrah again. We have learned to distinguish the sound of their guns from ours. Ari has joined his parents in their bed and it's very late, but they don't mind the clack-clack of my typewriter keys for it masks the noise of boom-boom and rat-tat-tat.

Duncan, at times like these I miss our gramophone. I had to sell it to pay for the typewriter with which I'm typing this letter. I don't regret the decision, but still . . . Now and then, I visit the fellow in Mea Shearim who bought the gramophone from me, along with our entire stack of records. He's a man with butcher's paws and laugh lines crinkling the corners of his eyes. He lets me choose an old favourite and sit outside his shed on a crate, while he tinkers inside with his machinery and the record spins. We barely speak or look at one another the whole visit, but, for the duration of the piece, our minds float on the same current. Yes, this grey-bearded, barrel-chested Hasid in gaberdine and skullcap and me—united by the amber throbbing of a Bach cello suite. To feed my hungry ears, sometimes I hover in the stairwell when Dr. Eisenberg's radio broadcasts a symphony. Other times, snatches of music just spring into my mind. Playful themes from Mendelssohn's Octet. The Andantino from Mozart's Violin sSonata (No. 26). In the stillness of the stuffy room, through sheer longing and the miracle of memory, I begin to hear a melody. It comes like an old friend with a tinkle of piano keys and the gentle sob of the violin. I have all the music in my head. How about some Chopin now? Do you hear it, Duncan? The Nocturne in B Flat Minor. The sigh and ripple and cascade of notes like the magic of a Jerusalem snowfall. Do you remember snow in Jerusalem, Duncan? How the low clouds hover—bloated grey clouds tinged with opal and green—and press close and let loose with their bounty? Snowflakes swirl, shower down, pile-up. Flakes settle on the shtreimels of the Hasids. Crystals lodge in the beards of the muezzins. Whiteness caps the ramparts, the domes, the steeples, the minarets. White shrouds the olive trees, the gravestones, the courtyards. It evens out the distance between mountain and valley.

It drapes gun barrels, armoured cars, helmets, badges and boots
and swallows the purple flashes of tracer bullets. Night falls, but not
the usual impenetrable wall of Palestine darkness. This snowy night
I conjure up has space and depth. And all the while, the Chopin in my
head glitters and showers all over the city and the trail of our two
sets of footprints softly vanish into the luminous gloom.

April 15, 1948
To Whom It May Concern

The road to Tel Aviv is blockaded. Jerusalem is cut off from the world. Throughout the night Bren guns chatter, shells explode, the hills shudder and, in our beds, we hold our hands to our ears. The racket is less lusty in the daytime, but still the bullets fly. When I set out in search of food, I sidle along the walls of the buildings for cover. I duck into stairwells at the sound of every whistle and bang. Yossi, the grocer, was killed the other day while crossing Gaza Road. Such stories are a shock, but with each one, the shock is just a bit more muted as death becomes a habit. The pressing problem of the day is the bread ration, the margarine ration, the hope for some potato or an onion. Most of the town's kerosene is gone and people cook on wood fires or use Flit and D.D.T. for fuel. There's no water in the taps. We must queue up for water now too. Milk is a luxury reserved for the children. Those cafés still open serve black coffee with saccharine pills.

Sometimes I catch sight of the boys and girls of the Haganah as they head off to their positions, youngsters in stocking caps and overalls or grey flannels, carrying a motley collection of arms. Yet they march like soldiers with a resolute stamp and their new song.

On the barricades we will meet at the last / And lift freedom high from the chains
of the past.

I see the youth of the splinter groups too, for they no longer hide their faces. Side by side with the Haganah, they staff the barriers, shoot from the cracks between the boards. Irgunists and Sternists in rag-tag uniforms take over swaths of the city, strut through the streets like lords. Can I deny they are fighting the common enemy? That they are people's protectors? They are immensely courageous, those two small bands of soldier-zealots. They will stand at their posts under the blazing sun, without food or a drop of water and shoot to their last bullet. Yes, yes, I know all that. And for such feats I admire them. But I know their other side as well. A few days ago, they captured an Arab village, leaving heaps of massacred men, women, and children to pollute the earth. They paraded the survivors in three open lorries, driving slowly up and down King George V Avenue. The mukhtar of Deir Yassin, his womenfolk and children and all the others stood with their hands over their heads, frozen in surrender, while the victors brandished their guns. I saw the horror-stricken eyes of the captives looking down at me over the slats of the truck walls and those eyes were my own.

Soon afterwards came the terrible reprisal. A convoy of medical staff bound for Hadassah Hospital was ambushed in Sheikh Jarrah and pinned down by merciless fire. Seven hours of bullets, bazookas, and Molotov cocktails. More than seventy-five dead—doctors, nurses, students, faculty members, including the hospital's director—people who were supposed to be immune from attack, with many bodies burnt beyond recognition and later buried in a mass grave. And the other burials had to be hasty, guarded affairs because of continued sniping around the makeshift cemetery.

"Don't worry," Shimshon's voice assures me. "We will answer in kind. Atrocity for atrocity. Two pounds of their flesh for every pound of ours."

I do not feel reassured.

All over our side of the city, men and women are quietly, without fuss, and perhaps even in secret, setting down their last will and testament. Just in case. The other day, while Liesel was out of the house, Manfred asked me to put my witness signature to his small but neatly handwritten list of bequests. And surely, in rooms and on rooftops around town, others are busy scribbling their memoirs as am I as I tap-tap my thoughts onto paper during the gaps between the hours of scavenging for food. It seems important to record these moments in my own and the people's history. Perhaps the recording of the moments makes us feel we can hold time still, keeps the unknown future at bay, fulfills the function of prayer. As during the Days of Awe when there is still a chance to alter the heavenly decree of who will be entered into the Book of Life for the coming year. And who not.

And now there is something more I must set down in writing. A story that all those other memoirists are unlikely to tell. I must put it down now, finally and irrevocably, before I lose my resolve. About the events that happened in early January 1947, as I stood on the corner of Mamilla and Princess Mary roads and a vehicle approached and rough hands snatched and I ended up bound and beaten on a cellar floor. The story festers beneath my ribs even though these ribs healed many months ago. I need to write the words and give them . . . to whom? Who wants to read this?

With a war of survival raging—the life of the nation hanging in the balance—this is not a time for stories like mine. People focus on their rations of oil and flour. They debate when to open those hoarded tins in the cupboard. They creep into the fields to pluck edible weeds. They exchange recipes for omelettes without eggs. They exchange rumours and dark humour. They cock their ears to the illegal broadcasts of the Haganah and the Voice of Fighting Israel. Give us stories about our sons and daughters in the militias, they say. Tell us whether the latest convoy will get through. How much water remains in the cisterns? What is happening to our isolated colonies in the Judean hills? How does one grow lettuce in flower pots? Is it true what they say about the secret weapon called "Davidka"? Tell us about Jewish unity, the feats of the defenders, the messages of support from America, the clandestine shipments of weapons, the airplane hidden in a cattle barn, the refugees who staggered off the boat in the dead of night and volunteered directly afterwards for military service. Yes, these are the concerns and preoccupations and longings.

Moreover, there are thousands in this land with the brand of the camps seared onto their arms. They have stories that make mine seem like a jaunt at the beach. Yet they don't talk about the horrors that stalk their sleep. They have the grace or the wisdom (or is it because of a horror too profound?) to keep their mouths shut. And if they spoke, who would listen? And if not to them, why to me?

Another matter too keeps my lips sealed. The other day, I read a report in *The Palestine Post*—just one tiny paragraph—that chilled me to the core. It told of a Jewish woman, whose neighbours suspected her of being a spy, kidnapped and shot by "unknown assailants." Nothing more in the article. No follow-up reports later in the week. If I hadn't saved the clipping I could convince myself my fevered imagination had dreamt it up. Yet why should I doubt the truth of the sordid tale? Rumours about collaborators circulate in stairwells. Who bats an eyelash about rough justice nowadays? Who cares to contemplate the problem of false accusations, the possible innocence of the victim? When such reports and rumours pop up, fear stalks me again, a beast breathing hard against the windows of my mind.

So this is not the time to broadcast my story. Later, I tell myself. When this is all over, when we've won and the state is established and there is calm. In the meantime, I must leave it be. Bury the words. Forget. All the same, the story churns in my gut. It begs for at least a glimmer of the light of day. And that's the real reason I've been typing, typing, typing these pages, even though they may never get beyond this rooftop.

Here are the facts: On the evening of January 10, 1947, men of the Lehi, the Freedom Fighters of Israel, also known as the Stern Gang, kidnapped me as I was reading a billboard. They took me to a cellar. Bound and gagged me. Left me in the dark for terrible hours. When they returned, they accused me of treason, of giving comfort to the enemy. For this they beat me senseless. In the name of the national struggle, but for no logical reason, I suffered violence at the hands of my fellow Jews. I witnessed the poison that can make brave, strong, idealistic youths plough their fists into a helpless dwarf of a woman. That's the whole thing in a nutshell. No witness can corroborate my statement, nevertheless my testimony stands.

I grieve for the self that was so cruelly battered. I weep for the youth that have lost their way.

And I do finally believe in something. Yes, I do. That if we win this war and the crisis of survival is past and we finally have our state, it will be the place of the better dream. Arab and Jew will find a way to live side by side. Peace will reign. Justice will prevail. The weak will be embraced as much as the strong. No longer will anthems blare about conquest and sacrifice. No more worship of blood and land. One day madmen like Shimshon will face a reckoning. The fanaticism of this era will become a relic of history. One day, when the big noise of battle and "necessity" subsides, I will tell what was done to me and the people will want to listen. They will agree that the suffering of one unremarkable citizen—though she's merely a dwarfling—deserves a hearing. They will say that, even though so much greater tragedy raged in those times of death and terror, any injustice is still one too many. And, also, that if the zealots were capable of such brutality against one of their own people, what other sins lie at their doors? How many innocents did they harm and how much force was truly justified and how can we make amends? The people will hunger for the truth, even its tiniest kernels. And they will judge between transgressor and victim and they will proclaim the verdict from the hilltops.

These things will come to pass, if not tomorrow, then the next day or the next. Though no objective evidence comes to my aid, I believe. For I have come to understand that belief is breath. Without it, the heart withers, the song of life dies in the throat.

Absurd and untenable such a thought may be, I believe a better world is dawning because . . .

Because *ein breirah*. I must.

Gabriella Goliger's first book, *Song of Ascent* (Raincoast Books), a collection of linked short stories, won the 2001 Upper Canada Writer's Craft Award. Her novel *Girl Unwrapped* (Arsenal Pulp Press) won the City of Ottawa 2011 Literary Award for Fiction. She was co-winner of the 1997 Journey Prize for short fiction and a finalist for this prize in 1995 and she won the Prism International award in 1993. She has also been published in a number of journals and anthologies including *Best New American Voices 2000* (Harcourt Inc.), *Contemporary Jewish Writing in Canada* (University of Nebraska Press) and *The New Spice Box: Canadian Jewish Writing* (The New Jewish Press).